Cursed
in the
Blood

By Sharan Newman from Tom Doherty Associates

Cursed
in the
Blood

SHARAN NEWMAN

A TOM DOHERTY ASSOCIATES BOOK
NEW YORK

1694 4132

This is a work of fiction. All the characters and events portrayed in this novel are either fictitious or are used fictitiously.

CURSED IN THE BLOOD

Map by Ellisa Mitchell

A Forge Book
Published by Tom Doherty Associates, Inc.
175 Fifth Avenue
New York, NY 10010

Forge® is a registered trademark of Tom Doherty Associates, Inc.

Library of Congress Cataloging-in-Publication Data

Newman, Sharan.
    Cursed in the blood / Sharan Newman.—1st ed.
        p.   cm.
    "A Tom Doherty Associates book."
    ISBN 0-312-86567-8 (acid-free paper)
    1. Scotland—History—1057–1603—Fiction. I. Title.
PS3564.E926C87   1998
813'.54—dc21   98-14608
                                                                              CIP

First Edition: August 1998

Printed in the United States of America

0 9 8 7 6 5 4 3 2 1

The book is for Jeff and Diana Russell,
for their years of support, advice, and friendship,
as well as for giving me a place to stay while I finished this book,
and for greeting me with champagne.
With love and thanks.

Acknowledgments

All of the people listed below have been of great help in advising me on this book. Any mistakes herein are completely due to my own perversity or lack of comprehension.

Dr. Tess Gerritsen, for not thinking I was crazy when I asked her about amputations and for giving me excellent advice on that grisly subject.

Prof. Bert Hall, University of Toronto, for setting me straight on windmills and for believing that Catherine and I both had the intelligence to understand his explanation.

Rebecca T. Hill, R.N., for telling me what to do until the *medicus* arrives.

Prof. Lester Little, Smith College, for finding the malediction from which this book is titled and for allowing me to use it.

Prof. Nicholas Howe, Ohio State University, for sending me the Durham poem and checking my Anglo-Saxon curses.

Prof. Brian Patrick McGuire, Roskilde University, Denmark, many thanks for all his advice and help on Aelred of Rievaulx.

Roger Norris, and also Wendy and Ivy; Cathedral Library of Durham, for allowing me to do research at the library, for getting the books and manuscripts out before I arrived, for finding a place to plug in my laptop so I could work and for providing a friendly atmosphere in which to work.

Prof. David Rollason, Durham University, for suggesting that I write about the bishops of Durham and then providing me with the chance to do the research there.

Prof. Jeffrey Russell, UC Santa Barbara, for enduring my questions, correcting my Latin and slogging through Lawrence of Durham's turgid imitation Vergil for me.

Prof. Richard Unger, University of British Columbia, for getting everyone across the channel without anachronisms. (I hope.)

Prof. Linda Voigts, University of Missouri, for help with *dwale* and advice on medieval medicine.

Prof. Alan Young, University College of Ripon & York, St. John, for allowing me to read his notes for his monograph, *William Cumin: Border Politics and the Bishopric of Durham 1141–1144* and for being so enthusiastic about having his work becoming the basis for a mystery novel.

Edgar's Family

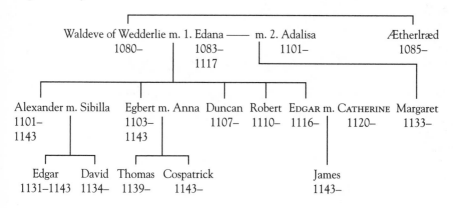

Waldeve of Wedderlie m. 1. Edana —— m. 2. Adalisa Ætherlræd
1080–   1083–   1101–   1085–
             1117

Alexander m. Sibilla Egbert m. Anna Duncan Robert EDGAR m. CATHERINE Margaret
1101–   1103–   1107–   1110–   1116–   1120–   1133–
1143   1143

Edgar   David   Thomas Cospatrick   James
1131–1143 1134–   1139–   1143–   1143–

Catherine's Family

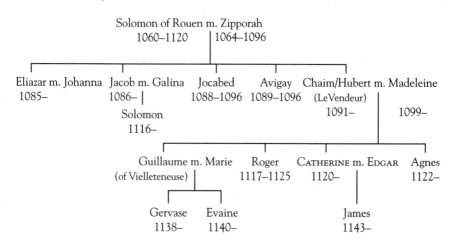

Solomon of Rouen m. Zipporah
1060–1120   1064–1096

Eliazar m. Johanna Jacob m. Galina Jocabed   Avigay   Chaim/Hubert m. Madeleine
1085–   1086– | 1088–1096   1089–1096   (LeVendeur)
                    Solomon   1091–   1099–
                    1116–

Guillaume m. Marie   Roger   CATHERINE m. EDGAR   Agnes
(of Vielleteneuse)   1117–1125   1120–   1122–

Gervase   Evaine   James
1138–   1140–   1143–

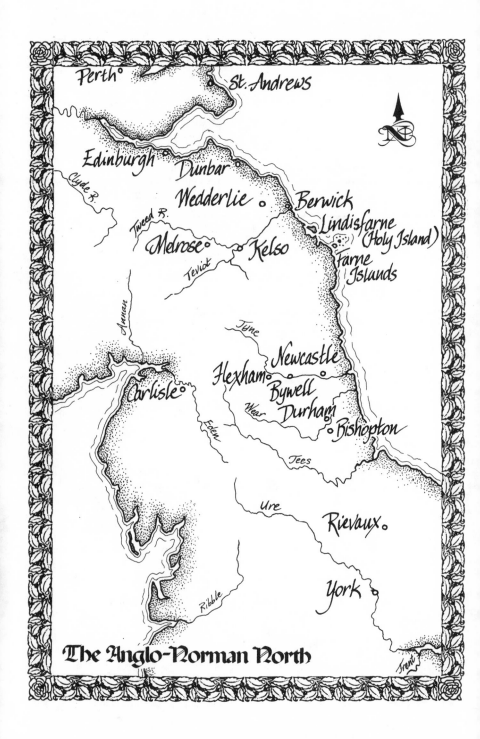

The Anglo-Norman North

One

A ditch on the north side of Hadrian's Wall, Scotland. Ascension
Thursday, 3 ides of May (May 13), 1143.

*aðwear afeallen thaes folces ealdor, Æðelredes eorl; ealle gesawon
heorðgeneatas that hyro heorra læg. Tha ðær wenden forð wlance
thegenas, unearge men efston georne: hi wolden tha ealle oðer twega.
lif forlætan oððe leofne gewrecan.*

Then fell in battle the people's lord, Æthelræd's earl; everyone
saw, all his hearthsharers, that their leader lay slain. Then went forth
the proud thanes, fearless men, hastened there gladly. They all wished
only one or the other, to lay down their lives or avenge their
loved one.

—*The Battle of Maldon*,
lines 203–209

$\mathcal{T}$his way, Lords!" The old man panted with exertion and fear. "You'll see. We touched nothing; I swear, by Saint Cuddy's cow! They're just as my boy found them."

"Stop mewling and get on with it!" the rider, Urric, shouted at the pair running before him. He muttered to himself as he watched them stumbling to keep ahead of the horses, "Stupid *neyfs!*"

"What's that?" His friend Algar guided his horse closer to better hear him.

"I said, they've not touched it? Those two must be cracked if they haven't taken anything. Insane to have come to us at all. Do they expect old Waldeve to reward them? He'll just as likely have them hanged from the portcullis for bringing him such news."

Algar nodded agreement, then his face changed as a sudden thought struck him.

"What do you suppose he'll do to us, then?"

Urric only grunted. It was too late to worry about that. The peasants had stopped, the older of them bent over breathless from the run across the hilly countryside. The younger pointed to a pile of branches and brush torn from the sides of the ditch.

"Under here, Lords," he told them. "Nothing has been moved. I covered them again as best I could, but it looks like the birds have been at that leg, already."

He paused, staring at the ravaged limb above the leather boot.

Urric's expression didn't change. "Get on with it," he ordered. "Show me."

The men on horseback waited while the peasants pulled back the branches covering what was left of the bodies. When the job was finished, they dismounted and examined the remains.

"It's them, for certain," Urric said after a moment. "Both of them. No doubt of it. The faces aren't that much marred."

"And the boy, as well," Algar added sadly. "Poor lad. His first time out with a sword. You can tell that they all went down fighting, though. Not that it'll be much comfort to the old man. His two eldest sons and his grandson, all slaughtered. This'll kill him."

Urric snorted, then gagged at the rising stench.

"Not that old bastard," he said. "I know him too well. Their deaths won't kill him. If anything, this will make him fiercer; it's hate that's kept him alive this long. No, we're the ones who'll die in the war this tragedy will cause."

Algar nodded, but not bitterly. It was right that murder should be avenged. As Lord Waldeve's man, it was Algar's duty to see that those who had slain his kin paid the price for their crime. If Algar died in the pursuit of that justice, he trusted his lord would see his own killer punished, as well.

Urric agreed in principle, but he was older and had seen more battle than Algar. Occasionally he wondered if the honor involved in blood feuds was worth the loss of so many good men. He had always firmly quashed such uncertainties. They stank of cowardice and the preaching of Norman priests.

He looked at the bodies again. The sight was enough to erase all doubt. These men hadn't just been his lords, but his friends. Those who had slaughtered them deserved not only to die, but first to feel the pain that Urric felt now.

"You!" he pointed at the older peasant. "Tell me again. How did you find them?"

"It was my nephew, here, that did." The man gestured toward the youth, who wiped his runny nose and looked up at them with a sullen expression. "He went to look for a ewe that escaped from the lambing pen. Thought she might have gone off somewhere private to drop it. They do that sometimes."

"I don't care about the habits of sheep," Urric warned him.

"Ah, yes . . . no, of course not." The man glanced nervously at the sword and knife Urric carried. "He saw the birds circling and thought it might be the lamb stillborn. When he saw what it really was, he pulled the brush back over them and ran for me. I sent for you at once, Sir."

"And it's just as he left it?" Urric asked. "Nothing touched since then?"

The boy shook his head vigorously. His uncle answered for him.

"What was here then is here now," he insisted. "Saving what the birds got."

Urric nodded. He bent over one of the bodies and motioned for Algar to do the same. Algar's eyes widened and his stomach contracted abruptly. He gripped Urric's arm in anger and disbelief. At the end of each right arm was only a ragged stump.

"Their right hands have been cut off!" he gasped. He looked around wildly for the missing parts.

"You won't find them," Urric said. "It was done after they died. See? No bleeding to speak of."

"Taken for trophies?" Algar asked. "But why hands? I'd have thought it would be their heads."

Urric shook his head in worry. "So would I. Worthy adversaries lose their heads. What reason could they have for cutting a man's hand off?"

The peasant assumed it was a general question.

"If they be thieves, Lord," he said. "Thieves and poachers, and oath-breakers of course."

Urric gave him a look that made the man wish he had kept his own counsel. He stepped back, away from the bodies. Perhaps he and his nephew could just slip away now.

Algar saw them edging off.

"Stop at once!" he shouted.

They froze.

"Help us wrap the bodies of the lords Alexander, Egbert and Edgar in those blankets," he ordered. "Algar, can your horse carry them all? You can ride behind me."

Reluctantly, the peasants complied. Urric watched them closely as they set each body on a blanket and bound it with rope. Death as such didn't bother him, neither did ambush and murder. He'd done plenty of that, himself. The Peace of God hadn't reached the North, and there were no roads safe from brigands. Or from one's enemies. And every man had enemies. But there was something wrong about this. Robbers stole everything, down to woolen hose and shifts. Enemies at least took weapons and jewelry as honest booty. Urric shook his head. Nothing had been taken from Waldeve's sons, not even their swords, now lying next to the bodies. The only things missing were their horses and their hands.

He shuddered, then quickly crossed himself, muttering a prayer of protection.

With much effort, the four men managed to get the bodies onto Algar's horse and tie them securely. The peasants turned back to Urric, looking at him with a mixture of hope and terror.

"You can see we took nothing," the older one pointed out. "Sent word to the reeve right away."

Urric had mounted and reached down to pull Algar up behind him. Algar paused. He gestured toward the peasants.

"They're harmless, Urric," he whispered. "They could have looted the bodies and hid them again. And, as you said, they'll get no thanks from Waldeve."

Grudgingly, Urric agreed. He reached behind his saddle for his pack. Rumaging through it for a moment, he brought out a square of linen. He balled it up and tossed it to the man.

"Here," he said. "It's to wear next to your skin. Softer than wool."

The man felt the material with a look of delight, stuffed it in his belt and with much bowing, backed away from the horseman until he judged he was far enough to turn and make a dash for home. His nephew was already well ahead of him.

As the men rode off, Algar nudged Urric. "Linen? What's he going to do with that?"

"If he's smart, give it to a pretty girl in exchange for her favors," Urric answered. "But it's just as likely that anyone so dutiful that he reports a body without stealing so much as a pair of boots will probably give his reward to the parish priest for the good of his soul. Idiot, I say!"

He spat against the wind. Behind him, Algar wiped the spittle off his cheek.

The peasants ran until they were sure they were out of sight of the horsemen. Then they stopped and leaned together to catch their breath.

"Do you think they believed us, Uncle?" the youth asked.

"Of course they did." The old man held up the linen with a laugh. "They think we're too much in awe of them to lie."

"Stupid bastards," his nephew said.

Waldeve, thane of the shire of Wedderlie, which consisted of three villages, woods, a good fishing stream and not much else, sat alone in his bed chamber. He knew before Urric and Algar had returned that the bodies found had been those of his sons and grandson. He'd known his boys were dead three days ago when they hadn't come back. His wife had tried to convince him that they had simply been overtaken by the dark and taken refuge in a village or a priory. But he'd have none of it. He was as sure of their deaths as if he'd heard the final screams and felt their souls flit through his body, hunting for a way around Purgatory.

He wanted to grieve for them, but he couldn't make himself feel anything, not even for Edgar, his eldest grandchild. A promising boy, almost as bright as the uncle he'd been named for. Waldeve swallowed the bile that rose with the memory. His fifth son, also Edgar, had been intended for the church. He could have been bishop of Saint-Andrews, or Glasgow, or even the new see at Carlisle. Instead the boy had gone mad while studying in France and married a nun, or something like that. He'd only seen Edgar once in the last twelve years, and that hadn't been a good meeting. The boy had come home only to announce that he was giving up his family and selling the land his mother had left him, all for a woman with no title whom he hadn't even slept with yet.

The old anger stirred Waldeve more than the immediate grief.

"My lord, Urric and Algar have returned."

The voice was soft and expressionless. Waldeve sighed. The fact that his wife had come to tell him instead of sending a servant sealed his certainty. He looked up. Adalisa stood just outside the curtain, her hand gripping the thick material so tightly her knuckles were white. Her face was blotched with tears.

"What do you have to grieve about?" he snapped. "They were none of yours."

Adalisa took the blow with little more than a flicker of an eyelash. He'd said crueler things.

"*Your* sons have been laid out in the Hall," she answered, the emphasis barely noticeable. "Do you wish to see them?"

He glared at her in response and stood up. He took a step, then stopped, his eyes closed. He swayed a moment. Adalisa put a hand out to support him, then drew it back. The old man took a deep breath, straightened his shoulders and raised his chin proudly. She held the curtain aside as he passed through, not touching her.

∞

Urric and Algar stood well back as Waldeve examined the bodies. The others in the hall were silent in horror. The only sound was the rustle of mice in the straw on the floor.

Finally Waldeve turned and faced his household.

"Someone's going to Hell for this," he said in a voice all the more terrifying for being so low and steady. "And I intend to send them there one piece at a time."

In the upper regions of the keep a woman began to scream. The noise was soon accompanied by wails and lamentations from the others. Lord Waldeve closed his eyes. He recognized the loudest. It was Sibilla, Alexander's wife. She had lost both husband and son. It was right now for her to mourn. He wouldn't rob her of it. He only wished she'd do it somewhere else.

"My lord, shall I call the priest?"

Waldeve started. He had forgotten his wife was still there. "Adalisa, I have work to do. We don't need that noise now. Can't you quiet them?"

"Of course not," she told him. "It's only proper that they should shriek their loss to heaven. I would rather you joined them than hold your cold silence, keeping these good men standing when they are no doubt tired, hungry, thirsty and heartsore themselves."

She gestured at the two soldiers.

Algar stood stiffly and tried to appear impervious to human needs. Urric's left eye twitched in what might have been a wink. Quickly, Adalisa turned back to her husband, who sighed and waved them away.

"Go." he said. "Wash, eat. Then sharpen your swords."

Gratefully, the men left. Adalisa let her shoulders droop. She knelt by Waldeve's chair and tried to put her arms around him. He pushed her away.

"Why are you weeping?" he demanded. "What has this to do with you?"

Adalisa stood.

"I was their stepmother. I arranged their weddings and took in their wives. I was the first after the midwife to hold baby Edgar. Nearly twenty years they've been part of my life. And you can't imagine why I should weep."

"They weren't your blood," he said, dismissing her and her grief with a gesture. "Now, go quiet those women. And, yes, send for the priest. Tell him I want Masses said for them without ceasing for the next month."

"And the burial?" she asked.

He swallowed. "At once."

Adalisa nodded and left. The bodies had to be washed and wrapped. It was the job of the women of the family to do it. But after three days in the open, the task might be more than Alexander's and Egbert's wives could endure. Adalisa stopped and leaned against the cold stone wall. Of course she would do it; there was no way it could be avoided. She was the lady of the keep. Her job was to see that everything ran smoothly, that there was food on the table, beds enough for guests. She held the keys to the larder and the store-rooms, to everything except the iron-bound box that lay beneath their bed. She was the mistress of Wedderlie and its slave.

So there was no time for weeping. And why should she grieve for her husband's sons? After all, as he had sneered, they had been nothing to her.

Nothing at all, she told herself as her tears began again.

The kitchen was full of people and clatter when Urric and Algar entered. The pot boy saw them first and stopped scrubbing. The silence spread out from him until the room was still enough to hear the roast sizzling. The soldiers saw the curiosity in twenty pairs of eyes as they came down the steps.

"Ale," Urric said. "And soup. We're frozen clean through with the wind and rain."

A space was cleared at the long table, between the chopped roots and the half-plucked birds. The men sat. No one said a word until each had drained a bowl of ale and made good headway into the trencher of soup.

"When do we ride?" The abrupt question was not unexpected. Everyone had been waiting for the order since word had come that the bodies had been found.

Urric shrugged. "The old man hasn't said."

"Who did it?" That was not as important.

Algar shook his head.

"No one saw." He poured another bowl of ale. "It wasn't for booty. It had to be retribution."

Everyone was silent again, trying to think which of the great families Waldeve or his sons could have offended.

"We're at war with no one now," the cook said finally. "At least, not that I've heard."

His tone indicated that he expected to be the first one told.

"There's plenty who'd like to pay back old wounds." The voice came from someone at the back. They all nodded. Memories of ancient insults were long as winter nights in the north. And tales told by the fire fanned resentment for years until only a spark was needed for it to explode into fury.

"Someone will know." Urric sighed and tried to straighten a kink in his back. "And they'll get drunk and tell someone else, or brag to some woman and she'll pass it on. No . . ." He stopped, wincing as his spine fell into place. "That's not right. Why should it be a secret? Whoever did this, they must want us to know. Why else kill them and take nothing but . . . ?"

"Their hands," the cook finished. "You don't need to be delicate. We all heard."

He rubbed his wrist as if to assure himself that his own hand was still connected. He wasn't the only one.

Algar finished his soup and got up. He'd just remembered something.

"With the lords Alexander and Egbert dead, that means Duncan's the oldest son."

He shivered. There was something about Waldeve's third son that made him want cold iron and holy water near him at all times, just to be safe, either way.

In the smoky kitchen more than one hand moved in the ancient sign to ward off evil.

Urric snorted. "That doesn't make him thane of Wedderlie," he said. "Alexander's got another son who could inherit, and there's always Robert."

The cook wasn't about to let this reassure anyone. "Alexander's son is a child still, and as for Robert, well, it seems to me Waldeve picked the wrong boy to make into a priest."

Everyone nodded.

The gloom in the kitchen was thicker than the smoke. A vision of life under Duncan of Wedderlie was terrifying to contemplate. When Duncan had gone off to Durham to cast his lot with the king's chancellor, William Cumin, in his fight for the bishopric, the household had cheered his going and prayed that he would never return.

Finally a spatter from the roast that was no longer being turned brought the cook back to the present.

"No point in borrowing trouble," he said. "There's enough here now. Lord Waldeve's got plenty of good years left. By the time he goes, young Ædmer will be old enough to take over. You! Gillecrist! Who told you to stop working? That meat'll be raw on one side and burnt on the other."

The servant hurriedly grabbed the spit and began turning it, wincing as the heat of the metal came through the cloth wrapped around his hand. The others made a show of getting back to their duties as well. But the air of disquiet remained. The horror of the loss was bad enough, but the fear of what it might lead to was worse.

Adalisa made her way slowly up to the women's rooms. She had consulted with the priest, overseen the preparing of the bodies, ordered food for the funeral and sent messengers to various kin, including Waldeve's cousin and lord, the earl of Dunbar. Now she had to go face the wives of her stepsons and their children, console them in their grief and calm their fear about the future.

She wished there were one place in this whole bailiwick where she could hide.

Reaching the top of the stairs, Adalisa drew back the curtain, steeling herself to endure Sibilla's wailing.

The widows sat in chairs by the window. Egbert's wife, Anna, held their new son. Her other boy was only four. He sat by the side of her chair, sucking his thumb. Anna knew that she would be given little time to mourn. She was heiress to a castle and five villages. Suitors would be arriving before grass sprouted on her husband's grave.

Sibilla was staring at the dust that was dancing in the afternoon sunlight. She had only one child left now, and he had been sent for fostering at the earl's court. Adalisa could only imagine the depth of her devastation.

Sitting between the women, cross-legged on the floor, the sunlight catching the gold in her red hair, was Margaret. She greeted Adalisa with a tremulous smile.

"Mama, I'm so glad you're back," she said. "No one will tell me anything."

The girl rose with a fluid grace and Adalisa realized as they hugged that her daughter was growing again. She could rest her chin on Margaret's head now. Nearly eleven. It didn't seem possible. She hugged the child more tightly.

"There's nothing to tell, sweeting," Adalisa told her. "The preparations have been made for the burial tomorrow. We shall keep vigil and pray tonight."

She stopped as Sibilla gave a low moan and covered her face with her scarf.

"I'm sorry, Sibilla," she added. "Margaret, there's something you can do for me. Run down and get some water. Then bring me my herb box. We all need something to ease the pain."

When the child had gone, Adalisa went over to the two women. She had no idea what to say to them. Sibilla looked up, her eyes red in her pale face.

"What's to become of me?" she asked. "Whatever shall I do now?"

"I don't know," Adalisa answered. "This isn't the time to think of it."

"And what else shall I dwell on? My poor child's body, perhaps?" Sibilla was well over the edge of hysteria.

"His soul, waiting for you in Heaven?"

Sibilla's response to that was less than devout. Anna looked up from the baby, shocked.

"Of course young Edgar is in Heaven!" she said. "Or will be soon. What had he to repent of? And we'll have the nuns pray for him night and day, just to be sure."

"Well, don't think I'll be joining them in the convent," Sibilla answered. "I've no intention of spending the rest of my days surrounded by women. Oh, dear holy Mother, what's to become of me?"

Adalisa sighed with relief as Margaret returned, carrying a pail of water in one hand and balancing the herb box against the opposite hip.

"Thank goodness," she said. "Here, give me the box. Pour some of the water into the long-handled pot and the rest into the bowl next to the brazier. Heat them both. Now, what do I need?"

She took out borage, vervain and wood betony, putting them into a linen square, which she then tied with string. When the pot boiled, she dipped the sachet in it until it soaked enough to sink. While she waited for the herbs to steep, she took out a small vial and dripped a bit of oil onto the steaming water in the bowl.

"Tincture of roses," she told the women. "Lean over it and breath. It will ease your minds."

While they were doing that, she brought a pitcher of strong Gascon wine. She mixed the herbal potion with it.

"Drink this, all in a draught," she ordered. "You need it. You must sleep tonight. Tomorrow will be long."

They obeyed. Adalisa gave some to Margaret as well, diluting the wine considerably for her.

"Will you stay with your sisters-in-law?" she asked her daughter. "I must see to your father."

Margaret nodded. Adalisa kissed her.

"I'll send one of the other women up soon. They're washing now."

Washing off the smell of death. Adalisa didn't add it, but something in Margaret's eyes said that she knew.

Waldeve had put on his riding boots. He paced back and forth across the hall, raising clouds of chaff. His men stood near the hearth, trying not to cough. They were desperate for action. All Waldeve had to do was give the order.

"Urric!" Waldeve shouted.

Urric sprang to attention. "Yes, my lord!"

"Has Robert been sent for?"

Urric sagged a bit. "Yes, my lord."

"Where is he, then?"

Urric looked over at Algar, who answered all in a rush, as if hoping to distance himself from the words as quickly as possible.

"Lord Robert said that he had something to finish, but he would be here by nightfall."

The men waited for the eruption, but Waldeve only tightened his lips and continued his pacing.

"Bring him to me as soon as he arrives," he told them. "Now, Algar, you'll need to go find my brother."

Algar stared. "Your brother, Lord?"

"Yes, you remember him." Waldeve stopped long enough to give Algar the full force of his sneer. "Tall man, red hair, beak like a puffin. Totally mad."

"Yes, Lord." Algar hesitated. "Where should I start looking?"

Waldeve considered. "Edinburgh," he said finally. "He's often there. If not, you'll have to search farther north."

"Yes, Lord," Algar answered. "I'll leave at first light."

Algar stepped back relieved. Urric closed his eyes. He knew what the next order would be.

"Urric!"

"Yes, Lord."

"You and Swein ride at once for Durham." Waldeve ignored the wince both men gave. "Tell my son Duncan that he doesn't need to fight for that Norman upstart anymore. He's just become my heir."

Satisfied that things were finally being accomplished, Waldeve stopped his circumnambulation of the room, sat down and called for wine. He had just finished the first cup when his fourth son, Robert, came in, a sleek hunting dog at his heels.

"Father!" he cried. "How did it happen? Who did it?"

Waldeve gazed at his son with contempt.

"If you'd been with them, you'd know," he answered.

Robert was brought up short. "If I'd been with them, I'd be dead, too. Did you send for me to tell me I should have been slaughtered?"

Waldeve held out his cup to be refilled.

"No, I sent for you to tell you that you're going to France." He waited for the shocked response, then smiled. "Edgar may have abandoned his family for his French whore, but his blood is still ours and it's his duty to come home and fight with us to avenge his brothers."

"He won't come, Father," Robert answered.

"You make him come," Waldeve said quietly. "Or don't bother returning."

Robert opened his mouth to protest, noticed Adalisa in the doorway gesturing for him to agree. He turned away angrily, but then gave in.

"Very well," he said. "I'll leave as soon as I can arrange for someone to oversee the spring shearing."

"You'll leave at once," Waldeve told him. "And return by the kalends of July."

Robert managed to get out of the hall before he gave way to his anger. Adalisa followed him. She put her hand on his arm, stopping him from pounding his fist against the stone wall.

"Please, Robert," she said. "Do as he asks. And come back quickly, as quickly as you can. Remember that until you and Edgar return, there will be no one to stand between your father and Duncan. And no one to stand between Duncan and the rest of us. Tell Edgar he must come. We need you both; all of us need you to protect us from him."

Robert shivered. She was right. Finding and punishing murderers was no more than usual summer activity here in Lothian. The real test would be to stand up to his brother Duncan. For that, Robert wanted all the support he could get.

"If I go, will you see to it that Lufen here is taken care of?" he asked Adalisa.

He bent over to rub the dog's flank lovingly. His stepmother smiled.

"I'll send her scraps from my own dinner, if you like," she promised. "And she may sleep here in the hall. I know how much you care for her."

"There's no one in the world that matters more to me," Robert answered. "She's the only one, besides you, whom I can trust."

"I know," she said. "So come back to us soon."

"By the kalends of July," he promised. "And Edgar will be with me."

Two

Paris, the home of Hubert LeVendeur, merchant, and his family.
Wednesday, 7 kalends June (May 26), 1143. Feast of Saint Augustine,
archbishop of Canterbury and missionary to the English.

"Sire," dist Evroïne, "n'alés pas co disans;
Il n'a en tot cest siecle arme nule vivant
Qui je creïsse mie a garder mon enfant."

"Lord," says Evroïne, "don't even suggest it;
In all the world there is no one living
Whom I would trust for an instant to care for my child."
—La Naissance du Chevalier au Cygne,
laisse 74, lines 2349–2351

*E*dgar sat happily in the back garden of his father-in-law's house, surrounded by wood shavings and walnut shells. He cracked open another nut, ate the meat and then rubbed the shell in a circular pattern against the wooden horse he was carving, smoothing and staining it at the same time. He worked slowly, meticulously. There was no hurry, and he wanted this to be perfect.

A shadow fell between him and the morning sun.

"Saint Joseph's splintered palms, Edgar! Are you making a child's toy or a reliquary?"

A shadow fell across Edgar's spirit as well. His wife's father stood over him, frowning in confusion. Edgar liked Hubert well enough. He adored Hubert's daughter Catherine enough to give up his country, his language and his family for her. But he knew that Catherine's father still found this new son an enigma. And when he couldn't understand something, Hubert's patience with it was small.

Edgar sighed. "I'm making a Trojan horse for James," he explained. "I don't want there to be any rough edges on it."

"Your son is but four months old," Hubert said. "It will be ages before he can play with it and then he'll most likely smash it."

Edgar nodded and went on with his work. Now Hubert sighed. He had come out here for a reason. What was it?

"Ah, yes." He made the effort and spoke in a more conciliatory tone. "About the extention. I've spoken to Prior Hervé at Saint-Denis and he's willing to let us have the stones you wanted for the foundation."

This caught Edgar's full attention. After weeks of argument, he had finally convinced Hubert to allow him to design and oversee the building of a room at the back of the house for himself and Catherine. It represented a great concession on Hubert's part, admitting both that Edgar had the skill to manage the work and that, despite his claim to be an English nobleman, he might have some use other than siring grandchildren. But much depended on the success of the project.

"And what does the prior want to charge you for the stones?" Edgar asked.

Hubert shrugged. "A cask of wine, not even the best. It's nothing."

"Except that the stones I want are leftover pieces," Edgar said in disgust. "Too small or misshapen for the church. Hervé would have had to pay someone to haul them away."

"I know that!" Hubert answered sharply, his trader's pride stung. "But for the amount of business we do with the abbey, it doesn't hurt to let them think they have the better of the deal."

The two men stared at each other, both trying to think of something that wouldn't drive a wedge into their cautious acceptance of one another. The sound of laughter saved them.

The walled garden they were in reached all the way down to a shallow stream that emptied into the Seine. On this warm morning the rest of the household had sensibly gone down to the water. Now portions of it were returning—damp, cool and content. In the lead was Edgar's wife and Hubert's daughter, Catherine, wearing only a shift that barely reached past her knees and carrying her son, James, who, at four months, was in danger of being thoroughly spoiled by adoring relatives.

Just behind her was the maid, Samonie, followed by her own three children. Hubert had not been pleased when Catherine had allowed the maid to bring her bastards, fathered by God-knew-whom, into the house. But he had to admit that they were well mannered and could be trusted with chores. The oldest girl, Willa, had taken over the care of baby James with tenderness and skill on the rare times when Catherine would release him.

She wasn't about to at the moment. James, wrapped only in a linen cloth, was making it clear to his mother that he was ready to eat.

Catherine stuck a finger in his mouth and he began sucking eagerly.

"That won't quiet him for long," Edgar said.

"I know, I'll take him in," she answered. "Samonie will see to the feeding of the rest of you."

James's face was turning red with frustration. Edgar patted his head, quite sure that this was the most remarkable child ever born into the world. His hair, what there was of it, was dark like Catherine's, and small curls were evident, but his skin was lighter than hers. His eyes were already grey like Edgar's, and curious. As for the rest, all the limbs were in their proper places, fingers and toes accounted for. That alone was worth the long journey they had made to the shrine of Saint James in Spain. They had asked the saint to grant them a living child and he had given them a miracle.

Just at that moment, Edgar was as content as he ever hoped to be in this life.

He should have savored the moment more. It was to be the last for many months.

It was early evening. The air had cooled and fog was creeping up from the river. Hubert had gone out to visit his brother, Eliazar, and taken Catherine and the baby with him. Edgar was dozing in a chair by the window overlooking the narrow alleyway next to the house, his feet propped up on a cushioned stool. Through half-closed eyes, he watched the people passing, their voices rising in an unintelligible mix. Suddenly, he sat upright, fully alert. It couldn't be. He kicked the stool aside to lean out the window for a better look.

The man was just rounding the corner. He entered the main road that ran next to the Grève. Edgar rubbed his eyes. He must be wrong. It was just another northerner. The man was tall and had hair a shade of blond much more vibrant than Edgar's pale straw color. But he only resembled Robert, that was all. Edgar hadn't seen the face. Probably just another English student in Paris, or a trader from Germany.

Then he heard the clanging of the iron ring at the door to the courtyard. With a sinking heart, Edgar went down the stairs slowly to meet the visitor. He didn't need to hear the stumbling French or the puzzled response of the maid to know that it was his brother. And if Robert had left his precious estate and come all the way to France then something terrible had happened.

"*Edgar! Hwæt sægest thu, Broðer?*"

Edgar blinked. It had been so long since he'd heard his own language that it took a moment to understand.

"Robert!" Edgar endured his brother's embrace. "I'm sorry. I couldn't believe it was you. What's brought you here? What's happened?" He switched back to French to shout at the errand boy. "Ullo, fetch some food and wine for my guest!"

Then he turned back to Robert. "There's no point in wasting time in greetings. Only catastrophe would being you here. Tell me. Now."

Robert did.

Ullo arrived with a tray of bread, cheese, strawberries and a pitcher of wine. He saw Edgar's face go stiff with horror and became frightened, himself, not knowing what this foreigner was saying. The sounds themselves were brutal to his ears.

"Shall I go find Master Hubert?" he asked.

"What?" Edgar tried to focus on the boy. "No, this has nothing to do with him. Put the tray down and go."

Robert broke off a piece of cheese. Edgar poured a cup of the wine for him and then another for himself.

"It's horrible," he said. The cup rattled as he set it on the tray and he realized he was shaking. "Who would have killed them all? Especially little Edgar. I'd almost forgotten I had a namesake. He can't have been old enough to wield a sword."

"He was a tall lad, and strong for twelve," Robert answered. "At least he had a weapon to defend himself. And he used it. All the swords were stained." He took a hunk of cheese. "Father sent me to bring you home. We need you."

"No." Edgar shook his head. "No." He backed away a step. "No."

"Edgar, I know what he said to you." The cheese crumbled in Robert's fist. "He was angry. He didn't mean it."

"It's not that," Edgar answered. "I forgave him long ago. After all, he doesn't know Catherine."

Robert wiped his hands of the cheese and any interest in Edgar's wife.

"Then how can you refuse, Edgar?" he demanded. "This is family. It's your duty to come back."

"And do what?" Edgar splashed wine in an arc as he waved his arms in anger. "I have no talent for warfare; you all told me that often enough. And if I couldn't fight for the good of the family, I had to pray. Well, I haven't become a priest, Robert. My prayers are of no more value than yours."

Robert's tanned face grew red, then pale. He bit back his sharp answer.

"Vengeance is more than battle. There are other ways to destroy an enemy," he said. "And we have enough priests at home. Too many, to my mind. This is about what you owe your family. Your brothers have been murdered, Edgar. It's laid upon you to come home."

"Robert, this is my home." Edgar turned toward the door. He had heard the steps and the whispers.

"And this is my family," he added as Catherine came in with the sleeping child in her arms.

She looked from Edgar to Robert, her blue eyes wide with surprise. Then she nodded to Robert.

"*Ic gief the greting,*" she said. "*Ic eom Catherine, Eadgardes wif.*" She glanced at Edgar. "Is that right?"

He smiled. "Close enough. He understood you."

Robert licked his lips. "*Jo Robert, le freres. Diex te saut.*" He muttered to Edgar, "You know I hate this tongue."

Willa appeared at Catherine's side and gently took the baby from her arms without waking him. Catherine turned back to Robert and smiled nervously.

"Edgar, I'm very happy to welcome your brother to our home," she said. "But why is he here?"

"I'll explain it all later, *carissima,*" he told her, "For now, would you arrange for a place for Robert to sleep?"

"Of course. He must be very tired," she answered. "I'm sorry."

"In the morning, Robert, we can discuss this," Edgar said. "I'll send whatever help I can, but I won't return to Scotland with you."

"You must," Robert answered. "Father needs all of us now, even you. I need you. It hasn't come to you yet, has it? With Alexander and Egbert gone, that means Duncan is the eldest."

Edgar froze. Catherine's stomach tightened as she saw the horror in his eyes. What were they talking about?

"Father would never let him inherit," Edgar stated, but there was uncertainty in his voice.

"He's already declared him heir. And when Father dies, who will stop him?" Robert asked. "We need someone who knows our laws and can argue at the court for the French custom of the eldest's son's son succeeding when he's of age. That's our only hope. I won't have Duncan as my overlord."

"Then find a new lord, or join the church," Edgar answered. "If

Father has decided Duncan is to get Wedderlie then there's nothing I can do."

"Edgar . . . for Christ's love! We're desperate! We need you! What must I say to make you see that?"

Catherine was becoming increasingly frightened by the conversation. The interchange was too quick to follow but the sound of it was to her like one of those sad tales about lost sailors and exiles that Edgar chanted sometimes. She shivered. What must this place be like that their language was made up only of words of anger and grief?

Edgar would allow no further discussion that evening. Robert was introduced to Hubert at dinner.

"I grieve with your father at the loss of his posterity," Hubert said formally, and waited for Edgar to translate.

Robert nodded his appreciation. Hubert glanced from him to Edgar. He could feel the tension between them. He guessed the reason. Everyone knew a man's duty at such a time. But would Edgar be persuaded to perform it?

After a few attempts at translated conversation, they gave up and ate in silence. After the meal, Robert was given a bed and shown where the privy was. When his brother had been settled and they had checked that James was safe in his cradle, Edgar and Catherine undressed and climbed into bed. Edgar closed his eyes and curled into his normal sleeping position, but Catherine had restrained her anxiety all evening and wasn't to be put off any longer.

"How dreadful for your brother to have to come all this way bearing such sorrow," she opened, still sitting up. "The loss must be devastating to you."

Edgar nuzzled his forehead against her thigh.

"So awful I can't bear to think of it," he mumbled.

She ran her hand through his hair.

"Yes, I understand that," she said. "We'll all pray for their souls and I'll write Mother Heloise, asking that the nuns add their prayers."

He raised his head. "I hadn't thought of doing that. Would you?"

Catherine smiled. "Of course. Now, Edgar, tell me the rest. I know your brother didn't come only to bring this news, however disastrous for your family."

Edgar saw that feigning sleep wouldn't work. He decided on an alternate route of distraction. Catherine's fingers tightened, pulling painfully on his hair before he could get very far. She slid down on the bed until they faced each other.

"I love you," she said quietly. "But before I show you how much, you have to tell me. These deaths were part of a blood feud, weren't they? Who does he want you to help kill?"

Edgar rolled over onto his back. Catherine could feel his anger but wasn't sure if it were at her or the situation. He was quiet so long, she wasn't sure if he would answer. Finally he swallowed and she understood that he had been trying to control his voice.

"No one knows," he said. "And it doesn't matter, not to me. They'll have to fight their own battles; I won't leave you."

Catherine moved against him. She had interesting curves to nuzzle with, he reflected anew. She waited until she was sure his attention wasn't on anything she was saying, but he heard it anyway.

"You don't have to," she whispered. "James and I will come, too."

He decided the argument could wait until morning.

Catherine and Edgar were still sound asleep when Hubert was awakened abruptly by his nephew, Solomon ben Jacob.

"Uncle!" Solomon whispered harshly. "Get up! Hurry! You must come with me at once."

Half-awake, Hubert's heart leapt in panic. "What is it? Have they come for us?"

"No, no," Solomon answered. "I'm sorry. No, we are in no danger, at least I hope not. But Uncle Eliazar has had disturbing news. He sent me to bring you now. It can't wait until daylight."

Hubert sagged back onto his bed. It took a moment to bring himself back to the present. He wasn't a child any longer, but a man in his fifties. And the Soldiers of Christ weren't at the door this time. It had been over forty years since they had broken in and dragged off his mother and sisters to their deaths while he hid in the cupboard. Forty years he had been a Christian, at least in the eyes of the world. But a sound in the night could still make him tremble. In every Easter sermon he could still hear the echoes of his mother's screams.

Solomon saw that Hubert's hands shook as he dressed. He

cursed himself for being so thoughtless. There had been no overt persecution since he had been born, but Solomon knew the stories from the days of the Great Crusade. He also knew how tormented Hubert was for the sin of baptism and for staying alive.

When Hubert was ready, they set off. They crossed the bridge over the Seine from the Grève to the Île de la Cité and felt their way down the dark and twisting streets of the old Juiverie to the house of Hubert's brother, Eliazar.

The gate was opened not by a servant, but by Eliazar's wife, Johanna.

"My poor Hubert!" she exclaimed softly. "We'll find a way out, I promise we will!"

Thoroughly frightened, Hubert followed her into the house and up the stairs to his brother's hall. Eliazar was sitting by the cold hearth. A solitary candle lit a circle about him. On the table next to his stool was a wine pitcher and three cups. He set down his own empty cup as they entered.

"Brother!" he cried and hugged Hubert. "We are in grave danger. Word has come that you have been reported to the bishop as an apostate."

"What?" Hubert blindly took the cup Johanna thrust into his hand. "Who? How? What proof have they given?"

His mind flashed to his other daughter, Agnes, who had discovered his secret two years before and had refused to live under his roof since then. She couldn't have betrayed him. She didn't hate him that much, did she?

"We don't know who," Eliazar told him. "But there can't be much proof or you would have been brought before the bishop at once."

"One of the canons is a friend of Edgar's and mine," Solomon explained. "He came to me this afternoon to tell me. He doesn't believe the accusation."

"But does Bishop Stephen believe it?" Hubert asked.

Eliazar shrugged. "We don't know. You've never hidden your birth, exactly."

"I've simply told no one that I was born a Jew, nor have I admitted to being your brother, as well as your partner." Hubert shook his head. "Most people assume that I'm the natural son of Gervase LeVendeur. There aren't many now who remember differently."

"Someone does," Solomon said. "Or thinks he does. We must convince Bishop Stephen that there's no truth to this accusation before it becomes public."

Eliazar agreed. "Even the rumor could destroy us, Brother. The other merchants would believe we had taken unfair advantage. Abbot Suger would never trust us again."

Hubert sat staring at his hands, but what he was seeing was his mother's face as the soldiers pounded on their door. Her beautiful dark hair and wide eyes. Her face so like Solomon's and so very much like . . . "Catherine," he whispered.

"What's that?" Eliazar had been lost in his own memories.

"She must leave Paris," Hubert said. "If a mob comes for me, I won't have her taken as well. I've seen it, an angry beast with no mind. No one will believe she's a Christian. They might even say we were trying to convert Edgar."

"Yes, it would be safest if she and your grandson were sent away," Eliazar agreed. He looked at his wife.

"Don't even suggest it," Johanna said. "I've stayed at your side through fire, flood and famine and I'll not leave you now."

"Catherine won't go, either, if she knows why," Solomon pointed out.

Hubert sighed. "I know that. She's more stubborn than Ballam's ass."

"Would she go to your son at Vielleteneuse?" Eliazar suggested.

"Too close. She'd be back at the first hint of trouble," Solomon answered.

Hubert agreed. "No, there's only one thing to do, much as it galls me. Edgar's brother has arrived with news of death in the family. I suspect that he wants Edgar to return with him. I must convince Edgar to go and take Catherine and the baby with him. And may the Holy One protect them."

"It will take a lot of convincing," Solomon warned.

"Not if I tell him the truth," Hubert said. "And not if you go with him."

Solomon's jaw dropped.

"I would never leave you two to fight this out alone!" he told them. "What sort of coward do you think I am?"

Eliazar grew stern. "My brother is right. Solomon, you are the last of our family who still keeps the true faith. If you're killed, then the seed of our father will never grow again. There are few enough of us."

"Absolutely not," Solomon said.

Hubert and Eliazar looked at each other in silent agreement. Solomon would go. They would make him understand that if it took them all night.

Edgar came downstairs before Catherine had wakened and, finding Hubert in the great hall, explained the situation. The response was not what he had hoped for.

"What do you mean, you think I should go?" Edgar was furious. He had expected support. "I know! You want to see your daughter widowed, don't you, so you can find her a more suitable husband?"

Hubert snorted. "Nonsense! Do you think she'd be any more tractable the second time?"

Edgar's lips twitched. It was a cogent point. "Then why, by the two halves of Saint Basilla, do you want me to go back there and fight?" he shouted. "What good will I be to them? I was trained for the church. Do you think I'll vanquish my brothers' murderers with *exempla?*"

"I want to send Solomon with you," Hubert replied. "To negotiate with the king of Scotland and the abbots there for our spices in trade for wool. The Flemish and the Danes are the only merchants in Scotland now. But with the war in England the usual routes are closed and we might be able to find new markets. You know the customs, speak the language. You could be of help to him."

Edgar blinked. His father-in-law knew him better than he had realized. The appeal to family loyalty would have been only a repetition of Robert's plea. But the prospect of being a part of Hubert's work, that was intriguing. Still, there was something odd about this. It was too convenient. Edgar tried another gambit.

"Catherine has said she won't let me go without her," he announced. If that didn't put Hubert on his side, nothing would.

To his astonishment, Hubert seemed pleased.

"That would be an excellent idea," he said. "It's time Catherine met your family."

Edgar sat with a thump. "I don't believe it," he said. "You're either mad or there's something wrong."

"You're right." Hubert gave him a hand up. "Something is wrong. I need your help and we must keep Catherine from knowing."

"To the first you are welcome," Edgar said. "As for the second, that will be much harder. Now tell me."

Hubert bit his upper lip, scraping it with his teeth in an effort to find the right words.

"In joining my family," he began slowly, "in accepting *all* of us, you've taken on a great burden, one, I admit, I've doubted you could carry. You think I believe you useless. That's not true. I believe you to be dangerous."

Edgar was stung. Hadn't he proved his loyalty many times over, not least on their recent journey to Spain? He reminded Hubert of this.

"It's one thing to stand by us far from home, where there is little chance of encountering anyone who could threaten our safety here," Hubert answered sternly. "It's another to risk being labeled a heretic or apostate by those who can destroy your life."

Edgar closed his eyes, pushing out the image of his mentor, Peter Abelard, forced to burn his own writings as heretical. It was too close to a vision of flames licking at his own feet, or Catherine's. He took a deep breath and opened his eyes again.

"I can defend myself and my wife against any charges," he answered. "Far better than you could. The question is whether or not I would betray you. I resent your even asking it."

Hubert gazed at his son-in-law in surprise. Although Edgar wasn't trained to be a soldier, he had been raised to lead, and the traditions of his class were woven into his being. In his world, betrayal was worse than apostasy.

"I apologize," Hubert said. "I'll tell you everything and then you may do as you see fit."

It was Edgar's turn to be surprised.

Sometime later Catherine came in and found them huddled at the end of the room, speaking in whispers. They both looked up guiltily when they saw her.

"Where's the baby?" Edgar asked.

"He's been bathed, oiled and fed, and Willa is swaddling him," Catherine told him. "Now may I join the discussion? I know it's about me."

She waited. Hubert shrugged and went over to sit at the open window. Edgar felt abandoned.

"Catherine," he began, "I've decided to go back with Robert and—"

"Don't you two tell me I can't come with you," she interrupted. "I've thought of another eight reasons why I should."

"No," Edgar said. "Your father and I agree that you and James will make the journey as well."

"What?" Catherine turned from her husband to her father and back again. "You think I should go?"

Hubert nodded. "You have a duty to your husband's family. I have no right to keep you from it."

Catherine frowned. That had been reason number three. Something was wrong here. It wasn't like either man to give in so easily.

"Why do you want me to go?" she asked suspiciously.

"I don't *want* you to go." The honesty in Hubert's voice was unmistakeable. "But I think you should. I shall miss you and worry about you every day."

"Really?" Catherine said. "I mean you really believe that it's my duty to go to Scotland?"

"With all my heart," Hubert told her.

"Edgar?"

"Your father made me see that it might be best if you met my family," Edgar said. He didn't sound as certain as Hubert had. "I have my doubts about it. There is war in England and the North is unsettled by it. The journey won't be easy."

"No journey ever is." Catherine dismissed that.

"I would miss you terribly if you stayed behind." This was said with more conviction. "If I must go, I would rather you were with me."

Catherine smiled. She wasn't sure how she had won so easily but she wasn't going to complain lest they change their minds. Time enough to ferret out the reason when it was too late for them to back out.

Suddenly Edgar spoke in English.

"You can come in, Robert. I can hear your breathing out there. And, yes, I've decided to come back with you."

Since he'd been found out, Robert pulled the curtain aside and came in. He rushed over and gave Edgar a bear hug. Then he hugged Catherine as well.

"I understand more than you think!" he said. "She's talked you into coming, hasn't she?"

He grabbed Catherine and lifted, whirling her around.

"Thank you, *bele soeur!*" he cried. "Thank you!"

Catherine grinned at Edgar as she flew past him.

"I presume this means he likes me?"

Edgar nodded, then went over to the window where Hubert sat. He stood there for a moment, looking out across the garden to the stream and the town of Paris beyond it. This was Catherine's world. She had lived most of her life by the hours rung on the bells of Paris. How could he prepare her for the emptiness, the wildness, of Scotland? Or for the bleak homecoming he expected?

Solomon prepared for the trip as well, but was determined to sulk through the whole process.

"So, what do I have to be this time?" he asked. "I doubt that Catherine could remember to call me Stephen."

"She won't have to," Edgar said. "There are men named Solomon in Scotland, and I'm certain none of them are Hebrew. We use the old names more than they do here."

"Ah, but you still don't think I could go as myself?" Solomon had expected this.

Edgar had managed to get his English friend John to take Robert out for an afternoon so that they could meet with Eliazar and discuss the monetary aspect of the journey.

"I hate making you pretend to be one of them, Solomon," Eliazar muttered. "There's no profit anywhere worth risking your soul."

Solomon patted his uncle's shoulder.

"No one is making me do this," he said. "After all these years, there's no chance of my converting. I promise you I'll not touch pork or take Communion."

Eliazar shuddered at the thought.

"It has to be," Hubert reminded him. "If he's going with Catherine and Edgar. His resemblance to her is too strong."

Solomon grinned at his cousin. The black curls, the olive skin, the straight, determined nose were the same in each of them. Solomon's eyes were green and Catherine's blue and Solomon's beard covered the chin that was also the same as hers, but no one seeing them together would believe they weren't related.

"Don't worry. I won't let anyone torment you," Catherine assured him.

"Except yourself, of course," he added, reaching out to tweak her hair. She moved to avoid him and fell off her stool.

Hubert glared at them both. "You are both too old for that sort of nonsense," he warned. "Solomon, no one is going to take you for a serious merchant's representative if you are seen pulling your cousin's braids. And, Catherine, you should remember that you're a married woman and keep those braids covered."

"Yes, Father." Catherine was tempted to pull her skirt up to cover her hair but decided that age did indeed bring wisdom and resisted the impulse.

"Now, have we finished with the school room long enough to plan what you'll need to take with you?"

Solomon and Catherine folded their hands like children and prepared to behave.

Everything was finally ready. Gifts assembled and wrapped. Clothing chosen and packed. Guards hired for as far as Boulogne, and Samonie convinced to let Willa go along as nursemaid to James, a decision that Catherine was infinitely grateful for.

"I truly couldn't bear to be parted from him," she told Edgar as they prepared for bed the last night before going. "But I don't think I could manage to take care of him on my own."

"I still think we should bring a wet nurse as well," Edgar said. "What if the travel causes your milk to stop flowing?"

"You know how I feel about that," she answered "All the authorities agree that a child needs to be fed by its own mother. Saint Ida found that a wet nurse had fed one of her sons and made him vomit the foreign milk. But it was too late; the other two sons became kings but Eustace was only a count."

"I'm sure that proves something," Edgar said. "But James has little chance of becoming even a count, in any case."

"Edgar." Catherine started to speak, then stopped and looked at the floor. Edgar realized that the subject was about to change radically.

"Catherine? What is it now? I know you." He bent down and took her chin in his hand, forcing her to look up. "Something is gnawing at you and you won't be content until it's been stopped. Now, what is it?"

She closed her eyes, her lips twisted in embarrassment.

"It's just that you still seem unhappy about my coming with you. . . . I keep wondering what there could be in Scotland that you don't want me to see, and . . . it really doesn't matter if you . . . especially before we met." She sighed again.

Edgar's sigh echoed hers. "Catherine," he started, trying to keep the exasperation out of his voice, "if that's what you're worrying about, don't. I left no bastards behind at home, no women pinning for me and no one I want to return for. Why don't you trust me?"

"I do trust you," she answered. "It's myself I doubt. What do I have to keep you here but your own sense of honor? The past few years have been so hard for you. You gave up everything for me."

"*Stulta carissima!*" Edgar hugged her tightly. "How many ways do I have to say it? I gave up nothing for you. I found everything, more than I ever dreamed possible on this earth. I love you sacreligiously. I adore our son. I want no life other than with you. There is nothing calling me back to Scotland but duty. Is that clear? Now, please stop moping."

She had buried her face in his tunic. When she looked back up at him, the imprint of his silver brooch was on her cheek.

"I know I'm being foolish," she said. "But I also know there's a lot you haven't told me and I have the feeling that there's something your brother isn't telling us, either. Whatever it is, we need to be together to face it."

"And James?" Edgar countered. "Would you risk him, as well?"

"It would kill me to leave him," Catherine said. "And I must go with you. So we'll have to have faith that the Holy Apostle who granted us the miracle of his birth will continue to watch over him."

"It may be that it's because of James that I even considered obeying my father's command to return," Edgar said. "No one could have warned me that I could feel so intensely about a being so small, useless and smelly. Every time I look at him, I want . . . ."

"I know." Catherine leaned against his shoulder. "I do, too. I'm sorry I'm acting so oddly. I don't really fear you'll want to abandon us for some woman of your own race."

"That's good," he said and put his arm around her, steadying them both.

"But, Edgar." She kept her eyes on the cradle and his rough hand, so huge next to the baby's. "I do sense something very wrong about all this, and although I intend to see it through, I'm still very frightened."

Edgar didn't respond. She had no idea of what they were running away from or what they were heading into. He did.

And he was terrified.

Three

The North Sea, a day out of Niewpoort, Flanders. Saturday, 2 ides of June (June 12), 1143. The feast of Saints Basilidus, Cyrini, Nabor and Nazar. Roman soldiers martyred under Diocletian.

Cernens autem Edgarus Ethlinge . . . ascensa navi cum matre et sororibus in patriam reverti, qua natus fuerat, conabatur. Sed summus imperator, qui ventis imperat et mari, mare commovet, et spiritu procellarum exalti sunt fluctus ejus. Saeviente vero tempestate, omnes in desperatione vitæ positi, sese Deo commendant, et puppim pelago committunt. Igitur post plurima pericula . . . coacti sunt in Scociam applicare.

Edgar Atheling . . . with his sisters and mother, boarded a ship, attempting to return to the country where he was born. But the Lord above all, who rules the winds and seas, disturbed its waters. The waves rose with the force of the tempest. In the raging storm, with everyone despairing for their lives, they commended themselves to God, and entrusted the boat to the sea. Therefore, after many dangers . . . they were compelled to land in Scotland.

—Johannes de Fordun,
Chronica Gentis Scottorum,
Liber V Captitulum xiv

I'm dying," Catherine moaned. "Edgar, for mercy's sake, please don't take a second wife who will be cruel to my son!"

Edgar looked down at her and laughed heartlessly.

"You're not dying," he informed her. "You'll be fine soon. It's a beautiful day. The winds are with us. We should see the coast of Northumbria by tomorrow."

Catherine lifted her head an inch off the deck and regretted the movement immediately.

"I hate you," she croaked. "Go away."

She turned her face back to the wall of the canvas shelter and tried vainly to pretend the world was still.

Edgar bent to give Catherine a comforting pat, but decided it was better simply to obey her and leave. He stopped at the doorway to check that Willa was not suffering as badly as Catherine and that James was content in his sling, which had been nailed to a frame on the deck so that he would stay steady as the boat rolled. The baby was sleeping soundly. Edgar went over to the windward rail where Solomon was leaning out, his black curls blown into Gordian knots by the breeze.

"Is she any better?" Solomon asked.

"She's able to speak," Edgar said. "Though I'd almost rather she weren't."

"Perhaps we should have taken the risk and gone through Normandy to Calais," Solomon said. "We could have made the crossing in just a few hours."

Edgar shook his head. "Absolutely not. That would mean another week going north on dangerous roads, with robbers at every turn and no guarantee of a safe place to rest the night. I wish we could sail even farther north and land at Berwick."

"It's that bad in England? What does your brother say? How did he make his way to France?"

"He came through York and out the Humber," Edgar told him. "He says the journey is better now than when I was last there, but still not worth the risk. No, the water is friendlier. Well, it is for most of us. Poor Catherine! I never thought she'd have such trouble with seasickness."

"Neither did she," Solomon answered. "Remember, she'd never seen anything wider than the Seine before this trip. It's not something one can describe."

"How will we ever get her home?" Edgar worried.

"We won't," Solomon told him. "Catherine will have to find the courage herself."

He looked out at the empty sea. "I only hope we have a home to come back to."

Catherine was miserable. Once the worst of the motion sickness passed, she felt a fool. No one else was suffering like this. What was wrong with her?

"It doesn't matter what's wrong, girl." Catherine bit back a curse. Sweet Virgin! Four years out of the convent and the voices of her teachers still haunted her. Catherine cringed, but the voices in her head continued. *"Stop whining! Bear your affliction with patience. You're a grown woman, with a baby to care for. What will happen to James without you?"*

Cautiously, Catherine sat up. She groaned. The long swells were pushing her stomach up and down with the boat. And the smell made it even worse. Thank God the traders were on their way to England to buy skins for tanning and not on the return. The cargo on this trip was finished cloth. She didn't think she could have stood the odor of fresh animal skin along with the tar and fish smells that permeated the air. Bile rose in her throat and she leaned over the bucket they had left for her. Why couldn't anyone see that she was in extremis? Edgar was cruel and unfeeling and probably had a new wife selected and waiting for him in Scotland.

"Willa?" she whispered.

The girl was beside her at once.

"Any better, Mistress?" she asked.

"Perhaps I'll wait until tomorrow to die," Catherine answered without conviction. "Is the baby all right? I haven't heard him."

"Fine," Willa answered. "He's awake now and watching everything. He seems to like the rocking of the waves."

"Little traitor," Catherine muttered. "He must get it from his father. Well then, he'll want to eat soon. Can you get me something gentle to drink before you bring him to me? Flat beer, perhaps? I'm worried that my milk will stop if I have nothing in my stomach."

"Of course." Willa raised the tent flap to leave. She hesitated, then spoke again. "It wouldn't make any difference if a wet nurse had come with us. She would likely have had the same problems as you."

Catherine smiled. "Thank you, Willa. How did you know I was regretting not bringing one?"

"I just guessed," the girl answered. "But you've no need for regret. Look at you, almost sitting up. You're much better. In your worry for James, you've overcome your own illness. So it's all to the good, isn't it?"

Her words cheered Catherine, even though they were inaccurate. She felt terrible. She was drenched in her own sweat. Her skin, normally a light olive-brown, was now an unripe-olive green. The boat crested a wave and slid into the hollow. Catherine shut her eyes and lay down again. Why had no one told her that the sea was so unstable?

Edgar was slurping down pickled eel, letting the juice drip onto a slab of rye bread balanced on his knees. He took a long swig of beer from the gourd that was being passed around and belched appreciatively.

The captain nodded approval. "You'd have made a good Viking," he commented. "Both of you," he added as he passed the beer to Robert.

Robert grunted and pretended to drink. He wasn't as good a sailor as Edgar but he'd be damned and fried if he let on.

There was one other passenger on the boat, a young cleric named Leonel. He took no part in the camaraderie. When he wasn't hanging over the side, he sat and glared at those who were obviously enjoying the journey. Seeing him so miserable, Solomon had tried to help him, but Leonel's only response was to moan and wave him away.

Solomon went back to the group and sat beside Edgar.

Edgar leaned back. "They say our family came to England with Hengst and Horsa," he said. "But I suspect there's a bit of Danish in us, too. We've lived in the North several generations now."

Solomon took a strip of eel and lowered it into his mouth. "Can't understand why Catherine's so ill," he said. "*We* come from a long line of Saracen pirates."

There was a silence from the sailors as they studied Solomon's dark features. Solomon grinned at them wickedly and Edgar rolled his eyes. At last the captain decided it was a joke and they all laughed.

"We don't get Saracens much in the North Sea," he said. "But there are still Danes who roam the coasts, especially north of the Humber. They haven't forgotten Viking ways."

"I've seen them in the east, sailing up the Dnieper," Solomon told them, serious now. "They aren't too fond of other traders. Board, steal, kill and sink seems to be their general strategy."

The captain agreed. "But we've had no trouble with them so far this year. Perhaps they decided that they had plundered Northumbria to the bone or maybe King David's justice has finally reached them. Whatever the reason, I'm grateful. We have a steady supplier in Wearmouth who saves the best of the skins for us. He's even promised a brace of hunting dogs that I can sell at a fine profit in Bouillon. I may be able to put out two boats by next Saint John's Eve."

He paused and gave them a nervous glance. "Forgive my blether," he added quickly. "I know men like you have no interest in trade, unless you hold the tithes for some seaport. If you do, forget everything I just said. Trade is terrible. The sea takes most of what I earn."

He regarded them with suspicion. Edgar laughed.

"Do I look like an abbot?" he asked. "Or an earl? We're lucky in my family if we can collect the cornage and have enough left over for conveth when the king comes visiting."

"Ah, yes. There's a lot of you like that now," the captain said. "The North's full of Saxon lords trying to hold on to what they can all the while hunting for a rich marriage with one of the Normans' daughters."

Edgar tensed.

"Our family doesn't have to marry to reclaim our own land," he said.

Beside him Robert wiggled uncomfortably. Edgar looked at him. "Are you ill, Brother?" he asked.

Robert was mildly queasy but he shook his head.

"You needn't take offense so quickly," he told Edgar. "The man didn't mean it as an insult."

"Of course not!" The captain was surprised. "I'd rather earn my land in a warm bed than in a battle any day, even if the woman were covered in warts and had the breath of a goat."

"A noble aspiration, sir." Robert passed him the beer jug. "I drink to your success."

The captain grinned and took the jug. "Wæs hael!" He gestured at them all, then upended the jug so that the beer poured into his mouth and overflowed to dribble through his beard.

When they were alone again, Edgar turned on Robert.

"How can you take that slander so lightly?" he demanded.

Robert shook his head in disbelief.

"What slander?" he asked. "Marriage has always been the best source of land and of assuring oneself of allies. Because you went mad and took a wife with no relatives who know how to fight, do you think everyone else should follow your example? If everyone married where their heart lay, what would happen to families? We'd soon all be left with nothing more than a toft on a hillside, too rocky even for sheep."

"That isn't what we were taught, Robert," Edgar muttered.

"Things have changed," Robert told him shortly. "You'll find that out soon enough."

Edgar didn't answer but stared out at the water, empty as far as the horizon, where a smudge of grey clouds was forming. He shivered. Once again he regretted letting himself be talked into this journey. Only his fear for Catherine's and James's safety could have done it.

It was so peaceful on the water. Edgar wished they could sail on forever, past Britain and out into the open ocean. The Irish said that there was an island far to the west of their own in which there was no sorrow or suffering. At the moment Edgar felt it would be worth the danger to seek it. Anything would be better than having to face his father again.

The smudge that was at the joining of sea and sky seemed to be growing. Edgar squinted, wondering if it was the first sign of land.

But there was nothing solid about it. The captain passed by and Edgar grabbed his arm, pointing to the spot.

"Yes," he said. "I've been watching it. You'd best stay under the canvas with your family tonight."

"If you need help . . ." Edgar started.

"Don't worry," the captain told him. "If it means saving us all, I'll order you to help."

"You'll get no protest from us."

Edgar went back to tell Solomon and Robert of the approaching storm.

"You've lived inland too long," Robert said. "I smelled it growing hours ago. We'll be all right, although your wife may not believe it. These men make the crossing five or six times a year. The boat is sturdy. The captain carries a cross with a fingernail of Saint Nicholas embedded in the wood."

Solomon snorted. Robert turned on him.

"It's true," he insisted. "He told me that it glows like a diamond in the sun when there is danger. It's warned him of pirates and frightened away whales with its brilliance."

"Then let's hope it also has control over the winds," Solomon said. "And I'll add my own prayers that these men are as skilled as you say."

Solomon wasn't the only one praying that night. Willa clutched her string of wooden beads and counted out *Nostre Peres* over and over. Catherine, too frightened to be sick, recited psalms in her head and tried not to let her mind stray to the book of Jonah. Robert and Edgar alternated between ancient songs of sea wanderings and exhortations in their own language to Saints Cuthbert and Kedigern. The poor cleric crouched next to the rail, soaked to the bone, refusing to move.

The canvas flapped about in the wind, giving them little protection from the elements. The wood of the boat creaked as if it were about to fly apart. From outside the flimsy tent there were shouts and curses as the crew endeavored to save the mast.

James lay in Catherine's lap. She was nursing him discreetly through an opening in her tunic and he had fallen asleep in midswallow. His swaddling reeked, as there had been no chance to change it, but it wasn't bothering him yet. Of all on board, he was the only one who was perfectly content.

Catherine felt his gentle breathing against her skin and was comforted. She leaned against Edgar, who had his arm around them both.

"Saint James won't let him die," she said.

Edgar felt for the baby's head and stroked it. How could anyone sleep so peacefully in all this cacophony?

"I wish I was as sure of his protection of us," he said. "I'm sorry, Catherine."

She shook her head, then gasped as a wave whapped against the boat and spun it.

"No," she said when she had regained her breath. "You mustn't be sorry. We're together. It's dying apart that I fear most."

How odd. Even with the storm whirling around them, when Catherine said that, the terror left her. She didn't like where she was. She prayed that she could step on steady land again, but she knew that she had spoken the truth. If death came it would take them all. She wouldn't have the gnawing grief of those left behind, of the women she knew whose husbands had gone off to the Holy Land or just on a trip to Reims and vanished forever with no one knowing for certain if they had died or where their bones lay.

From somewhere near the stern a man screamed as his hands were sliced by the line he was trying to control. Catherine decided Jonah wasn't such a bad choice after all.

"*Et proiecisti me in profundum in corde maris et flumen circumdedit me; omnes gurgites tui, et fluctus tui super me transierunt.*"

After a moment Edgar joined her. Solomon, after listening a moment, started the prayer haltingly in Hebrew.

The wind blew the words from their mouths as it raged even louder.

A storm of another sort was brewing in Scotland. It was easy for Lord Waldeve to order Algar to find his brother, Æthelræd. It was not even that hard for Algar to do so. The real problem was in convincing Æthelræd to come back with him.

Æthelræd had been the only member of the family to stand by Edgar's decision to marry Catherine instead of join the Church. It was popularly believed that he had done this only to thwart Waldeve. The reason most people gave for this was not on account of any animosity between the brothers but because Æthelræd had been born face down and so spent his whole life being contrary. He had never given anyone cause to change that belief.

After days of searching and several false trails, Algar had finally tracked Æthelræd down in Moray, at the home of a Culdee priest, one of the ancient Celtic order who stubbornly resisted the insistence of the Norman bishops that they give up their wives and houses and become Augustinian canons. Naturally, Æthelræd sided with the Culdees and did his best to see that they found other means of support when their lands and benefices were taken away. In return, they shared their dinner and gave him a bed whenever he happened to pass through.

"God save all in this house," Algar said politely as he entered. "I seek my lord Æthelræd, brother to Waldeve."

From the gloom a voice roared out.

"Tell that son of a one-eyed ogre and a narwhal that I don't want to be sought!"

Algar turned in the general direction of the gale. He bowed.

"It's Algar, Lord," he said. "Remember me? You used to give me honeycomb pieces for cleaning your boots. I'm not your enemy."

A hand reached out and pulled him down. Algar stared into a face that was mostly bright red hair, with fiery eyebrows bristling in curls around sea-grey eyes, a jutting nose and a flowing beard streaked like rime with pure white. The eyebrows almost met in Æthelræd's effort to recollect the messenger.

"You one of my sons?" he asked.

Algar shook his head. "Not according to my mother," he said.

"Good. Too many bastards in the world already," Æthelræd returned to his soup.

Algar waited. Finally, with a sigh, Waldeve's brother waved to him to sit.

"Ita! Is there enough in the pot to feed this boy?" he shouted.

In the shadows a woman moved. A moment later a bowl was thrust under Algar's nose. He murmured thanks and got out his spoon.

"Sir," he began again, "I've been sent to tell you of a most grievous tragedy."

"My eldest nephews are murdered, I know." Æthelræd waved that bit of news away as he crossed himself. "It's sad about the boy, especially, but life is uncertain. I'm sure Ita and Kessog, here, will pray for him. You can put me down for a candle at Saint Andrews, as well. Now eat."

Algar looked at his soup. It was cold and greasy with mutton fat. The day was warm and the ride had been long. He ate with relish. Æthelræd watched him impatiently. Finally he could stand the silence no longer.

"Very well," he demanded. "What does the old tyrant want from me?"

Regretfully, Algar looked up from the soup.

"Lord Waldeve wants revenge on the murderers," he said. "He calls you to fulfill your duty to the family."

This did not come out as sternly as he had intended. Algar returned to the soup, hunching nervously over the bowl and bracing himself for the outburst.

A deep sigh wafted from the opposite side of the table. It hit Algar with a force that told him Æthelræd had had ale with his soup. Æthelræd stood, blocking the light from the door. He reached for his short cloak and wrapped it around his waist. Algar blinked in shock. The old heretic had been sitting there naked, just like the barbarians of Galloway, who only put on clothes out of doors to protect themselves from the elements. And with a woman present! Algar was astonished that Ita and Kessog allowed such behavior in their house.

"I need to walk this out," Æthelræd said. "Finish your food and follow me up to the church."

Tying the makeshift skirt with a strand of woven leather, he stomped out.

Algar scraped the last of the grease from the bowl and gave it back to Ita with thanks.

"Do you know Æthelræd well?" he asked her.

The woman smiled. "Not as well as you're thinking, son, but we've been friends many years. He's not mad, you know, however it looks, only bitterly unhappy."

"About the murders?" Algar asked.

She shook her head. "A much deeper pain than that. We've tried to get him to pray it away, to let God ease his suffering, but we've had no success."

"Do you think he'll come back with me?" Algar asked. "I don't like to think what Waldeve will do if I return without him."

Ita pursed her lips in thought.

"Tell him that," she said at last. "He'll come to protect you. At least that will be a good enough reason for him to save face. I think he's secretly glad he was sent for. Go on now. He's had time enough to think."

It wasn't hard to find Æthelræd. Algar spotted him almost at once, sitting among the grave markers at the church at the top of the hill. It was obvious that he had worn little more than the skirt for weeks. His skin was bronzed by the sun; his hair flamed against the green of the vines running up the stone wall behind him. Climbing the hill to meet him, Algar felt as if he were one of the knights in the Arthur stories, about to face a giant. He rather liked the conceit.

Æthelræd stood as Algar neared the top of the hill. By some chance, his head appeared directly in the center of one of the stone Celtic crosses. The sunlight coming through the spaces sent a nimbus around him that obscured his face. Algar saw only the light and the form of the man with the dark cross jutting out behind. His breath caught and he hurriedly blessed himself.

Æthelræd stepped from the sun. He was frowning.

"What made you do that, boy?" he growled. "You think I'm some kind of demon?"

"No, Lord," Algar stopped, embarrassed. He had no explanation.

Æthelræd looked down at the young man. If Algar had been awed by the image of Æthelræd and the cross, Æthelræd was also moved by the face before him. Caught in the glow of the evening sun, Algar seemed so vulnerable. He looked up at the man he had come so far to find, blinking and guileless and far too trusting for a native Anglo-Scot. The sight made up Æthelræd's mind.

"Don't fret yourself anymore, son," he said. "I'll return with you. What I do after that is between my brother and me. But no blame will come to you from it. You've fulfilled your charge."

Algar sighed in relief and the two men started down the hill. It still seemed to Algar that he was walking with a legend, one of the Viking kings sired by the gods. He kept a respectful silence. It came as a surprise when Æthelræd gave a great yawn and spoke.

"So, which one of my dear brother's enemies are we supposed to kill?" he asked.

"No one knows," Algar admitted. "There was nothing to tell who had done it and we've heard of no man boasting of their deaths."

Æthelræd's eyebrows writhed with concentration.

"I can't believe that," he said finally. "In all of Scotland, Cumbria and Northumbria, I can't think of a man who wouldn't want the world to know if he'd managed to defeat my brother."

He continued walking. The sun still lay on the horizon in the long summer twilight, but the path was bordered by thick stands of fir and the way was dark. Algar shivered. The farther north one came, the stranger the landscape. Still, he considered, it was better than the task his friend Urric had been given.

Anything was better than having to face Duncan of Wedderlie.

Robert scanned the clear horizon. "I think you have your wish," he said to Edgar. "We're much farther north than Wearmouth." He shook his head. "I only hope we haven't been blown around Scotland altogether."

Edgar glanced over at Catherine, then remembered that she couldn't understand the conversation. But the Flemish captain could.

"Bilge," he said as he paused from scooping seawater out of the hold. "The sun's too low to have gone that far north. My guess is that we're somewhere south of the Firth, but beyond New Castle. And thanks be to God and Saint Nicholas, we managed to save the mast and most of the sail."

"How far out are we?" Edgar asked.

"We should see land by noontime," the man answered. "But not soon enough for your wife, I'd say."

Edgar smiled sad agreement. He felt terribly guilty, as if he'd raised the storm himself to torment her. He should have hunted for a better way to protect her, rather than to take her into a danger that might be as great as the one she had left. He should have left her at the Paraclete.

But in his heart, he knew he hadn't thought of those things because he hadn't wanted to. He didn't want to leave them, not ever again. He cursed his selfishness.

Edgar returned to the canvas shelter, now steaming in the growing warmth of the sun. Catherine and Willa were oiling James before putting him in fresh swaddling. The baby flailed his arms and legs about, glad to be free of the restricting cloth. And at that moment a miracle occurred. Catherine looked up at Edgar and laughed.

All the demons that had been pulling on him fled at the sound. He knelt by the baby and tried to catch his slippery hand.

"Look at your son!" Catherine said exultantly. "He grows fatter and stronger every day. All the tumult of the storm couldn't frighten him."

"And you?" Edgar pushed back her matted hair to peer into her eyes.

Catherine shrugged. "It was a blessing, really. Terror drove away all the nausea. It hasn't come back . . . yet."

"The captain says we're off Scotland now," Edgar reassured her. "He'll put in to the first village he spots and let us off."

Catherine couldn't suppress her sigh of relief. "And then what will we do?" she asked.

"See if we can buy a couple of horses and set off for Wedderlie," Edgar answered.

Catherine looked down at her stained clothing and felt her greasy hair.

"Are there bathhouses in Scotland?" she asked.

Edgar grinned. "No, but there are baths. We won't greet my family looking like beggars, I promise you."

He got up swiftly then, but Catherine had seen his expression. What were these people like? He had never spoken much about them, only a comment here and there. He seemed to have a great deal of affection for his stepmother, and the stories about Waldeve had always made him seem bombastic but in a comical sort of way. He had never even told her the names of his brothers that she recalled. She wished she knew enough English to talk with Robert.

"Mistress?"

Catherine woke from her speculations. Willa needed help wrapping the baby. He wiggled so. She held him still as the soft linen was wound around him. Soon he would be strong enough to leave his arms free.

"I wonder if we'll be home before he starts walking," Willa said.

The idea startled Catherine. "Oh, I hope so. Edgar says that winter is black and bleak here. I don't think I could bear the darkness."

But it wasn't the darkness outside that unsettled her, but her fears about the cheerless people they might be among. Selfishly, she didn't want to stay long in a house of mourning. She wanted to be among friends who would rejoice when James took his first step.

As she settled herself to feed the baby she had another disturb-ing thought.

What if Edgar decided it was his duty to remain in Scotland for-ever?

"Land!"

There was a rush to the port side of the boat. Catherine craned her neck to see where they were all staring. Willa got up and, a mo-ment later, came back to report.

"It looks just like the French side of the sea," she said. "Dark pine trees almost down to the water. Rocks sticking out near the shore. Birds just like ours. I saw no sign of roads or people."

From her tone, Catherine realized that she had been hoping for something altogether alien. Willa was still child enough to hope that a new country would have more magic than her own. Dragons or unicorns, it wouldn't much matter to her. But a new country should have its own mystery, not be a mirror of home.

Solomon came and sat beside them.

"I was hoping we'd see little men, painted blue, dancing on the rocks," he said.

Willa's eyes grew wide.

"Wood demons?" she asked.

Catherine answered before Solomon could embroider the tale.

"No, just men," she told the girl firmly. "Picts, they're called. And I don't think they live on this side of Scotland. If there are even any left. Edgar says Saxons have been living in this area for genera-tions now."

"Then perhaps we'll see some Saxon elves?" Willa wasn't ready to release her fantasy.

Catherine realized that this country, so frightening to her, was like a living *jongleur*'s tale to Willa. There might be monsters, but there would also be heroes. And God saw to it that heroes always won. Who was she to destroy someone's else's faith?

"We might," she told Willa. "We'll both keep watch for them."

Edgar had no hope of magic. As they drew nearer to the coastline, all he felt was dread. Somewhere on that soil the men who had killed his brothers and nephew lived in freedom. Part of him wanted to leave the matter to divine justice, as his early clerical training had dic-tated. But another side was surfacing. It astonished him that all the years of contented exile in France were slipping away, leaving him exposed to feelings he thought he'd cast out. He hadn't much cared for his family, but someone wanted to destroy them and that meant they wanted to destroy him, too.

How far would this reach? How many generations did the hatred last? Edgar thought of Catherine, lying miserably in the shelter of the tarp, and James happily watching the clouds sail by. Hubert had reminded him that he had taken on the enemies of her family when he married Catherine. He hadn't considered that she had done the same. The realization chilled him. If anyone tried to harm his family . . .

Edgar stopped himself. All the years of cathedral training fell away, and he knew that if Catherine or James were in danger, he could slaughter those who seeked to harm them and do it gladly.

Four

Durham, outside the bishop's castle. Monday, 18 kalends July (June 14), 1143. Feast of Saint Basil the Archbishop.

Anno MCXLIII: Rogerus, Prior Dunelmensis, et Ranulfus archidiconus, directa legatione ad Apostolicum, ei afflictiones ecclesiæ Dunelmi exposuere. Cujus auctoritate freti, convocaverunt ad se apud Eboracum in capella Sancti Andreæ, . . . paucos de personis diocesis Dunelmensis, quos vix habere poterant propter persecutionem Willelmi Cumin, in media Quadragesima. Consenserunt ergo omnes in electione Willelmi decani Eboracensis, qui in diebus cuidam concilio apud Lundoniam intererat.

1143: Roger, Prior of Durham and Ranulf, archdeacon, on a direct mission from the Pope, revealed to him the afflictions of the church of Durham. Fortified by his authority, they convened a few people from the diocese of Durham in the chapel of Saint-Andrew at York in the middle of Lent, . . . who were barely able to attend because of the persecution of William Cumin. Therefore, all agreed on the election of William [Ste. Barbe] a deacon of York, who was at that time attending a meeting in London.
—The Chronicle of John, Prior of Hexham

*U*rric hadn't really minded being ordered to go to Durham and roust out Waldeve's third son, although he grumbled about it loudly in the kitchens. The knight had long had a secret admiration for Duncan. It amazed Urric that anyone could be so absolutely certain of himself. Of course, Duncan had no sympathy for the weak or vacillating. His temper had been hardened by the fire of Waldeve's outbursts and then cooled to icy stillness. The man was nerveless. Urric had seen Duncan slice men in two in battle without seeming to notice their screams. He was as oblivious and uncaring as Death himself.

And yet, Urric trusted him. Duncan might be cruel but never without purpose. In this he was unlike his father, who seemed to thrive on making all those around him miserable. Waldeve hurt people for his own amusement and one never knew when he might be in need of diversion. If Duncan tortured a man, that man would know why long before the rope was tightened around his head.

Urric felt that the change in lordship might not be so terrifying as others feared.

That didn't mean that he had set off with eagerness. Durham wasn't a place anyone went to willingly these days. The county was a civil war inside the greater one being fought by King Stephen and his cousin, Matilda. Three years before, when Bishop Geoffrey of Durham had died, his acolyte, William Cumin, had convinced some of the monks to conceal the death until he could arrive from Scotland and claim the bishopric for himself. With the support of King David, whose chancellor he had been, Cumin managed to take over the bishop's castle and receive the homage of most of the barons of the county. But the majority of the monks of the cathedral refused to accept him as bishop and a bizarre struggle had begun, with the monks barricaded in the church and cloister, surrounded by

Cumin's men and yet protected by the patronage and the relics of Saint Cuthbert, who was the true lord of Durham in the eyes of the people.

Duncan had been Cumin's friend at King David's court and had joined him at once, hoping for the reward of land confiscated either from a recalcitrant lord or from the patrimony of Saint Cuthbert himself. Duncan's respect for the Church ended at property lines.

The past three years had not brought Cumin the recognition he demanded. King David had long ago withdrawn his support for the usurper. The papal legate had excommunicated him and there was a rumor that some of the monks had managed to escape the cloister and arrive in York, where a new bishop was to be canonically elected. But Duncan remained loyal to William Cumin.

That puzzled Urric. Did Duncan really believe that there would still be a reward for supporting the false bishop? What could be great enough to risk dying in battle while excommunicate? Urric couldn't imagine anything in particular but would be interested in discovering what was worth damnation and, if possible, getting a share of it.

Now he and his fellow messenger, Swein, stood at the barricade at Framwellgate Bridge. Above them on the right rose the escarpment that jutted into the middle of the river Wear. That was impressive enough. But what took their breath away was the sight at the top where the cathedral of Saint Cuthbert stood, solid as fate and, next to it, made of the same massive stone blocks, the bishop's castle, with guards staring down from every merlon.

As he was about to present himself to the watchmen, Urric felt a prickling on the back of his neck and turned away from the sight of the impregnable fortress.

Behind them in the road was a row of men, peasants and tradesmen by their dress. They carried no weapons but gazed at the knight and the serjeant with a hatred that pierced Urric's mailcoat and left him cold and frightened. Even knowing that Swein stood next to him, huge and Danish, was not enough assurance. Urric showed his pass to the guards and crossed the bridge. Whatever awaited him inside the usurper's lair couldn't be worse than the palpable anger of the tenants of Saint Cuthbert, cut off from the shrine of their lord.

From the far side of the bridge, Urric glanced back at the lowering men. The look on their faces was enough to send him hurrying up the steep path to the castle. He wanted thick walls and hard steel between himself and their fury. How had Cumin survived for so long with such opposition?

Catherine wasn't concerned with the politics of the English. All she wanted was for the ground to stand still. She didn't understand it. She had spent hours gazing hungrily at the coast as the boat searched for a safe place for them to come ashore and now that they had, the land seemed to be as untrustworthy as the waves had been.

"What's wrong with it?" she moaned. "Does your island roll like the sea?"

"The feeling will pass," Edgar assured her. "Sit down and close your eyes."

"Not until we're in a warm, dry, still place," she answered.

They had landed at the town of Berwick, not far from Wedderlie. Edgar was surprised at how the place had grown in the past few years. Trade must be improving. The boat had sailed up the Tweed to the docks of the town, newly enlarged. The tollhouse at the dock had also been enlarged, whitewashed, and it was well staffed, to the captain's despair.

"That's another reason I didn't want to stop in here," he muttered. "Tolls are much too high. And the place is full of monks. I have to trade with them or no one."

"What's wrong with that?" Solomon asked. He had spent the last ten years working for the abbey of Saint-Denis. He was used to monks.

The captain grimaced. "They pay with the thinnest coins I've ever seen. They can drive a bargain tight as a wedge and I can feel them wedging it in me already."

He sighed and scratched at a flea in his crotch. Solomon shrugged.

"You can set off back down to Wearmouth, if you wish," he told the captain. "Cloth won't spoil."

Having thoroughly irritated the flea, the captain turned his attention back to Solomon.

"I could," he said glumly. "But I need money now for repairs. I'll have to sell what I can here and hope that my supplier will take coin for his skins, instead of cloth. At least," he added, brightening, "I might get King David's silver instead of the half-weight coins Stephen is minting."

They were interrupted by Leonel, the clerk who had traveled

with them, weak from hunger and fear. "Captain," he said, mustering up all his strength in an effort to assert his rights. "I paid you to take me to Wearmouth, not Scotland. How am I supposed to get home?"

The captain stared at him.

"You should thank the saints you're still alive, on any shore," he answered. "I'll take you back down the coast with me, no extra charge, or you can see if the monks will give you shelter and then walk home."

"But I need to be at York in a week!" Leonel protested.

The passenger's complaint didn't really interest Solomon, to whom the story was an old one. All travelers and traders faced these problems and it was how one solved them that made the difference between wealth and poverty. He left the two of them to come to their own solution and returned to the rest of their party.

"Catherine?" He squatted next to where she was sitting. "Are you better now?"

She opened one eye and then, cautiously, the other one. She took a deep breath and then stood.

"Yes," she said at last. "Now what do we do?"

Edgar looked at his brother.

"The abbey of Kelso has a hostel on Waldesgate," Robert told them. "We can stay the night there. I'll arrange for horses and guards for the journey to Wedderlie."

"Is it far?" Catherine asked when Edgar had translated.

"A few more miles up the river is all," Edgar said. "We'll be there by tomorrow afternoon."

Catherine nodded and began to gather up their belongings. A hostel sounded fine. She wondered if there were a place where she and Willa could wash the salt from their hair and find someone to boil James's swaddling cloths. She was as tired as she could ever remember being and her face was chapped from the wind and spray. Even her nervousness over meeting Edgar's family was melting under her desire to be in one place, anywhere warm, dry and steady.

The men took the bundles and led the way as Catherine, holding James in one arm, took Willa's hand and followed.

They walked down Briggate, parallel to the river. Catherine looked around. There were shops and even two-story houses. There was a church, although she couldn't see to which saint. There actually seemed to be more monks in the street than lay people. It didn't look so different from home. Not Paris, certainly, but perhaps a village nearby, one dependent upon an abbey. There were more blondes and redheads than she was used to, but none of them wore that silly skirt that the Scottish students in France affected. Well, there were a few, she amended, as a group of men rounded a corner, dressed in nothing but the skirts with their tunics tied by the sleeves around their waists. Willa nudged her and giggled.

"Hush," Catherine said. "We may look just as odd to them."

But she didn't believe it.

Solomon nudged Edgar, but not for the same reason.

"Uncle was right!" he said excitedly. "We could make a fortune here. The monks are doing tremendous amounts of business. I've seen Benedictines, Tironians, Cistercians and some I don't even recognize. They must need spices and incense and fine silk. Well, not much silk for Cistercians, but the others certainly! Perhaps this journey wasn't as useless as I thought."

"Useless?" Edgar said. "Then why did you come?"

"To take care of you and Catherine, of course," Solomon answered. "How else do you think my uncles could have convinced me to leave them? I was also hoping you'd show me the lake with the monster in it."

"That's far north of here," Edgar said absently. "To take care of us! What sort of cracked-brain idea is that? You can't even speak English!"

"What difference does that make?" Solomon replied. "Do you think you'll talk your enemies to death? I'm here because you can trust me. Is there anyone else in this whole kingdom you can say that of?"

Robert looked at them quizzically, wanting to know what the argument was about. Edgar smiled an apology, then turned back to Solomon.

"You plan on being Olivier to my Roland?" he asked. "Thank you. I mean it. You're right. There are only two men in Britain that I trust completely. No, not even Robert. He's the best of my brothers, I think, but I'm not positive even of him."

"So, who are they?" Solomon wanted to know.

"Æthelræds, both of them," Edgar answered. "And both too far away. One is my uncle and the other a friend from when I was a page at King David's court."

Solomon's eyebrows rose. "It's always good to have a friend at court."

"This is even better." Edgar grinned. "That Æthelræd has gone to be a white monk, somewhere down near York."

"A Cistercian?" Solomon commented. "I hear that they're almost as powerful in England as in France. Still, York is a long way to call for help."

Edgar nodded. "So I'm glad you're here, in case any is necessary."

Just then Robert gave a cry and began running up the street. Edgar gave one look at the man who had just appeared from around a corner and, with a whoop of delight, ran toward him as well. Catherine stopped where he had dropped their baggage.

Willa bumped into her. She had been gaping at the man now being effusively greeted by her master and his brother.

"Mistress," she whispered tremulously, "I don't think we're in Paris anymore."

Catherine put a protective arm around her. Then she looked down at James, who stared up at her with Edgar's clear grey eyes.

"I suspect this is another relative of yours," she told him. "And I was worried about how Edgar would react to *my* family!"

She turned to Solomon, who had stayed with them.

"Do you think he's safe?" Willa asked, gesturing at the man.

Solomon grinned at her. "Not in the least," he answered. "So don't you think we should greet him very politely? From Edgar's reaction, I feel fairly confident that he's a friend."

Willa wasn't so sure. She had imagined magical creatures from the woods but they weren't meant to be so big.

"What does he eat, do you think?" she asked.

"Large amounts of meat, most likely," Solomon answered. "We'll have to be sure he gets enough, or he may take a bite of you."

"Solomon!" Catherine stopped him. "She's frightened enough!"

Solomon started to apologize when Edgar came racing back to them.

"It's my uncle!" he told them. "Æthelræd, the one I just told you about. Come meet him."

He tugged at Catherine, who advanced slowly, Willa hiding behind her. Æthelræd started toward them, then seeing Willa's frightened face peering around Catherine, he stopped with a laugh.

"*Ic beo manne, swa swa min broðorsunnu, Edgar! Ne forhtiað, cild!*"

Willa clutched Catherine to keep herself from running away. Even Catherine was startled by the sudden rush of alien words. The only one she understood was Edgar's name. Æthelræd turned to Edgar.

"What's wrong with them?" he asked. "Do I reek?"

"They don't understand you," Edgar explained. "French convents don't give English lessons."

He went over to Catherine and took the baby from her arms.

"Uncle says he's human, just like me," he told her. "You don't need to fear him. He's big but not dangerous . . . usually."

Not greatly reassured, Catherine still put out her hand in greeting. To her astonishment, Edgar's uncle bowed like a fine lord and responded in heavily accented Latin.

"*In nomine Christi te saluto.*"

Catherine gave a startled laugh. It was as if a trained bear had spoken. Then she blushed.

"Please forgive me," she said hastily, also in Latin. "I wasn't prepared to be honored with such a greeting. I thank you and greet you also in the name of Our Lord."

It was Æthelræd's turn to be startled. His forehead creased in his effort to follow her fluid speech. Then he grinned at Edgar.

"My informants told me she was educated," he said. "But they didn't say how well. Tell her I haven't read more than psalms and charters for thirty years and can't keep up with her refined phrases."

Edgar translated and Catherine blushed more deeply. They picked up the bags and continued toward the hostel. As they walked, Æthelræd nudged Edgar.

"She talk like that in bed, too?" he muttered.

"You should hear her periphrastics." Edgar leered.

Æthelræd gave a deep sigh. "You're a lucky man, nephew. Eyes like hers and Latin phrases, too."

Hubert was thinking of Catherine's Latin phrases at that moment, too. He was remembering how she could decimate pompous underlings, such as the one standing before him, with a few well-chosen insults.

"I have a right to know who accuses me," he told the man. "I'll answer nothing until I can face those who would slander me so and receive restitution from them."

The cleric from Notre Dame was a totally nondescript man, the sort one might imagine seeing half a dozen times a day because he looked like everyone else. It wasn't until he opened his mouth and spoke with his grating Occitan accent that he became an individual.

"My dear sir." The cleric waved his hands placatingly. "No accusations have been made, as yet. My Lord Bishop only asked me to investigate a rumor. Undoubtedly false, of course, but with your connections to the abbey of Saint-Denis, one that needs to be refuted completely. Nothing more."

"I do refute it," Hubert said. "No one among my Hebrew colleagues has ever tried to convert me to their pernicious beliefs. Our dealings have solely concerned business of mutual benefit, to us and the abbey."

He glared at the bishop's messenger, defying him to challenge him. The man only smiled.

"Certainly," he said. "But Bishop Stephen feels that there must have been some, quite innocent, action on your part that started this gossip. He requests that you search your memory for what it could be and report to him next week, so that he can assure the king and Abbot Suger of the solidity of your faith."

"He wants to see me?" Hubert repeated.

"At your convenience." The cleric smiled again.

Hubert wished again that Catherine weren't so far away. Her counsel would be useful in the coming week.

Catherine wasn't thinking of rhetorical arguments just then. Her thoughts concentrated on hot water and soap. They were greeted warmly by the monks at the hostel in Berwick. Catherine was relieved to find that a number of them were French or Norman so that she didn't need someone to go through the tedious job of repeating everything. One of them offered to take the sack of used swaddling to a nearby laundress. Another offered her some strips of worn linen to make new. The sexes were separated at the hostel, so she and Willa settled gratefully into the bed provided in the women's room, James snuggled warmly between them. Catherine closed her eyes. For the moment sleep was all that mattered. She felt the soft breath of her son upon her neck. Outside was an alien world. But here they were safe. The monsters could roar unhindered until the morning.

Coming up only a moment later, Edgar found them all sound

asleep. He dropped the bags quietly on the wooden floor and resisted the temptation to find his own bed. His muscles ached; his eyes were red from staring into the wind and sun. He wanted to sleep for a month. Instead he went back down to the dining hall, where Robert and Æthelræd sat and waited for him. A little apart from them Solomon had joined two of the French monks and was cautiously broaching the subject of the wool trade. Edgar sat next to his uncle.

"How did you know to meet us here?" he asked without preliminaries. "We meant to land far south."

It was almost an accusation. Æthelræd smiled.

"You know very well how," he answered. "I've always been able to find you. It never bothered you until those clerics stuffed you full of theology."

Edgar was having none of that.

"It always bothered me." He frowned at the memory. "No matter where I hid, you always pulled me out and put me to work. I believed you could sniff me out like a wolf."

Æthelræd laughed. "Maybe I can. You stink now of fish and stale beer. Anyone could have found you."

"From Edinburgh?" Robert had never trusted this uncle.

"Even from Orkney," Æthelræd answered firmly. "Or maybe I heard of your coming from our cousins, the seals."

Edgar paled beneath his sunburn.

"Don't you start telling those stories around Catherine," he warned. "I'll not have her thinking we still believe those pagan tales."

Æthelræd laughed. "I never said we did, nephew. But there's many who do. Your father seems to enjoy letting them think he's not quite human."

Robert nodded. "He glories in anything that will increase his hold on the countryside. And I'm not always sure, myself, that there isn't a touch of something in us. Grandmother used to say she knew when trouble threatened the family. I always thought you did, too, Uncle. Until our brothers went out to die alone and unprepared."

He gave Æthelræd an angry stare. Æthelræd set down his mug with a sigh.

"You think I could have warned your brothers of their fate?" he asked. "They wouldn't have listened. They never did." He paused. "I was too far away, in any case. I only knew something was wrong and God knows that's nothing new in your father's household. So don't reproach me, Robert. I'm not some damned prophet, you know."

Edgar shivered. He wasn't so sure. Perhaps his Gallowegian grandmother *had* brought with her the blood of demons. But there were saints in the family as well, at least according to the stories— abbesses and hermits, devout lords who fed the poor and only slept with their own wives. Æthelræd didn't belong with any of them. He was vulgar and gluttonous and not known for his abstinence in anything. But his eyes, so like Edgar's, saw far into things that only God should know. Not for the last time, Edgar wished he'd never been talked into coming back.

The next morning Catherine insisted on baths and hair washing for herself and Willa, at least. She also wanted to unpack all her clothes, shake them out and press them again.

"Catherine, that will take all day," Edgar complained.

"Easily," she answered. "But I'm not going to meet your father and stepmother looking like a castaway. So you can either wait or go on without me. You could use a wash and a shave, yourself."

Edgar took Solomon and retreated to an inn. He figured his ablutions wouldn't take long. He could make them that evening, when Catherine was finished.

"She looks fine to me," he told Solomon. "I don't see what all the fuss is."

Willa understood, though and listened intently as Catherine considered which of her *bliauts* would be most impressive and still survive the ride.

"It will have to be the linen," she decided finally. "I'll simply have to sit very carefully and try not to get too wrinkled. What do you think, Willa?"

"I like the roses on the hem," Willa said. "And the sleeves are so elegant, all edged in gold and the latest cut. Will you wear the gold chain belt and bracelets, as well?"

"I don't know." Catherine thought. "It might attract robbers. But I can't let them think I have no jewelry. I know. I'll put the bracelets and rings on just before we get there. My riding cloak should cover the rest."

She and Willa soaked in a large wooden tub and then poured water over their soapy hair until it was rinsed. They then spent the rest of the afternoon getting a comb to go through Catherine's black curls and braiding them quickly while the hair was still heavy with water and not as apt to spring away from the hairdresser.

"There," Catherine said finally. "What do you think?"

Willa looked at her in honest admiration.

"I think they'll say that you're as fine a lady as ever came from Paris, as fine as the queen, herself."

"Oh, I hope so," Catherine said. "Now if I can only keep my stomach steady, I may survive the meeting."

They said their prayers and went to sleep.

The next morning they all set out for Wedderlie. Catherine rode pillion behind Edgar. Her heart was beating with anticipation. Beyond a whistle at her appearance, Edgar had made no comment on the homecoming. It was only by the pounding of his heart beneath her hand that she knew he was as nervous as she.

The ride was far too short. It seemed only a few minutes before they rounded a bend and Edgar pointed out his home to her.

Catherine looked up at the stone keep on the hill. It thrust itself out above the trees and the village in a way that seemed as if it were just the tip of something greater attempting to break free of the earth. She shook herself. That was nonsense. She was allowing herself to be affected by Willa's fears and her own sense of being in an unearthly place. It was just a keep, probably as drafty and uncomfortable as the one her brother lived in at Veilleteneuse in France. Catherine only hoped that there would be a place out of the chill of stones where James and Willa could rest warmly.

At the edge of the town they dismounted and led the horses between the huts and outbuildings.

As they went up the path through the village, Edgar looked around in surprise. Had he been away so long or had he simply forgotten? There seemed to be more open land now, more fields of rye and barley ripening in the sun. The houses of the tenants were all in good repair, the fences mended and roofs newly thatched. What could have caused such obvious prosperity? He turned around to ask Robert but was stopped by a shout from ahead. Someone had seen the group and recognized them.

At first Catherine couldn't understand what was happening. The people in the fields dropped their hoes and started running toward them. From the huts women appeared, some still holding spoons or spindles. They all stopped and stared. Catherine clutched James more closely. Did these people never see travelers? What might they do next? Even a spindle can be a weapon, and these tall, sturdy women looked more than capable of wielding one with deadly skill.

Suddenly the villagers made a rush at them. Willa screamed and Catherine inhaled sharply, preparing to add her voice. There were shouts and wild, high cries. Why didn't Edgar and Robert do something?

Edgar stepped forward and held up his hands.

"No!" Catherine shouted.

A number of things happened at once. Æthelræd roared something at the crowd that seemed to agitate them even more. James, jostled beyond endurance, began wailing. Solomon leaped in front of Catherine and Willa to protect them, thus blocking their view. And Edgar was snatched by a dozen dirty hands and pulled away from them.

"Edgar!" Catherine screamed. "Solomon, move! What's happening? What are they doing to him?"

Solomon stepped back, still shielding them from the excesses of the mob. Catherine strained to see around him and calm the baby at the same time. Everyone was yelling.

Still looking for a way around Solomon, Catherine bumped into Robert.

"What are you doing here?" she said, forgetting that he couldn't understand her. "Why aren't you rescuing him?"

If Robert didn't know the words, the expression was all too clear. He laughed at her and tried to pat her arm.

Catherine was horrified. Edgar's fears had been realized. It had been a trap all along. Oh dear Saint Genevieve, she prayed, if you can hear me so far away from Paris. Please protect us from these evil barbarians!

With her free hand, she struck out at Robert, who laughed all the harder. He grabbed her wrist and spun her around so that she could at last see what was happening.

Edgar had been lifted to the broad shoulders of one of the men. He loomed far above the crowd as he was rapidly carried up the hill to the keep.

"Catherine!" he called through cupped hands. "Don't worry. I'm fine. They're friends!"

Friends?

Catherine looked around again. Now that they had captured

Edgar, the people had moved back a bit. She felt dozens of curious stares beating upon her, almost as frightening as blows would have been. She froze.

"Remember, Catherine. Your ancestors fought with Charlemagne! Don't betray them now with your cowardice!"

Catherine shook herself. Those damn voices. They had come with her even to this wilderness. And, as usual, they were right. She lifted her chin and tried not to think of the state of her hair and clothes after the ride from Berwick. She threw back her cloak so that the gold shone in the sunlight for all to see. James's howling subsided to whimpers as she faced the villagers.

At the sight of the baby, one old woman grinned at the friend beside her, who cackled in delight and muttered something that would have completely destroyed Catherine's poise, if she had comprehended it. Then the two astounded her even more by bowing and backing away.

The others did likewise, until the path was clear for them all. Solomon put his arm around her and stared suspiciously at the quiescent crowd as they made their way along the incline where Edgar had been taken. Willa came with them, holding the edge of Catherine's sleeve for dear life. Behind them, they could hear a booming as Æthelræd explained something to the people that made the laughter break out again.

Solomon patted her shoulder.

"It's all right now, Cousin," he soothed. "I think they were just glad to see him."

"I suppose so," she answered shakily. "Do you think the greeting inside will be as . . . forceful?"

He sincerely doubted it, from what Edgar had told him, but he kept silent as they crossed the bridge over the deep ditch and climbed the motte to the wooden fencing that enclosed the bailey. Inside, at the very top of the hill stood the keep, solidly stone behind a wooden palisade.

The gate was open. Catherine, Willa and Solomon paused. There were people in the bailey watching them, as well, standing unmoving, staring in what seemed to all three to be deep antagonism.

Solomon swallowed and set his shoulders proudly.

"Remember who we are, Catherine," he said.

Catherine gave him a puzzled glance. "We? But your ancestors didn't fight the Saracens," she said.

"No," Solomon answered without a trace of humor. "They fought the Pharaohs."

Catherine put that comment in the back of her mind for future debate. For now, she gave the baby to Willa, smoothed her robes and walked through the gate as if she had every right to receive the homage of all within.

It had taken Edgar some time to convince the men to put him down. He was elated to be greeted this warmly after abandoning his patrimony so long ago. But he didn't want to be carried into his father's presence like a roistering child, dumped sprawling into the straw.

"Alfred!" He kicked at the man beneath him. "Put me down! I'm not one of your sick sheep. This is no way to enter a house of mourning."

Alfred stopped immediately and let Edgar slide off his shoulders.

"You'll not find grief in there, my lord," he said softly. "Your noble father won't allow that sort of weakness." Alfred half feared he had overstepped himself. But Edgar had known the peasant all his life. This wasn't the first time he'd ridden on the man's strong shoulders. Edgar only nodded.

"The warning is welcome," he told Alfred, "but not needed. I know what I'm coming home to."

"For your sake, young Edgar, I hope so." Alfred bowed and backed away, leaving Edgar to meet his father alone.

It occurred to Edgar that this had been the man's intention all along. Alfred had meant for Edgar to arrive at his father's door, ahead of the others. The old shepherd had known that it was better to encounter Waldeve as one man to another, not encumbered by the need to curb one's words for the sake of his family. He climbed the steps to where the door of the keep lay open in the summer air.

Inside all was in shadow. The windows were narrow and deep inside the thick walls. No summer could ever penetrate this chill. Edgar stood at the threshold, letting his eyes adjust to the gloom. He wasn't startled, though, when she spoke. He had noticed her scent immediately.

"Welcome, stepson," Adalisa said quietly. "You have been greatly missed."

He saw her at once come out of the shadows, and embraced her tightly, marveling again at how small she was and how strong.

"If so, Stepmother," he answered, "it was not by my father."

Adalisa pulled away and looked up at him. She smiled. There was a set to his face that hadn't been there a few years ago, an assurance. She had opposed his marriage, for many reasons, but she could tell now that he hadn't been harmed by it. She wondered what sort of woman had drawn him away from his own people and kept him there.

He held her rough hands and smiled back.

"Catherine will be here shortly," he said. "Will you greet her and show her where we are to stay?"

She nodded. "Your father is in the chapel," she told him.

He took a deep breath. "Good. It's less likely he'll try to kill me there."

He released her and strode purposefully down the narrow corridor, feeling like Daniel walking into the lion's mouth.

Five

The keep at Wedderlie, Berwickshire, Scotland. Tuesday, 17 kalends July (June 15), 1143. Celebration of the deposition of the remains of Saint Eadburge, Virgin and martyr.

Siteð sorgcearig, sælum bidæled,
on sefan sweorceð, sylfum thinceð
thæt sy endeleas earfoða dæl.

The sorrowful one sits robbed of joy,
his mind in darkness, it seems to him
that his hard lot will last forever.

Deor, 11. 28–30

*T*here was little light in the chapel. The room had been dug into the foundations of the keep, far into the earth. Or perhaps the hill had grown to surround it. Only one narrow window near the ceiling kept it from being as black as the dungeon hole, where prisoners or provisions were stored. There was a small oil lamp beside the altar but it had not been lit. Waldeve was seated in the only chair in the room, as was his right as lord. He was quite alone.

He didn't look up when Edgar entered.

Edgar's eyes had grown used to the grey-brown gloom. He made out the shape, saw the muted glint of a ring on the knife hand. This is just a man, he told himself. My father. There's nothing at all to be frightened of.

"Father?" he said.

Still Waldeve didn't move.

"You sent for me, Father," Edgar said more loudly. "And I have come."

He waited. Finally the old man's head lifted and turned to him.

"I thought you'd lost all your honor," he stated. "Living with those *wæpnedwifstres* in Paris."

Edgar nearly smiled. "I haven't forgotten who I am, Father. And the bodies of the French are not half one sex and half the other, I assure you."

Waldeve stiffened. "Indeed? Well, you should know. Did you bring your whore with you?"

Edgar had expected this.

"My wife is with me," he answered. "Catherine came at her own request, not yours. She wanted to see the land that bore me."

"And discover how much of it you had surrendered for her?" Waldeve was irritated that he couldn't get a rise from his son. "Perhaps she also wants to find a way to get it back?"

Now Edgar did laugh. "I gave up a few *davoch* from my mother's land, hardly enough to feed a man in the best of years. And, even if she cared about such matters, Catherine has no need of our land. Her father could buy us all twice over."

Edgar realized his blunder as soon as the words were out. Waldeve rose slowly, like the tide. He faced his son, their eyes on a level.

"Buy us, could he?" the old man said too softly. "And sell us the next morning at a profit, no doubt. Gold before honor. So this is what you've come to, is it, boy?"

"I've come to be with you in your sorrow and to grieve for my brothers," Edgar said, forcing himself not to flinch. If he was going to be struck, he wouldn't give the old bastard the satisfaction of seeing him cower before the blow.

Waldeve tightened his grip on the sword. Edgar hadn't even realized he was wearing one. It didn't matter. He had feared his father too long. The old man could wound more deeply with words than with steel, anyway. But Waldeve only waited, looking at Edgar with contempt.

"Why did you send for me then, Father?" Edgar asked again. "You know I'm not trained for battle. I can't help you in your vengeance. Have I made this journey only so you can denounce and disown me once more? Did you send for me only to give yourself that pleasure amidst your pain?"

His father glared at him so long and fiercely that Edgar feared the answer might be yes. Finally Waldeve broke the stare and, the metal of the unsheathed sword clinking against the silver bands on the chair legs, sat once again with a long exhalation.

"You've changed, Edgar," he said. "You've finally become a man, but I'm not certain what sort. I called you back to stand with me, as is your duty, but not to fight. Since the time Henry the Clerk took the throne of England, we've needed men who know their way about a charter as well as a battlefield."

Edgar was confused by this sudden change.

"What have charters to do with my brothers' murder?"

Waldeve's left hand clenched and unclenched. "I don't know," he said at last. "But I don't believe that their death was all the bastards wanted. My sons and my grandson weren't killed for glory or sport. There's revenge at work here. Something hidden for years, like a curse written in blood upon parchment rolled up and left to fester at the bottom of a casket. Dark, deep hatred. I feel it."

Edgar could see that. But whose? His father hated better than any man he'd ever known. Who could match him?

"Name your enemy, Father," he replied. "And if he can be defeated by words alone, I will challenge him."

Waldeve gave a grim smile. "Your priests say words are stronger than speartips. I know some that bite more deeply. But I cannot name the enemy. Do you think I'd be sitting here like an old woman, if I could?"

"Then what am I to do?" Edgar almost shouted his exasperation.

Waldeve leaned forward, grabbed the string of Edgar's tunic and pulled him down with vicious force.

"Find the bastards," he hissed. "Find the *orcðyrs ordbana*, you dolt! Search the documents; talk with those men in *wifscrud* you're so fond of, those monks. Find the ones who did this and bring them to me. And when you do, you can slink back into your wealthy wife's bed and earn your keep in *firenlust*. Show me the man who did this. Find out who among my enemies is wicked and desperate enough to take this revenge. That's all."

His hand lashed out, and gripped Edgar's wrist. The fingers were cold and hard as shackles.

"Only find them. Nothing more, your hear? Give me their names, but you may not harm them. I intend to kill them myself." Waldeve tightened his grip until Edgar's hand went numb. "Is that understood?"

Edgar understood all too well.

Adalisa waited at the door, as she promised, for Catherine to arrive. She shielded her eyes, trying to make out the faces in the approaching group. She recognized Robert, in the lead, and fiery Æthelræd was unmistakable. Between them, huddled together as if under guard, were three other people. The child was too old to be Edgar's, a servant perhaps. The woman was undoubtedly his wife, though, carrying a bundle of some sort. And the man . . . she squinted, what a strange-looking person! Lean and dark with his head a mass of unruly black curls that blended into his beard. What could he be, some enslaved Saracen prisoner? No, not the way the woman was holding his arm. Who, what, was he?

She waited. Dignity and training overcame curiosity. They would reach the door soon enough.

A small hand slipped into hers.

"Is that my sister-in-law, Catherine?" Margaret asked.

"I believe so." Adalisa smiled on her daughter. "Let me look at you. Are you presentable? Oh, Margaret, you're barefoot! You're old enough to know better. Run get some shoes on quickly. What will she think?"

Margaret ran. Surreptitiously, Adalisa examined her own apparel. She knew Waldeve's loudly voiced opinion that this Catherine was some scullery maid who had seduced Edgar and made him believe she was a well-bred convent-reared lady. But Adalisa wasn't so sure. In any event, she didn't want to appear like a peasant, with bare arms and feet and straw in her hair. She wished she'd bothered to do more than braid it today.

This is nonsense, she told herself. I'm the mistress of this castle. These people are my guests, not my judges.

As Catherine drew closer, Adalisa realized at once that her own dress was hopelessly out of fashion. Belts were being worn lower now, the sleeves longer. The cut of the neck, with the *chainse* showing a bit of embroidery above the collar of the long *bliaut*, these were the little touches that someone who lived in the Paris of Eleanor of Aquitaine would have learned. Her nervousness increased tenfold.

As the party reached the base of the steps, Adalisa stepped into the doorway so that the sun shone on her. Catherine looked up and met her eyes. She smiled wearily. Adalisa looked down and saw the burden she carried. Her concerns vanished.

"*Ma douce broiz!*" she exclaimed. "You poor thing, traveling so long and with a child so young! Come in, come in at once and rest!"

"Thank you," Catherine answered. "We are very worn and dusty from the journey. You are Edgar's stepmother?"

She made it a question because Edgar had never mentioned that Adalisa was so young, not nearly as old as her husband must be.

Adalisa nodded. "Yes, my dear. We can wait until supper for the formal introductions. But this is . . . ?"

She held out her hand to Solomon, who bowed and kissed her fingers. Adalisa shivered. His beard was soft, as silky as the fringe on the altar cloth.

Catherine introduced them. Adalisa nodded.

"I would have known you were related," she said. "Cousins, you say?"

Solomon confirmed this. His eyes lowered from her face to her waist and he grinned. Adalisa felt at her sleeve. Was something showing? Then she felt the head poke under her arm.

"Mama," Margaret said. "I put my shoes on. Now may I meet Catherine?"

Catherine stopped at the final step. She gaped at the lovely elfin face almost even with hers. Then she pulled herself together, promising to have a long talk with Edgar in which she would do most of the talking. Why in the world had he never told her he had a baby sister?

Then her mind made another revolution. Both mother and daughter had spoken in French, and not even Norman French but good, clear Francien. In all of his diatribes about his proud Saxon family, Edgar had never once mentioned that his stepmother was French.

That talk was going to be very interesting.

For the moment, though, Catherine was only glad to be greeted in her own tongue. So much so that she found herself in tears.

"Oh, my dear!" Adalisa exclaimed. "I've kept you standing here, tired and hungry, like a beggar at my door. Forgive me! Come in, all of you. Come in. Welcome!"

As she showed them their beds and ordered hot water and warm food, Adalisa was also busy revising her opinions about Catherine. But she had no intention of discussing them with her husband.

Supper did not begin well.

"Where the hell is Robert?" Waldeve began, even before the blessing had been said.

Æthelræd was the only one who dared answer him.

"Robert said he'd been away from his land too long; he needed to see that all was well." Æthelræd grinned at his brother. "Admirable, wouldn't you say, to take such care of what you've entrusted to him?"

Waldeve signaled for the nearest retainer.

"He's gone to see his damned dog!" he shouted. "Cares more about a good hunter than his own family. Bring him back at once! I never gave him leave to go."

"Now, now, Brother," Æthelræd soothed. "It can wait until we've eaten. There's plenty of daylight left. Let me fill my belly and

I'll go for him, myself. Lufen is a fine animal. I don't blame Robert for wanting to be sure she was well."

But Waldeve would not be placated. The hungry servant was sent out on the run, leaving his tray of dried olives and apricots on the window ledge, where it remained until found the next morning.

"Now all stand for the blessing," Waldeve continued, as if nothing had happened. *"In nomine Patris et Filii et Spiritus Sancti."* All crossed themselves. "Lord God, bless this food and poison the meat of any man who goes against me. Twist the entrails of the unholy murderers of my sons until they scream horribly and beg for death. And then deliver them to me so that I may do the same. This we beg in thy name. Amen."

He sat and reached for the salt cellar. The servants brought in the trenchers of bread and trays of roast geese. Everyone reached gratefully for the food.

Except Catherine. She stared down the table at her father-in-law, who was stuffing his mouth as if stoking a fire. He hadn't even looked at her when he came in, hadn't greeted her at all. At the moment, she was too relieved to be insulted. And what had been the text of the Saxon prayer that everyone reacted to it as if the meal had been profaned instead of blessed? She wished she could have stayed up in her alcove with Willa and the baby.

At the other end of the table, Edgar was wishing, once again, that he had never brought her to Scotland.

Adalisa knew that it was her place to make cheerful conversation to aid in the calm enjoyment of the food. She surveyed the grim or nervous faces around her and decided, perhaps tomorrow. So the meal took place with only the sound of chewing, gurgling and occasional fights among the dogs for the bits dropped to the floor. Adalisa tried to eat, but nothing could get past the tightness in her throat. She concentrated on keeping back tears. Years of practice helped her.

At the far end of the table, next to Catherine, Solomon watched Adalisa. It seemed to him that Edgar's stepmother was a delicate French rose, planted in a desert and somehow expected to bloom. He wondered if, after so many years, she still felt like a foreigner in this land.

They had reached the fruit and nut stage when Robert arrived, with his dog. He was wearing old leather breeches and a tunic without sleeves that was stained with sweat. Waldeve glanced at him and his jaw set. He put down the sticky sweetmeat he had been gnawing.

"You look like a *neyf*," he said. "No. Worse. Like a slave, without pride or sense."

Robert shrugged.

"I've been away from my holdings for weeks," he stated. "They
needed tending to. I need to work to survive on the pittance of land
I have. I'm too busy for family dinners. The only reason I've come
at all is that I have news for you."

He raised his voice, although the hall was quiet enough for him
to be heard in a whisper.

"There was a messenger waiting for me," he told them. "He had
information he was afraid to deliver here."

For a moment Waldeve's shoulders sagged, as if an iron yoke
had been dropped on them. He regained himself quickly though.

"And what did your cowardly messenger fear to tell me?" he
asked.

Robert looked around the room, savoring the attention.

"The horses have been found," he said. "At Hexham. Alexander's still wore the bridle the king gave him at Carlisle."

The silence became uproar. Men shouted and pounded their
knives and cups on the table. Alexander's wife shrieked and began
to wail. Æthelræd didn't bother to try to push through the confusion to get to Robert. He simply stepped up onto the table, making
it creak alarmingly, sending dishes flying and spattering sauce across
the room. He jumped off the other side and faced his nephew.

"Where are they?" he asked. "Who has them? Who did it?"

"At the priory," Robert answered. "In the care of the priest. I
don't know. They were left in the church, tied to the rood screen, in
the middle of the night."

That brought the room to silence again. Edgar shivered and
crossed himself. So did many others. Solomon and Catherine
looked at each other. Would no one tell them what was happening?

Waldeve leaned forward over the table. A pitcher of ale tipped
over, causing a foamy waterfall to spill to the floor. His mouth
opened and closed twice. Finally, he found the word he wanted.

"Why?" he asked. "Who is playing with me like this?"

For once Robert almost pitied his father. He seemed to have
aged in the past few moments, crumpled. Adalisa put a hand on her
husband's arm. He turned and stared at her as if at a stranger. Then
he looked at Edgar.

"Is it God?" he asked. "Is this a divine punishment for my sins?"

The question startled Edgar. When had his father ever worried about his sins? And what answer could he give? How would he know God's mind? He was thankful that Catherine couldn't understand. She'd try to explain her theories on divine retribution. But Waldeve didn't want theology, he wanted reassurance.

"More likely someone in league with the devil," Edgar decided. "After all, if the Lord wished to punish you, he wouldn't need swords."

Waldeve nodded, comforted. It pleased him to think that he was so powerful his enemies needed to league themselves with Satan in order to combat him.

"But why Hexham?" Edgar wondered. "Robert, was there anything, a message, a sign, anything at all attached to the horses? Did they seem to have been abused, ridden hard?"

Robert threw up his hands. "I've told you all that was told to me," he said. "And now I must get back to my work."

He turned to go.

"Stop at once!" Waldeve roared. "We're leaving at first light and you're going with us."

Robert sighed and shook his head, but kept walking. The door was open to let in the summer sun. This close to the solstice, it shone almost horizontally into the room. He paused at the threshold, black against the glare, then shook his head again and left.

For a moment, everyone simply stared at the space where he had been, then all heads turned to Waldeve.

Deliberately, Waldeve pushed back his stool. He walked the length of the table, ignoring his stunned household. He crossed the room to the doorway and pulled down a crossbow from the wall. As they watched in horror, he slid the bolt into the weapon and raised it, aiming out into the courtyard.

Æthelræd leaped forward, knocking his brother over as the arrow was loosed, shooting up into the sky.

"Have you gone mad?" he asked Waldeve. "You have no sons to spare."

Waldeve lowered the crossbow and spat on Æthelræd's bare feet.

"I have a dozen sons better than that one," he answered calmly. "No man turns his back on me."

Æthelræd looked at him with scorn.

"You mean, no man dares to," he said. "Robert has done your bidding long enough and he's no traitor. Any man brave enough to tell you 'no' to your face will never betray you."

Waldeve looked around his brother to the people gathered at the table. His eyes scorched them. Finally, his gaze stopped at Edgar.

"Will you go to Hexham?" he asked.

"I will," Edgar answered. "Not for you, but for my own satisfaction. You haven't answered my question, why there? I want to find out."

"Husband," Adalisa interjected. "Your son has only just arrived. He needs to rest before setting out again."

"He'll have the night," Waldeve said. "Take the women and retire to your rooms, Wife. We don't need you here."

She clenched her teeth and opened her eyes wide to keep back the tears. She wouldn't disgrace herself before all these people. Adalisa raised her chin, then bowed her head slightly.

"As you wish," she said.

Catherine was startled at being rushed so abruptly from the hall. But she was also relieved. Now she could find out what all that had been about. She also hoped that James was awake and hungry. She was more than ready for him to eat. As they left, she snatched a hunk of dripping bread from the table and hid it in her sleeve. No one would have thought to give Willa any food.

Adalisa moved with dignity, ignoring the whispers of the other women as they moved up the stairs together. Inside, her heart was thumping so hard that her ears ached with the sound of it. She was frightened and she was hurt, but most of all, she was angry.

They reached the women's rooms. Sitting on the floor by the window was Margaret along with Anna's son. They were dutifully rocking the cradles of the two babies, both of the children watching with rapt delight as Willa's long fingers tied bits of string, cloth and sticks into figures. A horse, a monk, a knight with a sword, these were already set on the floor next to her. As she worked, Willa hummed a song from Champagne. The children didn't look up as their mothers entered.

The tears Adalisa had fought so hard to control came rushing out. Quickly she went to her clothes chest, opened it and began rummaging in its depths as if looking for something. There the tears fell from her face onto wool acrid with dried herbs.

Willa stopped her song when they entered. She smiled at Catherine.

"James is awake, Mistress," she said. "The other baby is sleeping still. Did you have a good dinner?"

There was no answer to that. Catherine took out the bread and gave it to the girl, then bent over James's cradle. Her son looked up at her with his father's eyes.

"What cursed place have we come to?" she murmured, as she lifted him and settled herself to give him his dinner.

Anna and Sibilla watched her with something between contempt and wonder. Catherine ignored them. She was used to the belief that only peasants breastfed. But all the scholars agreed that weaknesses and flaws in the character could be drawn in with strange milk, so she held to her determination. Edgar had assured her that King David's mother had nursed all her own children. If a sainted queen could, she told people, so could she.

The women lost interest in her oddity after a moment and retreated to a corner to discuss the events of the afternoon. Adalisa emerged from the woolens, her emotions conquered. She seated herself on the rushes next to Catherine and gestured to Margaret to join her.

The child came, still clutching her new toys. Adalisa wrapped her arms around her and rubbed her face against Margaret's soft, bright curls. Then she gave Catherine a rueful smile.

"There are too many men in this family," she announced.

Catherine smiled back.

"Perhaps that's why we really send our sons out for fostering," she suggested. "They're too much like their fathers to all live together in unity."

Adalisa nodded with a sigh. "Now, I imagine you want to know what all that was about."

"Among other things," Catherine answered.

Adalisa gave her a puzzled glance, but went on to explain the gist of the argument that had gone on below. Catherine listened while James fed contentedly.

"I see," she said when the story was ended. "It's strange. I don't know the customs of this place, but it appears to me as if these deeds are the act of someone deliberately trying to demean Lord Waldeve. His sons murdered and mutilated like felons, his horses returned as if worthless. Is this usual behavior in Scottish feuds?"

"Not in the least," Adalisa said. "Revenge is brutal here, even with the efforts of King David to make people bring their grievances to his court. But it's also straightforward. A man has a grudge against his neighbor and he kills him in the open and sticks his head above the gate for all to see. This . . . this desecration, it's unnatural."

Catherine agreed. "And you have no idea who would want to behave so?"

It seemed to her that Adalisa hesitated.

"No," she said. "My husband has never felt the need for friends, but in his own way, he is honorable. He has never betrayed his lord, which is almost a miracle in these times of shifting allegiances. He isn't kind to those under him, but he is just, I believe. He's more cruel to his family than to his slaves."

Catherine had seen enough in her short time at Wedderlie to believe this. She shifted James to the other breast and asked another question.

"Why do you think the horses were returned to Hexham? Where is it?"

"Southwest of here," Adalisa answered. "Just past the Roman wall."

"Is it in Scotland or England?" Catherine asked.

"That depends on whom you ask," Adalisa said. "At the moment, King David and his son, Earl Henry, have the greatest claim. But the church of Hexham is under the protection of the archbishop of York."

"Does Edgar's family have any connection there?"

Again a hesitation. Was Adalisa preparing a lie or simply trying to remember?

"Edgar and Robert had a friend who grew up at Hexham," she said at last. "Robert gave some money for the rebuilding of the church of Saint Peter there. Waldeve, of course, refused. It's not much of a connection but there's nothing else that I know of."

"Could this have something to do with Robert, then?" Catherine asked. "Might this be an attempt to place blame on him?"

Adalisa sighed. "I have no idea, Catherine," she said in exasperation. "This does not seem to be the work of sane men, so how can I imagine their reasoning?"

Catherine finally took the hint and subsided.

James was dozing now. In the unfriendly silence Catherine was having a hard time staying awake herself. She felt that Edgar's step-mother wasn't telling her the whole truth, but everything here was too new and confusing for her to risk more questioning. What she wanted was time alone with Edgar.

Gently, she made James release his grip. His arms twitched beneath the swaddling. Soon, Catherine reflected, they would have to make some little shirts so that his upper body could move freely. She placed him back in the cradle and stood.

"Do you think the men have finished their council?" She asked. "If we are leaving again in the morning, I need to speak with Edgar."

Adalisa seemed startled. "Catherine, you aren't considering going to Hexham, are you? The road there isn't safe at all. And what they find there may be even more dangerous."

"We came here as a family," Catherine explained. "Edgar won't let us be parted now."

"If you say so." But Adalisa seemed unconvinced.

"Catherine," Edgar began, in the voice of one who expects to have to continue talking for some time. "There's no reason for you to come to Hexham with us and every reason for you to stay here."

"My safety? James's?" Catherine asked, knowing that they were both good reasons but not enough to sway her.

"Yes, of course," Edgar answered. "But much more than that. If I go with my father, I can investigate the situation at Hexham with him and, perhaps, prevent him from striking out at the first person he sees."

"That makes sense," Catherine admitted.

"And, more important," Edgar continued, "I want you to stay because my father won't be here."

"Oh . . . oh, yes!" Catherine understood. "I can be of help, then, can't I? People will speak more freely if he's not here. Little Margaret can translate for me."

"Yes, *carissima*, you can." Thank the saints he had married such a perceptive woman!

He kissed her in gratitude and she returned it, for love's sake, but she wasn't through with him.

"Now that that is settled, *carissime*," she whispered seductively. "You can explain to me why you never told me that your proud

Saxon father took a French woman for his second wife and more-over, why you never mentioned that absolutely adorable little sister."

"Ah." Edgar bit his upper lip. "That's a long story. Do you think it could wait until morning?"

He kissed her again and started working his way down the side of her neck, fumbling with the strings of her *chainse*. Catherine cursed him silently and then herself, for she knew she was going to let herself be persuaded.

Anyway, she considered, morning came very early this far north.

But even dawn wasn't soon enough for Waldeve. It was still the grey of constant summer twilight when everyone was rousted out.

Algar woke Edgar with an apologetic shake of the bed curtains that set the rings rattling.

"My lord requests that you be ready to leave within the hour," he told Edgar.

Edgar stared at him blearily. "What the hell hour is it?" he asked.

"I heard the bells at the monastery ring for Matins not long ago. I haven't heard Lauds rung, yet."

"Saint Servanus's risen pig!" Edgar roared. "Even the birds are still asleep, man!"

As if to flout him, at that moment a cock crowed. Edgar swore again, but swung his legs over the edge of the bed.

"Catherine." He pushed at the coverlet. "Catherine?"

She wasn't there. He vaguely remembered her climbing over him some time ago, but this was a normal nightly activity. She had always returned before.

Algar coughed. "Um, Lord Edgar, I believe your wife is already down in the hall, preparing your things for the journey."

Edgar frowned. That was so like what an obedient, dutiful wife would do that it made him nervous. In any case, it appeared that he was doomed to stay awake.

The half light of a midsummer morning tended to muffle vision rather than clarify it. There were shapes moving about in the hall and more in the courtyard, but they all appeared the same. Edgar found Solomon first by tripping over him.

"What are you doing still on the floor?" Edgar asked.

"I was sleeping," Solomon answered. "I'm not going anywhere, so there seemed no reason to leave my bed, such as it is. Obviously I was mistaken."

He let Edgar help him up. Together they went out into the misty air.

"I'm glad you'll be here with Catherine," Edgar said.

"I knew you'd appreciate me sooner or later," Solomon answered.

Edgar gave him a worried glance.

"The two of you aren't planning something, are you?" he asked.

Solomon laughed. "Don't worry, *vieux compang*. I'm staying because your brother and I have some ideas about the wool trade we want to explore. It's good that your stepmother can translate. Why didn't you tell us she was French?"

Edgar shrugged, then his attention turned. "There you are!" he said in relief.

He hurried toward Catherine.

Catherine was shaking out his heavy cloak from his pack so that it could be refolded and repacked. It seemed a pointless task to Edgar but he had learned that women do such things. The scorn shown him when he asked had taught him to accept that it was part of the arcane feminine rituals that even Catherine excluded him from.

Catherine looked up at his shout and waved them closer.

"I've almost finished," she told them. "The packhorse we bought in Berwick is loaded and your father says you're to find your old saddle for the other one. Do you know where it is?"

"It wasn't in the stables when I was last here," Edgar answered. "It must have been put in the storeroom. I'll get a lantern and go look."

Adalisa had come up in time to overhear the last of this conversation.

"No, Edgar," she said at once. "You'll never find it amidst all the barrels of provisions. I'll send Algar."

"That's all right," Edgar told her. "Algar is busy with his own work. I'm sure I can find it."

"No!" she said, so sharply that they jumped. "I don't want you rummaging around upsetting things. Algar can be spared for a few minutes."

She went off to see to it, leaving the other three staring at each other in confusion.

"I'm sure all the turmoil here has upset her," Catherine hazarded. "All this coming and going as well as the strain of grief . . ."

Edgar looked after her. "I suppose so," he said slowly. "Solomon, don't leave Catherine and James alone for a moment. Promise me."

"Of course not," Solomon assured him. "Don't worry. Nothing will happen to us here."

"That's right; we'll be fine," Catherine agreed. "It's you who needs to be careful. It's your family that someone has attacked."

Edgar forbore mentioning that it was now her family, too. Perhaps it wasn't, though. The events of the evening before had made him doubt that it was even his family anymore.

"Catherine," he began.

She looked at him, then looked down quickly, but it was too late. He had seen the terror in her eyes.

"Come with me," he said.

She shook her head without raising it. "No, it's best, if I stay here," she said softly. "Imagine taking your wife and child in a war party. James and I will be safer here."

She started fussing with the mail shirt they had found for him, settling it so that the links didn't stick into his tunic. Edgar took her hands.

"I'm not going to get myself killed," he said.

"Of course not." Her lip trembled.

"Oh, *carissima*." He held her close, oblivious of the people bustling around them. "I am so sorry. I never should have brought you here."

"Do you think I'd worry less in Paris?" Catherine reminded herself that this was women's fate, to wait and worry. Her job was not to make his harder. But she hated it. She hated everything about it.

"I see no glory in battle," she told him. "But if you must fight to save yourself, then do it. Anything you must do to return safely to us. Promise me."

Edgar smiled down at her. "With pleasure, my love. I have strong beliefs about keeping my skin whole."

"Saint Drostin's dripping tears, Edgar! Kiss her good-bye and get your ass in the saddle or I'll have you tied to it!"

Edgar clenched his teeth.

"I'm coming, Father," he said.

He turned back to Catherine. She put her hand over his mouth.

"I don't know what he said," she told him. "But it's clear he wants you to go. There's no sense in making this worse."

He kissed her good-bye and mounted his horse.

The sun was hanging just over the horizon as they left the castle. They threaded their way down and across the motte, between the tumble of huts and onto the road.

The morning grew warmer as they rode south, toward the Roman wall. Edgar was just considering taking off his leather mail shirt when they rounded a bend and were brought up short by a force of ten men strung across the road and into the woods, all in mail and helmets. Their swords were drawn. Edgar clutched at his knife.

Waldeve let out a roar.

"About time you got here! Saint Macarius's maiden mare! What took you so long?"

"My Lord Bishop didn't want to spare me," the leader answered, pulling off his helmet. "It took some time to convince him that filial obligation came before my vows to him. Now, Father, I'm at your service."

Edgar closed his eyes. Life had just become infinitely worse.

His brother Duncan had come home.

Six

The road to Hexham. Wednesday, 16 kalends July (June 16), 1143.
Commemoration of Saint Julitte, martyred for being Christian, and her son,
Cyrus, age three, martyred for kicking the Roman governor in the stomach.

Est in Northanhymbrorum provincia, haud procul a Tine flumine, ad
austrum site, villa quædam, nunc quidem modica, et raro cultore habitata,
sed, ut antiquitatis vestigia tenantur, quondam ampla et magnifica.
Hæc . . . Hestild vocatur.

There is, in the province of Northumbria, not at all far from the River
Tyne, on the east side, a certain village, now rather ordinary, and
sparsely inhabited, but it holds the traces of antiquity, at one time
important and magnificent. This is called Hexham.

—Richard of Hexham,
History of the Church of Hexham,
Capitual I

*D*uncan grinned at the stupefied expressions of his family. The grin grew wider as he recognized Edgar.

"Baby brother!" he exclaimed. "I can't believe they would bother to drag you back home. Father must truly be desperate. What do you intend to do, preach our enemies to death? Or has Father decided that our brothers were murdered by demons and sent for you to exorcise them?"

Edgar was too stunned to respond. He had tried very hard to forget the effect his brother Duncan had on him. But again he found himself feeling like a calf about to be slaughtered, listening to the scrape of the sharpening knife. He knew he should have fled, but now it was too late.

"Greetings, Brother," he managed. "Are you coming with us to Hexham?"

If he wasn't, Edgar intended to turned around now and hurry back to Wedderlie. He wouldn't for all the world risk letting Catherine fend for herself in the same household with Duncan.

To his relief, Duncan nodded. "We were on our way here when word came to us that the horses had been found. So we decided to wait for you so that the family could arrive in force in case the canons should decide to fight."

"Don't mock, Nephew," Æthelræd shouted. "This could be a trap. Do you want us to be caught unprepared?"

Duncan looked from Edgar to Æthelræd. His eyebrows raised at the sight of his uncle. He scanned the group of warriors, noting the familiar faces among Waldeve's men-at-arms. Bastards, all of them, some his own. All tied to them by blood oaths as well as blood. He smiled his approval. "For once, Uncle, you make sense. Very good. The murderers will know we stand together. All but Robert, I see. Father, how did you dare to leave that plotting weasel behind?"

Waldeve snorted. "That *bædling!* He can do no harm. I left him tilling his fields like a peasant. Adalisa knows better than to give him any control over my keep, and he hasn't the *hangelles* to take it."

Duncan smiled again, but said nothing. He knew that Wedderlie was as good as his now. To Edgar, that smile was a smirk of triumph and he longed to knock his elder brother sprawling in the dirt.

Their father was well aware of this. He looked from one son to the other with satisfaction, noting Edgar's barely suppressed anger. About time he showed some, to Waldeve's mind. This last son of his might turn out to be worth something, after all.

"Well, then," Waldeve said. "If you've been waiting for us, you must be rested. Let's waste no more time. We can be fording the Tyne by noon tomorrow."

As they started off again, Edgar saw Duncan working his way back to where he and Æthelræd were riding.

"Stay near me, Uncle," Edgar muttered, as his brother approached. "I want no trouble with him today."

But Duncan was in a jovial mood. He reached out and gave Edgar a brotherly punch that nearly toppled him. Edgar winced, wondering if Duncan had read his thoughts, but said nothing.

"I can't believe you're back!" Duncan laughed. "We all thought you'd abandoned us for that French *galdricge* of yours. What happened? She discover just how much use clerks are in bed?"

Edgar bit his tongue. He took a deep breath. "My wife is quite well, thank you. I will give her your regards."

"Maybe I'll come over to France and give her more than that," Duncan told him.

Edgar gave him a long, cool stare. If this were the best Duncan could do, perhaps his fear had been groundless. Still there was no need for him to know just how nearby Catherine was.

"Before you plan your visit, Duncan," Edgar said, "I think we should finish the matter at hand. Who do you think killed our brothers?"

"How should I know?" Duncan shrugged. "I've been at Durham the past two years. Hardly home at all. Any feuds Alexander and Egbert began had nothing to do with me."

"What about feuds that you began?" Edgar asked.

Duncan's eyebrows raised.

"Me?" he said in surprise. "I have offended no man. I serve my

Lord Bishop faithfully. All I do is at his command. Who would wish to revenge themselves upon me?"

Æthelræd leaned across so that Duncan could see him. "What about the villagers of Durham town?" he asked.

Duncan bridled. "We did nothing there but collect the tithes due the bishop."

"You burned their homes," Æthelræd reminded him.

"At Bishop William's orders," Duncan insisted. "And only those belonging to the traitor archdeacon, Rannulf. Anyway, this deed wasn't the work of villeins. How could they kill men with swords? Nor were the murders directed against me. If anything, I profit from them. No, look to our father's sins, if you want reasons."

Much as he hated to admit it, Edgar suspected that Duncan was right. But it would have given him such pleasure to lay the blame at his older brother's door. Then he could stop all this pretense and go home with no qualms at all.

Wistfully, he wondered what Catherine was doing.

With the departure of the men, the atmosphere at Wedderlie lightened considerably. Grief was still with them, but now it could be attended to in the proper fashion, with prayers and weeping. Catherine's sisters-in-law could give full vent to their suffering without being shouted into silence by Waldeve.

Sibilla, who had also lost her firstborn, refused consolation. She had sent word to her father that she was returning home and made preparations to do so.

"Don't you think you should stay here?" Adalisa asked her, as she furiously packed. "Eadmer is safe for now with Earl Cospatrick, and by Norman custom he has a right to inherit as well as Duncan. You should fight for him."

Sibilla didn't pause.

"I intend to," she said. "And the best way to do that is to return to my own kin. If you want to help me, just keep that old goat of yours alive long enough for Eadmer to reach his majority. As for me, I'm glad to be rid of the lot of you."

Adalisa nodded. She expected no loyalty from Sibilla. The sons of Waldeve had never been known for their kindness to their wives. She wondered how Edgar had escaped being like the others. He must have done so, somehow, for Catherine's devotion to him was obvious. Such love could not live with fear.

Adalisa felt the tears rise again and bit her lip. What would it be like to be married to a man one didn't fear?

As she went down the stairs to the hall, Adalisa heard laughter, children's laughter, mixed with growling and the barking of excited dogs. She came in to find her shy mouse of a daughter riding around the room on the back of Catherine's cousin, Solomon, who was on all fours. They were chasing Catherine, who had tied her skirts up between her legs so that she could better evade them. Willa was sitting on the windowsill, bouncing the baby in her lap and watching the fun. The dogs were running circles around them all.

As she came in, Solomon caught up with his prey and they all went down, rolling on the floor.

"Margaret!"

Her daughter looked up. She saw the astonishment on Adalisa's face and took it for disapproval. She hurriedly got to her feet, brushing the straw and dried flowers from her clothes.

"Mama, I'm sorry," she spoke quickly. "Solomon was my bear and Catherine was the hunter and we were chasing her out of the forest."

Solomon also rose, helping Catherine up with him.

"I apologize, my lady," he said. "We were playing as we do at home. It was unforgivable to forget that this is a house of mourning."

"Yes," Catherine added. "It's my fault. We should have taken the children out instead of disturbing my sisters-in-law."

Adalisa shook her head.

"I don't believe they heard you. I'm not angry, only surprised. Such behavior isn't common here."

Unfortunately, she added to herself.

Catherine took her hand. "I can take all the children out to the meadow, if no one will object. Come with us. It's such a beautiful day."

"Is it?" When had Adalisa last noticed the weather? She couldn't remember. "No, I have things to see to, but please enjoy yourselves. You're guests here. There's nothing you need to help with."

As soon as they were safely away from the keep, Solomon looked at Catherine and raised his eyebrows.

"This is what our Edgar grew up in?" he asked. "Even the cloister must have been appealing by contrast."

"I don't think he spent much time here, even before he came to France," Catherine answered. "He was sent first to the court of the

Scottish king and then to the cathedral school at Durham. But perhaps it's only like this here because of the tragedy."

"Cousin," Solomon chided. "Two days at Wedderlie and I know that the real tragedy of this place is its lord. You know it, too."

"Yes," Catherine answered slowly. They were near the meadow now, the children running ahead. Willa had already spread out a blanket for James and was unwrapping him. "But look about you. For all his cruelty, Waldeve can't be that hard a master. The village here is clean and the people seem strong and content, what I've seen of them."

It occurred to her that she'd seen very few people near the keep, after the excitement of their arrival. Of course, this time of year, they were probably all working in the fields or with the flocks in the hills.

"The peasants seem better off than the masters," Solomon admitted. "I've been in many strange lands, Catherine, but this unsettles me more than any other. It doesn't look that different from home, but it feels alien, almost ensorcelled. Does that make any sense to you?"

"Yes," Catherine said. "There's some wrong here. Something in the roots of the place. I think Edgar feels very much the same."

"I, for one, don't care about finding out what it is or even who was responsible for the killings," Solomon concluded. "I just want to finish my business and return to France as soon as possible."

Catherine, feeling cold even in the bright sunshine, fervently agreed.

Edgar's journey to Hexham was uneventful. Although banditry was rife in the area and they often heard scurryings in the woods that were too clumsy to be deer, the party wasn't attacked. A force this strong and purposeful was in little danger from the outlaws of the forest. Only an army could have gone against them.

Speaking only English again seemed strange to Edgar at first, but as they went deeper into the country, the years in France began to fall away from him. He felt himself once more the little boy in awe of the warriors who controlled his universe, wishing with all his heart to be like them and bitterly resentful of his preordained fate. It was as if his wish had finally been granted. Here he was, riding with the *feolagscipe* of his family, to avenge their own. He felt powerful, dangerous, invincible.

He felt like a fool. A complete impostor. Still, for a moment, there had been a touch of glory.

As Waldeve had predicted, they reached Hexham late the next morning. They had taken advantage of the summer twilight to ride far into the night. The town was perched on several levels of rock and earth on the south bank of the Tyne. As they approached the ford, they could see the burnt remains of the carnage wrought by King David's soldiers five years before, as they retreated back across the wall after their defeat at the Battle of the Standard. But on the other side of the river, within the ring of sanctuary crosses, the village had been spared.

The ruins in Hexham were old. Roman buildings destroyed by the Saxons; Saxon buildings destroyed by the Danes. Danish, now English, homes destroyed in William the Bastard's harrying of the North seventy years before. Now new homes of timber lay within ancient boundary markers. Trees grew from the cracks in the stones of the courtyard at the old monastery. Pigs snuffled around the remnants of vines planted by homesick legionaries.

Normally a troop of twenty armed men would send the inhabitants of a village running to the keep for protection, but the people of Hexham only glanced at them and went on about their work.

Duncan shook his head in wonder.

"They still think they're immune to invasion," he said. "Unbelievable."

"Who would attack them now?" Urric asked. "Everyone knows that Saint Wilfrid and Saint Cuthbert protect the whole town. What else could have saved them from King Malcolm and then King David but a miracle?"

Duncan spat his derision.

"Sudden fog and flood in this land are no more miraculous than the sun coming up," he said. "If Malcolm's army had been kept away by a rain of frogs, I might give some credence to it."

Urric was silenced, but unconvinced. Hexham had twice been spared destruction by the Scots because of its devotion to Wilfrid and Cuthbert and that's all there was to it. Anyone could see where the line of devastation ended. All the same, the soldier was impressed by Duncan's skepticism. This was a man who would let nothing keep him from what he wanted, not even the power of the saints. Urric had no intention of damning himself along with his lord, but there might be a way of grabbing some of the spoils for himself before it was time to repent.

Edgar was looking around, as if searching for someone.

"I keep expecting to see Æthelræd here," he told his uncle. "This is his home. You remember your namesake, don't you?"

"Of course I do, boy," Æthelræd answered. "Only he calls himself Aelred, now that he's become a Cistercian."

"Aelred?" Edgar's lips tightened. "Another concession to a people who won't bother to learn to pronounce the *eth*."

Æthelræd laughed. "What of it? It may be that he just likes the name better. He's become a new man with his conversion to the monastic life. Why shouldn't he have a new name, as well, easier for the French monks to pronounce? You've been gone too long, Edgar."

"Yes." Edgar sighed. "It seems I have. Still, I miss him, whatever he calls himself. He might be able to help us. Æthelr . . . Aelred always knew all the gossip. Perhaps Robert should go see him. They were always such devoted friends. I can't believe he's changed that much."

Æthelræd considered this. "I agree someone should speak to him," he said. "But not Robert. They had some sort of falling out when Aelred decided to become a monk. Robert won't speak of it, but since then, he's not been back to court. He stays on his lands and devotes himself to his crops and his dogs. If we have no luck here in discovering the answer to this, I'll ask your father to send us down to Rievaulx to talk to Aelred."

"Edgar!" The voice so close startled them both.

Edgar's head came up. "Yes, Father."

"We're almost at the priory," Waldeve called back to him. "Get up here. I want someone to talk to these canons in their own language. Earn your keep, boy! Spout some Latin! Let them know we're not illiterate *neyfs* that they can fool with fancy speech."

"Certainly, Father," Edgar answered. Beneath his breath he muttered, " 'Spout some Latin!' Do you want words at random or maybe a whole sentence? You wouldn't know the difference, you old *irrumator*."

Grumbling all the while, Edgar obeyed his father. He dismounted and pounded the iron knocker on the priory gate.

The door was opened and Edgar scowled at the friendly smile of a canon of about his own age whose expression changed swiftly to alarm. Hurriedly, Edgar regained his composure.

"My apologies," he said. "I am Edgar, the son of Lord Waldeve. We understand that some horses belonging to our family were left here."

"Ah, yes," the man answered. "I'm the porter here. My name is Meldred."

Meldred. A good English name. Edgar continued in that tongue.

"In that case, Meldred, my father would like to speak with you."

Meldred opened the door all the way.

"Of course, with Prior Richard's permission," he answered. "But you and your party will need to rest and wash first, I'm sure. We don't have space to house you all here, but perhaps somewhere in the town?"

"I believe that my father would prefer information at once," Edgar answered. "Is the prior available?"

The porter thought. "Yes, I think so," he said. "He may be working on his history but I know he'd understand the need for the interruption."

He looked over Edgar's shoulder at the troop of men, so obviously related and all so large and well armed.

"Perhaps just you and your father could come in?" he asked timidly. "So many would disturb the peace of the cloister, especially with the horses. You can see how little space we have. We had to take our own horses out of the stable to care for yours.

"Of course," the canon added as they waited for Waldeve to dismount and join them, "we thought at first that the horses were a gift."

His voice rose in hope, but Edgar knew better than to assume his father would donate three good war horses for the use of clerics. The priory would be lucky if he gave them even a part of their worth as alms.

Waldeve did not appear in a benevolent mood as he strode through the gate. The porter had some trouble staying ahead of him as they headed for the prior's residence.

"We've fed and groomed them, my lords," he told them. "It's been years since I've seen such fine horses. Raised in Durham, were they?"

Waldeve shut him up with a look.

"How did you know they were mine?" he snapped.

"The bridle, Lord," Meldred stammered. "By the crest on the silver. I come from Wedderlie. I can see you don't remember me. I'm one of Alfred's grandsons. I knew that it belonged to one of your sons."

He nodded at Edgar. Waldeve growled.

"Not this one," he barked. "Alexander. Murdered, with his brother and son. Now, tell me, how did my horses get here? Who did this?"

Meldred was beginning to feel as if between the jaws of a mastiff. He cringed inside his robe and backed into the priory.

"Perhaps Prior Richard would be the one to speak to," he quavered.

But Waldeve wasn't ready to let him go.

"Was it you who found them?"

The canon shook his head as if shivering.

"No, Lord," he insisted. "It was the sacristan, come to light the candles for Matins."

"Bring him to me at once."

"Lord, this is his hour of meditation . . ." Meldred began.

Waldeve roared. "Bring him to me now or you can meditate on the toe of my boot up your ass!"

Meldred backed away quickly. As he scurried through the doorway to the churchyard Edgar murmured to him.

"Remember, the meek shall inherit the earth."

Meldred paused and shook his head.

"Only six feet of it, I fear," he answered.

Waldeve snorted as he left.

"I've no use for clean-shaven men," he muttered. "Including, you, Edgar. You're not a monk. You should grow your mustache like a proper Saxon. Now where in hell is that prior? You'd think he'd have come out to see what the noise was, if nothing more. Useless, the lot of them."

"Perhaps not so much as you think."

Waldeve froze, then turned around slowly. Prior Richard was standing directly behind him.

The prior was almost as tall as Waldeve and his glare nearly as angry.

"I understand you come to apply for my position." Prior Richard spoke between clenched teeth.

"What are you babbling about?" Waldeve shouted back at a distance of three inches from the prior's nose.

"Your orders to my porter could be heard from here to Edinburgh." Richard's voice rose to match Waldeve's. "Who are you to tell my people what to do? You have no right even to enter without my permission!"

Waldeve stopped. He didn't like being attacked unawares. He was the one with the grievance. He tried to take back the offensive.

"I'm after the men who ambushed my sons, you arrogant ass!" he said.

Now Prior Richard was confused. "Meldred told me that a force of Scots had arrived to retrieve the horses that were left with us."

"And so we have," Waldeve motioned Edgar to him.

Edgar came forward cautiously. He didn't know this man. The prior in his day had been old Canon Asketill, a seasoned administrator who never needed to raise his voice.

"Prior Richard." He deliberately spoke softly so that the man would have to concentrate on his words. "My father, Lord Waldeve, is devastated by the loss of my brothers. He believes you know something of the men who killed them. Forgive his outbursts."

The prior made a visible effort to throw off his anger.

"I see," he said and took a deep breath. "I was unaware that you had come, personally, to investigate this. We all grieve for your loss and will pray for your family. I am sorry that Meldred didn't make the matter clear to me. You shouldn't have been made to wait."

Waldeve might be tyrannical and nasty but he was not ill bred. He accepted the apology graciously.

"An understandable mistake," he said. "We shall not speak of it again."

The prior led them to his room.

"I've sent for wine and food for you," he told them. "And I can send some ale to refresh your retainers, if you'll permit."

"They can drown in it, if they like," Waldeve said. "They won't be needed today. Have them set up a camp. We'll go no farther until I have reached the heart of this matter."

"Father," Edgar whispered. "I don't think Duncan and Æthelræd appreciate being left outside."

"*Hie hie fulbrecon mægon,*" Waldeve answered.

Edgar suspected that both of them could, but not in public. However, it was clear that his father didn't want either man sent for.

They settled themselves with cups of wine and a platter of fruit and bread.

Prior Richard opened his mouth to speak but Waldeve stopped him.

"I don't want to hear any more expressions of sympathy," he said. "And yes, I'll make a donation to the priory for the rest of their souls, but not of land, you hear. I'll think of something. But not now. Just tell me what you know."

The prior accepted the rebuke with dignity.

"There's little enough to tell, my lord," he said. "It's a mystery to us. The gates had been barred for the night, and as you have seen, the church is within the walls. My sacristan came in before dawn and found the horses. He thought that perhaps they belonged to Saints Wilfrid and Cuthbert and that it was a sign that we were about to be invaded again."

Waldeve started to say what he thought of that, then changed his mind. He motioned for the prior to continue.

"That's all I can tell you," Richard went on. "He was soon convinced that they were not from heavenly realms. They had been well fed, the only mark on them was the cropping. And we have cared for them well, while they were in our charge."

"I have no doubt of it," Waldeve said, then stopped. "The what?"

Prior Richard seemed puzzled. "Didn't the messenger tell you? Their tails and manes had been sheared off, almost to the skin."

Waldeve leapt up, knocking over the wine and splattering it on the monk's robe.

"Edgar!"

"Yes, Sir?"

"Talk to him. Get the whole story. I'm going to see to my horses."

With that Waldeve left the room, leaving Edgar wondering how to begin.

"Prior Richard—"

"Don't apologize for him," Richard interrupted, wiping the wine off with his hands. "He's not the worst, not at all. These are wicked times and men become hard to survive them. I am accustomed to their brusque behavior."

"Nevertheless," Edgar continued, "my father believes 'hoc voluit, *sic jubet, sit pro ratione voluntas.*' I've been away from home a long time. I had forgotten how much a lord he is."

Prior Richard smiled. "I haven't read Juvenal in years. So you think that your father makes his own laws?"

"At Wedderlie, it is his justice that prevails," Edgar said. "It's destroying him that he can't find any for my brothers. Those who killed them aren't acting according to custom or tradition. If my brothers had been killed for profit, then their bodies would have been stripped. If for revenge, then their heads would have been taken, and the horses and weapons considered honorable booty. This has no logic. It's as if someone were taunting him. Was there anything, any message attached to the horses when they were found?"

The prior shook his head slowly. "Nothing that I could see. I have no idea, unless the fact of their being brought here is a sign. But I don't recall your family having anything to do with Hexham."

Edgar shook his head. "The family doesn't, apart from a few bequests in my grandfather's day. But when I was studying at the cathedral at Durham, sometimes my friend, Æthelræd, would bring me here to visit. It was when his father still lived. I was very fond of old Eilaf."

He paused a moment, remembering the kindly old man who had seen his whole way of life reviled and taken from him and in the end had not let bitterness master him.

"But this crime has nothing to do with me," he continued. "I've been away since I was fourteen. Nearly fifteen years, now. The few who remember me only knew the boy I was."

Prior Richard considered this.

"Perhaps this deed has its beginnings in that time," he said at last.

Edgar sat up straight. "But I did nothing!"

"I didn't say that." Richard held up his hands for silence. "But memories are long in the North and more than one man has been raised to avenge a wrong done to his father."

Edgar had no refutation. He sipped his wine, idly reflecting from its quality that the prior must have connections in Burgundy.

That cup also crashed to the floor as Waldeve burst back into the room.

"What kind of monsters could have done this?" he shouted.

"You know who they are, don't you? They paid you to keep silent. Tell me now, or I'll choke it out of you!"

He grabbed the prior by the neck strings of his robe and began to pull them tight.

"Father!" Edgar moved to help, but he wasn't needed. Prior Richard would not be moved.

"Take your hands off me, Lord Waldeve." His voice was steady and menacing, his breathing labored as the strings tightened. "Or, for your ill treatment of this servant of God, Saint Andrew, Saint Cuthbert and Saint Wilfrid, I'll curse you and your family to a fate that will make what has happened to you seem a blessing."

He stood motionless, staring fearlessly into Waldeve's fury. There was a long moment during which no one breathed. Then Edgar's father released his grip. He looked away.

"Cursed," he whispered. "I need no more disaster called down upon me. Not now. I am cursed enough."

The prior adjusted his robe where Waldeve had crumpled it. Edgar could see him struggling to regain his composure. Finally, he spoke.

"Forgive me, Lord Waldeve," he said. "My words grew from anger at your act. I was born, like you, to command, not serve. The hardest thing God has asked of me is humility."

"Accepted," Waldeve answered. "Now come with me and see what care you and the other servants of God have taken of my horses. Edgar, examine them. There must be something to tell us why they're here."

The horses were standing in the court in front of the church. Edgar felt a pang as he saw them, the finest horses his father owned, now reduced to almost comical figures. Somehow, the sight made him more angry than the death of his brothers. Men fought each other constantly here in the North. It was part of life and Alexander and Egbert and even young Edgar had been trained for it. But the horses had done nothing to be so abused. Their dignity had been taken from them. Someone wanted to humiliate the lord of Wedderlie as much as they wanted to destroy him.

For the first time since Robert told him the news in France, Edgar found himself truly compelled to discover the reason for all this. There had to be an answer.

What had his father done to create this kind of enemy? And, even more, how much farther would this enemy go?

It hit him with the force of a battering ram.

All the fighting men of Wedderlie were here. Apart from a few guards, there was no one left to defend the keep.

He had left his wife and son behind, thinking them safe.

Instead, he had left them unprotected from attack. Edgar felt a wave of panic. The danger at Wedderlie might be worse than that they had left Paris to escape.

Seven

The keep at Wedderlie. Friday, 14 kalends July (June 18), 1143. Summer solstice and the feast of Saint Gemma, who preferred losing her life to losing her chastity.

> *Ne thæt aglæca ylden thote,*
> *ac he gefeng hraðe forman siðe*
> *slæpendne rinc, slat unwearnum,*
> *bat banlocan, blod edrum dranc*
> *synsnædum swealh; Sona hæfde*
> *unlyfignendes eal gefeormod,*
> *fet ond folma.*

> That demon thought not of delay
> but first swiftly snatched
> a warrior sleeping unaware,
> bit off his limbs, drank his blood,
> swallowed great chunks; Soon he had
> consumed all the corpse,
> feet and hands.
> —Beowulf, 11.739–744

*T*he clouds lay over the land, diffusing the sunlight so that the colors of the world were muted into shades Catherine had never known existed. The fog lifted slowly, the light breaking through here and there in sudden stabs of gold. She had no idea of the hour. From far away there were bells but they might have been for anything from Matins, in the middle of the night, to Prime, just after dawn. The sun hadn't done more than dip below the edge of the sky for the past two days. It one sense, it was beautiful. In another, the strange light only intensified the feeling that this was a place not wholly of the earth.

"It seems that the fog would lift and reveal fairies, dancing by the river." Solomon appeared next to her at the window; he wore only his tunic and his black curls were tousled from sleep. Catherine leaned against him, so sure and familiar.

"I'd like to see that," she said softly.

"So would I." He grinned. "The stories all agree that they dance naked."

The world became real again.

"What are you doing up so early?" Catherine asked him. "James woke me a while ago, wanting his breakfast, but he barely managed to finish before he was back asleep. I've heard no one else stirring."

"The light pulled me from sleep, I think. Or perhaps it was the dream." His voice became serious again. "I thought I heard someone weeping, calling for help with no hope of anyone hearing. I could almost taste their tears."

Catherine turned his chin down so that she could see his face. Solomon met her eyes. She saw no laughter in his look. He wasn't teasing her with a dramatic tale. But it wasn't like him to be bothered by dreams.

"Do you think it's a warning?" She tried to keep her voice calm.

He shrugged. "Do I look like Joseph? I can't interpret dreams. I only know that I didn't want to stay in bed any longer with the memory of it."

"Perhaps it's only the quiet," Catherine said. "Now that Sibilla and Anna and their women have left, as well as most of the men, the hallways echo with emptiness. The only guards left are the few from the village. A dropped boot sounds like the tread of a hundred soldiers."

She sighed. "I wish Edgar would come back. I wish we could go home."

Solomon put his arm around her. "He'll return soon. In the meantime, I need to continue my negotiations with Robert and his friends. The Flemish are already establishing themselves in settlements here. They'll control the wool trade completely if I can't convince the natives that we can offer them more in return."

"I can't imagine you as a merchant." Catherine shook her head. "When you go off on your journeys, I always believe you're battling pirates and dragons all day and spending your nights in disreputable inns."

"All inns are disreputable," Solomon assured her. "But I do my best to avoid dragons and pirates. I have enough trouble with ordinary bandits and pretty girls with ugly fathers and brothers. Trade is what I do, Catherine. It's not noble, but it is useful. And I need to be good at it. We're being driven out of every other occupation. The extra tithes on Jews and the laws controlling us grow stronger every year."

"I know," she said, but Catherine didn't want to hear it. To her the answer was simple; Solomon should become a Christian. But the only times she had ever seen him truly angry were when she had tried to convince him to convert.

It was safer to change the subject.

"What do you think of my stepmother-in-law?" she asked.

"I think she's the saddest woman I have ever met," he answered. "Perhaps it was she who cried in my dream."

Catherine nodded. "I can't imagine anyone being happy married to Waldeve. I wonder what Edgar's mother was like. Edgar doesn't remember her at all."

"The people of the village could probably tell us," Solomon said. "I wish we spoke the language. It's not that far from German, but just enough that I can't follow what they say. I *know* they're gossiping about us. I can hear them whispering behind me every time I pass."

"I don't mind that," Catherine said. "It's the feeling that everyone but us knows what's going on. I just can't believe that Waldeve could have made such a vicious enemy and not know who it is."

"I can't either," Solomon said. "Do you feel that you've been thrust blindfolded into the center of a storm?"

Catherine sighed. "Ever since I left Paris."

"Don't you think we should start finding out what direction the storm is blowing from?"

"Yes," Catherine said. "And, most important, if it is anything that can hurt Edgar."

"For once, we agree." Solomon laughed. "Now, how do we do it without understanding the language?"

Catherine considered. "Margaret."

"That child? What can she do?"

"Speak both French and English," Catherine said. "And also, the people of the village know her and treat her kindly. I've watched. I think they pity her."

Solomon considered this. "Pity? Why? Her lot is no worse than others of her class and a damn long way better than that of a peasant."

"I don't know the answer to that, either," she answered. "But I see it in their eyes. Yes, I'll take Margaret into the village with me today. Is Robert coming here?"

"Yes, Adalisa will translate for me." He yawned. "You know, I think I could manage another stretch of sleep, after all."

"Go on, then." Catherine gave him a push. "I think I'll watch the fog a little longer."

She stood watching the swirls for some time, feeling that she was half in a dream already. Then she blinked, blinked again and leaned dangerously far out of the window, trying to make out the thing she had seen.

"What is that?" She breathed. It was huge, whatever it was. She could make out no shape, only a dark mass, undulating across the road. It seemed to be made of the skins of a dozen animals. Antlers poked out the front and it had what looked like a unicorn horn. As she watched it paused and gave out a roar that should have brought people tumbling from their homes.

Nothing.

Catherine tried to call out, but could only gasp like a fish on the riverbank. As she watched in horror, the thing lurched on and vanished into the forest.

She closed her eyes. "Saint Maurice and all your soldiers, protect me from that thing," she whispered.

The ribands of fog curled around the place where the monster had disappeared.

Just a few years ago Catherine would have run out to investigate. She would have unbolted the door, gone down the stairs shoeless, across the bridge of the motte, slid under the portcullis and been out in the road hunting for the trail of the beast before it had time to vanish completely.

Now, she told herself, she was learning caution and good sense.

In her mind there was a phantom sniff of disbelief from the voices of the convent.

Very well, she was learning to be more circumspect before raising the household with tales of monsters in the morning mist.

She tried to remember exactly what she had seen. The image was hard to recapture, distorted by the variations on sunlight and fog. There seemed to be a head, the end with all the antlers. Did it have feet? She couldn't recall. It had moved in a slithery fashion, like a giant serpent, only with fur.

Oh, dear, she could just imagine what Solomon would say to that.

Was it real or had she imagined it? Was it a dream conjured out of Edgar's Saxon tales? The great monster living in the lake, for instance. Saint Columba was supposed to have exorcised it centuries ago, but Edgar said it still lurked in the dark water. Could this be a land-bound cousin to that demon?

"Logic, Catherine," she told herself. "Think rationally. Organize the information. Form a clear and reasoned hypothesis."

She could almost hear Mother Heloise standing next to her, leading her through her lessons.

"I must get down there and examine the ground," she decided. "If it left tracks, it was real. If it was a demon, then I can only hope God will protect me."

Her clothes were all in the women's rooms. Catherine looked around as she hurried down to the door. There was a cord hanging on a hook that she could use to belt her shift, and a clean tablecloth that she could use to cover her head, as was proper to a married woman.

There was no hope of finding shoes.

At the last moment, she also snatched up something to defend herself with.

No one noticed her as she took the bar off the door and went down the steps. The only sign of the guards at the gate was their snores. Catherine was both relieved and chagrined to see that the portcullis hadn't been completely lowered the night before. There was enough space to go under if she crouched.

Catherine did spare a glance of disgust at the sleeping guards. These people were in charge of protecting her child? Better to arm Willa.

The pebbles in the pathway bruised her feet. Catherine went as quickly as possible down through the collection of huts and then stepped onto the soft verge, damp with dew.

Now, where had the thing come out of the wood? She walked more slowly now. Nothing that big could pass without leaving a trace.

There. Clear as if an army had come through. Catherine pushed back the torn branches of a fir tree, hoping to see the trail leading back to the monster's lair. There was nothing but a deep depression in the ground, wildflowers squashed flat. Their scent rose to greet her.

Catherine puzzled over this. Had the thing been lying in wait and then, lacking prey, got up again? She moved to the other side of the road, noting how the dirt had been disturbed and the ruts of the cartwheels dented.

So, it had crossed here, just as she had seen. And vanished among the trees.

Catherine hesitated. What if it were still there? What if it attacked her?

I shouldn't be doing this, she thought. If I'm killed, what will happen to my child?

Still, she peered into the forest, looking for a glimpse of the monster as it retreated, she hoped.

The branches shook. Catherine leapt back to the other side of the road. She raised her weapon as the leaves parted.

Two women came out of the woods. They were carrying baskets of strawberries. When they saw Catherine, they screamed and then threw themselves face down on the grass.

Catherine started toward them, to help them up. She stopped as both women began chanting at her, loudly, holding the berries out before them.

> *"Ic on sunu thinne sodne gelyfe*
> *hælenda cyning, hider asende . . ."*

What were they doing? Catherine froze. Was it some sort of curse they were setting on her? Would it help to run? She was willing to try.

The women went on, neither one looking up.

> *". . . thone Gabriel, godes ærendraca,*
> *sanctan Marian sylfre gebodode. . . ."*

Wait. Those words sounded familiar. "*Sanctan Marian?*" Oh, no.

Now Catherine did run. Those women had taken her for an apparition of the Holy Virgin Mary. Horrible! She was much more afraid of committing sacrilege than being cursed. She prayed she would be out of sight before the women dared to lift their eyes. How could they have made such a foolish assumption?

"*How do you think, Catherine? Look at yourself! You should be ashamed.*"

The voices of the convent pierced through the thumping of her heart. She slid under the portcullis again, took the steps three at a time and, landing inside the doorway, barred it shut and leaned on it, gasping for breath.

Then she looked at herself: bare feet, white shift, a blue tablecloth over her head and, worse and worse, in her hands a sword left behind by Anna's son. It was a very simple toy, just two strips of wood lashed together. It looked very much like a cross.

She dropped it guiltily. It clattered on the stone threshold.

"What's that?"

Adalisa looked up from a table by the hearth. It was littered with papers. When she saw Catherine her mouth opened in astonishment.

"Good morning," Catherine said quickly. "I was just . . . just . . ."

Adalisa shook her head. "It doesn't matter. I don't want to know."

"No!" Catherine was alarmed. "It isn't like that. I thought I saw something in the woods. I went out to investigate."

"Of course," Adalisa answered. "And what did you find?"

"Nothing," Catherine said. "Just broken branches."

"A deer, probably." Adalisa bent back over the papers.

Catherine blushed, more in anger than embarrassment. This woman didn't believe her! She thought Catherine had gone out for some sort of assignation.

My God, she thought. From the Virgin to the Magdalene, and all before breakfast.

Catherine could see it would be no use to defend herself. She crossed the hall to the stairs up to her room.

"Catherine?"

Catherine stopped. "You wished something more, my lady?"

Adalisa sighed. "When you're dressed, I could use some help going through these. Please. And, Catherine, you have nothing to fear from me. I would never betray you."

Catherine spoke between clenched teeth. "I have done nothing that would cause me to fear you. I shall be happy to help. Let me check on the baby and put on my *bliaut* and shoes."

James still slept, but Willa was awake.

"Did you dance with the fairies, Mistress?" she asked.

"Have you been talking with Solomon?" Catherine asked sternly.

"No, Mistress," Willa said. "I saw you from the window. Next time, may I go, too?"

Catherine wondered how many others had seen her and what they thought she had been doing. Any chance she may have had of being thought of as a respectable French matron had been shattered by one rash act. Her only consolation was that Edgar would probably think the episode amusing.

She dressed carefully, although she doubted that proper attire would salvage her reputation with Adalisa. Then she descended to the hall.

A servant had brought a pitcher of ale and a platter of meat and bread. Adalisa had poured a bowl of the ale, but left the food untouched. Her finger was moving slowly across a square of vellum that kept trying to roll itself up again. She looked up when Catherine entered.

"Eat first." She waved vaguely at the small table set up to hold the food. "Then help me with these. There's some language in this charter that makes no sense to me. My Latin is only the little our parish priest could teach."

Catherine poured a bowl of ale. It was more sour than French beer but she was becoming accustomed to it. The bread was softened by the meat sauce, and she tore off a piece from the edge and nibbled at it as she read over Adalisa's shoulder.

"Which is the troublesome part?" she asked.

Adalisa pointed, moving over so Catherine could see.

Catherine put down her bread and bent over the text. As she did, a suspicion struck her.

"This isn't some sort of test, is it, to see if I'm what I claim to be?"

Adalisa almost laughed. "No, or I'd have set you a task I could better judge. I've known Edgar since he was a boy, better than his father does. He could never abide stupid women, stupid people, actually. A pretty face might hold him a few nights, but to abandon home and family, he would have to have more than his privates interested. I'm sure you have the education he claims for you. Now, please look at this."

Catherine returned to her task, somewhat reassured.

"*Sciatis me concessisse et reddidisse . . . ego pro delicitione Dei et redemptione anime mee. . . .*" She looked up. "It seems a fairly standard charter of gift."

"Not that part," Adalisa said. "Farther down. After Saint Cuthbert."

"Let me see." Catherine read further. It wasn't a very neat copy. There were places where words had been scraped and reentered. She held the page up to the light. "*Sancto Cuthberto et Willelmo Cumino, episcopo.*"

She looked up again. "I thought William Cumin was never elected Bishop of Durham. Isn't that what Edgar's brother Duncan is fighting about?"

"Yes, it is," Adalisa said. "But that hasn't stopped Cumin from issuing charters and giving away church land. That's not what's bothering me. It's the next bit.

"Very well." Once again. "*Unam carractam terre de feudo meo in . . .* is this the Latin for Berwick? Berwick, then . . . *pro escambio terre de*—"

"That's it!" Adalisa said. "*Escambio*, what is it?"

"In exchange for," Catherine answered. "It's fairly straightforward. Waldeve gave land in Berwick to the bishop of Durham in exchange for three horses, fully shod and caparisoned. From what I've seen of my father-in-law, it's not unlike him to disguise a sale as a gift. Is the land in Berwick worth three horses? It seems a lot to pay for only one carractate."

"I don't see how it could be," Adalisa said. "That's part of what bothers me. I knew nothing of this. He told me he had bought the horses at the fair at Roxburgh. The land at Berwick is only a toft, with a small house. It was part of his first wife's dower. I didn't even think it was his to give. I thought it had gone to Robert."

Catherine looked at the signatures of the witnesses.

"Robert hasn't signed this," she said. "Duncan did, as well as the other two brothers. It says the transaction was done at Durham, but not when. Perhaps the property went to one of the others instead. Or one of them may have traded Robert for it."

"I don't think so," Adalisa said. "I wonder how old this is? Waldeve keeps the family papers in a casket under our bed. While I hold the keys to everything else, he's always kept this one until now. I think he felt that his family was none of my business."

Catherine heard the tightness in her voice. Adalisa's fate was a cruel one, to have a husband who gave her so much responsibility and so little respect.

Adalisa continued. "This is the first time I've opened it alone. But it occurred to me that the reason for the persecution might lie in some agreement my husband made long ago. Perhaps someone felt they were cheated of their birthright."

"You suspect that Robert is getting revenge for the alienation of his land?" Catherine was aghast. "That's rather drastic, don't you think?"

"Robert?" Adalisa brushed the idea away with a flick of her fingers. "Poor Robert probably doesn't even know about this. No, don't you see? You said it before, William Cumin is not the canonically elected bishop. He tried everything to make the canons choose him, including imprisoning them in their own cloister, but they wouldn't do it. Yet he still behaves as if he's bishop."

"I don't understand," Catherine said. "Does that mean that the charter is invalid? Were the horses stolen, then?"

"I don't know," Adalisa answered. "No, what frightens me is the fact that more men of our family than Duncan are dealing with Cumin at all. King David supported him at the beginning but almost no one does now. The town is under siege with the body of Saint Cuthbert held hostage. Horrible things have been done there, I've heard tales of torture and rape and houses put to the torch."

"But surely all of those who stand with this Cumin aren't being murdered," Catherine argued. "Why would this family be singled out? Hardly because Waldeve bought some horses."

"Perhaps it was because those horses were used to bring my stepsons to Durham to commit those atrocities. The past few years, they've all been gone for long stretches. They said they were with the king or Earl Cospatrick. What if they weren't?"

Adalisa started rolling up the various papers and tying them with ribbons. She rubbed at the marks the wax seals had left on the table.

Catherine could see that there was no point in arguing, but in her mind the theory had a hundred flaws. The greatest was the idea that anyone who owed knight's fee to the king could escape it. If Waldeve and his sons hadn't been with the court, someone would have come looking for them.

Now *that* was a thought. Men who reneged on their military feu might well be given a traitor's death.

Suddenly, from no reason for the murder of Edgar's brothers, Catherine now had too many. Were any of them the true one? And, oh, Saint Genevieve, was Edgar safe from this evil, especially traveling with his own family?

Edgar was perfectly safe at that moment, but bored and thoroughly disgusted with his family. He had amused himself for a while trying to remember which of the men-at-arms were his brothers and which his nephews. He wondered if any of them resented Waldeve's legitimate sons enough to kill. But there was no way he could find out, so he was left to sit in the makeshift camp outside the priory and endure their bombastic talk and various demonstrations of prowess.

Duncan sat next to him. Edgar reflected that there were worse things than boredom.

"This must all be very crude to you, after your soft life in France." Duncan smiled.

Edgar thought of the six-month journey he had just made to Santiago del Compostella. He thought of the dangers he and Catherine had survived only through God's grace. He didn't feel like telling Duncan about them.

"They call us Scots barbarians, in Paris," he said. "*Crude* is one of the kinder words."

"It must be degrading for you to have to admit that you belong to such a race," Duncan said.

"I've always been proud both of being a Saxon and a Scot." Edgar knew he was being baited. Damn. Duncan always knew how to make him rise to it.

"There are monks in Durham who remember you," Duncan continued. "They say you were an indifferent student."

"Perhaps they were indifferent teachers," Edgar answered.

"Perhaps. Do you remember a certain Lawrence?" Duncan's voice took on a sharper edge.

"Yes, of course," Edgar answered. "Very fond of Vergil, he was. Is he well?"

"The last I heard," Duncan said. "He's one of those malcontents who refuse to submit to my Lord Bishop William. They have barricaded themselves in the cloister. Did he ever take you into his bed?"

"What? Of course not!" Edgar jumped to his feet. "What are you getting at?"

Duncan's smile widened. "Nothing, little brother, only you did spend a considerable time with clerics and, of course, you were also a friend of Aelred."

"Aelred taught me the Latin that Canon Lawrence couldn't," Edgar said. "I've always admired him greatly, even more now that I know he's become a white monk."

"And you don't mind that he corrupted your brother," Duncan said.

Now Edgar understood at least part of what Duncan was doing. He not only wanted to make Edgar angry, he was also seeking information to discredit Cumin's enemies.

"You thought I didn't understand the nature of Aelred and Robert's friendship?" he asked. "I wasn't that much an innocent. They weren't the only ones at King David's court. I was in more danger from the men there than from those in the monastery. You won't get me to betray the canons at Durham for your own ends. They did nothing worse than beat Latin verbs into me."

Duncan stood up, as well, not bothering to conceal his anger.

"They are all catamites and cowards," he hissed. "If the bishop had taken my advice, we'd have slaughtered every one of them and installed men who would do as they were told."

"Fine cowards they must be, then," Edgar said. "To resist armed men with no weapon but faith."

Duncan glared at him, trying to come up with a rebuttal. When he couldn't, he swore loudly, turned and walked away.

Edgar hadn't felt so elated since the night James was born.

With a renewed sense of well-being, Edgar returned to the priory, where his father was spending the day making life miserable for the canons.

"Someone must have heard something!" he was shouting for the hundredth time. "Someone must have seen them. You can't all be idiots."

Edgar left him to it. At this point, no one was likely to suddenly remember a sound in the night. And anyone who might wasn't likely to tell Waldeve. Edgar wasn't sure there was anything to find here at all, but he thought the best thing to do was examine the horses, yet again.

The stables were warm on this summer morning, the smell of the animals strong. Edgar inhaled deeply. There was something so comforting about the familiarity of it. He went over to where the horses stood. They were new since his time, but obviously from Durham. The area was famous for the quality of its horse breeding.

He examined their hooves, not having any idea what he was looking for. He ran his hands over their flanks and withers. Nothing was unusual apart from their poor, shorn manes and tails. Edgar went over to the place where the gear had been stored.

The saddles and blankets weren't the best, and hadn't been intended for fighting. The pommel and cantel were low to allow the rider to mount and dismount more quickly. They wouldn't have provided support in a fight. The bridles were unadorned, except for Alexander's. Edgar picked it up. The silver disk was clearly engraved with the seal of the king. Edgar studied it closely, with professional interest. He had once posed as a journeyman silversmith and the training period he had spent learning the craft had been one of the happiest times of his life.

It was crudely done, but the silver was good quality. There was no message scratched on it. Nothing at all to indicate who had taken the horses and then returned them. Edgar hung the bridle back on its hook and stared at it in disgust. The metal jingled as it swung.

Edgar's eyes narrowed. There was only one silver disk. Shouldn't there be two, one on each side? He hadn't spent much time learning horsemanship but he thought he knew that much. He examined the bridle again. Yes, how could he have neglected to notice the rough edge where the metal had snapped?

So now he knew that there was a piece missing. What of it? He'd ask if it had been lost before Alexander was killed, which was possible, but even if it had been taken by those who killed him what use was that to know? He could hardly hunt through the possessions of every man in the North for a bit of silver. Most likely, it had already been melted down and used for something else.

"Edgar! Where are you?" Waldeve was shouting from the courtyard. "Never around when you're wanted. Get out here, boy!"

With a long sigh, Edgar went out to face his father. Now what?

Waldeve was putting on his riding gloves.

"These imbeciles know nothing," he grumbled. "I'm leaving a few of the men here to watch, in case anything more happens. You come with me."

"Are we going back to Wedderlie, then?" Edgar asked, hope rising.

"Hardly," Waldeve said. "I've been talking with your brother. We need more help. I'm going to Durham."

Durham?

"But why, Father?" Edgar ran after him as he strode out to the camp. "Isn't there trouble there? They won't be able to spare any men."

"Cumin owes me," Waldeve told him. "He'll help or see even more trouble."

"Shouldn't someone go back to Wedderlie to see if all is well there?" Edgar asked.

"I'm sending someone," Waldeve said. "No, not you, so you can put away that thought. I've never seen anyone so unnaturally attached to his wife. If she's that good, I'll try her, myself."

Edgar's fists clenched. Waldeve laughed.

"A joke, boy, just a joke."

Edgar didn't believe him. Waldeve continued.

"In any case, Duncan and I will take the rest of the men to Durham while you and your uncle head for York."

"York? Why?" Edgar was becoming dizzy from the abrupt changes in direction.

"All right, Rievaulx, then," Waldeve said. "If these fools here at Hexham know nothing, then maybe Robert's friend can help us. He grew up here. He knows our family. I thought you'd been itching to see him since you got back."

It was true. Even if he had Frenchified his name to Aelred, Edgar still wanted to see his old friend. And Aelred might know something that could help them solve this.

But Rievaulx was far to the south, that much farther from Catherine and James. They had come to Scotland because they wouldn't be parted from him. Now they were as remote as if they'd stayed with Hubert in Paris. Had he taken them from one peril only to put them in a greater one?

"Once again, I've made the wrong decision." He sighed. "Forgive me, *carissima*."

Eight

*Wedderlie. Wednesday, 9 kalends July (June 23), 1143. Saint John's Eve,
and the feast of Saint Æthelthrytha, Saxon queen, who was married twice,
yet died a virgin.*

*Heo wearð geuntrumod swa swa heo ær witegode
Swa that an geswel weox on hire swuran
mycel under that cynn-bane and heo swiðe thancode gode . . .
"Forðan the ic on iugoðe frætwode minne swuran
mid mænis-fealdum swur-beagum and me is nu gethuht
thæt godes arfæstnyss thone gylt aclænsige."*

She was stricken with illness, as she had foretold
So that a swelling grew great on her throat
under the chinbone and she thanked God exceedingly . . .
"For in my youth I adorned my neck
with manifold neck jewels and now it seems to me
that God's mercy may cleanse my guilt."

Ælfric, *Homilies*,
"Life of St. Æthelthrytha," 11 49–58

*A*re you sure, Margaret?" Catherine asked again. "None of the people in the village has ever seen this creature?"

"Quite sure, Catherine," Margaret answered. "They laughed at me when I asked."

"I don't understand," Catherine said. "No one? Did you describe it?"

"Yes, Sister." Margaret spoke slowly, wondering if her brother's wife were a simpleton. "They say that you must have seen the men going down to the river to fish. The salmon rise to the surface at dawn and the fishing is good then."

"Fishing?" Catherine was less sure than she had been two days ago. It had been foggy. Sheil nets and bob nets, with their rings and hooks, carried on the backs of men along with their small river boats, might have seemed like one great beast if the men had been very close together and wrapped in rough wool cloaks against the morning chill. Perhaps.

"But why was the grass all trampled?" she wondered aloud. "Why did they cross the road instead of walk down it?"

"Oh, I know that," Margaret told her. "They keep the nets and fishing boats in the hollow there. There's a path on the other side down to the river. Didn't you see it?"

"I saw nothing like a path that morning, nor when I looked again in the afternoon," Catherine said.

Margaret rolled her eyes. "Well, I could find it easily. Why didn't you ask me to go with you?"

"I didn't want the monster to get you." Catherine smiled. "Next time I see it, I'll remember and call you first. I feel somewhat foolish now. The explanation seems so obvious."

Margaret sighed. "I knew there were no monsters around here. Only ghosts."

"Ghosts?"

"Yes, one in the keep and more by the pagan stones. But they don't hurt anyone." Margaret took Catherine's hand and led her back toward the keep. "They just moan and cry."

"Oh." Catherine said hesitantly. "That's good."

Margaret stopped. "You won't tell Mother I know about them, will you?" Her small, pale face was worried. "She thinks I'd be frightened, but I'm not. I have a feather from one of Saint Cuddy's birds and it protects me."

Catherine was relieved to know that the child did not spend her nights cowering in her bed. She wasn't sure she could have been that brave at ten. Of course, this was the only world Margaret knew. Perhaps ghosts were so natural that they didn't concern her. They may have seemed more friendly than her own father.

And as for the thing she had seen, somehow the explanation seemed just a bit facile. She may not know much about the customs of Scotland, but she had grown up by the Seine and she had never heard of fishing equipment being left tangled in a pile by the road. Nor did she think that men going fishing in the early morning started out with a roar.

On the other hand, it was much more plausible than great hairy beasts prowling the countryside unnoticed.

Back at the keep, Robert and Solomon were continuing their bargaining. The two man sat at opposite ends of a table, with Adalisa in the middle. It had been a long session but Solomon felt that they had made progress.

"It would be much more convenient for you if you dealt with us," he said. "Lady Adalisa, tell him that we could bring spices directly into Berwick from France. But we'd need some sort of reduction of the import toll." Solomon waited for the translation.

Robert answered, "I might be able to convince some of the abbeys, like Melrose, that it would be to their advantage to get the king or Earl Cospatrick to grant you an exemption. Could you get incense, as well? The churches must have it and the cost is high."

"We bring it in through Spain," Solomon told him. "Carried across Africa from the East, always by traders I know. I go to Saragossa, myself, to get it. Our prices are far below what the Flemings will charge."

Adalisa gave him a strange look, then told Robert what he had said.

Robert nodded. Then he stood and gave Solomon his hand.

"I'll contact some friends," he said. "I think we might be able to arrange something. Melrose and Jedburgh, perhaps even the canons at Saint-Andrews would be interested. I'll send out messengers at once."

"*Thanc the*," Solomon said. "Let me know as soon as they return."

"I shall," Robert answered. "Come, Lufen!"

The dog had sat silently under the table for the whole of the session. Now she rose gracefully and followed Robert out like a devoted shadow.

When he had left, Solomon sat back down with a sigh. Adalisa poured him some ale and then a bowl for herself. He drank his in a gulp.

"Trading is dry work." He grinned. "And one daren't quench the thirst until the deal is made."

"You're skilled at this, I can tell." Adalisa rubbed the back of her neck. "You didn't let yourself become distracted by Robert's maunderings about his friends or how Waldeve is cruel to him."

"I've learned to let them go on if they need to confide," Solomon told her. "But I don't invite confidences."

"Or give them." Adalisa tried to reach the crick in her back.

Solomon watched her a moment.

"With your permission?" he asked. He got up and stood behind her, rubbing the tight muscles between her shoulder blades. "I have no grievances or secrets to share," he told her. "Ask Catherine."

"If that is true, you're a very fortunate man," Adalisa answered. "Oh, yes, that feels wonderful! However, I doubt that you're entirely without sorrow or secrets."

"Nothing of consequence, I assure you," he answered.

He moved his hands up to her shoulders, thumbs massaging the back of her neck. Adalisa tensed, then closed her eyes and let her head slip forward. It had been so long since anyone but Margaret had touched her without causing pain. The room was so still that she could hear the curlews outside crying as they flew over on their way back to the sea.

Solomon noticed the way her hair had escaped from her braids in small tendrils that were soft between his fingers. There was a wisp of the scent of eglantine as he disturbed the curls. With a start, Solomon brought himself back to reality. What had he been thinking? She was Edgar's stepmother and a lady, not some cozy innkeeper to play with for a night or two.

"Ow!"

"I'm sorry, Lady." In his panic, he had squeezed too tightly. He let go at once. "Is that better?"

"Yes," Adalisa answered. "The stiffness is entirely gone. I'm grateful for your ministrations."

"Since the discomfort was caused by the time I made you sit here, it was my duty to try to relieve it," he answered. "I appreciate your help. It's rare to find a translator one can trust to get the sense of the conversation on both sides. You are most kind to give so much of your time to helping me."

She looked up at him and smiled. Edgar's stepmother, Solomon repeated to himself.

"I find the discussion interesting," she assured him. "But now I must return to my household duties. I think I hear little James crying. Perhaps I should see if Willa needs any help."

"He's probably hungry again," Solomon said. "He seems to need an amazing amount of sustenance, considering his size. I'll go see if Catherine is on her way back, yet."

He made his way shakily to the doorway. Clearly he had been celibate too long, if he could react that strongly to the scent of a woman so far outside his rank and so completely forbidden by all custom and law. He wondered if it might not be prudent to return to Berwick for a few days. There was a tavern there where he could get whatever he liked at a price he could far better afford.

Adalisa climbed the stairs to the women's quarters. She could tell that none of Willa's ploys were reducing the level of James's crying. Hopefully, Catherine would return soon. That was one of the problems in not having a wet nurse handy.

She twisted her neck as she went, luxuriating in the lack of tension. Solomon was such a nice boy, and very astute in his business. Kind, as well. He wasn't just a relation of Catherine but a good friend to Edgar. It had relieved her mind about having Waldeve's youngest so far away to know that he had people who cared about him.

So it was a pity that she was beginning to suspect that Catherine's cousin was not all he pretended to be.

She wondered if Edgar knew about it or if he was being cozened by his wife's family. If that was the case, then poor Edgar might be as much in danger in Paris as at Wedderlie.

She could feel the muscles in her neck tightening all over again.

"Are you sure this is the right path?" Edgar asked his uncle as another branch was slapped back into his face.

Æthelræd laughed. "It's a back way into the valley. The main road is full of carts, loaded with stone. These monks are always building."

"Uncle, I think this is nothing but a deer trail and that we're completely lost."

For answer, Æthelræd pushed aside another branch and held it up until Edgar reached him.

"There." He pointed. "Rievaulx Abbey."

Edgar looked. He gave a sharp intake of breath. For a moment he felt a longing for the life he might have had in a place like this. Below them lay a valley hidden at the bottom of a circle of wooded hills. Rills spilled down into it, and the monks, like all good Cistercians, had already diverted the resulting stream to provide water for the monastery. The abbey buildings were encircled by a rivulet that passed under and around as needed. There were a number of makeshift huts, a low stone fence with a gate and a gatehouse and, of course, a church half constructed. Men were coming and going in good order, oblivious to those watching from above. It was a portrait of monastic peace.

"It's perfect," Edgar said. "I can see why Æethel . . . Aelred was captured in one visit. I would be tempted, as well."

"You dragged your wife from the convent." Æthelræd grinned. "Would you be so cruel as to leave her to enter one, yourself?"

"Hardly," Edgar answered. "If we hadn't married, we would surely have burned. But sometimes it seems so restful to be a monk and have each day ordered, circumscribed by the hours and the will of the abbot. Especially now, when nothing out here in the world makes sense."

Æthelræd laughed, a great exuberant sound that echoed across the valley. Edgar stared at him, affronted at being mocked.

"Nephew." Æthelræd chuckled still. "If all your yearning for the monastery was to have someone else think for you and tell you when to shit, I'm glad enough that you avoided it. And as for the world making sense, what makes you think it's supposed to? I never heard such a pile of seagull droppings."

He plunged down the trail to Rievaulx, leaving Edgar standing at the top of the hill, half-angry and half-embarrassed. Only Master Abelard had been able to make him feel such a puerile fool. He sighed and accepted the rebuke, then looked down at the way his uncle had gone.

"He's mad," Edgar said. "Why should I doubt it? This isn't even a deer trail. Saint Martin's cackling goose! Uncle! Come back! You'll be killed."

The only response was another laugh from halfway down the hill.

Edgar sighed and shifted his pack to a more comfortable angle. He tried to see the route Æthelræd had taken, then gave up and plunged after him into the brush.

They both burst out at the bottom at top speed, laughing and shouting so that they startled a young novice into dropping his water buckets.

"*Libera nos a malo!*" he cried as they advanced on him, slipping in the mud of the spilled water.

"Don't curse, man!" Æthelræd shouted. "We've just come to visit one of your brothers."

"*Veritem dicit!*" Edgar added as he slid past the openmouthed monk. "We want to see Aelred!"

The monk was reassured enough to bend over to get the buckets, then wring out the hem of his robe.

"Brother Aelred is at his meditations now," he told them. "But if you'll come to the porter's lodge, I'll have someone tell him you're here. Who are you?"

They told him, and then dripping, torn, bruised and caked with mud and twigs, they followed him to meet their old friend.

Some of the faces of the monks they passed on their way seemed familiar to Edgar, but he couldn't put a name to any of them. He wondered if, like Abbot Bernard, Aelred had convinced his friends and relations to join the monastery when he did. Or the men might be boys who had studied with him at Durham. It bothered Edgar that among the monks there might be people he had once known well. And now they were strangers with totally different lives.

"Edgar! My dear boy!" He was suddenly enveloped in a bear hug. "You're looking well, albeit a bit worn from the journey."

"Aelred?" Edgar stepped back to look at him. "I hardly know you. I mean, you look well, too, but so different. Much thinner, of course."

Aelred laughed. "Once I got out of King David's kitchens and stopped sampling everything that went to his table, I was amazed to find how many more notches I had to put in my belt."

Edgar smiled back. But the change was more than weight alone. Aelred was only four or five years older than he, but there were lines in his face that made him seem of another generation. There was a streak of grey in his hair. Edgar wondered if his friend now regretted his decision to join this most rigorous of orders. And yet, there was also a lightness about him that Edgar had never seen before.

Some of the twigs had attached themselves to the monk's robe. Edgar tried to brush them off. The robe was slightly damp and the bits stuck. Aelred stopped him from fussing.

"These aren't courtier's silk, Edgar," he said. "They won't be spoiled by a little dirt. I am so glad to see you."

Edgar's smile faded. "I wish I could say that I've come all the way from Paris just to see you," he said, "But Uncle Æthelræd and I need your help. You've heard about what happened to my brothers?"

"Yes." Aelred became serious at once. "I was terribly grieved for your family. Do they know who did it?"

"We haven't a clue." Edgar sighed. "That's why we've come to you."

"Me?" Aelred seemed shocked. "What would I know? I've spent the past year on a journey to Rome. I've only just returned, like you."

Æthelræd had kept silent during the greetings but now he came forward.

"Aelred, I've known you all your life." He loomed over the monk. "And there's no man in all of Northumbria who keeps his ear closer to the ground. If there's any gossip at all about this, you will have heard it."

Aelred's welcoming expression faded. "Not anymore, Æthelræd. I have no time for such things, now. I'm the novice master here and there's some talk of sending me to Lincoln to be abbot of a new daughter house. Moreover, Abbot Bernard of Clairvaux has asked me to write a treatise that is straining my meager scholarship to the full."

Edgar gently pushed his uncle away from Aelred. He stood close to his old friend and put an arm across his shoulders.

"Aelred, please," he begged. "Someone is trying to destroy my family. The only clues we have lead to Hexham and, perhaps, to Durham. You know both places well. You know the situation there. Is there anything my brother Duncan might have done to cause someone to wish to take revenge on us all?"

Aelred looked at him for a long moment.

"Edgar," he said at last, "is there anything Duncan might *not* have done?"

Edgar felt a coldness at his back.

"You do know something, don't you?"

Aelred sighed. "I might. Come with me. We can't talk standing out here."

He led them to a small room in the gatehouse. There was only a rough wooden bench to sit on. Someone had left a pitcher and three bowls on the windowsill, and Aelred poured them each some water. To Edgar it seemed a mockery of the service the monk had once performed at court.

Æthelræd sniffed suspiciously at the bowl.

"Water?" he said. "What have you come to, Aelred? Your father would have given us wine and meat."

Aelred refused to take offense. "My father was from another time, my friend, when priests kept wives and gave their benefices to their sons. But even he converted in the end and died a monk of Durham."

Æthelræd subsided, glumly staring at the water as if expecting a sea monster to rise from it.

Edgar would not be put off with reminiscences.

"Duncan, Aelred," he said. "Tell us what he's been up to."

Aelred took a deep breath and let it out.

"I got most of this from Archdeacon Rannulf," he warned them. "William Cumin drove him from the cloister when Rannulf and the others refused to elect him bishop. It may not all be true."

"Aelred . . ."

"Very well, Edgar. It is said that Duncan is the man that Cumin put in charge of subduing the town and collecting the rents and tithes from the dependent villages. He and his men have been given free rein to terrorize the people as they wish. The stories of torture, rape and sacrilege are too horrible to mention."

"Really?" Æthelræd asked, interested.

"I don't understand," Edgar said. "There's no question that Duncan is capable of such things, but what have his actions in the service of his lord to do with the death of my brothers?"

"It is said," Aelred continued, "that Duncan has been particularly harsh concerning the property of Roger de Conyers, the only local lord who actively opposes Cumin. Roger has power and friends north of the Tyne."

Æthelræd could stand it no longer.

"Aelred, I don't believe it," he interrupted. "Roger de Conyers is a man of honor. If he struck back, it would be at Duncan, not his family. Have any of Conyers's family been ambushed and murdered by Duncan?"

"No," Aelred conceded. "Only the buildings burnt, the livestock stolen and the tenants tortured and killed."

"That's war," Æthelræd said. "It happens everywhere. This murder is different."

Aelred stroked his chin, rubbing at the stubble. "The only real difference is that the one responsible hasn't claimed credit for the death of your brothers. It's not as if they were killed unarmed or unprepared. Someone should be bragging of this."

"What about one of Conyers's men?" Edgar asked. "Could Duncan have singled someone out for particular ill-treatment?"

"I don't know," Aelred answered. "You've been away, Edgar. You don't know what it's been like since King Henry died. With Stephen and the Empress battling for the crown, there's no order anywhere. Minor barons build castles and ravage the countryside and no one stops them. The chancellor of Scotland usurps the see of Saint Cuthbert and holds the monks prisoner in their own cloister and only one lord of the county is brave enough to fight him. I only thank God my father died before this final insult."

His voice broke. Edgar stood and patted him clumsily on the back.

"I'm sorry, Aelred," he said. "I forgot how devoted your family is to Cuthbert."

"My ancestors cared for him for hundreds of years," Aelred answered. "We were the priests of Cuthbert, not Durham, and I would have been, too, if my birth hadn't denied me the right. I still serve him as much as my father and grandfather ever did."

"I'm sorry." Edgar meant it. "I believed that you had changed your allegiance when you changed your name. Forgive me."

Aelred forced a smile. "I'm more English than you, Edgar. Don't forget that Cîteaux was founded by an Englishman, for all it seems so French. Half the monks here are Saxon. We don't forget our race; we have only found a greater brotherhood in God."

Edgar sat back down, abashed. "I shouldn't have come to you with this, Aelred. I can see you've left all that behind."

The monk gave Edgar a long appraising stare. Then he smiled. It changed his whole face and Edgar realized that the alteration he had marked at their meeting was not so much of the body as of the spirit. At Durham and at the court, Aelred had performed his duties meticulously but without joy. Here, he was happy.

Edgar and Æthelræd got up to leave, but Aelred stopped them.

"Tonight is the vigil of Saint John, who knew the truth before it was revealed to the world," he reminded them. "Stay with us and join our prayers. Tomorrow, with the abbot's permission, I will go with you to Durham."

"Aelred!" Edgar was astounded. "But why? You have no obligation to us."

Aelred's smile trembled. "I think I do. When I entered Rievaulx, I left someone behind without preparing him properly for my loss. I've regretted that and think that perhaps I'm finally strong enough to face him."

Edgar understood. "Robert stayed behind at Wedderlie. He won't be at Durham."

"Oddly, I have a feeling that he will," Aelred answered. "But, in any event, I also owe Saint Cuthbert the same devotion my father and grandfather gave him. If the death of your brothers is a part of this desecration of Cuthbert's church, then it is my duty to help you discover how and why."

Edgar closed his eyes as relief washed over him. He hadn't realized the burden he was carrying until it was lightened by Aelred's offer to share it for the sake of old friendship.

"Thank you, Aelred," he said. "Thank you."

Catherine was finding living at Wedderlie extremely frustrating. She was used to considering herself a well-educated woman and enjoyed showing off her knowledge. But half the people she met here weren't impressed by Latin and considered her rather dull to speak no English. It was a new and unpleasant feeling, although the convent voices reminded her that humility was a lesson she needed badly.

She was sure that there was something strange going on in the village. How could she find out what was happening if she had to pass every question through Margaret? And what could she ask? Why is everything so orderly here? Why do I never see anyone working alone? Even in the gardens behind their huts the women were always in pairs. The men went in a group to the fields. Were they afraid of something? If so, what? The younger men and boys had taken the sheep to the hills for the summer and the guards were mostly with Waldeve, but the few men left were enough to fight off thieves or wild animals.

Or was there something worse lurking in the forest?

Catherine wondered what the hour was. She had heard bells when James had wakened her, but in this light, they could even have been for Matins. There were sounds from below of people stirring, but Willa still slept in her corner. They had the women's room to themselves now and it was restful but lonely. Catherine had too much time to ponder while she fed her son. Despite the disapproval of other women it gave Catherine great satisfaction to have him curled up against her and to know that she was still his source of sustenance.

But now he was asleep again and she was alone with her thoughts. Her mind strayed to another niggling worry.

What was the matter with Solomon?

He had spent the past few days either roaming alone out in the countryside, something Catherine felt wasn't safe despite Margaret's explanation of the monster, or sitting at a table making lists in that odd half-French/half-Hebrew script of his. He rarely spoke to her, never teased her and only seemed to come alive while playing with the children. When she asked him what the problem was, he only shrugged and said that he didn't like waiting for people to make up their minds.

Catherine had to be satisfied with that and it was true that Robert seemed to be taking a long time in contacting his friends about the trade agreements. But she had known Solomon too long not to recognize when something was gnawing at him.

Last year he had been much involved in Saracen magic and divination. Far too much, in Catherine's opinion. He hadn't mentioned it in a long time and Catherine hoped he'd gotten over his obsession to know the future and the pattern of existence. Perhaps this strange place had caused it to surface again.

She shivered, but not from cold. The castle was stone only in its foundations and ground level. The upper parts were of wood and the summer sun warmed the rooms quickly. There was something wrong at Wedderlie. Even with Waldeve and his sons gone, the place had an air of watchfulness and anticipation. Not just the keep but the village, as well. What, or whom, was everyone expecting?

James woke again, this time ready to play. Catherine considered waking Willa to take care of him, but the girl looked too peaceful to disturb. She had walked back and forth with him on many a fretful night while Catherine slept.

She left the soiled swaddling in a bucket and wrapped him more loosely from the waist up, leaving his arms free to explore. The first thing he did was grab and yank at her hair.

"Ow!" Catherine said. "No more of that, young man. Now, you've eaten well, but I'm starving. Let's go see if there's any cheese or bread in the kitchen."

She carried him down the rickety stairs. In one corner of the hall, Solomon slept deeply on his back, his mouth hanging open. Catherine hurried by him and on down to the stone portion of the keep, where the kitchens were.

The fire had been stoked and a kettle put on. Catherine sniffed it. Oat porridge boiled in whey. She wasn't that hungry. There was no one tending it. Where had the cook and his helpers gone?

From the narrow window, she couldn't see any signs of activity. Had they all gone fishing? Were they at an early Mass? It was doubtful. Few peasants had the time or inclination for church services, except perhaps at Easter.

"Well, James, it appears we're on our own," she said. "There must be a cut round of cheese somewhere."

The rafters were strung with herbs and fletches of meat and other mysterious bundles. Catherine didn't feel she could break into what might be a winter store. Where would they keep the fresh cheese?

"There's a storage room dug into the hill next to the chapel," she said. "Shall we hunt for the door?"

James looked bored and tried to catch at the dusty sunshine as it hit Catherine's chest.

The door wasn't too difficult to find. It was low and set into the corner across from the window. The hinges were well oiled. The cook's helpers probably used it a dozen times a day. There was a ladder inside. Catherine knelt and peered in.

"No light at all," she muttered. "Now, how can I get down there with a lamp and you, as well?"

James belched.

"Not helpful, *mon mignot fils*," she said. "But I can't leave you in the kitchen. There's nothing to put you in here."

She fashioned a sling for him from her scarf and then found an oil lamp and lit it from the fire. Her stomach grumbled as she backed down the ladder. The things one did in the extremes of hunger!

It wasn't that difficult. She soon felt the earth beneath her feet. She held the lamp up and turned around.

There was a whimper and a frantic scuffling from an arched alcove. Cautiously, Catherine shone the light in that direction.

A white form crouched against the stone wall. Huge dark eyes stared at her. A skeletal hand covered them at once as the thing cringed at the light.

Catherine screamed.

Nine

The cellar at Wedderlie; an instant later.

Fere vero antiqui tales aegros in tenebris habebant, eo quod iis contrarium
esset exterreri, et ad quietum animi tenebras ipsas conferre aliquid
iudicabant. At Asclepiades, tamquam tenebris ipsis terrentibus, in lumine
habendos eos dixit. Neutrem autem perpetummn est. . . .

The ancients usually kept such ones [violent madmen] in darkness,
for they judged that it was contrary to their well-being to be terrified
and the darkness itself is calming to the spirit. But Asclepiades said
that they should be in the light for the darkness itself is frightening.
Neither of these is always true. . . .

—Celsus, *De Medicina,*
Book III, part 18

*T*he apparition screamed even louder than Catherine, a horribly high-pitched keening.

James began to cry.

Catherine stopped her noise, but the other two went on. The figure before her shrank away from the light, long white hands over its eyes. It stopped only when it was trapped in the corner and remained there, huddling against the wall.

Since it didn't seem to be preparing an attack, Catherine took a hesitant step forward, still holding the lamp, all the while patting James with her other hand and muttering wordless soothing sounds.

After a moment, the thing slowly took its hands from over its eyes and stared at her in terror, blinking in the light.

"What are you?" Catherine breathed.

It made no answer.

She swallowed. "By the Father, Son and Holy Spirit tell me," she said. "Are you flesh or demon?"

The apparition stared at her, then at its hands and finally for answer made a clumsy attempt to bless itself. Catherine felt better. It was at least a Christian demon. She came closer. As she did the thing cringed away from her even more and tried to scramble back into the corner of the celler.

Clearly, it was much more afraid of her than she of it. In wonder and pity Catherine stooped to examine what must be Margaret's ghost.

What she saw was enough to break her heart. It was human, or had been once. It was probably male, although there was no beard. His hair was long and tangled, as pale a blond as Edgar's. His skin was also pale, as white as maggots in meat. Catherine had thought she was starving, but this man truly was. Here, with provisions all around, he looked as though he hadn't eaten in months. He seemed more a skeleton covered in flesh than a person.

James was calm, now that the tumult had stopped, and was watching the flicker of the lamp with rapt attention. Catherine moved closer to the man and put her hand out to touch him.

"I won't harm you," she said as he began to shriek again.

She moved away. He subsided to a whimper.

"Who are you?" she asked gently. "Why are you here? What did you do to be treated like this?"

The only answer was a vacant stare.

Catherine put the lamp on a barrel and knelt beside him. James twisted in the sling to see and reached out for the man's matted hair.

"No, James." Catherine took hold of his hand. She wasn't sure if she were more afraid of James frightening this sad creature or of it somehow hurting him.

At the sight of the baby, the man's face lost some of its emptiness. He seemed puzzled. Very slowly, a long bony finger reached out to touch the child's dark curls. Catherine tensed, ready to pull away at the first sign of evil intent. But the touch was soft and swift. The man closed his eyes and Catherine saw tears glittering on his cadaverous cheeks.

What should she do?

She came even closer. There was a shackle about the man's ankle, and from it a short chain ran to a ring in the wall. She didn't think she could break it. If only she knew who he was. A felon? A hostage? A captured enemy? Or some poor madman locked away for his own protection?

Whom could she ask? Most of the people at Wedderlie must be aware of the prisoner. The cook and his helpers went down for foodstuffs several times a day. She sniffed. There was only a slight smell of urine through the odor of straw, salted meat and brine. Someone must be taking care of some of his needs, even if they weren't feeding him. She wondered how long he had been kept here, chained in the darkness.

And then another thought struck her like a blow.

Did Edgar know about this?

She didn't believe it. She wouldn't. He'd been away from home most of his life. A thousand things could have happened here that he would be ignorant of. Edgar would never countenance anyone being treated so cruelly.

Catherine looked at the man. He was simply staring at the light. He no longer seemed afraid. She wasn't sure if he were even aware of her. He had made no other move since he reached out to James. He had made no sound other than the horrible keening that had greeted her. She wondered if his tongue had been cut out.

She had no idea what to do. Her heart told her to release this poor suffering creature but sense reminded her that he had been put here for a reason. Dared she ask Adalisa?

James wiggled against her, trying to grab at the light. Catherine realized that she had to come to a decision quickly.

"You'll have to stay here a little longer," she told the man, not sure whether he understood. "I'll come back for you soon. I promise."

She climbed back up the ladder and into the kitchen. This time she found it occupied.

"Lady Catherine!" The cook dropped his carving knife in astonishment. "What are you doing in the storeroom? Here, let me help you."

He took the lamp and gave her a hand as she climbed out.

"I came down early," Catherine said. "There was no one here. I was looking for something to eat, but all the cheese was sealed."

She wondered if that sounded as odd to him as it did to her.

"Of course the food in the storeroom was sealed," he answered. "There's a box here for cheese and bread."

He pointed to a hinged wooden box nailed on the wall to keep it safe from rodents.

"Of course," Catherine answered. "How silly—" She stopped. "You're French, too?"

He shook his head.

"Flemish," he said. "But I apprenticed at the court of the count of Poitou. I came to Scotland with Lady Adalisa."

Which meant that his allegiance might be to her, rather than Waldeve. Catherine studied him. He didn't appear concerned that she had been in the storeroom beyond being shocked that a lady and a guest would be somewhere so inappropriate. He must know there was a prisoner down there. Did he think she knew it, too? Or was he hoping that she hadn't got far enough among the boxes to find him?

"I see." She made up her mind. She wouldn't mention this to

anyone until she talked with Solomon. "Thank you, then. Should I wake up hungry again, I'll remember where to find food."

"You should have called one of the servants or sent your girl down," the cook told her sternly. "This isn't the place for you."

"Yes, I know." Catherine sighed. *This isn't a place for anyone,* she thought. *If only Edgar would come back and take us home!*

She went slowly back up the steps to the Great Hall, nibbling at the hunk of cheese the cook had given her. She couldn't understand it. There was such beauty here—wildflowers in the nearly perpetual sunshine, fields of oats and barley ripening, a river full of fish—and yet everywhere she went, Catherine felt only sorrow and secrecy.

"This is what enchantment must feel like," she told James. "I hope this is really cheese and not an illusion."

She took another bite. It tasted like cheese. She reached the top of the steps, where the sight of Solomon sitting on the edge of his bed and scratching beneath his tunic brought her back to the real world.

"Good morning, Cousin." She came over and sat next to him. "Do you want some cheese?"

"Not before I've had some beer," he said. "Here, give me the baby. You're dropping bits on his head."

He settled James on his lap and bounced him gently. Catherine brushed the crumbled cheese off her tunic.

"Solomon," she said. "There's a prisoner shackled in the storeroom. I think he's insane."

"I'm not surprised," Solomon answered. "If we stay here much longer, I think it highly likely that I shall go insane, myself. Is there room for two down there?"

"Solomon, I'm serious!"

"A prisoner." Solomon stopped bouncing James, who then took an interest in the drawstrings dangling from the neck of his shift. "Does this madman have a name?"

"He couldn't tell me," Catherine said. "You wouldn't laugh if you had seen him."

"I'm not laughing," Solomon assured her. "He's probably some hostage waiting for his ransom to be paid."

"If so, it's been delayed a long time. I don't believe the poor thing has seen sunlight in years."

"Catherine." There was a warning in Solomon's tone. "It's not our affair. Waldeve has the right to judge and punish his people as he sees fit. You may grieve for him now, but the man could be a vicious criminal."

"Then he would have been hanged, or mutilated and released," Catherine insisted. "And why would Margaret not know about him? She thinks there's a ghost in the celler."

"Would you tell a child there was someone chained to a wall in your home?"

Catherine clenched her jaw. Her cousin had an answer to everything. He could be very iritating.

She was trying to think of a rebuttal when the servants came in to take away the bedding and set up the hall for the day.

"Adalisa will be down soon." Solomon looked nervously at the staircase. "There's nothing for me to do here today. I think I might ask if I could take Margaret and ride over to Robert's estate. Perhaps he's had word from his monks."

Catherine looked at him sharply.

"There's a man in chains starving here and you can only think about business?"

He returned her look. There was a hardness in his glance that made her shrink away.

"Catherine," he said, "there are people in chains and starving everywhere. Some of them deservedly. You can't free them because they're pitiable now. If it grieves you so, then ask our hostess why he's down there. The answer may alter your view of him."

"I will," Catherine said. "But I doubt that it will affect my feelings. I can't bear to think of anyone in chains."

Solomon shook his head. Sometimes he considered it a minor miracle that Catherine had survived outside the idealized world of the convent. She was soft enough to pity Satan himself.

Catherine continued back up to her chamber, where Willa was now awake and collecting James's dirty swaddling to take out to the courtyard to boil.

"Willa, has the Lady Adalisa been up to see me yet this morning?" she asked.

Willa shook her head. She was beginning to tan in the sun but this morning her skin had the pallor of fear. "I've seen no one today, but a little while ago, I heard a dreadful wailing, like a soul rising from the grave." She paused, her chin trembling. "I don't think I like it here."

Catherine came to her and put her arms around her, James hugged between them.

"It's all right, Willa, the noise was just me, shrieking at a rat in the kitchen," she told the girl. "I'm sorry it frightened you. I don't like it here much, myself. As soon as Edgar returns, we're going home. Until then, I won't let any harm come to you. Trust me?"

Willa nodded and tried to smile.

"Now, we have work to do." Catherine looked dolefully at the bucket. "First I'm going to find Lady Adalisa and ask if we can give all this to her washwoman."

She left Willa playing with the baby and returned to the hall. Solomon was gone and Adalisa sitting at the table giving orders to the servants for the day. Catherine waited until she had finished.

"Your cousin has gone to Robert's," Adalisa began. "He took Margaret to speak for him. I sent a guard with them. It will be all right, don't you think?"

"Solomon will take good care of her," Catherine answered. "Adalisa, did you hear a screaming this morning?"

"Yes," she said. "The cook told me it was you. What was wrong?"

"I went into the storeroom, looking for something to eat," Catherine said. "No one told me there was a prisoner down there."

"A what?" Adalisa seemed astonished.

Catherine told her of the man she had encountered.

"That's nonsense, Catherine," Adalisa was firm. "You must have been dreaming. There's no one being held captive here. I would certainly know, especially if he were in the storeroom. I'm often there, checking on the state of supplies."

"I was not dreaming!" Catherine was indignant. "I know quite well what I saw. Come with me and I'll prove it."

But even as she spoke, Catherine knew there would be no sign of the prisoner now. She followed Adalisa down to the kitchen and looked as she was shown the room, empty of all but the most innocent barrels and bundles. She should have made Solomon go with her immediately after seeing the man. There was nothing to do but apologize and admit that she must have been mistaken. Margaret had spread the tale of the monster in the mist so that it was easy to add this to her growing list of eccentricities. Catherine could imagine the laughter in the village when the story was told. She just wondered if they would be ridiculing her insanity or her credulity for being so easily tricked.

Wedderlie was becoming increasingly unsettling. Catherine began to think about taking Willa and James and returning to the protection of the monks in Berwick until Edgar returned.

Margaret was extremely proud of her sudden transition from "that child" to a person of importance. It had never occurred to her that the ability to understand both French and English would be of use to anyone. But first Catherine and now Solomon seemed to find her indispensible. It was such a new sensation that she didn't know what to make of it.

"What if Robert uses words I don't know?" she asked nervously as they arrived.

Solomon held up his arms to help her down.

"He won't."

"Are you sure?"

"Yes."

Margaret wasn't, but Solomon was an adult and knew how things were done so she could only trust him and hope that she wouldn't fail when the time came.

She was further disconcerted when Solomon put her hand on his arm and led her to the house, just as though she were a grown lady in jewels and a veil.

Robert's dwelling was only a few steps in quality above that of his tenants. There was a fence around a yard, where chickens scratched, but no guard. The building itself had two levels, storage on the first and living quarters on the second. As they let themselves in the gate his dog, Lufen, started barking.

Solomon felt the girl's hand tighten on his arm, but she lifted her chin higher and ignored the dog as it ran toward them. It was the first time he realized that she had something of her father in her, after all. No child of Waldeve would ever dare show fear.

Robert came out when he heard the dog and called it off at once. Margaret's hand relaxed.

"Tell him we've come for a friendly visit," Solomon asked her. "I was bored and wondered if there was any news from the monks about the trade for wool and spices."

When she had translated Robert shook his head.

"But tell Solomon that I expect word soon," he said. "Since you're here, do you want some ale and bread? I was going out to check the rabbit snares. You can come with me or wait here."

Margaret opted to wait. "I don't mind rabbit stew," she explained. "But I hate to see them wiggling in the noose."

Robert shook his head at such fastidiousness.

"Lufen!" he called and the dog came running. The two of them started across the garden toward the wood.

Halfway across Robert stopped and bent over. Just as he did the dog pounced on something in front of him, gave a jerk and fell to the ground howling. Robert cried out as if he, and not the dog, had been hurt.

"Stay here," Solomon told Margaret.

He ran to where Robert was kneeling, trying to extricate the dog's leg from the teeth of an iron trap.

"Lufen! Lufen!" he cried as the dog snapped at his attempts to free her. *Thu ert mine heahgesceaft! Hilpst me, Solomon!*"

Solomon pulled off his tunic and handed it to Robert.

"Cover her head with it," he shouted. "Hold her!"

Robert understood his gestures and managed to restrain the dog. Solomon unsheathed the knife he always kept strapped to his arm and inserted the point between the teeth of the trap.

Having ignored his order, Margaret appeared beside him.

"What can I do?" she asked Solomon.

"Tell Robert to keep the damn dog still or she'll lose the leg before I can release her," Solomon panted.

"I'm trying to!" Robert said when she'd explained. "My poor Lufen is in agony. She saved me! My beautiful, noble Lufen sacrificed herself for me!"

Finally, the trap eased open enough for the dog to pull her leg out. Robert gathered her up in his arms and carried her to the house. All the way he murmured reassurance to the wounded animal. But Solomon had seen the shattered bone. He knew there was no way Lufen could be saved.

Robert shouted for the guard they had brought with them.

"Ride as fast as you can back to the keep," he ordered. "Tell my stepmother I need her to come at once. Have her bring some *dwale* for the dog. Hurry!"

The man left at once.

Robert set Lufen in her box near the hearth and went to look for a blanket. Margaret knelt next to the box. Lufen was now shivering and her eyes were glazed with pain. Solomon had followed them.

"Margaret," he said softly. "Robert isn't going to try to save the poor thing, is he?"

"He loves Lufen more than anything on earth," Margaret answered. "He doesn't care if she only has three legs."

"But she won't survive the amputation," Solomon insisted. "He'll just put her through more suffering for no reason."

"If the *dwale* doesn't kill her, she might survive," Margaret explained. "Don't you use it in France? It's a strong medicine that puts people to sleep so they don't feel even horrible pain. But sometimes they sleep so deeply that they don't wake up. Mother explained it to me a long time ago and warned me never to mistake her jar of it for wine."

Robert returned with the blanket and knelt next to his dog, gently rubbing her behind the ears and murmuring words of comfort.

"You can't die, Lufen," he wept. "Aelred is lost to me. If I lose you, too, then why bother living? Be strong, noble heart. Help is coming."

"Robert?" Solomon had to raise his voice before Edgar's brother remembered him.

"What is it?" he asked through tears.

"How did this happen?"

Robert never stopped caressing the shivering animal as he spoke. The anger in his voice never reached his gentle hands.

"There was a piece of cloth on the ground," he said. "In among the vegetables. I reached for it to see what it was, but Lufen leapt at it instead, and. . . . My poor, brave girl!"

"Why would there be a trap like that in your garden?" Solomon asked.

Robert spoke to Margaret for a long time. When he finally stopped, she turned to Solomon.

"Robert doesn't use such traps," she explained. "Only snares for the rabbits. This was put there by someone who knows that Robert has few servants and works his garden mostly by himself."

"You mean it was intended for him." Solomon's forehead creased in consternation. "And, with the cloth fluttering above it, they would expect him to do exactly what he almost did, reach for it and catch his hand in it."

Margaret nodded.

"And, while he likely wouldn't have died, he probably would have lost his hand." Solomon shook his head. "We should send word of this to your father. Whoever killed your brothers must be somewhere nearby."

As soon as the words left his mouth, Solomon wished them back.

"Of course," he added quickly. "They may also be far away by now."

The child's lips tightened, but she said nothing.

Since Robert was doing all that could be done for the dog, there was nothing Solomon and Margaret could do but wait. They settled themselves on a log by the main gate to watch for a messenger from Adalisa.

"This *dwale*." Solomon was intrigued. "I never heard of it. Is it often used on animals?"

"I never heard of anyone doing so," Margaret told him. "But I haven't been many places, so I don't know."

Solomon smiled. "Where have you been?"

She thought. "I was at King David's court at Carlisle, once. And I've been to Berwick. That's all."

She seemed to feel it was inadequate experience.

"Where have you been?" she asked wistfully.

Solomon considered hedging, but she was only a child. What harm could there be? "I've been to the edge of Spain," he told her. "And across into Africa, where the Berbers rule and the land is nearly treeless. I've been into Rus, where they still worship pagan gods and eat their meat uncooked. I've seen mountains so high that it's always winter at their peaks and heard spirits in the fog on the ocean trying to lure our ship onto the rocks. I've been to Rome and almost to Constantinople."

Margaret was staring at him openmouthed in wonder. He laughed.

"And I've never seen anything as pretty in all the world as you, little one," he finished, pulling on her braid to show he was teasing.

Nevertheless, Margaret blushed. He smiled. She seemed less nervous now. How stupid he had been to frighten her like that. She was so composed that he often forgot she was only a little girl.

The sound of the hoofbeats approaching made her tense and

grab his sleeve. The hardness of the knife in its sheath reassured her. She was even more relived when the rider appeared and she saw her mother sitting behind the guard, a leather bag hooked over her shoulder.

She slid from the horse and gathered Margaret in her arms.

"*Ma douz.*" Adalisa kissed her. "I've left Catherine alone at the keep. I want you to go back with Oswin, here, so that you can explain to her what's happening. I've given her instructions so you should obey her as you would me. Do you understand?"

"Yes, Mother." Margaret clung to her for a moment. "When will you return?"

"In the morning, I hope," Adalisa told her. "I'll have to sit with Lufen tonight."

"I'll go back with her," Solomon offered.

"If you don't mind, I'd rather you stayed," Adalisa told him. "Oswin needs to organize the men to guard the keep and I will want someone to help hold the dog. I fear Robert may not be able to watch what I'll have to do."

Solomon swallowed. He wasn't sure he had the stomach for it, either.

"Do you know how?" he asked.

"Yes."

She didn't say where she had learned such a skill and he thought it best not to ask.

He hoisted Margaret into place behind Oswin, who patted her hands reassuringly as she wrapped her arms around his waist.

"I'll not let any harm come to her," he promised Adalisa.

When they had left, Adalisa took a deep breath and turned to Solomon.

"Is there a fire in the house?" she asked.

"The hearth is cold," he told her.

"Build one for me, please," she said. "I'll need white-hot coals for the cautery."

He followed her into the house, marveling all the while at her steadiness. Where had she learned to do an amputation? Even on an animal as small as a dog, sawing through the bone required strength and accuracy. It wasn't something he felt competent to do.

Adalisa knelt and examined the dog while Solomon worked at striking tinder for the fire. She then sent Robert out for a jar of wine and a large bowl.

"Do you think you can save her?" Solomon asked.

"I don't know," Adalisa answered. "But if I can't, at least she'll die quietly and without more pain."

She ran her hand along the dog's side, stopping at the heart. She bit her lip in worry.

"At least Robert remembered to tie off the leg," she said, "or Lufen would have bled to death by now. Has the fire caught?"

"Yes," Solomon said, "but it will be some time before there are coals."

"That's all right. I need to have her asleep first," Adalisa said. "I only pray that I can get the dosage right."

Robert returned with the wine. Adalisa got up and took a small vial from her pack. She set the bowl on a table and poured it half-full with with wine. Then she added only a few drops of liquid from the vial. Solomon watched in fascination.

"What is this *dwale?*" he asked.

"It's something the Saxons use," she answered. "Not very often, though, as it can kill all too easily. There's hemlock in it and poppy juice. It will cause the dog to fall into a sleep so deep that she won't feel the saw."

"Amazing!" Solomon said. "And it's drunk? I've seen people breathe in the scent of a potion from a sponge, but to drink it! How long does the sleep last?"

Adalisa didn't look up.

"Sometimes forever," she said. "I have to sit with her tonight to watch her breathing. If she gasps and chokes, then I'll need to try to wake her."

She picked up the bowl.

"Now, the difficult part," she said. "I have to get enough of it into the dog."

In that, Robert was invaluable. He coaxed Lufen to swallow a few drops from his fingers.

"Is that enough?" he asked.

"We'll have to wait and see," Adalisa answered. "Better too little than too much. She should become more calm soon."

Adalisa eyed Robert's hands, shaking with worry and apprehension.

"Robert," she said firmly, "I'm going to make up a draught for you, as well. There's nothing more you can do but fret and make me vexatious. I want you to sleep tonight so that you can care for Lufen tomorrow."

"I must be with her!" Robert protested.

"No, it would grieve you too much," she said. "Solomon will help me. If the *dwale* works, Lufen won't know whether you're here or not."

"When she's asleep." Robert gave in. "Then I'll sleep, as well."

It was twilight before Robert was convinced that Lufen was safely under the effect of the *dwale*. But Adalisa had secretly put valerian and a little poppy juice in his wine sometime before so that he went off to bed quietly and was soon heard snoring.

"Now, set that lamp so that I can see clearly and hold the poor thing's leg," Adalisa ordered Solomon.

She took a small saw from her bag, of the sort used for pruning new branches from fruit trees. As the light glinted on it, Solomon had a sensation that it was alive and hungry. He shook it off. This was not the time to give way to fancy. He knelt next to Adalisa. In the heat, she had taken off her long tunic and only wore her *chainse*, the neck strings loosely tied. Solomon jerked his glance from the way her breasts curved beneath the thin cloth and forced himself to concentrate on the dog.

"Make sure the tourniquet is tight," Adalisa said. "Now, hold her and pray."

It was over in a moment, the wound then cauterized and bandaged. Beyond a feeble whimper, Lufen hadn't moved.

Adalisa bent for a moment and let out a long sigh. Then she straightened and got up to wash the blood and hair from her hands.

"You cut with great skill," Solomon said. "You've had to do this before."

"Once," Adalisa said. "On a man."

Solomon opened his mouth to ask if the man had survived but changed his mind.

"Now what do we do?" he said.

"I must wait and watch." She came back and sat next to the dog, her back against the wall. "You can sleep, though. You must be exhausted."

It was good advice, but Solomon instead brought all the pillows and bedding he could find and made up two pallets on the floor.

"You may as well sit on something comfortable," he told her. "I'll just doze a bit and you can nudge me if you need me."

She nodded and closed her eyes a moment, her head thrown back against the wooden wall. Solomon watched her. A strand of hair was sticking to her cheek. Some impulse made him lean over her and pull it back. Adalisa's eyes flew open. Her whole body tensed.

"I didn't mean to startle you," he said.

"No, it's all right." She relaxed. "I shouldn't have been so near sleep. When you touched me I thought it was Waldeve."

That would explain the sudden alertness. Solomon felt such pity for her, living with a man whose touch she feared.

He hadn't moved. She looked up at him. What she saw in his eyes made her open her mouth in wonder. It was too much for Solomon. Casting away all reason, he kissed her.

He half expected her to push him away with outrage. Instead, after a moment of surprise, she responded passionately, putting her arms around him and drawing him against her.

The thought of what would happen to them if they were caught flew across Solomon's mind and vanished. He slipped the *chainse* from her shoulder and felt the relaxing of her muscles as his fingers caressed her skin.

With a sad smile, she eased him up so she could undo first his belt and then the drawstring of his *brais*.

In the room above, Robert slept on. Next to them, Lufen didn't stir, not even when Solomon bumped against her box in his haste to remove his boots.

Ten

Paris, the home of Hubert LeVendeur. Sunday, 5 kalends July (June 28), 1143. Feast of Saint Emission, bishop of Nantes, who died leading the soldiers of Christ against the Saracen invaders.

Erat autem miles quidam Rogerius de Coincneris, vir bonus et fidelis; hic non acquievit communicare actibus Willelmi Cumin. Unde in possessione sua, scilicet in Biscoptum, firmavit sibi munitiunculam, quia locus congruebat.

There was a certain knight, Roger Conyers, a good and loyal man; he had no wish to take part in the acts of William Cumin. So he strengthened the fortifications at his castle in Bishopton nearby.

—Simeon II, Chapter IV
of the poem of Durham

$\mathscr{H}$ubert knew it was too soon for any word from Catherine. They must have arrived in Scotland by now, he told himself. He wouldn't think of pirates or storms at sea, brigands on the roads or wolves in the forest. Absolutely not. She was fine. They were all safe and far from the storm that was brewing here in Paris.

The bishop hadn't bothered to see him personally, when Hubert had arrived as requested. But one of the episcopal secretaries had questioned him for several hours as to his relationship with one Eliazar, Jew of Paris.

"He's my partner in business," Hubert had told the man. "This is all well known. His family and mine traded together in Rouen, where I was born."

"So you're Norman, then?" the secretary asked. "Your father was also a merchant? Did he have Jewish partners?"

"Yes, he traded in the north, for fur and ivory," Hubert explained. "Eliazar's father traveled to Spain and Italy for cloth and spices. They combined forces to sell to the Normans, including those in England. Many of Eliazar's family were among those Jews that Duke William settled in London when he conquered the English. When I was a young man, my father sent me south to Paris. It was arranged that Eliazar and I continue the family partnership."

Hubert waited for the man to make notes on his tablet. The story was essentially true, except for the fact that Gervase LeVendeur was Hubert's adoptive father. Except for the fact that Gervase had tried to erase all memory of his Jewish past from his new son. Hubert's father had been in Paris when his wife and daughters had been killed and Gervase sent him word that Hubert had died, too. Grief had shortened the poor man's life and he was long dead by the time Eliazar found Hubert and reclaimed him to the family.

There weren't many people left who remembered what had

happened or knew that Hubert wasn't the son of Gervase. Hubert's oldest child, Guillaume, had no idea. Guillaume had named his first son after the man he believed to be his grandfather. Edgar, Catherine and her sister, Agnes, were the only Christians who knew that Hubert and Eliazar were brothers. So who could have denounced him? Hubert wanted to ask but knew it would only increase suspicion. For now, all the secretary told him was that the bishop was concerned that there had been Jews proselytizing the students and Hubert's connection with the community was being investigated.

"So, you see," Hubert concluded, "my association with Eliazar is of long standing. Our business benefits from the separate contacts we have."

The secretary didn't answer. He made a few more notes. Finally, he looked up.

"If you had heard of any attempts to make Christians renounce the faith, you would have reported it, of course?"

"Of course!" Hubert did his best to appear shocked. "But I can't believe there is anything like that going on in Paris. The Jews here are too devoted to the king and grateful for the kindness of the bishop."

"So we have always believed," the secretary said.

He took his leave then. Hubert was left to fret. His first impulse had been to run to Eliazar with the news. But then he feared that someone might be following him to see if he did just that.

What was wrong in Paris lately? There had always been animosity in some quarters against the Jewish community, but they had been living here almost a thousand years, always protected by the crown and the church. Now it seemed that this protection was slowly eroding.

Hubert felt chilled despite the summer heat. He had no idea how to combat this denunciation by rumor.

He was only grateful that Edgar, Catherine and the baby were well out of danger.

Edgar was feeling that he had walked weaponless into the lions' den as he, Aelred and Uncle Æthelræd waited nervously to meet with the one man who had resisted William Cumin, and by extension, Duncan and Waldeve, for the past three years. It had surprised Edgar when Aelred had suggested a council with Roger de Conyers before trying to penetrate the fortress of Durham.

"Don't you think he's more likely to hold us for ransom than to help us?" he had asked.

"I don't think so," Aelred had answered. "He's a man who believes in justice. He's been loyal to Durham and Saint Cuthbert even though all the other barons capitulated to Cumin."

"But that's why he's the most likely to have ordered the murder of my brothers," Edgar reminded him. "Especially if Duncan has attacked his vassals and family."

"Nevertheless, I think we should first give him the opportunity to prove his innocence before we proceed further." Aelred answered. "Your uncle thinks Conyers is a man we can trust, as well, don't you, Æthelræd?"

"From all I've heard of him, yes," Æthelræd hedged. "But I'm not giving up my sword, yet."

Aelred's determination to come to see Conyers had convinced Edgar when they were safely at Rievaulx but here, in the bailey of the castle at Bishopton, he wasn't so sure. The men around them all wore chain mail, even in the summer heat. They appeared ready to attack at any moment. Neither Aelred nor Æthelræd seemed at all concerned, but Edgar felt very vulnerable. He was glad he had left Catherine and James back in Scotland, although he missed them terribly. He looked around at the amount of sharp steel surrounding him.

"Aelred!" a voice called out. "I thought you were at Rievaulx. What are you doing here? Have you heard the news about the election?"

The man who addressed them came over and greeted Aelred warmly. Then he noticed the monk's companions.

"Æthelræd! By Saint Gall and his builder bear! I thought you were living in a cave in Moray!"

Æthelræd grinned at him. "I came out for the solstice, Rannulf, to see what kind of woman I could catch in the field on Saint John's Eve. Instead, I spent it in the company of monks."

The man smiled back at him. "Just as well, Æthelræd. I'd have thought you'd have worn it out by now, anyway. And who's this?" he added, staring at Edgar.

Edgar put out his hand. "Archdeacon Rannulf, don't you remember me?"

"*Enondu!* Young Edgar!" he exclaimed. "Now you, I know, went off to Paris years ago to sit at the feet of that heretic, Abelard. I didn't know you'd come back."

He stopped and studied all three of them.

"To bring all of you here," he continued, "something dreadful must have happened, something more personal than the desecration of my father's see by that usurper, Cumin."

Aelred told him.

Edgar felt suddenly shy, seeing Archdeacon Rannulf again after so long. He had always been in awe of this man. It was an open secret that he was the son of Bishop Rannulf Flambard, who had not let his election to the see of Durham interfere with his amorous activities. The bishop had left behind nearly as many acknowledged children as Waldeve. But his son had followed a career in his father's church, undaunted by the obstruction of his illegitimacy. And this Rannulf had proved himself more worthy of the priesthood than the old bishop had been. As archdeacon of Durham, he had shown himself to be an honest administrator and a loyal supporter of whomever was bishop. He had an air of authority and a way of staring at the boys of the school as if he knew and condemned each of their sins.

But Edgar's timidity was completely overcome by the sincere outrage and sympathy Rannulf showed when the situation was explained to him.

"If it's true that these cowardly murders are connected to events here at Durham," he stated, "then that's one more tragedy to add to those laid at the door of William Cumin. I once thought he was merely ambitious and greedy. Now I believe he has become demonic."

Edgar swallowed a lump of fear in his throat. He had never had illusions about the sanctity of his relatives, but neither had he faced the possibility that they might actually be damned. All those who followed Cumin had been excommunicated with him of course, but that could be retracted. However, if the stories were true, and Edgar saw no sign that they weren't, Duncan had built up a mountain of atrocities during his service at Durham. Edgar doubted that anything short of a martyr's death could wipe away such black sins.

"And so you've come here to find the killers of your brothers?" Rannulf asked him.

"I came home because my father ordered me to aid him in his revenge, but I'm not sure I believe in it anymore." Edgar sighed. "I'm beginning to fear that if I find the killers, my first thought will be to protect them from my father's wrath."

"That's a proper Christian thing to do," Rannulf said. "They should be turned over to the king's justice."

But Edgar wasn't sure about that, either.

Aelred sensed his distress and guided Rannulf away from the others, asking him about the recent election in York of William of Saint-Barbe to the see of Durham and how the unfortunate Saint-Barbe proposed to take possession of his new office when the city was in the possession of Cumin and his army.

Edgar turned to Æthelræd.

"What are we doing here?" he asked. "I feel that I'm flopping about like a fish on the riverbank. If my father is working with Duncan in support of Cumin, perhaps Alexander and Egbert were, as well. It may be that their deaths were in just retribution."

Æthelræd shook his head.

"If that were true, someone would have claimed responsibility," he said. "It always comes back to that. Blood feuds are celebrated. Men proclaim their victories and have *scops* make up songs to them. This was murder and we must find out why before anything else will make sense."

"Well, I hope we find the answer here," Edgar said wearily. "I want to be home before autumn."

His uncle gave him a sharp look, realizing that Edgar didn't mean Wedderlie, but Paris.

Edgar didn't notice. He was remembering the horse he had begun for James. If this wasn't resolved soon, his son would be old enough for a real horse before it was finished. He wished he could do something at once that would bring all this to an end. His desire for revenge was definitely fading.

When Solomon awoke, the air was still grey around him. He could barely make out Adalisa's silhouette as she knelt by Lufen's box.

"How is she?" he asked, trying to keep his voice steady.

"Still asleep, but breathing well," she answered, with a catch in her own voice.

"Adalisa . . ." he began.

She came to him in a swift movement and kissed him deeply.

"Don't apologize," she said. "And don't fear that I'll expect anything more of you. For twenty years I've wondered what it would be like to really make love, instead of simply perform my duty as a wife. Now I do, and I'm so grateful to you."

This wasn't the first time a woman had told Solomon this. It was just the first time he believed that it was the truth. And the first time he cared.

"I had no right," he said.

"None at all." She almost laughed. "Neither had I. I'm probably mad to have given in to this, especially when I know you're not what you pretend to be, but last night, it didn't matter. And today . . . today it still doesn't."

Solomon rose to one elbow.

"What do you mean?"

She sat up again.

"You're a Jew," she said in a matter-of-fact tone. "I suspected it before, but now, of course, I'm sure. At least that you were born one."

Solomon closed his eyes and nodded slowly.

"I will die one, as well," he said. "So, now that I've confirmed your worst fear, what are you going to do?"

"Nothing." Adalisa turned from him and felt the dog's flank. "I think she'll survive now. We should wake Robert and let him care for her."

"Nothing?" Solomon repeated.

Adalisa turned to face him again. "I suppose I should feel defiled. I suppose I've just compounded the sin of adultery with something worse. But at the moment, I feel no guilt, no revulsion, only thankfulness. Does Edgar know about you?"

Solomon nodded.

"And he's remained your friend?"

"My best friend in the world, I think."

"And Catherine, is she Christian?"

"Firmly so." He sighed. "She is constantly trying to convert me."

"I shall pray that she succeeds," Adalisa told him. "But I have no intention of betraying you as long as you promise never to reveal to anyone at any time, what we did last night."

"I'm not a fool, Adalisa," he said. "Nor a traitor. I know we would both be killed if this were known. Don't worry."

"Swear it," Adalisa commanded.

"My people don't take oaths," he said. "But I will promise and that is binding enough."

"Very well," she stood and brushed straw from her *chainse*. "I'll go wake Robert now, but before I do, just one thing."

"Yes?"

"Kiss me again."

Solomon did. It took a very long time.

Although Catherine understood why Adalisa had to go and although she was sure Margaret would translate carefully, she still felt as though she had been heartlessly cast to her fate. Being surrounded by strangers who spoke a foreign language frightened her more than she dared show. She retreated up to the women's room with Willa and James.

"*Look at you, cowering in the sunlight.*" Catherine should have known the voices of the convent wouldn't stay quiet. "*Shame on you!*" they scolded. "*We brought you up better than that. Do you want these barbarians to think you're afraid of them?*"

But I am, Catherine argued in her head. These blond men with their long mustaches and these tall women with their curious eyes. They don't like me and I have no words to persuade them otherwise.

"*Then convince them by your courage and your piety,*" the voices told her. "*Are you not all Christians here?*"

I wish I could be sure of that, Catherine thought. "I wish Edgar would come back," she said aloud.

"So do I, Mistress," Willa agreed.

Thinking of Edgar reminded her that she had been left behind, not just for her own safety but to discover as much as she could of the undercurrents in the life at Wedderlie. So far, she had only started and she hadn't bothered to sit down and analyze her discoveries rationally. The voices were right to chide her.

Margaret had explained to them about what had happened to Lufen, along with Solomon's comments about the trap having been intended for Robert. Catherine had tried to assuage the child's fear, as well as her own, but it was disturbing. There was some comfort in knowing that the guards at the gate were being augmented by the men left in the village. But, she wondered, could they be trusted?

Willa was telling Margaret stories as she rocked James's cradle. Catherine used the lull to go through her clothes and take out those that needed mending and to make some simple tunics for James, so that he could start stretching his arms all the time now. While her fingers stitched, her mind worked on organizing the few facts she had.

Murder was the first. Edgar's brothers and nephew had been killed and mutilated. That was a fact. Their horses had been taken, but then returned to Hexham. That was a fact.

Edgar's father was an arrogant, selfish man who had made many enemies. Well, the latter part was fact. The first was only Catherine's opinion. If the murders had been committed by someone her father-in-law had known years ago, then there might be any number of reasons that she had no way of discovering. But the trap set for Robert indicated that it was someone who knew the whole family. Perhaps even someone in the family.

Robert might have set the trap to draw attention away from himself. He couldn't have known that the dog would spring it. Would Robert kill his brothers so that he could inherit Wedderlie? It didn't seem likely. If Scotland were anything like France, land passed to the one who could hold it or at the will of the king. Being the eldest son was important but not always the deciding factor. Robert would be challenged by his nephews when they were old enough or by their maternal relatives as soon as Waldeve died.

And there was that odd charter. Land that was legitimately Robert's had been traded for horses, perhaps the very ones that had been taken. Did Robert know or care? And why should this Durham bishop want a house in Berwick so much that he would trade valuable animals for it?

Added to that, Catherine was unsettled by events at Wedderlie. What had she really seen in the mist that morning? Fishermen or a monster? Logic chose the former, but the roar she remembered hadn't sounded human.

Finally, who was the young man held prisoner in the keep? No amount of denials could make Catherine believe she had imagined him. His piteous state haunted her more than anything else. Eager as she was to return home, she felt it would be impossible to leave without trying to save this pathetic creature. Where could they have hidden him? Why was he captive in the first place? Why would no one admit he existed?

Catherine couldn't help but feel that he was the key to everything. Waldeve could lead his men from one end of the land to the other hunting for answers, if he wished. But more and more Cather-

ine believed Edgar's father was lying to them, and perhaps to himself. The answers were here at Wedderlie, hiding in the mist or en-
tombed in the bowels of the keep.

And now Robert had been attacked, probably. Catherine was
most concerned that this new threat had come as a trap and not an
open challenge. It reinforced her growing belief that this was more
than the enmity of the blood feud, but a deep hatred born of some
shameful act. Robert might well have survived the iron trap, but
almost certainly would have been maimed. Why the determination
to cut off the sword hand? Were the family cowards, traitors? Of
course, she reflected, the right was also the hand with which one
took an oath or made one's mark. Yes, that could be it. Waldeve had
broken faith, and as a result some disaster had occurred. But for
whom?

She wished she could talk this over with Edgar. They worked
better together.

She looked over at James, now fussing in his cradle, his dark
curls damp in the heat. She got up to loosen the confining linen
wrapped around him, smiling once again at the wonder of him. Yes,
she and Edgar did everything better together.

Edgar had never met Roger de Conyers and wasn't prepared for the
man now sitting before him. The sole baron to hold out for the past
three years against William Cumin was a small man, fine-boned. He
was probably in his late forties and his grey-brown hair was thinning.
He looked more like a clerk than a lord. When he at last had time
to meet with them, he had asked to see Edgar alone. Æthelræd had
protested, but Aelred convinced him that it was best to submit to the
lord's wishes.

Conyers looked up at him. His eyes were mild, as well, as they
settled on Edgar.

"I was grieved to learn of the deaths in your family," he began.
"The North has seen too much meaningless slaughter in the past
few years."

Edgar licked his lips. "This is true," he said, "and I fear that my
brother, Duncan, has been responsible for a part of it."

Conyers's eyebrows lifted. He nodded gravely.

"A large part, here in Durham," he agreed. "The people of the
town have good reason to fear him."

"Is there anyone who hates him enough to take revenge on his family?" Edgar asked.

The eyebrows went higher. "You're very direct, young man." Conyers almost smiled. "I don't know the answer. Who can read another man's heart? There are many who have lost their homes and families, many whom your brother has tortured to get them to reveal where they hid their gold. I'm sure there must be those whose hate burns strongly enough. But how many would have the courage or the means to ambush three armed men? How many would have known where to find them?"

Edgar had no answer. Conyers finally motioned for him to sit.

"Wine?" he offered. "It's not the best. The war has made it difficult to get shipments from Normandy, anymore."

Edgar shook his head. He was still pondering Conyers's last question. Why hadn't it been asked before? Who knew where his brothers would be? In the shock of their deaths, Edgar hadn't thought to ask what they had been doing or where they had been going when they were attacked. Waldeve had been so sure that the action had been directed at him that too many other points had been ignored.

"Thank you, Lord Roger," he said. "You've given me something to think about."

"Have I said anything to convince you that I wasn't involved?" Now Conyers did smile.

Edgar smiled back. "I believe that my friend Aelred was right. It's not the kind of revenge you would order."

"Perhaps," Conyers answered. "But the fact is that I have too much to occupy me here. Word had just reached Durham that a real bishop has been elected. They say Cumin's mad with fury and is taking it out on the monks still in the cathedral. I also know that your father and brother, with their men, were admitted to the town a few days ago. You can report to your brother that I am fortifying my position here and he won't find us as easy to intimidate as unarmed villagers."

Edgar was startled. "You are allowing me safe passage to Durham?" He wasn't sure he wanted it.

"Archdeacon Rannulf has vouched for you and your uncle," Conyers told him. "Aelred I trust implicitly. He's known to be a friend of the monks and won't be allowed to enter the city but the

two of you might be able to reach them with a message. Do you remember the chanter, Lawrence?"

"Very well," Edgar said.

Lawrence had been the one at the other end of the cane when
Edgar had misbehaved in class. He had been a pompous man, fond
of misquoting Vergil, although Edgar hadn't known the quotes were
wrong until many years later.

Conyers noted the wince in Edgar's reply. "I can see that you
do." He smirked. "He's one of the monks still inside. Until recently,
we've been receiving letters from him, lowered down over the cliffs
to the river in a basket. But there's been nothing for the past few
nights. Either he's been discovered or the monks are now unable to
get out of the cloister area at all."

Edgar tried to think of Brother Lawrence being that brave. He
had always thought the man a pompous bully, but perhaps misfor-
tune had brought out a nobler side.

Conyers watched him. "He may have been tortured, or even
killed."

"I wouldn't like to think of that happening," Edgar said truthfully. "Minor humiliation is the worst I've ever wished on him. And
I have some fondness for others among the monks, as well as a great
respect for Saint Cuthbert. No one, including my brother, should be
allowed to defile his land or desecrate his shrine."

"Then you will help me?" Conyers asked.

"I'll not hinder you," Edgar answered. "I'll give your message to
the monks and do what I can to protect them from Cumin's wrath.
But I cannot lift my hand to my brother or my father, no matter
what they might have done."

Conyers stood and offered Edgar his hand.

"I wouldn't have believed you if you had said you could," he
told Edgar. "I want nothing more than to have Brother Lawrence
know of recent events and a report brought back as to the situation
within the cloister."

"That I will do," Edgar promised. He shook Conyers's hand. "I
swear it."

"Then you may have safe passage to the gates of Durham,"
Conyers replied.

Edgar returned to Æthelræd and Aelred and reported his conversation with Conyers.

"It hadn't occurred to me that I might be too well known to be

allowed in," Aelred said. "But I believe Lord Roger is right. Someone might suspect you if you were known to be with me. I have permission to be gone from the abbey as long as necessary, though. I'll
stay here at Bishopton for now. There may be something I can help
you with when you've returned."

Æthelræd scratched his chin through his beard. "I have no love
for the canons of Durham," he said. "But they serve the saint and
should not be molested. I came on this expedition to watch over
you, Edgar, and to thwart any schemes my dear brother, Waldeve,
might have for random revenge. It bothers me to be drawn into all
this political warfare. But." He sighed. "I suppose it's too late now.
Tomorrow, then, we enter the hellmouth, armed only with our pu-
rity of heart and quick tongues."

Edgar looked at him. "We'll try not to rely too much on the former," he said. "I think Saint Cuthbert would prefer not to have to
protect us based on our rectitude"

"You have a point," Æthelræd conceded.

Catherine was so relieved when Solomon and Adalisa returned that
she didn't notice the constraint between them.

"Did you save the dog?" she asked as Solomon let Adalisa down
from his horse.

"It will be some time before we know for sure," Adalisa told
her. "But it seems so. Robert will care for her as you would James."

"I'm glad of that," Catherine said. "The guards have been dou-
bled and Margaret says that the villagers are putting a barricade
across the road."

"Yes, we saw them at it as we arrived." Solomon had dismounted and handed the reins to the stableboy. "It won't stop a
real attack, though."

"I know," Catherine said. "But it seemed to please them to be
doing something."

Adalisa had left them and gone into the keep, looking for Margaret. Catherine moved closer to Solomon.

"Do you think we should send for Waldeve to return?" she
asked.

"I suggested that to Adalisa," Solomon answered. "She found
the idea horrifying. 'What if he came all the way home and found
there was no threat after all?' she asked me."

Catherine shivered. "What if there is one?"

Solomon didn't try to reassure her. "I've been thinking about that," he said. "Setting a wolf trap for Robert is the action of someone working alone, or with only a few cohorts. We're well enough defended against that."

"But?" Catherine said.

"But, I'd feel better if you came down to the hall to sleep, all of you," Solomon continued. "Or at least to Adalisa's room. I think it's better to stay together."

"You fear that one person might get in when an army couldn't?" Catherine asked.

"Exactly," he said.

"But we don't even know if whoever it is wants to hurt us," Catherine argued. "They may only be seeking Waldeve's sons."

"I hope so," Solomon answered. "But you don't want to wager your son's life on that, do you?"

The answer to that was self-evident. "Will you sleep in front of the doorway?" Catherine entreated him.

"I won't sleep at all," he promised.

Solomon kept his word. He stationed himself in front of the door to Adalisa's room, where Catherine, Willa, Margaret, and James had crowded in. Oswin, the soldier in charge of the guards, insisted angrily that he could keep watch without the assistance of a guest in the keep.

"I hope you can," Solomon told him. "But I prefer to guard my cousin myself."

"As you wish," Oswin said. "If I find you asleep, I'll be sure to leave a pillow by your head."

He stomped off to shout reprimands at a couple of village men who were whiling away the time playing at dice.

Night finally came and with it silence.

Comforted by the knowledge that Solomon was watching over them, Catherine fell asleep almost at once, Willa snuggled beside her and James lay in his cradle. It was several hours later when she was wakened by the shouting and by Solomon shaking her.

"Hurry, Catherine!" he cried. "We've got to get out at once!"

"What?" She tried to focus on him.

Then from Adalisa's bed there came a cry.

"Oh dear Lord, save us! We're on fire!"

Eleven

Wedderlie, the hour before dawn. Monday, 4 kalends July (June 28), 1143.
Feast of Saint Ireneus, bishop of Lyon and adversary of heretics.

In ðeos burch breoma geond Breotenrice,
steppa gestaðolad stans ymbutan
wundrum gewæxen. Weor ymbeornad,
ea yðum stronge, and ðer inna wunað
feola fisca kyn on floda gemonge. . . .
Is in ðere byri eac bearnum gecyðed
ðe arfesta eadig Cudburch . . .

At this walled town reknowned throughout Britain
the firm foundations surrounded with stones
wondrously grew. The water rushed around it
With waves strong, and in there were
Fish of many kinds mingled in the flood . . .
And it was to this place as it is proclaimed
pious ones first came bearing blessed Cuthbert.

—The poem of Durham

*C*atherine immediately reached for James. She could smell the smoke and hear the cries now. The narrow window faced east but the light was that of the wooden palisade around the keep as it blazed in a dozen places.

"Willa!" The girl was next to her. "Gather up all the covers and clothes you can carry. Don't overload yourself. And don't waste time!"

Adalisa was already up. She had thrown a cloak over her *chainse* and had Margaret in her arms.

"Are the stairs aflame?" she asked Solomon.

"Not yet," he said. "Here, give Margaret to me. She's too heavy for you. Is there any water in the pitcher?"

Willa checked. "A little."

"Soak a cloth in it and tear it into six strips, if you can. Each put it over your face to breathe through. Quickly!"

Catherine took the damp cloth and put it over James's face. He twisted to avoid it but she kept it on him.

"Ready?" Solomon said.

It didn't matter if they were or not. There was no more time. Following Solomon, they entered the wooden stairwell.

The steps were warm under Catherine's bare feet but the smoke wasn't thick. As they descended, the air became more dense. Willa started coughing.

"Hold on to my robe," Catherine told her. "Close your eyes and feel your way down."

The steps made a sharp turn before reaching the main hall. The walls below were of stone and earth but everything above was made of wood. One side of the hall was burning. Pieces had fallen out of it and the night air was rushing in, fanning the flames. They raced across the hall to the door out. Solomon lifted the bar.

He looked down into emptiness. The outside staircase had vanished. The fire hadn't reached this far. There were splintered bits of board at the bottom. He didn't take time to wonder what had happened.

"Is there a ladder?" he asked Adalisa.

"In the larder, but we can't reach it from here," she was pale with terror but remained in control of herself.

"Can we get to the chapel?"

She looked around. "Yes, but then we'll be trapped down there. It's below the earth."

"This isn't a time for secrets, Adalisa!" he shouted. "There's no other way out."

Her immediate terror won over her fear of Waldeve.

"Follow me," she told him.

She nearly bumped into Catherine as she turned and led them to the passage down to the chapel.

The air became cooler as they descended but Catherine knew it was just a matter of time before the fire caught on the ceiling and burning chunks rained down on them. She shifted James in her arms and kissed him, murmuring wordless comfort.

They reached the little chamber. It was pitch dark, but Adalisa felt her way along the wall to the stand by the altar where the priest washed the instruments of the Mass. She pulled at the stand until it swung open.

"You'll have to crawl," she called to the others.

"Go on, Margaret, after your mother." Solomon put her down. "Willa, after Margaret, Catherine . . ."

"I can carry James." She knew where they were going. It was only a brief shuffle through to the storeroom, where they could hear the frightened yips of the prisoner.

Adalisa was already mounting the ladder to the kitchen.

"Wait!" Catherine stopped her. "We can't leave him to die."

It was too dark to see faces, but there was despair in Adalisa's voice. "We have to. I don't have the key. It's still upstairs."

"Go on!" Solomon's voice came from behind them. "There isn't time!"

Adalisa pushed open the entrance to the kitchen. "There's smoke here, but I don't see any flames. We just need to reach the door to the courtyard."

"But we can't . . ." Catherine began.

The smoke poured into the storeroom. Then Catherine knew she could. It would be on her conscience forever, but saving her son was all that mattered. She followed Adalisa and the girls up the ladder, across the kitchen and out the door into clean air.

The four of them huddled together at the edge of the motte. The bridge across was gone.

"Where are the guards?" Catherine said.

"I don't know," Adalisa answered. "They can't have run away, leaving us to die!"

Catherine looked around. "And where's Solomon?"

"He was right behind you, wasn't he? Oh, Saint Janvier! Solomon, what have you done? *No!*"

Adalisa started toward the door they had come through, but Catherine held her back.

"He's gone for the keys, hasn't he?" she asked, hoping Adalisa would say no.

"They're on my belt, hanging from the bedframe," Adalisa said. "He knows where they are. But there isn't time!"

Now, above the roar of the fire, Catherine heard the clash of metal against metal. In the bailey below them, a struggle was going on.

"We're being attacked," she shouted to Adalisa. "We have to get away before the guards are overpowered. Solomon!"

She screamed his name in a voice already hoarse from the smoke. Finally, there was a movement within the darkness of the doorway and Solomon emerged carrying something wrapped in a blanket.

"Thank God," Catherine whispered.

"He can't walk," Solomon told them as he reached them. He looked over the ditch to the bailey, where five or six guards were fighting off what seemed to be a horde, some with swords, but more carrying pikes and torches.

"Who is it?" Adalisa wailed. "Who is doing this to us!"

"The men are fighting well," Solomon decided. "But they're far outnumbered. I've got you get you all out of here and someplace safe."

Someplace safe, Catherine thought. *This* was supposed to be someplace safe.

"Can we make it down the other side to the river?" she asked Adalisa.

"Perhaps." Adalisa thought. "I don't know if the girls can."

"Yes, I can, Mama," Margaret piped up. "I know the way. I've done it lots of times."

"Margaret!" Adalisa realized that this wasn't the time to scold. "Show us."

They looked like a scene from some damnation frieze, the five of them crisscrossing down the side of the motte, outlined and then hidden by the fires. The trail Margaret went down was suitable only for goats and sure-footed children. Catherine did a large part of it by sliding, grateful that the other noise masked James's howls as he was swung abruptly in her arms. Solomon went down like a hunchbacked bear, the prisoner slung over his back.

They reached the bottom at last. The battle sounds were more remote now. Whoever was attacking them hadn't thought to set a guard at the rear of the steep motte. The river was across an open field. There was nothing for it but to pray and run.

"Into the woods," Solomon panted. "Don't look back!"

They splashed through the shallow water and into the shelter of the trees. Suddenly, Margaret halted.

"We're heading for the pagan stones," she wailed. "The ghosts will devour us there."

They stared at her. She had been so calm up to now. She clung to Adalisa in terror, tears streaming.

"We don't have to go that way," Adalisa told them. "We should be heading for the coast and then south. If Robert has escaped this, there's one place he'll go to look for us."

Margaret looked up. "Saint Cuddy's?"

"Yes, my love." Adalisa wiped the child's face. "We should try to reach Holy Island."

Catherine didn't know what or where it was, but the name itself was a refuge. She wondered how long it would take for a party such as theirs, barefoot, with no provisions, slowed by children and a man who could neither walk nor speak, to come to this sanctuary. But it was a beacon to follow. She wrapped James more securely in his blankets and prepared to set out.

The town of Durham is built on a rocky peninsula jutting into the river Wear. The cathedral and the castle were intended from the beginning to withstand attack. The custodians of the relics of Saint Cuthbert had been driven across the country by Danish invaders and wanted never to be forced to move again. The land for miles around had put itself under the protection of the saint and the bishop had become the lord of the county.

It was late in the morning when Edgar and Æthelræd reached the southwest gate. Unlike Urric and Swein, who had arrived on horseback fully armed, they were dressed no better than the farmers around them and came on foot. By preference, Æthelræd still wore only his Scots skirt wrapped around his waist. He had been coerced into putting a short tunic on, as well, but he complained that it itched and told Edgar loudly that he'd be glad when this was all over and he could run naked again.

They didn't seem to be a threat to anyone and were admitted within the walls without incident.

Edgar knew the way up to the castle well. He had climbed it often enough as a boy. But as they passed through the town, he was horrified at the changes made during the three years that William Cumin had been in control. Houses had been destroyed and left in ruins. The shops were mostly boarded up. Stones had been pried from the main road leaving holes that made riding impossible. What few people they saw in the streets were clearly in a rush to complete their errands and get back home. No children played in the common field at the base of the escarpment. The only people who seemed at home were the soldiers.

One of them approached Edgar and his uncle.

"You there!" he said, in a way that made both men stop and turn around slowly, not with fear, but annoyance.

Æthelræd smiled in amusement.

"We are indeed here," he told the soldier. "And who might you be?"

The man paused, confused. He wasn't used to being addressed in this way by peasants.

"That's no concern of yours," he blustered finally. "What do you think you're doing, wandering about the city?"

"We're not wandering," Edgar explained. "We're heading for the bishop's castle."

The man gave a snort. "And what business would you be having with his lordship, the bishop?"

Æthelræd was beginning to enjoy himself.

"I don't want to see the bishop," he stated. "I'm looking for my brother. Have you seen him?"

The soldier looked him up and down with contempt. "I've seen nothing that looks like you," he said. "Not since we chased the Gallowegians back over the border at the Battle of the Standard."

Æthelræd nodded. "I was proud to stand with them," he said mildly. "My brother was in the rear somewhere, with the king. We were in the front ranks."

Edgar tugged at him. "Uncle, this could take all day."

"Listen to the boy, 'Uncle'," the soldier sneered. "And be on your way. No, not that way," he added as they set back up the hill. "The way you came."

He drew his sword. Æthelræd looked at it as if he'd never seen one before. Then he shook his head sadly and, in one movement, unwrapped his skirt and spun it around the soldier's arms, pinning them to his sides and causing him to drop the sword. Edgar picked it up.

"Uncle," he said. "You're naked from the waist down."

"Try to keep the women off me until I've dealt with this." Æthelræd grinned. "Now, my boy. I'm not going to kill you just because you're insolent and don't know how to speak nicely to your betters. I'm going to kill you because you mocked the Gallowegians."

The man glared at him and began to shout for help.

"Uncle," Edgar said wearily, "there are easier ways of finding my father."

"This one is the most fun." Æthelræd twisted the cloth more tightly.

There was the sound of boots on the cobblestones as the soldier's cries were answered.

"Æthelræd!" A familiar voice rang out. "Cover your ugly ass!"

Æthelræd released the soldier and tucked the length of cloth back into his belt.

"I hope the man isn't one of ours," he said. "I'd have drowned a runt like this at birth."

Leaving the sputtering man without a backward glance, Æthelræd went to greet Waldeve. Edgar followed, still carrying the sword.

"Have you found the bastards?" was Waldeve's greeting.

"Hello, Father," Edgar answered. "No, Aelred had heard nothing that would help us. Have you found any answers here?"

Waldeve stood uphill from Edgar, making him feel smaller and younger than he was. His father was flanked by men-at-arms, each staring blankly into God-knew-what private dream. The sun was almost overhead and light penetrated every corner of the narrow street. But it seemed to Edgar that his father stood in shadow, his face a blur.

Waldeve's answer was short. "Just more questions. Come on, both of you. Enough playing, Æthelræd."

It seemed there would be no more explanation until they reached the castle. Edgar and Æthelræd followed Waldeve, who had turned and started back up without further conversation. Behind them they could hear the profanities of the embarrassed soldier.

"We've made an enemy," Edgar told his uncle.

Æthelræd shrugged. "A man like that, I wouldn't want to call me friend."

When they reached the top of the escarpment, Edgar nearly cried out in dismay. The changes to the town below were nothing to that in the space between the bishop's castle and the cathedral. What had been a greensward was now covered with tents. The entrance to the church had been blocked and was guarded by several men. Refuse pits had been dug on one side and the stench was overwhelming.

"Saint Ethelwold's venomous wine!" Æthelræd exclaimed. "What have those men been eating?"

Waldeve spoke without turning around. "The bishop has ordered the burial of all those who have died since he was excommunicated. The canons have refused to do it, or to celebrate the Holy Office, as long as he is under interdict."

Edgar tried to imagine Brother Lawrence defying armed men in this fashion. Others, yes. Many of the boys he had studied with who had stayed to join the canons were from families of warriors, as he was. They would find it in many ways easier to stand firm against the usurper than to submit to him.

"But, Father," Edgar took long strides to catch up. "William of Saint-Barbe was consecrated at Winchester three days ago. There is no way Cumin can consider himself the rightful holder of the see."

Waldeve stopped and spun around. "He's living in the bishop's castle, sitting on the bishop's throne and marking his letters with the chapter seal. He's collecting the tithes of Durham. And he's sharing them with his followers. That makes him the bishop."

They were standing on level ground, now, eye to eye, and Edgar realized with a start that he was now taller than his father.

"And are you one of this man's followers?" he asked.

"Hardly." Waldeve sneered. "I'm one of his leaders."

The eyes Edgar stared into were grey, like his own, like James's. But the man who looked out of them had no kinship to him.

"You have allied yourself with a man who has defied both the Pope and the holy saints?" Edgar said in disgust. "Perhaps my brothers were struck down in dívine retribution."

Waldeve gave an involuntary shudder.

"The Pope is in Rome and only knows what the minions of the archbishop and the legate tell him," he answered. "And if Saint Cuthbert disapproved of William Cumin, then why hasn't he smote him with lightning by now? Maybe the saint prefers the new order."

"Heaven is more subtle than that," Edgar told him.

"It was living men who killed my sons and grandson," Waldeve answered firmly. "Men with evil and hate in their hearts. Don't try to confuse me with your cleric's logic."

"Very well," Edgar conceded because he was sure that, in this at least, his father was right. But there was retribution at work here nonetheless. Which of Waldeve's sins were coming home to roost? He followed glumly as he and Æthelræd were led to the bishop's castle.

"You'll have to sleep in the hall with the knights," Waldeve told them. "It's either that or share a tent with the soldiers."

"Where is Duncan?" Edgar wanted to know.

"He's patrolling the walls," Waldeve said. "He'll be back this evening."

"And now that I'm here," Edgar asked. "What do you intend for me to do, spout some Latin?"

Waldeve's look grew crafty.

"Maybe, or write some for me. I'll tell you when the time comes."

He left Edgar and Æthelræd to settle their packs among the others and to find a place to wash.

"It would be just our luck to roll out our beds next to the man you embarrassed on the way up here," Edgar commented.

"Well, he's seen what I have to offer." Æthelræd chuckled. "Maybe he'll decide to make friends."

"I'm finding a place next to the wall," Edgar decided. "What do you think my father is plotting?"

"No good, as usual," Æthelræd said. "But for now I'm only concerned about one thing. Where's the nearest alehouse?"

"There used to be one built on the other side of the cloister wall," Edgar said.

"Take me there at once," Æthelræd begged. "I've a thirst from the road that's overpowering me. We can speculate on your father's wickedness just as well there."

Edgar showed him the way, but he wasn't thinking of his father at all. The only thing on his mind was Catherine. How was she? Was James well? He sighed. And how long before they could all be together again?

In her confusion and terror, Catherine had planned no more than the next step, wanting only to put as much distance as she could between herself and the men with swords and torches. But once she'd had time to collect her thoughts, she realized that they couldn't go far without help and rest.

They had found a hut in the woods, made and abandoned by some charcoal burner. It was far enough away that they couldn't hear the shouting anymore, but Catherine feared it was still close enough for anyone who had seen their escape to find them. Still, they were all exhausted. Catherine's feet were bruised and cut and she feared Willa's were the same.

Solomon set down his burden. The prisoner sat in the folds of the blanket, shivering and staring around him with wide, wild eyes.

"Who is he?" he asked Adalisa.

"I don't know his name," she answered. Her face was hidden from him as she knelt by Margaret and examined the cuts on the child's feet.

"How long has he been down in that hole?" Solomon tried to keep his anger at bay, but he had carried this creature for over a mile. The man had made small sounds of terror the whole time. He was lighter than Margaret and his bones had poked in Solomon's back like sharp sticks.

Adalisa leaned back on her heels and closed her eyes. "Almost ten years," she admitted. "It was just after Margaret was born. Waldeve brought him home, tied over a sumpter horse. He put the shackles on himself, and forbade anyone to come near him. I was still confined to my room, but I could hear the screaming, the pleading. It seemed to go on for days."

"And you never asked who he was or why he was being treated so?" Solomon's voice showed his disbelief.

"I tried to find out from Urric," Adalisa said. "But he was under orders to say nothing. Once, a few months later, I went down to the storeroom and tried to speak with the boy; he must have been about twelve, then. But he only whimpered at me. I was discovered there and Waldeve beat me hard enough that I didn't try again."

She glared at Solomon and Catherine both. "You've lived here only a few weeks, but that should be enough time to tell you what it's like. I feared for my life. I feared even more for Margaret's."

She put her arms around her daughter.

"Solomon," Catherine said, "it doesn't matter now. He's here with us and we'll have to care for him as best we can. But we have to care for ourselves, as well."

"Yes, I know," Solomon said. "If anyone survived from the village, where would they go?"

Adalisa considered. "If they were afraid to return to their homes, Berwick is the nearest safe place for them, but it would only be temporary. I had thought to go there only long enough to get horses and provisions and to send a message to Waldeve. It's clear that someone wants to destroy us completely. So the only true refuge is with the monks at Holy Island."

"How far is it?"

"Less than a day from Berwick, if we can ride," Adalisa paused. "Longer if we have to walk."

Catherine looked at the prisoner, then at Willa. Willa tried to smile, but her chin was trembling. This was more adventure than she had expected. And James, where would they find swaddling for him? What if she were too worn to supply him with enough milk? Catherine was close to tears, herself.

"Where is your faith, child?" Those nagging voices were, for once, almost kind. *"Where is your courage?"* That was more normal. *"Are you any different from any poor refugee of war? Women have endured such things from the beginning of time. You're young and strong. You can survive, and care for your child, too."*

Catherine could almost feel the voices shouting inside her head, drowning out fear and doubt and the knowledge that many women and children did not survive. She would concentrate on those that had. It would have been helpful, she reflected, if the voices had come up with some solid suggestions as well as encouragement.

"If we follow the stream here," Adalisa told them, "it joins the Tweed a few miles on. Following that, we should reach Berwick by tomorrow afternoon. It twists around a bit, but the forest isn't too thick in this area. I think it would be better not to try to go by the road."

They all agreed.

"Do you think we dare ask for help if we come across anyone?" Catherine asked.

Adalisa looked at Solomon. He shook his head.

"I don't know. If we knew who we were running from . . ." he raised his eyebrows at Adalisa.

"I swear, by the veil of the Virgin, I don't know," Adalisa answered wearily.

"We'll have to decide when the time comes," Solomon said. "Now, we need to make something to protect your feet."

He had slept with his clothes and boots on and so was better prepared than the others. He started to take off the boots.

"Don't be silly," Catherine said. "Your feet are much bigger than ours. We'd fall more often than walk in those."

She took one of the covers that Willa had grabbed and began tearing strips of it. Adalisa got up and began examining the nearby trees.

"Solomon, I need your knife," she called a moment later. "Birch bark should come off easily enough. The sheep have no trouble destroying it."

In a moment she had pulled off a long strip of the bark, which she sliced into lengths. Then she took the cloth Catherine had torn and wrapped it around a piece of the bark.

"Margaret, give me your foot," she said.

The girl sat on the ground as her mother wrapped the rest of the strip of cloth around her foot, making a crude shoe with a bark sole.

"I don't know how long it will last, but it's better than nothing," Adalisa said.

She and Catherine finished covering their feet and Willa's. Then they looked at the prisoner. He hadn't moved from the place where Solomon had set him. Nor had he made a sound.

"I can carry him," Solomon assured them. "There's hardly any flesh on him at all."

They tested their new shoes. They were a little lumpy, but not uncomfortable.

"We should try to go as far as we can, today," Solomon said.

"It's high summer. We should have no trouble finding berries in the wood and fish in the river. We'll be fine."

"I never doubted it," Catherine said. "But could I take a moment to change the baby before we set out?"

Solomon sniffed the air. "I think we'd all appreciate that."

While she did, using the last of the cover she had demolished, Catherine wondered again about the man from the storeroom.

"He should have a name," she said. "Even if he doesn't respond to us. We can't keep saying 'him' or 'the captive'."

"His name is Lazarus," Willa said at once.

They all turned to her.

"It is? How do you know?" Adalisa asked.

"Look at him," she said simply. "What else could it be?"

She was right. The white skin stretched over bones and the astonished stare resembled nothing more than a resurrected corpse, confused and terrified at being dragged back into the world.

"Well then, Lazarus." Solomon bent down and picked him up. "We'd best be on our way."

Edgar stood up and threw down his ale bowl in disgust.

Æthelræd looked at him in mild curiosity.

"You don't like the ale?" he asked.

"The ale is fine, Uncle," Edgar answered. "Just as I remembered it. But I didn't come to Durham to sit in a tavern and guzzle ale. We've been here three days and have done little else."

"I say, don't complain when things are going smoothly," Æthelræd cautioned him.

"They're not going smoothly, Uncle. They're not going at all," Edgar sat again but continued fuming. "Every time I ask my father what I should be doing, he puts me off. I've tried to get permission from Cumin to visit the monks but I can't even get an audience with him. What am I doing here?"

Æthelræd finished his ale and belched.

"I wondered when you'd get tired of waiting," he said. "Why don't we do a few things without permission?"

He reached inside the scrip hanging from his belt and took out a key. Edgar began to grin.

"Where did you get that?" he asked. "I thought Cumin had confiscated all the keys."

"Apparently he missed one," Æthelræd answered. "Every monk has a key to the north door. The archdeacon took his with him and happened to give it to me."

"Why did you wait?" Edgar said in exasperation.

"I didn't know how much trouble you were willing to get into," his uncle said. "If we're caught in the cloister by Cumin's men, we may join the men who wouldn't pay the tithes. The ones hanging outside their homes on Silver and Saddler Streets."

Edgar had seen them, dangling not by their necks, but by their waists, with weights hung from hands and feet. It takes a long time to die that way.

"I know every place a boy can hide in the cloister and cathedral," he said. "We won't get caught."

They decided to go the following morning, reasoning that two men wandering about the cathedral would be less remarkable by day. That night Edgar ate his fish stew with more appetite than he had since coming to Britain. At last he was doing something, not letting himself be blown about on his father's whim.

The man he sat next to seemed vaguely familiar. Edgar had seen him among his father's retainers.

"I don't remember you from when I lived at Wedderlie," he admitted. "What's your name?"

"Algar," the man answered. "I remember you, though. I'm Alfred's grandson. When I was little, I used to run errands to the keep. Once, you gave me a honey cake."

"You remember that?" Edgar was astounded.

"It was an act of fellowship, not charity." Algar smiled. "You confessed that you'd stolen them from the kitchen."

"I probably had." Edgar thought back. "There were never any left after the men had eaten, although sometimes my stepmother managed to save me a few. Are we . . . uh . . . related?"

Algar grinned. "Your uncle asked me the same question. My mother says not and I believe her."

"She should know." Edgar offered his hand. "I'm glad to meet you again, Algar. It is nice to know there's one man in my father's company who isn't my brother or nephew."

Edgar studied the face before him. Algar must be five or six years younger than he. The incident he remembered must have occurred on Edgar's last visit home before he left for France. Fifteen years ago and yet that small act had remained in this man's mind. This was someone he should pay attention to.

He woke the next morning with his head full of plans about how to reach Brother Lawrence with the message he had been charged to convey. He didn't pay much attention to the commotion in the outer bailey. Then he heard someone call his name.

"Edgar, come quickly." It was Æthelræd, looking unusually grim. "There's news from Wedderlie!"

Edgar rushed out to find a crowd of men gathered around a rider who hadn't had time even to dismount. He then recognized Oswin, who had been left in charge of the guards at Wedderlie. His heart began pounding.

"Where is Lord Waldeve?" Oswin shouted. "Lord Edgar, where is your father? He must know at once. Two nights ago we were attacked. We drove the invaders back but most of the men were killed and the keep has been burnt to the ground."

Edgar felt all the blood drain from his head. He only stayed upright because of his uncle's strong arm around him.

"My wife?" he yelled across the tumult. "Where is she?"

Oswin's face was still blackened by smoke and there was a bandage around his head that was oozing blood.

"I don't know, Lord," he said miserably. "We fear they were all trapped inside."

Edgar stared at him, uncomprehending. This wasn't happening. The man was mistaken. Catherine must have escaped. He had left her there so that nothing could harm her and James. Oswin couldn't have meant that they had been hurt.

"Why are you here?" he shouted. "Why aren't you back home protecting my family?"

"My lord." Oswin was weeping. "Forgive me, but there's nothing left to protect."

Twelve

An abandoned cottage outside of Berwick. Thursday, the kalends July (July 1), 1143. The feast of Saint Serf, a Briton, about whom nothing is known.

Quae vero pestis efficacior ad nocendum quam familiaris inimicus?

And truly what plague is more powerful in hurtfulness than a member of one's household who has become an enemy?

—Boethius
Consolation of Philosophy,
Book III part V 11 41–42

*S*olomon should have been back by now," Catherine fretted.

"Do you think he's been attacked by brigands?" Willa asked.

Catherine immediately regretted voicing her worry. Willa had been so brave through the past few days, even when her teeth were chattering from terror. It would be cruel to add to her burden.

"No, I don't," she told the girl. "I think he probably had trouble finding someone who could understand him well enough to explain what has happened."

"I should have gone with him." Adalisa was fretting as well. "The monks at the hospice there know me."

Catherine shook her head. "No, Solomon was right about that. If someone wants to destroy the whole family, it's best that no one knows we survived the fire."

Adalisa was trying to comb her hair with her fingers. She yanked at it in frustration.

"Why are they such cowards?" she cried. "How can we fight an enemy without a face?"

The image gave Catherine a frisson at the back of her neck. That was the worst of it. Since they didn't know who was after them, they had no idea whom to trust. Even asking for help was dangerous, which was why Solomon had insisted in going into the town alone.

There was nothing for it but to wait. Catherine gazed at James lying naked on a blanket in the warm morning sunshine. He seemed content for now, but they had only been able to rinse out his swaddling in the river and hang it to dry on the bushes nearby. There were red chafe marks on his poor little bottom already. They had nothing to oil him with and no clean cloths to wrap him in. The ones they had used to make shoes with were filthy.

On the other hand, James was the only one of them who wasn't hungry. They had found berries and edible plants enough, but they hadn't managed to catch any fish and had no way to cook one even if they had. Catherine had been imagining bread with mutton drippings for the last hour so strongly that she could almost smell the fat.

"If Solomon doesn't find someone who will loan us a horse," she asked Adalisa, "do you think we can manage to reach your Holy Island, with the children and with him?"

She nodded toward the corner where Lazarus was curled, fast asleep. Berries had apparently satisfied him. He had rolled them in his mouth and bit into them with a joy that was almost painful to watch. But he had still said nothing and his legs were clearly too weak to support even his fragile body.

Adalisa had been trying to think of a way that she and Catherine could carry him, but she knew that even if they made a stretcher to put him on, they could only go a mile or so before they would need to rest. At that rate, it might take a week to reach safety. With Margaret and James to care for, especially James, a week would be too long.

She stroked Margaret's vibrant hair as the child slept, her head in her mother's lap.

"If Solomon doesn't return soon," she decided, "we'll have to take him into town ourselves. Our enemies will certainly find out then that we're alive, but if we stay here much longer, we won't survive and then they will have won."

Sadly, Catherine agreed. She watched James kicking happily in the sun, tended by Willa. Her duty was to care for both of them. The weight of it was crushing. When she had left the convent, all she had considered was Edgar, the love and, to be honest, the lust she felt for him. Mother Heloise had left her own son to be raised by his father's family when she had taken the veil. Catherine knew she couldn't do that. She had no wish to go back. But why had no one told her of the terrible responsibilities of love?

Late in the afternoon they heard someone moving in the woods. In a moment, they had gathered together, Adalisa holding the long knife Solomon had left as meager protection. Her relief was overwhelming as he appeared, leading a mule loaded with provisions. She dropped the knife and rushed to embrace him.

"It's all right," Solomon said over and over as she wept. "I'm sorry I was so long."

Catherine was surprised by how tenderly he comforted Adalisa and by how certain she seemed to be of receiving it. The way he smoothed her hair and wiped her eyes. And the way he smiled into them! Catherine looked away, unsettled by the sight.

She turned her attention to the provisions he had brought.

"Does this mean we can't go into Berwick?" she asked, gesturing at the laden mule.

"Word has already come that we were killed in the fire," Solomon told them. "A few of the people from the village have taken refuge at the hostels for now, but they're returning to Wedderlie soon. I don't think any of them saw me. The trader I talked with told me that the taverns were full of the news. They're calling it a judgment on Waldeve, saying how strange it was that the castle was destroyed and the village left unharmed."

"I'm glad of that," Adalisa said. "Even if it does seem to confirm that our enemies only care about killing us. But why? What have we done?"

"Did you learn anything about Robert?" Catherine asked.

Solomon nodded. "His farm was torched, as well, but he escaped. The rumor is that Waldeve and his men have gone to Durham. Robert is supposed to be going there himself, to bring the news. I hope the dog survived."

"Robert must have saved her," Adalisa said. "Or else he'd have died trying to."

"But that means Edgar will think he's lost us!" Catherine said. "We can't let him, Solomon. It will kill him!"

"We have to, Catherine," Solomon said. "There was no one there I could trust to send a message to him. Once we reach Holy Island, then I'll go myself to Durham. But first we must find all of you a haven from this nightmare."

Catherine knew he was right, even though the thought of what Edgar would be suffering was horrible. The only thing was to reach the island as soon as they could.

They ate the cheese and dried meat he had brought and Catherine rubbed grease from the cheese paper on James's bottom and wrapped him in the dried swaddling. Solomon didn't need to tell them to hurry. But he watched with impatience. He had another reason for wanting to be on their way as soon as possible. While in the tavern in Berwick, he had been surprised to see Leonel, the cleric who had come with them from France. The man had recognized him, he was sure. But, instead of greeting him, Leonel's face had paled with alarm and he had quickly gotten up and left. Solomon didn't know what to make of his actions. Had the cleric believed he had seen a ghost? Or was there another reason? Why was the man still in Berwick when he had made such a point of wanting to go to York?

Solomon tried to think of an innocent reason for Leonel being there, but could come up with none. Only one possibility rang in his mind. That the man hadn't traveled with them by chance, but had been sent to follow them. And the only reason he could think of for that was that someone wanted information on him and, perhaps, on his relationship with Catherine.

What if Leonel were to go back to Paris and tell the Bishop that he had been posing as a Christian and that Catherine and Edgar were in collusion with him?

He knew that his first job was to see that they all arrived safely at Holy Island. But Solomon couldn't help but wonder if there would be any haven for him or his family, should word of this reach Paris.

Edgar felt numb. He sat staring into emptiness, not letting himself comprehend what he had just been told. This hadn't happened. Catherine was fine. She had survived so many dangers before, even giving birth to James. God wouldn't give them to him and then take them away. There was no sense in such cruelty.

All around men were shouting, crying, raging at the air, demanding that Oswin tell them if their families had escaped.

"Only the keep was burned," he told them. "But the people are scattered. I don't know who survived."

Waldeve watched it all, uncharacteristically silent. But Edgar paid no attention. He was lost in his own world, trying somehow to make this news mean something else than what had been said.

"Edgar." Someone was shaking him. "Edgar, come back. They're not dead, I tell you. They're not dead."

Edgar blinked and looked into the shaggy face of his uncle.

"Listen to me," Æthelræd said carefully. "You know I've always known where to find you? I came to meet you at Berwick, even though you hadn't planned to land there. I felt it when your brothers died. I knew when my father had died, although I was in Denmark then. No one in this damned family dies without a piece going out of me. Your son survived; I'm sure of it. Margaret, too. And if they did, then it stands to reason that their mothers are also alive."

"Catherine?" Edgar still didn't understand.

"They didn't die in the fire," Æthelræd said again. "Nor did Robert. I would stake my soul on it. Edgar!"

Æthelræd shook him again. "Do you hear me?"

"Yes," Edgar said from far away. "You say they're alive. Of course they are. They have to be, or I've died, too."

Æthelræd sighed and rubbed his forehead. The boy was too far gone into shock to talk with now. The best thing was to get a sleeping draught into him and hope he'd be more aware when he woke.

They were inside a silent bubble in the middle of chaos. Æthelræd helped Edgar to stand and walked him over to the gate of the bishop's palace. With his free arm, he pushed aside anyone who got in the way.

"I need your infirmarian," he told the guard at the gate.

"We don't have one," the guard said. "There's a monk in the cathedral who tends to our wounds. That's all. But you can't go there without permission from the bishop."

"Fine," Æthelræd answered.

He shouldered Edgar once more and went back to the crowd, pushing his way through. From there he eased out the other side and toward the path leading to the cloister.

As they were about to vanish among the trees, Waldeve spotted them.

"You two!" he shouted. "Get over here. There's work to be done!"

Æthelræd ignored him and steered Edgar to the north door of the cloister. Taking the key from his scrip, he opened it and dragged Edgar in.

Waldeve watched them go with impotent fury. He couldn't reach them through the mass of men around him, begging him to take them back to find their families. He had nothing but contempt for his followers. Men who vented their feeling like this were of no use to him. Grief must become anger and anger hate or a man would lose the desire to fight. He had to regain control of them at once.

"You, stop that howling!" he screamed, hitting at the nearest man with the flat of his sword. "Crying won't avenge them. And going home will only take us into a trap."

The man only winced and continued sobbing.

Waldeve's anger grew. "Saint Finian's flying farts!" he bellowed. "Aren't there any men left here?"

"Waldeve, leave them be."

Waldeve looked up. Standing in front of him was William Cumin, erstwhile bishop of Durham. "They are torn with fear for those they love. You have lost much more than they. Why aren't you grieving with them?"

"My Lord Bishop," Waldeve said perfunctorially. "I learned years ago that my tears bring no one back. They only sap my strength, leaving me too weak to fight. My men are no good to me in this state."

"If you let them voice their sorrow, they'll be all the stronger when you lead them into battle," Cumin said. "I'll say a Mass for the souls of your wife and child tomorrow morning. Have the men attend. It will do them good."

Waldeve forebode mentioning that half the men would refuse to participate in a Mass said by an excommunicant. He was doubtful himself about the efficacy of any devotions Cumin might give for someone's soul. Mightn't they rebound and actually cause the soul to endure more hellfire?

He could see there was no way to get anything done until the first waves of emotion had abated. Waldeve returned to his tent and ordered a flask of wine from one of the bishop's servants. While he waited for it, he wondered if any of the horses had been saved. It was good that the best were with him. They would be harder to replace than his wife.

Edgar woke up slowly, unsure of where he was or why he felt as if the world had just ended. There was a familiar face hovering over him, one that he thought he had left behind years ago.

"Brother Lawrence?" he whispered. "What's happened? Why are you here?"

The monk patted his arm gently. "Don't worry about that, my boy. Just rest for now. I'll tell your uncle that you're awake."

Edgar ignored the monk's advice and sat up. Yes, he was in the old infirmary at Durham. The last time he had been here was when he had the spotted fever. He'd been delirious for days, they told him. He wondered if the same thing had happened again. He looked at his hands. No spots. Also, he realized that they were the hands of a man. He wasn't a student here anymore. He hadn't become a priest after all. He had gone to France and met . . . Catherine.

It all came back to him with tidal force. His hands balled into fists that he beat against his forehead, trying to drive the knowledge out. It was all his fault. No matter what the danger in Paris, they would have been safer there than in Scotland. If they had died, at least it would have been together, as Catherine had wanted. Now she and James were both gone and he was left behind. What was he to do?

Æthelræd came in and grabbed him, pinning his fists down.

"Edgar, listen to me," he said. "Please believe me. Your wife and son are alive. They escaped the fire. I know it. You must stop this. I need you to be calm. Everyone else from Wedderlie has gone mad, including your father."

Edgar stared at him dully. "Uncle, I know you mean well, but this isn't one of your games. The keep was attacked and destroyed completely. There's no hope."

"Nonsense!" Æthelræd exclaimed. "What do you mean 'my games'? I have the sight, just as my grandmother did. How can you doubt it? I saw you in Berwick and I felt the deaths of your brothers. And I see Robert now, heading toward us. He didn't get here before Oswin because he's carrying that dog of his, but he'll arrive by afternoon."

He sounded certain of himself, Edgar allowed. What was even more convincing was that Æthelræd also sounded exasperated at Edgar's scepticism. Edgar wanted desperately to believe him, but he knew he couldn't bear hoping and then having to face the truth again.

"Robert is coming this afternoon?" he asked.

Æthelræd nodded decisively.

"Before the bells ring for Vespers, he'll be here," Æthelræd's forehead creased in puzzlement. "I just don't understand why he's carrying that damned dog."

Catherine had thought they were an odd-looking group: one man, two women, two young girls, a baby and a pale, pathetic creature tied to a mule to keep him from falling off. But the people they passed on the road gave them little more than a glance. Once a pair of soldiers rode by, causing them to jump quickly into the brush and nearly toppling Lazarus from the mule.

"What's wrong with them?" Catherine protested, as she checked to see that the dust of their passing hadn't blown into the baby's face. "Couldn't they see we need help?"

It was Willa who explained it to her.

"We're just more peasants and refugees," she said. "Look at us, Mistress. We're no different from most of the others on the road. No one stops to help them."

Adalisa agreed. "The North is full of people just like us, thrown from our homes by the wars. In a way, it's our best protection. No one will look closely enough at us to recognize us. But, oh, how my feet hurt!"

"Is it much farther?" Solomon asked.

"I don't think so," Adalisa said. "We should be there by tomorrow. Then we only have to wait on the tide."

Catherine stopped in dismay. "I forgot it was an island! We'll have to take a boat."

"No, no, don't worry, *ma douz broiz*," Adalisa reassured her. "The island can be reached twice a day, when the tide is out, on foot. We only have to be careful that we aren't caught by the incoming water."

Catherine found that much less frightening than the thought of setting out to sea again.

"What will happen when we get there?" Solomon wanted to know. "Do any of the monks there know you?"

"No, but I think I can convince them of who I am, and they will take us in in any case," Adalisa said. "We can send a message to Durham from there. And we can stay on the island until someone comes for us. After that, I don't know. Waldeve will tell us."

Solomon had no intention of waiting on Waldeve's whim. As soon as he was sure that his charges were in good hands, he intended to set out again, first to Durham to report to Edgar, then on a quest of his own. There was a man in Berwick who shouldn't be there. He had to find out what that man knew and whom he planned to tell. There was no point in surviving this if they were to be arrested as soon as they got back to Paris.

Catherine wasn't thinking of Paris, except in a wistful sort of way, as she remembered the wooden tub in the back garden. She wasn't really even thinking about Edgar, except as a pang of loneliness. All her concentration was on James. He had become fretful in the past day, quiet only when eating, which he wanted to do more often than usual. She didn't know what was wrong. Wasn't she supplying him enough milk? Or were the sores from the swaddling hurt-

ing him? Perhaps all this moving about had brought on an illness. He
had no fever, as yet, but what could she do if he developed one?

"My love, my precious, my darling child," she sang to him,
"Saint James, protect him. Keep him safe. Keep him well."

Lazerus whimpered constantly, as well. The jolting gait of the
mule upset him and he threw up the little they had gotten him to eat.
He kept his eyes shut tightly until Margaret suggested that the sun
might be too bright for him. They made him a hat of willow
branches that Willa wove together. She put it on his head and tied
it under his chin with the string from her *chainse*.

He twisted back and forth to rid himself of it, then slowly
opened his eyes. His hand moved up to investigate. Willa stood
close by, in case he should try to remove it. He didn't. After pulling
on the string a few times, he let it be. A few moments later, Willa noticed that he was sitting up straighter and looking about.

"Lazarus is waking up," she said to Adalisa.

"He is, indeed." Adalisa smiled. "Perhaps he will awaken
enough to tell us who he is someday."

"You really have no idea?" Catherine couldn't believe a woman
could be that ignorant of what was going on in her own household.

"Truly I don't," Adalisa answered.

"But there must have been someone that Waldeve was having a
dispute with at that time, some neighbor or follower of his lord,"
Catherine insisted.

"Yes, but there always was," Adalisa explained. "Waldeve isn't
alive if he isn't asserting his rights over someone. The only thing I
can remember from then was some trouble with the villagers, something about the way the tithes were assigned."

"That sounds normal," Solomon commented. "Everyone com-
plains about that."

"That's true, but this seemed worse than usual," Adalisa said. "I
could hear them shouting from my room. Waldeve threatened to
have the leaders hanged, but no one was."

"And he brought Lazarus home soon after this?" Solomon
asked.

"At night, I think," Adalisa paused. "It was so long ago and I
was still weak from the birth. Margaret was reluctant to enter the
world, my dear wise child. But I seem to remember the sound of the
horse coming back later than usual. I suppose I thought Waldeve

had simply been with one of his women. Then I heard the crying and pleading."

"He spoke?" Catherine asked.

"I'm not sure anymore," Adalisa closed her eyes to see the past better. "It may have been just the tone. The words would have been indistinct anyway."

"How long had Waldeve been gone?" Solomon asked.

"Since Tierce, or thereabouts," Adalisa said. "He wasn't away overnight all that month. Oh, I see!"

She looked on Solomon with admiration. "I never thought of that. Lazarus must have come from nearby. But then why did no one come for him?"

They all turned to the bony figure balanced on the back of the mule. Lazarus was staring at the light slipping between his fingers. He held his hand up so that the afternoon sun beat against it. He seemed completely enthralled and oblivious of the others.

No one said anything. But each of them wondered if the boy had been as simple as the man appeared to be. Who, then, would make an effort to rescue him?

They had left the forest now and were traveling across the marsh. Adalisa pointed out the plants that grew between the wood and the sea.

"That's liverwort," she told Catherine. "We call it *pérèlle* in France. If you gather and dry it, pound it to powder and mix it with urine, it comes out a lovely purple that you can use to dye wool."

"I must remember that," Catherine said.

The gulls and curlews were swooping overhead. The land was open and empty except for the wind that came off the sea, filling the air with the scent of brine. Even on this warm day, it cut through them. They had all wrapped themselves in the cloaks or blankets that they had been able to grab in the fire. James was whimpering, but there was nothing to be done for him until they found shelter for the night.

"There's a plant that grows only on Holy Island that one can get both oil and salt from," Adalisa continued. "In ale it's good for dropsy, and if one inhales the aroma of the oil, it reduces hysteria."

Catherine thought they might all have need of it soon. She understood why Adalisa was rambling on so. They were no longer hidden. On this landscape, anyone watching from the land above could spot them at once. They all felt it. Willa and Margaret walked together, holding hands. Solomon kept looking over his shoulder. Adalisa talked and Catherine shivered.

"Only one more day," she told herself. "One more day and we're finally safe."

If only Edgar knew they were all right. Catherine couldn't bear to think of what he must be enduring now. Then an even worse thought struck her. What if he were in danger, as well? Oh, why hadn't they stayed together?

Edgar was asking himself the same question, over and over. Despite the protestation of Æthelræd that Catherine and James were still alive, he despaired. He had lived too long in rational France to have any faith in family legends of vision and prophecy.

He took no solace from the fact that without any effort on his part he had been able to tell Brother Lawrence the message he had been charged with, of the election of William of Saint-Barbe as bishop of Durham and the massing of an army to come free them.

Brother Lawrence didn't seem terribly surprised by this.

"I knew Saint Cuthbert would take care of us," he said.

Edgar reflected that he had always been unbearably sure of himself.

"What am I doing here?" he complained to Æthelræd for the hundredth time. "If Saint Cuthbert can take care of his own, then I don't need to bother. My father certainly shows no need of me. All he's asked me to do is talk to clerics, all of whom he could have conversed with easily himself. I say, damn them all. Let me at least go back to Wedderlie and give my wife and child a proper funeral."

His tears splashed into his winecup. Æthelræd had thought he was doing well to get Edgar out of bed and down to the tavern, but Edgar took it as just another way to deaden his pain. The wine was strong and he hadn't been cutting it with water at all.

"Edgar." He touched his nephew's shoulder. "I wish you could trust me. Your grief is unnecessary."

Edgar looked up blearily. "Right," he said.

There was a commotion in the street outside the tavern. People were laughing and taunting someone. Æthelræd turned to see what it was. Laughter of any sort was rare in Durham these days.

The doorway was blocked with gawkers. Æthelræd went up to see over them.

"What is it?" he asked.

One of the men turned around.

"Just some poor fool in rags heading up to the cathedral," he said. "Looking for a miracle, no doubt. Got a three-legged dog on his back."

"Hope it's not a bitch." Another laughed. "Everyone knows Saint Cuthbert can't tolerate females at his shrine."

Edgar raised his head. Æthelræd looked smug.

"It's Robert, you'll see," he said. "Carrying the dog, just as I said. Now do you believe me?"

It was ridiculous but a tiny flare of hope started in Edgar's heart. He got up and went after Æthelræd who was already pushing his way through the gawkers to reach the man climbing up the street.

"Robert!" Edgar shouted at the man's back, on which poor Lufen was strapped.

Robert turned around.

"Edgar!" It was more of a wail than a greeting. "They burnt my farm and trampled the fields. Lufen and I escaped with our lives, but look at her! If she dies because of this I'll have someone's head."

They had caught up to him now. Robert embraced his brother and uncle, his tears dripping onto their tunics.

Edgar took him by the shoulders. "Robert, did you see Catherine? What happened to the people at the keep?"

"I don't know." Robert shook Edgar off. He wiped his face with his sleeve. "I only had time to scoop up Lufen and run into the woods. I hid by the river until morning. I started toward Wedderlie, but I could tell from the smoke and the silence that nothing was left."

"You didn't even check to see if anyone was still alive?" Edgar was furious.

"I met Alfred on the road," Robert told him. "He said there was no one left inside the bailey and the people from the village had taken refuge in the woods. He advised me to head here to find Father."

Edgar looked at him in disgust. As Robert started to respond his eyes suddenly glazed and he swayed and would have fallen if Æthelræd hadn't caught him.

"He's exhausted," Æthelræd said. "By the look of him, he's walked all the way here. Don't condemn him until you know the whole story."

"He put that dog before his own kin." Edgar had no pity for Robert's travails.

"The dog loves him more," Æthelræd said simply. "Here, help me get him up to the castle. You take Lufen."

Between them they got Robert and his dog safely away from the scofflers in the street and up to their father's tent outside the bishop's castle.

They sat him down and Edgar got a dipper of water to splash in his face. Robert came to with an indignant sputter.

"You didn't have to yell at me," he protested. "If something could have been done to save them, Alfred and the other men would have done it. I'm sorry; I liked your wife. But he told me to save my own skin and it seemed a good idea."

Edgar raised his fist, but Æthelræd stopped him.

"It doesn't matter," he said. "Robert did the right thing. I tell you they were long gone by the morning."

"Really." Edgar was unconvinced. "And where did they go?"

Æthelræd squinted, as if he could see them in the distance, then shook his head. "I don't know. It's easier when there's danger. Right now, they must be somewhere protected."

He seemed so certain. Edgar wanted desperately to believe him. But that was why he couldn't let himself do so. It was better just to accept the fact that his life was over along with Catherine's and James's.

Æthelræd turned his attention back to Robert.

"When did you last eat?" he asked.

"I don't know." Robert didn't seem interested. He fell to his knees beside the unconscious dog. "She didn't have time to heal before we were attacked. I tried to be gentle, but the road was so hard. Is there nothing you can do for her?"

His misery was so consuming that even Edgar felt a twinge of sympathy. This increased when Robert looked up at them, struck by a sudden, hideous thought.

"Oh, God, I'm going to have to face Father now, aren't I?"

Thirteen

The marsh flats on the coast of Northumbria. Saturday, 5 nones July (July 3), 1143. Feast of Saint Mustiola, Virgin, martyred by the Romans by having a spindle hammered into her head.

Venienti igitur ad se episcopo, rex locum sedis episcopalis in insula Lindisfarnensi ube ipse petebat, tribuit. Qui videlicet locus accedente ad recedente reumate bis quotidie instar insulae maris circumluitur undis, bis reundato littore contiguus terrae redditur. . . .

Therefore, when the bishop arrived, the king gave him the island of Lindisfarne for his episcopal see, where he had requested it to be. At this place the tide, ebbing and flowing twice a day, is like an island surrounded by water, then twice restored to attachment with the shore.

—The Venerable Bede,
Historia Ecclesiastica Gentis Anglorum,
Liber III, Cap. III

*J*ames wouldn't stop crying. He had kept them awake all night. Catherine was at her wit's end. She had nursed him so often that her nipples were sore. Everyone but Lazarus had taken a turn walking with him, but nothing would stop the wailing. He even whimpered during his short naps.

"I know it's because of the swaddling," Catering moaned, "but I can't change him here. There's nothing left that's clean and the wind would freeze him."

"We'll be at Lindisfarne soon," Adalisa said. "The causeway to Holy Island is just over there."

She pointed to an area at the bottom of the dune where they were standing. A road led into the sea, it seemed, covered in places with kelp and sand. Not far away there was a wooden lean-to, where a few other people had taken shelter.

"They're waiting for the tide," Adalisa explained. "It looks clear to me, but it must be coming in or they would have gone by now. That means we'll have to wait here until the tide goes out again. But we should be able to cross before dark."

Catherine was too exhausted to rejoice. She stumbled after the others as they went down to join those waiting for the water to recede enough for them to pass.

Solomon was worried about Catherine more than the baby. If she sickened, he wouldn't survive long. She had never really recovered her strength after all the miscarriages that came before James was born. If anything happened to either of them, Edgar would kill him. Solomon silently cursed his friend for suddenly deciding to become a warrior. It must be something born with them, he decided. One would think that fifteen years a scholar would cure him of wanting to fight.

Solomon turned his attention back to the present. From the

shore, he could make out the long shadow on the horizon that was the island. There was one high point at the northern end of it, but the rest didn't seem that far above the water. Nevertheless, it had become a goal as desired as Jerusalem. For the first time in his life Solomon was eager to reach a place full of monks.

As they drew closer, they saw that the other travelers were two men. Their horses were tethered behind the lean-to provided for those waiting. They had built a fire from driftwood and were sitting before it, cloaked against the wind. The smell of the smoke reached out to the group as they came across the sand. With it was mixed another scent that made them all move more quickly. It was that of fish cooking.

"Do you think they'll share?" Catherine asked Solomon.

"I'm not going to give them a choice," he answered. He shaded his eyes to see the people better. The two men seated before the fire were motionless except for the wind ruffling their cloaks. Their faces were hidden by their hoods.

Something about the figures made him uneasy. They were probably pilgrims or even monks returning home, he told himself. But he unfastened the clasp holding his knife in place all the same. A poor defense if the men had swords, yet better than being unprepared.

The only person who noticed his movement was Willa. She was trudging behind Catherine, carrying the few things she had snatched as they ran from the fire. She had been trying hard to be strong. Catherine needed her. Her mother had impressed upon her many times how kind Catherine had been to them all. Not many people would take in a woman with three bastard children and give them all a home. She wanted to do all she could to repay the debt. But the past few days were telling on her. She was cold and aching and terrified. Knowing that Solomon felt there was danger ahead of them was too much. She began to cry, silently and steadily.

"Saint Genevieve," she prayed, "just bring us back to Paris safely and I will honor you all the rest of my life."

They were close enough now for the men to spot them. One pointed in their direction, but neither bothered to move. They both held sticks laden with spitted fish over the fire. The sight and smell was enough to overcome any hesitation Catherine may have felt about strangers.

Margaret had fallen behind the rest. She caught up to Willa and took her hand.

"I think I know them," she said.

"Those men?" Willa asked, fear growing. "How could you?"

"No, not the men," Margaret answered. "Not with the hoods over their faces. The horses. They look like two that father has."

All horses looked alike to Willa. Different shades of the same animal as far as she could see. They were mostly large things in the road that she had to try to stay clear of as the nobility cantered by. So she didn't place much credence in Margaret's statement.

"Maybe these men got their horses in the same place," she said. "Oh, hot food! Herring, it looks like. I'm so hungry!"

She pulled Margaret along to catch up to the rest.

Solomon motioned them back and went up to the men. Catherine gave him a look of alarm.

"God be with you, Goodmen," he said. "I don't suppose either of you speak French?"

One growled something back. Solomon looked over his shoulder to Adalisa, who came to stand next to him.

"They think you're Norman," she said.

"*Hal beo thu!*" she began. "We are pilgrims, like yourselves, bound for Holy Island. We have only cheese to share with you, but we will do so gladly, for a bit of your fish for the children."

The men looked at each other. They nodded. Then one of them stood up.

"You've been long enough about it," he said.

Adalisa's eyes widened as she saw the face inside the hood. "What are you doing here? Why . . . oh, Sweet Jesus!"

She turned around quickly, grabbing the reins of the mule from Solomon. With a swift movement she set Margaret on its back, behind the startled Lazarus. She gave the reins to Catherine with one word.

"Run!"

Solomon had the knife out. He was relieved to see that the men didn't have swords, only knives, smaller than his own and clubbed sticks. But there were still two of them. He backed away, moving the blade in slow curves in front of the men.

"Who sent you?" he demanded.

"Ask her," the first man said with a humorless laugh. "She knows, don't you, my lady?"

"You're insane," she answered. "You have no cause for this."

"We have a hundred," the second answered. "I'd tell you their names, but I don't want you to live that long."

He lunged toward her. Solomon stepped in his path and slashed at his knife hand. The man was too quick. He dodged sideways and the blade cut through his sleeve, grazing the skin. He was thrown off balance, and fell to the sand. Solomon advanced on him.

Adalisa cried out as the first man came toward her. She looked around frantically for something to fend him off with. As he rushed forward, she stooped and snatched up a length of seaweed, snapping it like a soggy whip at his face.

The edge of it caught him in the eye and he stopped, howling in pain. But not for long. He came at her again, rubbing his eye with his left hand, his knife still steady in the right.

Solomon's opponent rolled into the fall and was up again at once, jabbing at Solomon as he regained his footing. Solomon heard Adalisa call. Desperation made him reckless. Ignoring the threat of the other's knife, he thrust his directly at the man's left side, turning it sideways in the hope of slipping between the ribs. He felt a burning along his own side at the same time as the man's face changed to astonishment, then emptiness.

Solomon's knife slid out as the body fell.

"Adalisa." He turned around, looking for her.

She was running along the shore, not following the causeway, but leading her attacker away from the others. From far out he could hear Margaret's shrill "Mama! Mama!" growing fainter as the mule carried her toward the island.

Solomon ran after Adalisa. She was ahead of the man but her skirts were tripping her up. As Solomon raced toward them, she slipped and went down. The man was on her at once. The knife glittered in the sun as he raised it.

"NO!" The sound was wrenched from Solomon's dry throat.

He leapt at the man as the knife came up again, shimmering with red.

The crash threw both men down onto Adalisa. Solomon rolled, dragging the attacker off her. Without a second thought, he grabbed the man's hair, pulled his head back and cut his throat.

Blood spurted over his arm and soaked into the wet sand. Solomon repressed the need to vomit. There wasn't time.

"Adalisa," he whispered.

She was still alive. One hand reached out to him.

"Margaret," she gasped. "Tell Catherine. Take her home with you. Waldeve mustn't . . ."

Solomon took off his tunic to staunch the flow of blood. He didn't notice that it was already drenched with his own.

"I'll get you to the monks," he told her. "They'll take care of you."

"Yes," she murmured. "I'm so cold."

The blood was pouring out of her.

"You're not going to die!" he ordered.

Her hand dropped over his as he tried to force her life back into her body.

"Solomon." Her voice was almost too faint to make out. He bent close to her face.

"Kiss me good-bye."

Without moving his hands from over the wound, Solomon pressed his lips against hers.

He felt the last spark of warmth inside her dissipate as her body went limp. Ever after Solomon believed that she had breathed her soul through him, leaving a part of it within his own. He never spoke of it to anyone, but the conviction stayed with him for the rest of his life.

He picked her up and started to follow the others across the causeway. The bodies lay behind him on the beach. As the wind shifted for a moment, he caught the smell of burning fish.

Catherine didn't need Adalisa's warning. She took the reins in her free hand and raced for safety, forcing the mule to trot after her. From behind, in between Margaret's plaintive cries for her mother, she could hear Willa panting for breath.

"Willa, can you make it?" she called.

"Y-yes," the answer came between gasps.

They were over halfway along the raised path before Catherine let them slow to a walk. She turned and saw the figures of the man grappling with Solomon and then Adalisa running. She bit her lip to keep from adding her tears to the others. There was nothing she could do. Her first duty was to the children.

"Holy Virgin Mother," she whispered. "Protect them from evil."

Then she looked down. A wave had splashed over her foot. The men had been waiting for them, not the tide. But now it was coming in.

They had no choice now but to try to reach the island as rapidly as possible.

"Willa, can you take James for a moment?" She tried to sound calm. Then she took Margaret off the mule.

"If you sit in front of Lazarus," she explained to the child, "and Willa behind him, she can hold him steady and you can grip the halter. The mule is strong enough to carry all three of you. Willa, get on. You're too tired to keep your footing on this slippery path. There, give James back to me."

They set off again. Catherine could see now that each wave came up a little higher. There was a dip in the road just ahead that was already under the sea. The icy water hit her ankles and splashed up her legs as she went through it.

It was like a nightmare, where one tries to move but can't and everything is distorted, including time. Catherine felt that they were the only beings left on earth and that soon the flood would engulf them. God was punishing the world again and they weren't going to be allowed into the ark.

Willa sat on the mule, her arms around both Lazarus and Margaret. Her head was pressed against the man's filthy tunic and she could hear his heart beating above the sound of the ocean. Like Catherine, she was too numb even to pray.

Margaret held on to the mule's scraggly mane, repeating "Mama, Mama" over and over. She didn't think she was going to a place of safety. The only refuge she had ever known was lying behind them on the beach.

As they neared the island, Catherine dared turn around to look again. She saw Solomon far behind them wading through the waves, Adalisa in his arms.

Someone from the priory had seen them and there were people just ahead, waiting to welcome them. Seeing their struggle, two of the monks waded out to help them.

"My cousin," Catherine said. "He's behind us, carrying a woman. I think she's been hurt. Please help them."

"We'll take the boat out, if they aren't here before the water reaches knee level," the monk told her. "We can't before then. We run aground."

He said something in English to the people on the shore. One boy ran off. By the time they were on solid land, a party of women were hurrying toward them, armed with woolen cloaks and a jug of spiced ale. One saw James in Catherine's arms and cried out something. Then she turned and ran back toward the village.

"What did she say?" Catherine asked Margaret.

"*Ic hæbbe cildclathas,*" Margaret said through her tears.

"No, dear, I mean in French." Catherine could see Margaret was spent. She prayed that Adalisa's injury wasn't bad. The poor child couldn't take much more.

"Oh." Margaret yawned and rubbed her eyes. "She said, 'I have some swaddling.' "

It was too much. Catherine sank to the ground, sobbing.

"You're going to be fine now," she told James. "Just fine, my sweeting. The lady has nice, dry *cildclathas* for you."

Someone took her by the shoulders and helped her up.

"*Thanc the,*" she said. "I don't have much more English."

The woman next to her just smiled and patted her cheek. Catherine decided that she had no more energy for distrust. She allowed herself, with the children and Lazarus, to be led over the barren field to the tiny cluster of houses nestled in the shelter of the priory. As they left, she looked around for the man who had spoken to her in her own language.

"My cousin?" she called to him.

"The boat is going for them. We'll not let him drown."

Catherine believed him. She was on Holy Island at last. Who here would lie to her?

Solomon felt the wetness dripping down his side, but didn't realize that it was his own blood. He understood vaguely that it was growing more difficult to walk, but it hadn't hit him that it was because the water was rising around him. Adalisa's arm swung with each step, sometimes hitting against his leg. He wanted to fold it back over her but was afraid to put her down to do it.

He suddenly remembered that today was the Sabbath. It troubled him that he was carrying something when the Law forbade it. How long had it been since he had truly observed the day of rest? There were so many rules, he couldn't remember all of them. But he knew one shouldn't carry anything. Of course, in that case, he shouldn't have had his knife. By the laws of France he should never have a weapon at all. He wondered if killing people on the Sabbath with an illegal knife was twice as bad as doing it on another day. It was something he would have to ask Uncle Eliazar about when he got home.

A rogue wave washed over him, almost knocking him over. Solomon blinked out of his stupor and shifted Adalisa so that her head rested on his shoulder again. Where was he? Why was he walking into the sea? Who were those people rowing toward him? He wondered if it were possible that he was dead and this was the road to *Sheol*.

The boat came closer. The people were calling to him, but he couldn't understand them. Finally, they drew near enough so that one man could jump out and take Adalisa from his arms. The man gave a start as he realized that she was dead, then laid her gently in the bottom of the boat. Then he pushed Solomon in as the other rower pulled. Somehow, they managed not to swamp it.

Solomon lay half-unconscious, balanced in the prow to be out of the rowers' way. He would have to tell his uncle that he could now say with certainty that the afterlife was wet and freezing cold. A puffin flew by. And remember to tell him that it had birds. He was learning all sorts of new things. A pity he was dead.

Demons had lifted him and were carrying him off. Someone was shouting. A new torment.

"That's a bad cut," it said. "We're going to have to stitch it."

"Dead people don't bleed," Solomon muttered.

"Then you must not be dead," the voice responded smugly.

Solomon thought about this. It was probably a trick. He should . . . he should . . .

Finally, consciousness deserted him.

Catherine had turned James over to the woman who had brought them to her home. She watched as her hostess unwrapped him, exclaimed over the sores and washed and oiled him with experienced hands. Margaret and Willa were seated by a fire, each wrapped in a dry blanket and holding a bowl of steaming liquid. Catherine took a few sips, enough to warm her and restore her awareness. Then she got up.

"I must see if my cousin is safe," she explained.

The woman looked at Margaret, who translated. The woman smiled and waved her out, gesturing that she would take good care of the children.

Catherine went to the priory gate. It had been left open, and in the outer court monks and lay people were milling about. She stopped the first one who came close and asked, in her faulty English, what had happened to the people taken from the sea.

To her relief, she was answered in accented, but fluent French.

"They were taken to the guest house," he told her. "You were traveling with them? Were they close to you?"

"My cousin," she answered. "My husband's stepmother. *Were?* What do you mean, 'were'?"

The man took her by the elbow and guided her through the crowd to the guest house on the other side of the court.

"I'm sorry," he told her. "I didn't mean to be so blunt. The woman was dead when we came ashore. The man is very weak and feverish, but the infirmarian thinks he has a good chance."

"Adalisa? Dead?" It was one shock too many. To the horror of her companion, Catherine fainted into his arms.

It was only through the force of his presence and the fact that his men had learned to fear him almost from the cradle that Waldeve kept them from returning to Wedderlie as soon as they heard the news about the attack. Even then, it was only because William Cumin spoke to them himself, promising to add his own troops to hunt down the marauders that they agreed to stay.

"All I ask of you is a few days," he pleaded. "Our enemies are fortifying Bishopton as I speak to you. And how do you know that it isn't the allies of Roger de Conyers who have done this? The man is capable of anything in his impious need to vanquish me. You may well be avenging your families at the same time as you protect the patrimony of Saint Cuthbert."

Edgar was astonished that the men agreed to stay so readily.

"How can they not insist on leaving at once?" he asked Æthelræd. "For all they know, their wives have been raped and their children left to starve or be devoured by wolves."

"It surprises me too," Æthelræd answered. "Some of them grumbled a bit, but none demanded the right to go. It may be that no one dares defy both Waldeve and Cumin openly. They've seen the bodies hanging from the eaves of the houses. They've heard the screams from the suspected traitors when the ropes wound around their heads were tightened until their skulls cracked. I might think twice before risking such punishment. My death would only leave my family worse off."

"I suppose." Edgar wasn't convinced. "But it seems odd to me. What use is it to fight, if there's no home to return to? All the same, there's no reason why I shouldn't go. I'm not a soldier, remember?"

"You have to stay here because this is where they will send word to you." Æthelræd sighed. How many times would he have to explain it?

"Oh, yes, if you're right and they survived." Edgar sighed in return. "Uncle, you have no idea how much I want to believe you and that's exactly why I can't."

Æthelræd shrugged. He knew when he was beaten.

"Very well," he said. "Have you told anyone that we were at Bishopton before we came here?"

"No one has asked me. Why?" Edgar answered.

"Someone is passing information. Cumin knows that the castle is being fortified," Æthelræd told him. "That's why he's so intent on attacking at once, before it becomes impossible."

Edgar looked at the cloudy sky.

"It won't be a higher motte or a deeper ditch that could stop an attack, but a good summer rainstorm," he said. "The land around Bishopton is hard now, but a downpour would turn it into mud the consistency of bean soup. Even horses would have trouble getting through. It would be amusing if the bishopric were decided in the end by an act of God."

Æthelræd didn't see the humor of it. In fact, the bitterness in Edgar's voice chilled him. Up until now Æthelræd had hoped his nephew had escaped the family penchant for turning pain into anger and lashing out at the world. But once the first horror has passed, Edgar had become too calm. It was from such serenity that Waldeve's worst violence exploded.

Fortunately, Robert interrupted them before Æthelræd's reflections became too dismal. Edgar's brother was anything but calm.

"You have to talk to the monks for me, Edgar," he insisted. "Those officious cretins won't allow me to bring Lufen to Saint Cuthbert's shrine. They say it's only for people."

"It is in a church," Æthelræd reminded him.

"Lots of the lords and bishops bring their hunting dogs to Mass with them," Robert answered. "I've seen them."

"Can't you just pray to Saint Cuthbert for Lufen's recovery?" Æthelræd suggested.

"I don't just want her to recover," Robert insisted. "I want the saint to give her back her leg. For something that big, I need to be praying right over his bones."

Æthelræd turned to Edgar for help.

"Explain to this dolt how miracles work," he said.

Edgar hadn't appeared to be listening. He looked at both his relatives.

"Miracles?" His voice was flat. "They're all a sham. Saint James gave me my son. Then just when I thought my life was perfect, he took everything away. Don't ask Saint Cuthbert. He'll give Lufen back her leg only so that she can be destroyed more horribly later."

He got up, turned and walked away from them.

Both men stared after Edgar in near horror.

"That's blasphemy!" Robert breathed. "Isn't it?"

"Even worse," Æthelræd answered. "It's despair. We'd better keep an eye on him. God, I wish Aelred were here. He could sort Edgar out for us."

Robert winced. "You'll not get him out of his cloister for anyone," he said.

Æthelræd responded without thinking. "Oh, we have already. He's at Bishopton, if he hasn't gone on to Hexham. He was very concerned that our horses had been left in his father's church, as well as worried by the troubles here at Durham."

Robert went pale. "He's where? So close?"

Æthelræd swore under his breath. How could he have forgotten? "Yes, he came with us to Bishopton. I believe he's still there."

Robert nodded slowly.

"I believe I shall ride with my father to Bishopton," he said. "I haven't been as dutiful as I should recently. I'll do as you suggest and leave Lufen in the care of the bishop's master of hounds. I can pray for her anywhere."

When he had left, Æthelræd sat for a long time with his head in his hands. Why had he ever let himself be lured out of the North and back into this most unsettling family?

Waldeve was astonished to see all three of his remaining legitimate sons at the front of the ranks of his men. It was true that Edgar carried no sword, but he wore chain mail and a helmet. The helmet was too small and perched on his head like an inverted hornet's nest. Waldeve started to laugh, then caught himself. It was the first sign of loyalty the boy had shown. No sense in discouraging him.

"Urric." He called the soldier over. "My *preostlic* son seems to have decided to fight, after all. Keep an eye on him."

"To guard him, you mean, Sir?" Urric said carefully.

"Yes, from his own clumsiness mostly," Waldeve answered, equally carefully. "He'll likely not try to wield a sword. But I don't want him left behind after the attack because he's lost his sense of direction and wandered too near the castle."

"I understand," Urric answered. "I'll not let him out of my sight."

Waldeve then turned his mind to the matter at hand. Cumin came out to give them his blessing. He was dressed in riding gear, but had decided that his presence wasn't needed at the moment. Waldeve approached him and bowed over his hand. The ring of office wasn't there but the fiction was maintained that Cumin wore it under his glove.

"How many men can we expect to meet us?" he asked.

"Earl Henry has promised fifty from his mercenaries," Cumin told him. "With my loyal barons and your men that should be more than enough to take Bishopton and destroy Conyers once and for all. My nephew will be arriving from Northallerton to meet you outside the castle walls. He'll also fend off any help Conyers might be expecting from the south."

"That should be enough to make Conyers think twice about his resistance," Waldeve said. "When we take the castle, do you want it destroyed or turned over to your nephew to hold?"

"Burn it and raze it," Cumin answered.

Waldeve forbore asking if the bishop wanted the ground sown with salt, as well. The man was obsessed with the need to annihilate all those who would deny him legal right to the see. Waldeve found this a waste of energy. However, as long as he collected the tithes of the county and took the silver from the mines, Cumin served a purpose. Whether he won or lost, Waldeve could still take his share of the booty and return to Scotland. No retribution would reach him there.

Unless. Waldeve paused. Unless it already had. All the attacks

on his family could stem from their support of William Cumin. In
that case, he could kill with even less conscience that usual. It
wouldn't be combat or slaughter, but justice.

When Urric sidled up next to him and smiled, Edgar knew exactly
why he was there. Urric had been Duncan's shadow since they had
arrived at Durham. Either his father or his brother had set their
lackey to spy on him.

Edgar smiled back. "Good day for fighting, don't you think?" he
said. "Not too hot, cloudy enough to keep the sun out of one's eyes.
I'm looking forward to it."

Urric looked him up and down.

"What are you planning on fighting with?" he asked, noting the
lack of a sword.

"I was thinking of hurling anathema down on the enemy," Edgar
answered. "Far more potent than steel."

Urric hurriedly crossed himself.

"Exactly." Edgar approved the gesture. "And the power of God
shall be my shield."

Urric stepped back from him. Edgar was either mad or possessed by divine authority. Urric didn't know which frightened him
more. This task was going to be much harder than he had foreseen.

Æthelræd came over to check on them. He was wearing his short
skirt still but had added a leather shirt on which small pieces of
metal had been sewn. He jingled as he approached. From somewhere
he had found an old, round Viking helmet. His wild red-and-grey
hair sprayed out from beneath it like a flaming bush.

"Pity we don't have any Gallowegians," he said. "I'll have to
make the first charge all alone."

Urric backed even farther. At least he had always known Æthelræd was crazy. But two of them together could cause some freakish
aberration in nature. He decided he could probably keep an eye on
Edgar from a distance.

Æthelræd noticed the soldier backing off. He gave a short laugh.

"If we terrify our own troops, just imagine what we'll do to the
enemy," he said to Edgar.

Edgar leaned closer to him and lowered his voice.

"Just who is the enemy?" he asked. "I'm planning on getting lost
in the woods on the way and getting a warning to Conyers."

"You won't be given the chance." Æthelræd nodded and smiled at Urric.

"Then how can we keep Cumin's men from taking the castle?" Edgar asked.

Æthelræd put his hand on Edgar's forehead. If the boy wasn't insane, he must be fevered.

"What made you think we could?" he asked. "It's up to Roger Conyers to protect Bishopton."

"But my father's men alone have more horses and weapons than we saw at Bishopton," Edgar said. "And if Earl Henry and William of Aumale send more, how will Conyers survive?"

Æthelræd considered.

"Perhaps we should leave that up to God," he decided.

Edgar was not disposed to rely on faith. So far it hadn't been of much use.

But at that moment it began to rain.

Fourteen

The Isle of Lindisfarne. Sunday, 15 kalends August (July 18), 1143. The sun in Leo. Feast of Saint Thanay, stubbornly unwed mother of Saint Kentigern.

Nec mora: jam tristes pœnas et pallida vexat
Gens tormenta, truces plena furore manus
Ecce! catenarum tristi plus pondere vinctos,
Qua nexu juvenes pœna timenda vocat. [sic]

Delay no longer: now grievous pain and pallor tax
The tormented people, a hand filled with mad slaughter.
Behold! The fearful penalty summons the conquered
with a sadder weight of chains than with such bonds it summons the young.

—Lawrence of Durham,
Diologues,
Book II 11 307–310

Solomon, I'm worried about Margaret." Catherine nudged her cousin out of his doze. "I know that she needs to grieve for her mother but she isn't eating and her sleep is full of monsters. Can you think of anything we can do to help her?"

Catherine was worried about Solomon, too. The knife cut had been a clean one and was healing well. That couldn't be the problem. Something had happened to him that she didn't understand, something to do with Adalisa. It wasn't just guilt at being unable to save her. He had sat vigil by her body as if he had been family and had stood outside the priory church door with his head bowed all the while the funeral Mass was being said. It seemed as if something inside him had broken; not a vital part, but a piece that helped him keep his distance from the alien world in which he must survive.

Margaret sensed that he shared her loss and it was to Solomon that she ran for comfort. The two of them took long walks, round and round the edge of the small island, looking at the birds and talking. Sometimes they would just sit by Adalisa's grave in the village cemetery, Margaret leaning against Solomon and the two of them looking out to sea as if waiting for a traveler to come home to them.

Catherine was saddened by Adalisa's death, but try as she might, she couldn't grieve for her. It was inexcusable that she felt so little. What was the matter with her?

Finally it came to Catherine that part of her was glad that Edgar's stepmother was free of her own sorrow. In this world the best hope she could have had was to become a widow, but then she and her dower would have been prey for someone just as cruel to her as Waldeve had been.

Solomon hadn't answered. She nudged him with both hands this time.

"Solomon?" she said again. "What can we do for Margaret?"

At last he noticed that she was in the room.

"Give her time," he answered. "She has no one now to care for her."

"She has us," Catherine answered without thinking. "We won't desert her, will we?"

Solomon looked at her with a flash of his old self.

"Never," he said. "She's not going back to her father. I don't care if I have to abduct her to do it."

"I'm sure we can find a safer way!" Catherine was alarmed. He sounded as though he would really do it. The very idea was horrifying. A Jewish man stealing away a Christian girl, even with her permission! Solomon would be lucky if he were merely hanged.

"I promised her mother that the child would never be returned to Waldeve," Solomon said. "I won't break faith. Adalisa suffered enough without having to worry about Margaret from beyond the grave."

"Yes, she did." Catherine knew she was treading near an open wound, but wasn't sure where it lay. "And we couldn't help her. But there must be something we can do now for her child."

Solomon got up. "Let Margaret know we care. There's nothing else possible. This kind of pain only heals from within."

That closed the door on that topic. But it didn't stop Catherine from wondering. Just what had happened between Adalisa and Solomon? She knew her cousin's charm worked on Christian women as well as Jewish, but she assumed it was always women who weren't . . . women who tended to . . . not someone like . . . oh, dear! She supposed that, after all, Adalisa might be even more susceptible than beer brewers and innkeepers' daughters. Poor thing! And was Solomon grieving because he'd taken advantage of her loneliness or because he hadn't?

"Do you really think that's your concern, child?"

Ah, it must be the influence of the nearby monastery. Those voices sounded most righteous regarding her unchristian thoughts. Catherine went on to ask Solomon to help with her next problem.

"The prior doesn't seem concerned that the man he sent to tell Edgar we were safe hasn't returned, yet. But it's been two weeks. Don't you think we should send someone else?"

Solomon was standing by the window to the hostel. It looked out onto the North Sea. Even in calm weather, the waves frightened Catherine. On the softest of days, the sea off Holy Island always seemed menacing. The wind roared over the water, creating a turbulence that increased as it hit the shore. Not even trees could withstand it and there were few on the island, all tucked into sheltered corners. Catherine had never lived in a place where one could see so far. In a way, it was comforting, after all they'd been through. One could see an enemy approaching. But an enemy could also see her.

Solomon took a while to answer her last question. It was as if he needed to recall his spirit to his body each time he had to interact with another person. Catherine was trying to be patient, but it had never been one of her virtues. "Do you want me to go look for Edgar?" he asked at last.

"Well." She paused. "You did say that was your plan. That is, if you're strong enough."

"My health isn't the problem," he answered. "It's the fact that this evil seems to be following us despite my attempts to convince everyone that we were all killed in the fire. Now I think we should stay together. I don't want to leave you and the children unprotected."

"We're as safe here as we're likely to be anywhere in Britain," she argued. "Solomon, I'm not worried about us anymore, it's Edgar. There are people who seem determined to murder everyone in his family. He may not know about the fire or the trap set in Robert's garden. Or, even worse, he may and not know that we escaped. Do you want him to believe that all of us are dead?"

"Of course not," Solomon said. "But neither do I want him to find that you've been attacked again while I was out searching for him."

Catherine's whole body tightened in frustration. She wanted to hit something. Solomon was the obvious target. But she knew his reasoning was accurate. It wasn't fair to take her anger out on him. She compromised by stamping her foot.

"I can't stand this!" she shouted. "There must be a way! Oh, Solomon, I don't care what these people do to each other. I just want to find Edgar and go home!"

She burst into tears. Solomon put his arms around her.

"I know, Catherine," he said patting her back ineffectually. "I wish I could make it happen."

He also wished he knew what was happening at home. There had been no messages from Hubert or Eliazar. It was entirely possible that Paris was as dangerous for them as Scotland had turned out to be. Then where could they go?

"Why don't we bundle James up and take Willa and Margaret down to the other end of the island," he suggested. "We can watch the sea birds fighting over their catch. Perhaps we'll even see a puffin."

Catherine sniffed and tried to smile. Solomon thought her attraction to the silly-looking birds was bizarre. She had never seen one before this journey and had found their oversized beaks and quizzical eyes endlessly droll.

"All right," she agreed. "But if we don't have word of Edgar soon, I intend to wrap up James and set out to look for him, myself."

Edgar was feeling much the same. But he had no idea where to start looking. In the meantime, he had become trapped amidst the soldiers trying to take Roger Conyers's castle at Bishopton.

If they had started a day sooner, they might have had a chance. But two nights of torrential rain had made the countryside a bog for miles around. Progress was slow. Solid ground turned to marsh at a misstep and horses had to be pulled from the mud. When the defenders came forth to engage Cumin's men, they found that there was no place where either party could stand long enough to fight.

Cumin had decided on a siege, counting on the men being sent by Earl Henry of Huntington to augment his forces before long. It wasn't a popular decision. Many of the men only owed a few weeks service and wanted to go home and tend to their crops. Waldeve's troop was kept from deserting only by his threats of what would happen to those who did when he returned to Wedderlie.

However, it was the state of their souls that worried the soldiers most. Word was out now that a new bishop had been consecrated. Cumin had no hope of ever gaining the see of Durham. He had been officially excommunicated and his benefice at Winchester taken away. There were also rumors of his ill-treatment of the canons still left in the cathedral cloister.

"It's one thing to torture a man for his money," Edgar overheard someone say. "But forcing a priest to say Mass at knifepoint, that's the sort of thing that brings down fire and pestilence on a land. I want no part of it."

Edgar agreed. Even the officious Brother Lawrence didn't deserve to be so used. Of course, he thought with a smirk, this would be the canon's chance for martyrdom. Not many were able to have that these days without going on an arduous journey to the Saracen lands.

Now where had that come from? Edgar scratched his head. It was just the sort of comment Catherine would make.

The pain that hit him was worse than any sword could make. He didn't want to remember her laughing, teasing him, making fun of the pompous clerics in the schools of Paris. One memory like that just led to another and another, until they came crowding in, demanding his attention, reminding him of all he had lost forever.

It made him seriously doubt the mercy of God.

The mud under his boots was thick with leaves and broken plants. People didn't walk so much as slide. All their clothing was caked with the stuff. This was the glory of battle that the *scops* always sang about? Edgar made his way through the encampment and finally reached the place where Robert had set up his lean-to.

"Sit down, Brother," he greeted Edgar. "Any spot will do. They're all equally wet."

Edgar sat and Robert handed him a mug from which steam was rising. Edgar sniffed.

"What is this stuff?" he asked, wrinkling his nose.

"Some herbal concoction," Robert told him. "A woman down the road makes it. Suppose to keep away creeping fungus."

Edgar put the mug down. "I don't doubt it. Are you sure it's supposed to be drunk? It might be better just rubbed into leather."

"Hmm . . ." Robert took the mug back. "Maybe she did say that's what you did with it after it was heated."

Edgar grimaced. "If you're back to playing tricks on me then Lufen must be better."

Robert smiled. "The keeper of hounds sent word that she's up and eating well and that the other dogs haven't set on her, even though she's weak and crippled. I'd like to see a pack of humans behave so."

"Is that why you spend more time with dogs than people?" Edgar asked.

Robert's smile vanished. "No dog has ever betrayed or abandoned me," he said. "Do you think Aelred is still inside the castle?"

Edgar understood that the question wasn't a change of subject.

"So I've heard," he said. "He's waiting for William of Saint-

Barbe to arrive to take over the bishopric. Aelred will represent the abbey of Rievaulx at the welcoming ceremony."

"It will be an interesting ceremony," Robert said. "With the clergy all in mail shirts under their copes. Even if Cumin can't take the castle, he can keep Saint-Barbe from getting in to the cathedral. Durham is one of the strongest fortresses in England."

"Robert." Edgar moved closer. "Do you really care who wins this? Does it matter to you who the bishop is?"

"Of course not," Robert answered. "I'm here now only because it's just possible that the gate to the castle might open and the bridge come down and Aelred walk across it and greet me as he used to when we were . . . friends."

"That I understand," Edgar admitted. "It made no sense to me that you stayed even under Father's threats. I only wish I thought Catherine and James would appear in the same way."

Robert looked at him quickly and then looked away.

"I'm sorry," he said. "I forgot."

Edgar shook his head. How could anyone who had known them forget? It was amazing to him that the sun hadn't turned black and gone out. He sighed at his brother and left him to his vigil. Waldeve should put Robert on the watch since he spent all his time staring at the gate anyway.

Edgar stopped. Damn. Would he spend the rest of his life thinking of things that Catherine might have said?

If so, he hoped the time would be short.

Catherine's hair blew across her eyes. She tried to tuck it into her hood but it always escaped. Willa and Margaret had hair that obeyed. Willa's deep brown braids and Margaret's red-gold ones swung as they walked together ahead of Solomon and Catherine. Solomon had taken James and was singing to him as they walked.

"What is that?" Catherine asked him. "It sounds so mournful."

"Just an old Hebrew song," Solomon said. "Aunt Johanna used to sing it to me and I think my mother did too, before she died."

"What does it mean?"

Solomon covered James's head from the wind, but the baby seemed to like it. He shut his eyes from the force of it, but he was gurgling happily at the feel of the breeze on his face.

"I am my beloved's and he is mine," Solomon said, looking away from her.

It was a full minute before Catherine started laughing. "They sang you the Song of Solomon!" she gasped. "No wonder you grew up to be so arrogant."

"I am not!" he protested. "Just because I don't let you get away with your nonsensical logic when we argue!"

She laughed again. That was better. The old Solomon was creeping out from the cave of misery he had hidden in. Now if Edgar would only come home to them, they might start repairing their lives.

They climbed out of one of the hollows in the rolling land. Catherine glanced across the island and stopped short, frozen in terror.

"Saint Felicity's seven sons!" she exclaimed, pointing at the edge of the stone hill at the north end of the island. "It's followed us here! Solomon! Look! Over there! It's the monster I saw!"

Solomon was fussing with James's wrapping, which were going from damp to sodden. "Of course, Catherine, monsters."

Willa screamed. Solomon looked up. He saw what Catherine was pointing at.

"What in hell is that thing?" he said.

It seemed to be a huge brown beast with wide-swinging arms and a dozen legs. It had a long tail dragging behind and, as they watched, two men popped out from under the monster and detached it, following behind with the tail now over their shoulders.

Solomon turned to Catherine. "This is what you saw?"

"In the mist I couldn't see that the legs were human," Catherine protested. "Even if I had, I might have believed it to be some demon. What would you have thought?"

Solomon studied the contraption that the men were apparently trying to set up. He had to admit that it could be mistaken for some crude dragon costume.

Up until now, Margaret had said nothing. Since the death of her mother, she hadn't appeared to notice anything happening around her. Now she spoke up.

"It's a secret," she said. "You mustn't tell."

"Hell of a big secret," Solomon said, looking at the monstrosity.

"Margaret, what do you mean?" Catherine asked.

"I'm sorry." The child twisted nervously. "I promised Alfred and the other people in the village that I wouldn't tell anyone. I swore on my Saint Cuddy's feather! They were very angry with me."

"Margaret—" Catherine began, but Solomon interrupted.

"If we ask the men what they're doing and you translate," he suggested, "that won't violate your oath, will it?"

Margaret didn't think so. So they all followed the "monster" as it moved up the hill and stopped at the top, where a thick log had been buried upright in the ground and secured with three wooden legs also sunk into the soft earth. Catherine had noticed the post before and wondered if it were for a cross to be erected on holy days.

The men noticed them watching. One of them gestured for them to come closer.

"Ask him what it is they're building, Margaret," Catherine said.

"Oh, I know already," Margaret answered. "It's a windmill."

"A what?"

"It's a mill for grinding flour, but instead of being pushed by the water, it's pushed by the wind," she explained. "The man wants to show you how it works."

"He doesn't seem to think it's a secret," Catherine said.

"No," Margaret agreed. "I wonder why not. Alfred was very clear that I mustn't say anything to anyone about the one at Wedderlie."

The man was practically dancing in his eagerness to demonstrate the wondrous new machine. The others had removed the canvas over the thing and now Catherine saw that it was a small house, only large enough for one or two people to stand in. Attached to it were four long arms, with lengths of greased cloth nailed to each. With much effort and several near-disasters, the men managed to perch the house on the top of the pole in a hole designed for it.

The wind had caught the arms before the house was even in place. But it wasn't until the tail was reattached and one of the men turned it slowly into the wind, that Catherine saw what an amazing thing it was.

"My goodness," she said. "It's like a bird or a ship, flying on the air. And there are wheels inside and a quern to grind grain?"

Solomon was staring in openmouthed astonishment.

"You can hear the millstones turning, even through the noise of the sails," he said. "This is fantastic! Where did it come from?"

Margaret asked the man who seemed to be in charge.

"He says," she told them, "that it's a southern invention, from east of London. It's new. The farmers there built one because they lived too far from . . ." She paused and asked the man to explain again. "A reliable source of swift water," she concluded.

"Amazing." Solomon couldn't take his eyes off it.

"Edgar should be here to see this," Catherine said. "He loves machines."

"It doesn't seem very stable, though," Solomon commented. "If the wind catches it from the wrong side, the whole thing will go over. I don't think it has much of a future."

"I still don't understand why the peasants at Wedderlie wanted to hide this," Catherine was getting dizzy from watching the arms spin. "I see now that this is what flattened the grass on the side of the road there. But they couldn't have gotten it down that narrow path on the other side. Where did they take it?"

She looked at Margaret, who tightened her lips and shook her head. Her eyes were frightened. Catherine knelt by her.

"You mustn't break an oath," she told the girl. "I would never ask it of you. It doesn't matter, anyway. I was just curious."

"Are you sorry it wasn't a demon?" Margaret asked.

"Of course not," Catherine said. "I'm relieved, of course. Why do you ask?"

Margaret fiddled with her braid. "I used to dream that a great dragon would come and lay waste all the countryside and then Mama and I would fly off on its back to the Western Isles, where it's always summer and no one shouts at anyone. I guessed the windmill was your monster but I was hoping for the dragon."

This came out as a confession. Catherine wasn't sure how to respond. Solomon did it for her.

"I know about that dragon," he told her. "I spent many a night in Paris listening for the sound of its wings swooping through the air. This mill sounds much like I imagined it would. A pity that it grinds flour instead of taking us to magic countries."

Willa had not said a word since they had seen the mill. When it was set up, she had walked around it at a safe distance, and then sat down to study it more intently. Now she got up, brushed off her skirts and held out her arms for the baby.

"It's just a machine, after all," she said sadly. "It doesn't even have a heart. I thought it might be a magical mill that a brave knight had stolen from the elves. But it isn't even very well put together. Oh well, let's go back."

Catherine would rather have stayed and learned more so she could explain it all to Edgar, but James was in danger of floating away in his swaddling, so she followed the others back to the priory.

There was still no message waiting for them when they returned. Only one of the monks, a Brother Hugh, greeted them. From the day they first arrived, he had taken the care of Lazarus on himself, teaching the poor prisoner how to sleep in a bed and eat with a spoon and a hundred other things he had forgotten in his captivity. Or perhaps, things he had never known.

"Your companion is growing stronger." He greeted them. "He may be able to walk soon. He learns quickly and seems almost to understand my speech."

"Thank you, Brother Hugh," Catherine said. "He's said nothing, himself, though?"

"Not a word," the monk said. "But he does make noise when he's startled so he's not completely dumb. Perhaps he doesn't want to speak, yet. He must have endured a long time in dark silence."

"I'm afraid so," Catherine said. "Where is he now?"

"I left him on the grass by the church," Brother Hugh told her. "You can hear the brothers singing Tierce now. I should be with them, but I wanted to wait until you came back. He seems to like our attempts at music."

"So do I," Catherine said. She wished she could join them as well. The familiar psalms were comforting and reminded her of the days at the Paraclete. She had been eager to leave with Edgar and didn't regret her choice. But sometimes she wished for the guidance of Mother Heloise and even of the termagant Sister Bertrada. The responsibility for the lives in her care was weighing on her almost as much as her worry for Edgar.

"I don't wish to keep you from your devotions," she said, "but do you know if anyone has arrived with a message for us?"

Brother Hugh shook his head. "But the tide is going out now. Perhaps word will come when the road is safe again."

"Yes, of course." Catherine could see that he was more concerned with missing singing the Office. He smiled an apology and hurried off.

Catherine left Willa to attend to James and went over to where Lazarus sat in the lee of the church, squinting at the light. She knelt down beside him.

"You need your hat." She looked around for it, and Lazarus fussed at the cord as she put it on him.

"No, don't take it off." Catherine gently moved his hands away. "Your skin is too pale to stand the sun. You don't want to get a fever from it, do you?"

She peered into his eyes for some sign that he understood. Was it her imagination or was there a flicker of comprehension there? It vanished so quickly that she wasn't sure.

"Lazarus?" she said. "Do you know who you really are?"

There was no answer. He seemed to have become enraptured by the tiny white flowers in the grass. He lay full length to brush his cheek against them. Catherine picked one and gave it to him. He sat up, took it in his hand and folded his fingers over it. When he opened them, it was crushed and broken. He looked at it a moment, then closed his eyes and dropped it back onto the earth. Then he returned to his supine position and went back to caressing the growing plants.

Catherine gave up. Perhaps Brother Hugh could find a way into Lazarus's lost soul. She hadn't a clue how to reach him.

Willa brought the baby back to her.

"I only swaddled him from the waist down," she said. "He seemed to want to move his hands about. And it's warm enough if we stay out of the wind."

Catherine took him gratefully. At least most of the time James was easy to decipher. Feed him, burp him, change him and cuddle him. The only mystery was how someone so perfect could have come from her. She looked down into Edgar's grey eyes and felt tears start again.

That wouldn't do; she sniffed them into submission. Edgar would find them and they would all go home together. Everything would be all right.

"*And what of Margaret?*" Her voices intruded. "*And what will become of Lazarus?*"

How did they always know when she was thinking selfishly? Catherine saw that Margaret was with Solomon again and Lazarus had gone to sleep, a daisy against his nose. For now, they were safe, because she and Solomon had brought them this far. No, she couldn't abandon them now. Edgar wouldn't want her to.

But she wished someone would send her a revelation, for she had no idea what to do next.

The ebbing of the tide brought no messenger. This was too much for Catherine. Everyone had told her that the journey to

Durham was only two or three days, even on foot. The man had had time to reach Edgar and be back many times over. And there was nothing she could do but plead with the prior to send someone else.

Waiting only soured her disposition even more. She snapped at Willa and was rewarded by an increased feeling of guilt from the hurt in the girl's eyes. James became fretful again and she was sure the frustration had soured her milk, as well.

"Why don't you ask if you can use the priory library?" Solomon suggested when she had annoyed him thoroughly with her pacing. "Perhaps you can find a collection of sermons on bearing one's trials with fortitude."

Catherine didn't think it likely that she would be permitted to rummage through the scrolls and codices but Solomon was insistent that she needed something to distract her. She asked Brother Hugh if the prior would see her.

In her borrowed clothing, she appeared more a kitchen maid than a scholar but the English prior had already noticed that she preferred speaking with him in Latin rather than endure his ungrammatical French.

"All the books are kept in a closet next to my chamber," he explained. "And that would not be appropriate for you to visit. However"—he raised his hand to forestall her protest—"I can allow Brother Hugh to bring you something to read in the guest house."

"That would be wonderful." Catherine hadn't realized how much she had missed the pleasure of the written word. "Do you have Bede's history? I've only read his commentaries. I'd like to learn more about the past of this region. There's so much I don't know."

The request pleased the Englishman a great deal, and to the relief of everyone, Catherine now spent her afternoons poring over the codex in search of anything that might make the actions of her husband's family clearer to her.

Out of curiosity, Solomon used the empty time to watch the men in their struggles with the windmill. While he admitted that the idea was intriguing, the problems of construction seemed insurmountable. He supposed that a mill that could be set up anywhere the wind blew would be beneficial, if it could be made to work. But how could man expect to catch the wind and train it, as one did with weirs and dams on the rivers?

The builders didn't share his concern. When the greased cloth of the sails tore, they patiently mended it. They hauled the heavy box and clumsy arms across the island every morning, and each time they had made small adjustments and improvements, stronger supports, a better fitting for the long pole that turned the mill on its post until the great sails began to spin, a slight angling of the sails themselves so that they turned even more rapidly.

"They really believe that this will be as useful as a water mill?" he asked Margaret one day as the sail had knocked one of the builders flat as they were positioning the box.

"They say so," Margaret answered. "The people of Wedderlie seemed to think it would be even better."

"But they have all the water power they need." Solomon puzzled. "Why bother with something so clumsy and uncertain?"

Then his merchant's mind woke to the situation and he realized both why the villagers might bother and why it had to be such a deep secret.

Mills were always the property of the lord. Not only did the peasants pay a tithe of every bag of flour ground, they were also at the mercy of a ruler who could close the mill or forbid them to use it.

A windmill that could be put up by anyone, anywhere, was as dangerous to the order of society as armed revolt.

Fifteen

Near Bishopton. Sunday, the kalends August (August 1), 1143. Feast of Saint Ethelwold, builder, bishop, translator and fairly good cook.

Innocentius e.s.s.D. dilecto in Christo filio David illustri regii Scottorum s.e.a.b. Nobilitatem tuam ignorare non credimus quod Dunelmensis ecclesia pro invasions W. Cumin plurimum est gravata et tam in temporalibus quam in spiritualibus imminuta, unde tam ipse quam complices sui exommunicationis sunt vincula innodati. . . .

Innocent, bishop, servant of the servants of God, to his beloved son in Christ, David, illustrious king of the Scots, salutations and benedictions. We don't believe your nobility to be unaware that the church of Durham is oppressed by the many invasions of W. Cumin and as diminished in the world as well as in the spirit that he and his cohorts are overwhelmed by the chains of excommunication.

—letter of Pope Innocent I to
King David, c. spring 1143

We're never going to take that damned fortress," Duncan complained to his father. "There are as many defenders outside as in. My own brothers would be conspiring with the traitors if our men weren't watching them so closely."

"Your brothers don't worry me. Edgar is so sunk in grief he longs for death and Robert is only here so that I won't take away the little land he has." Waldeve chewed one end of his drooping mustache, a sure sign of perturbation. "Conyers has done a good piece of work," he admitted. "A dozen men could hold Bishopton keep against an army. When we rebuild Wedderlie, I'll see that the ditch around the motte is deeper, maybe even divert the river to fill it."

"Better to plant brambles at the bottom," Duncan suggested. "We can shoot invaders from above while they're stuck in the thicket."

He let Waldeve think on this for a moment, then added casually, "Do you think you can rebuild the keep before winter? It's getting late in the year to start something like that."

His father understood what he was getting at. "I'll rebuild whenever I've a mind to and damn the weather. Don't think you'll be rid of your obligation to me for some time yet. I haven't forgotten what's been done to us. I'm not returning until I find the people responsible for all these atrocities against me and punish them with my own hands," he said firmly. "Somewhere, someone is mocking me for my inability to protect what's mine. No man may do that and live. The only way you can get me to leave Durham is by finding the bastards and setting me on them."

Duncan was afraid of that. Having Waldeve around lessened his authority with his own men. How could he issue orders with any confidence if his father was at his shoulder, telling him loudly to do something else? Just because the stolen horses had been left at Hexham didn't mean that the criminals were in the lands of Saint Cuthbert. He suspected that the old man was here mainly because there was fighting and he could hit someone who would hit back. Not having an identifiable opponent was driving him mad.

In spite of his annoyance, Duncan smiled.

"Have you considered that your enemy may not be human?" he asked. "Why else would no one at Wedderlie recognize those who burned the keep? It would also explain why nothing was taken from the bodies of my brothers and nephew, and even why the horses were returned shorn."

Waldeve looked at him in disgust. "What do you think it is then? Elves and demons? *Orcneas?* Pagan nonsense!"

Duncan stood his ground. "Everyone knows that there are demons, Father. And half the men here are sick from elf-shot after camping in this misbegotten marsh. You can't deny the evidence of your own eyes. I think it's the only logical answer."

Waldeve's eyes narrowed in thought. "No, I don't believe it. I've done nothing to anger the old gods. I left the pagan stones standing even when Bishop Rannulf told me to tear them down." He paused. "I've had too many good nights out there at midsummer not to appreciate their use. Come to think of it, so did he, the hypocrite."

"And what if someone has bound the old spirits to themselves in order to gain your destruction?" Duncan would not be put off. "Then you might never see the man responsible, only the results of his minions' work."

Waldeve appeared to waver. Then he shook his head.

"There's human evil behind this," he insisted. "And I'll find the human hand responsible."

He glared at Duncan defiantly, letting him know that not even his own family was above suspicion. Duncan knew that quite well. Distrust was the first thing he had learned from his father's example. Keeping his rage in check was the second. The former had kept him alive and the latter had made him strong. More so than Waldeve would ever be. Duncan prayed every night that the next death in the family would be Waldeve's. He considered it his primary filial duty.

If the old man would just die, then there would be nothing to stop him.

∞

Edgar had gone back to Durham, leaving Robert to continue his fruitless vigil of the gate at Bishopton.

Each day the impact of his loss had grown stronger. He had tried to believe Æthelræd's insistence that James and Margaret, at least, had survived, but as the days passed and no word came of them, he had given up even that slim hope.

After the first shock had worn off, leaving raw pain, he had thought of going back to Paris. Some part of him believed that he would find Catherine there, waiting for him to start work on their rooms in Hubert's house. Then it came to him that this was impossible. He was forced to imagine facing his father-in-law with the news that all those who had been entrusted to his care were gone. And it wouldn't be just Hubert. He would have to tell Samonie that Willa had died with Catherine and James. And the thought of confessing to Eliazar and Johanna that the nephew they had raised from a baby had been killed for a family that wasn't even his in a feud he had no part of, that was too much. Solomon shouldn't have died because Edgar hadn't been there to protect his own. No, there was no longer a home for him in Paris. So where?

Edgar stood in the great cathedral, the solid stone pillars holding the ceiling so high above him that the tops were lost in the shadows. He leaned against one. The summer heat hadn't penetrated the building, and the granite was cold enough to feel through his tunic. He wished it would freeze him entirely until there was no feeling left.

Now that Cumin was keeping the monks under strict guard, the place was empty between the Offices. Edgar was alone in the immense church surrounded by all the saints of Durham: Cuthbert who held all the land between the rivers Tyne and Tees in his protection. In the tomb with him was the head of the martyr king, Saint Oswald. There was the body of Ethilwald of Farne and another head, that of King Ceolwulf, to whom Bede dedicated his monumental *Ecclesiastical History*, and then there was the Venerable Bede, himself, brought to rest here at Durham with the other saints of the region by Aelred's priestly grandfather, Alfred Westow.

Edgar had been taught all their life stories when he was a student here. Their courage and holiness were meant to be examples to the boys. But, try as he might, Edgar couldn't remember one among them who had been asked to bear such a loss as his. What sort of comfort could they give?

And yet the stillness of the place and the sense of being removed from the outside world did ease Edgar's grief a little. The proximity of the saints was oddly soothing and helped him to the resolution that had been growing in him since the horrible news had come.

As soon as the siege was lifted he would go to Aelred and ask him to speak to the abbot about letting him become a novice at Rievaulx. Perhaps it was cowardly to flee the world, but all he wanted now was to prepare himself to join those he loved.

At least, among the Cistercians his gift for carving wood and working in metal would be welcomed instead of scorned.

Edgar looked up at the diffuse light from the clerestory windows. He remembered the day he had given Catherine her ivory cross and admitted he had made it himself. Her reaction had been pride in his skill, the first time anyone had told him such a thing. She wore it constantly. He wondered where it was now.

"Everything I do and make from now on will be for you," he vowed. "For the good of your soul and the remission of your sins."

Although, at this point he had forgotten that she might have had any. The very human Catherine was in danger of becoming a saint in his memory.

At the same time that Edgar sat alone, wallowing in murky despair, an exhausted, wounded lay brother of Lindisfarne was climbing the hill to the bishop's palace. He had been set upon by brigands and robbed of all he possessed, including his clothes. They had clouted him on the head and left him for the wolves but he had been rescued by a man gathering wood. The man had balanced poor Brother Clarence on top of his handcart and taken him to his hut, where the lay brother had slowly regained first his health and then his memory.

The importance of the message entrusted to him had been impressed on Brother Clarence, and so instead of returning to Holy Island, he had borrowed tunic and trews from the peasant as soon as he was fit to travel and set off to complete his mission.

The only official at the palace was Archdeacon Ralph, one of the few clerics who supported William Cumin. Clarence was unable to convince the guards to let him see anyone in authority. His clothes and bandaged head made them think he was some beggar or simpleton. They gave him bread and drove him away.

Still slightly addled from his injury, Brother Clarence didn't know what to do next. He drifted toward the cathedral because it was familiar. He heard the first notes of Vespers beginning and followed them. Many times he had been allowed to leave his work and stand in the priory church to add his silent prayers to the melodic ones of the monks. Surely someone there would tell him what his next course of action should be.

The monks were all on the other side of the altar, where the laity wasn't permitted to go. Brother Clarence composed himself to wait until the Office was over. There was only one other worshipper in the church, a poor exhausted pilgrim, by the looks of him. He had fallen asleep at the base of one of the columns, his head on his knees. Clarence thought he looked terribly uncomfortable.

"Goodman?" He touched the man's shoulder. "May I help you?"

The man's head flew up and Clarence realized that he hadn't been asleep, but crying. He had interrupted someone's private act of atonement.

"I'm so sorry!" He backed away.

Edgar wiped his eyes with his sleeve. He noted the bandage Brother Clarence wore.

"Are you looking for the leech?" he asked.

"No, I . . . I don't know." Brother Clarence felt his head. "I'm fine. Can ye tell me where to find the lord of Wedderlie?"

"What?"

Edgar stood so quickly that his head spun. Clarence realized too late how odd his question had sounded. Edgar grabbed his shoulders.

"Lord Waldeve is my father," he said. "What do you want of him?"

"A message, Lord, only that!" Clarence's voice rose over the chanting. "The prior of Holy Island sent me to tell him that his family has found refuge with us."

"What?" This came from Edgar as a croak. "Who? Which ones?"

"It was all written on a paper the prior gave me," Clarence said. "The thieves took it with my clothes. But I saw them, a woman and two men, two girls and a baby. There was another woman, but she was killed. I helped dig her grave."

The leaps and plunges from hope to despair were keeping Edgar from regaining his balance. He leaned against the solid pillar again as he asked, slowly and carefully, "The woman who lives, do you know her name? Can you describe her?"

"Oh, yes." Clarence was eager to help. "I didn't hear her name, but she's dark, like an Italian. The man is, too. I think he's her brother."

"Cousin," Edgar whispered. "He's her cousin."

Without realizing it, he had slid down the pillar and was sitting on the floor. He looked up at the lay brother.

"They were all well when you left?"

"Yes, Lord, except the woman we buried, of course."

Edgar's head felt back with a thunk against the stone. Æthelræd had known all along. They were alive and in a safe place. He could go to them now without waiting to die. The wonder of it rolled over him like a giant wave and he felt robbed of breath and sense.

Clarence bent over him. "Will you take me to your father, then? I'm to wait for an answer."

Edgar let the lay brother help him to his feet.

"There's no need to find him," he said. "The message was for me. And you don't need to take an answer. I'm coming back with you to deliver it myself."

Catherine was sharing James's afternoon nap when the messenger arrived. She lay on her side with the baby cradled in the arc of her body. In his new little tunics, he seemed to have changed, grown. They had wrapped the swaddling around his waist and up between his legs and he was fascinated by the sight and feel of his newly revealed toes. He had wakened before her and was happily waving them in the air when Willa came in with the news.

She shook Catherine gently.

"Mistress, a man has come from Lord Waldeve with news of Master Edgar."

Catherine was awake and standing before she finished the sentence.

"Is he all right?" she asked.

She rushed out to the courtyard where a strange soldier was talking with one of the monks. He looked from her to the baby on her hip.

"Yes, you'd be the one," he said. "Lady Catherine?"

"Yes," she answered. "My husband, is he well?"

"Fine when I left," the man told her. "He is greatly relieved to know that you survived the fire and wants you to join him at Durham as soon as possible."

"Let me get my shoes on," Catherine said.

The messenger blinked. "I'm sure you have other things to pre-pare," he said. "But I can be ready to accompany you by the first low tide tomorrow."

"Tomorrow," Catherine said. "I suppose I can wait that long. Did he say why he wanted us to come to him? I'd have thought he'd return with you. He is all right?"

"Oh, yes," the man said. "But he's needed to help Bishop William in his battle against Lord Roger. He said you'd be safer from your enemies in the fortress at Durham."

"Yes, I suppose so," Catherine was doubtful.

Just then she saw Solomon and Margaret coming back from their walk. She beckoned to them to join her.

"Solomon, this man has come from Edgar," she explained. "He wants us to meet him at Durham. We leave tomorrow."

Solomon looked doubtfully at the messenger. He was dressed as a foot soldier with a rough leather vest and cap as his only armor. His French was Norman with an English overlay so that his speech was hard to follow. He was a head taller than Solomon and well muscled. The man could probably protect Catherine and the children as well as anyone, but he would also be a formidable opponent if Solomon were forced to confront him.

"I don't understand," he told the man. "Why does Edgar want us at Durham, where there's open warfare? Perhaps I should go back with you, alone, and ask him myself."

The man shrugged. "If you insist, Lord, but my instructions were clear. He said something about wanting to go on from there to York and thence to the coast and France."

"Home!" Catherine's eyes lit.

Solomon was still unconvinced. "Did he give you a written mes-sage or a token so that we know you really come from him?"

"He gave me no paper," the soldier said. "We were in the marsh when the man you sent found us. I was pulled from my post and told to come fetch you."

"Who told you?" Solomon asked sharply.

"Lord Edgar." The man was becoming angry. "I know him well enough. He said, 'Bring them back at once. I've had enough of this. I'm taking them home.' "

Catherine looked at Solomon. He raised his hands in doubt.

"My cousin and I need to discuss this," she told the man. "I'm sure you want to rest from your journey. We'll let you know what we decide."

When the messenger had left, Solomon took Catherine's arm and guided her well away from the buildings and any eavesdroppers.

"The words sound like his," he said. "But it doesn't feel right. Why didn't Brother Clarence come back? Why didn't Edgar come? I'd think his first impulse would be to see you and assure himself that you really were safe."

"His father may have prevented that," Catherine was torn between caution and desire.

"No, Catherine." Solomon had made his decision. "We can't take the risk. We're in a foreign country where most of the people don't speak our language. We know little of the customs. I want to send the man back to Durham with another message from you, in your own hand. Write it in Latin. Tell Edgar that you're safe here and will only leave when he comes for you."

Catherine considered this. It might annoy Edgar, but more likely he would understand her reluctance to trust their lives to a stranger.

"Yes, you're right," she said. "I miss Edgar so terribly that I wasn't thinking clearly. Thank you, Cousin."

The man wasn't happy with this decision. He pleaded that it would go hard with him if he returned without them.

"Not if you give my husband this note," Catherine assured him. "The monks here have kindly offered us a refuge. We shall remain in it until he comes to take us back to France."

There was nothing the messenger could do but take the letter and leave, which he did at once and with bad grace.

"We did the right thing," Solomon said as the man threw a last curse at them as he rode away.

"Yes, I'm sure we did," Catherine answered. "But I'm even more worried than before. We still don't know if Edgar is alive and well. We don't know if he knows that we are the same, and even worse, we have no idea who else may have sent this man or why."

Solomon put his arm around her. "That seems an accurate summation of the situation. And I say, when you don't know which way to jump, it's best to stay put as long as the ground beneath your feet remains."

"Considering the nature of this island, that may not be long." Catherine watched the sea roll over the road the messenger had just crossed, cutting them off from the rest of Britain. She would be quite happy to have it remain so, if only Edgar were safe on this side of the water.

Edgar was facing his own frustrations. His uncle had found him in his tent as he was making preparations to go to Lindisfarne. His first mistake had been in telling Æthelræd that he had been right all along.

"Holy Island? Best place for them." Æthelræd beamed. "Now will you learn to trust my sight? Can't think what sort of gibberish you learned in those schools that you no longer have faith in me."

"I apologize, Uncle," Edgar said. "If I'd believed you, I'd have been spared the blackest moment of my life. I promise never to doubt you again, no matter how preposterous your tale may be."

Æthelræd grunted. "That's not exactly a solid sign of your confidence, but considering what you've been through, I'll accept it."

"I hope I remember the roads to take to Lindisfarne," Edgar continued. He was busy stuffing his belongings into a leather bag. "I wonder if I can get some cloth in Wearmouth. Brother Clarence says they arrived with nothing but what they wore. Poor Catherine, all those fine clothes she brought to impress my family gone up in flames."

"Hold, nephew!" Æthelræd blocked Edgar with his arm. "You're not thinking of setting out alone just after telling me that a poor monk couldn't even make the trip here safely?"

Edgar pushed Æthelræd aside. "I'm taking a horse and will be well armed. And I don't plan to rest until I get there."

"I see," Æthelræd mocked. "You're counting on speed to hide the fact that you haven't a clue how to use those weapons you'll be carrying."

"Exactly."

Edgar continued his packing. Æthelræd chewed the end of his mustache, proving he had more in common with Waldeve than either of them would admit. Finally he thought of another argument.

"It won't work, Edgar," he said. "Bandits will attack you if they think you can't fight back. But this whole area is patrolled by soldiers, as well. And they'll only attack you if they believe you can threaten them."

"I'll get a safe passage from Cumin and another from Conyers,"

Edgar insisted, but Æthelræd heard the beginning of uncertainty in his voice.

"Ah, that would be fine, to be caught with letters from two implacable enemies. Whichever side finds you will decide you're a spy and hang you right there."

Edgar threw down the pack in fury. "Then what should I do, Uncle?" he cried. "I thought they were dead. Now I have to see for myself that they still breathe. I can't stay here and do nothing. It's not as if I had a purpose in Durham beyond annoying my brother. And you do that better than I."

"I agree with that." His uncle laughed. "But I believe you do have a purpose here and it's not to let yourself be slaughtered in battle or on the road. What could I tell that wife of yours if I let you ride off to your death?"

Edgar, remembering his own terror of telling Catherine's father of her death, took this to heart. He knew he had lost. He gave the bag at his feet a savage kick that lobbed it against the tent wall and scattered clothes and coins everywhere.

"There must be a way to get a message to her, at least," he muttered, as he bent to pick up the detritus. "A pity she doesn't have your sight, as well."

"With eyes like that, I'm surprised she doesn't," Æthelræd commented.

Edgar looked at him in astonishment.

"I'm old, I'll grant you, lad," his uncle added. "But I'm not dead, especially to a pair of blue eyes that gaze at me as if I was stripped to my soul."

"A message," Edgar reminded him.

"Let me think on it." Æthelræd turned abruptly and went out, leaving Edgar to collect his belongings and wonder when he would ever see his family again.

Catherine was chafing equally under the enforced inactivity. Beyond caring for the children and reading such books as the prior thought suitable—mostly saints' lives she had read before—there was nothing to do but watch the road as it was hidden and exposed and wonder if Edgar would ever come across to get them.

She knew Solomon's advice was sound. But she knew that if it hadn't been for James, Willa and Margaret she would have borrowed a pair of *brais*, looped her braids around her head and ridden off long ago. This was an aspect of parenthood that hadn't occurred to her.

Although she was wrapped up in her own worries, Catherine couldn't help but notice that they weren't the only refugees on Holy Island. People came and went with every tide, but the ones who stayed seemed to be the most wretched. They were starving with the kind of hunger that has gone on for months. Some were maimed or wounded. At first Catherine thought they were pilgrims, hunting for a cure, but she eventually realized that they were there for the same reason she was. War had destroyed their homes and crops. They had been forced to flee with what they could gather up, driving their cattle before them. Margaret told her that many of the women and girls had been raped, and the child's matter-of-fact attitude toward this shocked Catherine as much as anything.

"It's what men do whenever they can," Margaret told Catherine, upsetting her even more. "Mama explained it to me long ago. My brothers would laugh about it at dinner. They thought it was fun, but I don't think I'd like it."

"No," Catherine managed to stammer. "I'm sure you wouldn't. Neither would I."

She repeated this conversation to Solomon late that evening.

"What kind of life has that child had?" Her voice was tight with anger. "I knew nothing of that sort of thing at her age."

"You didn't need to, Cousin," Solomon said. "You were guarded every moment. When your father took you to the fairs with him, there were always men assigned to do nothing but watch over you. The lectures I was given on not letting you come to harm!"

"You!" Catherine was incredulous. "You tormented me constantly."

"Well, how would you like to be told you had to watch out for a stupid Christian girl when you wanted to have fun on your own?"

Catherine had never considered it from that angle.

"Very well," she said. "I see that I was protected more than most children. I should have been more grateful, I suppose."

Solomon made a disrespectful sound.

Catherine kicked him gently in rebuke and continued.

"But it's Margaret we're talking about. I understand now why Adalisa didn't want her returned to her father. If Edgar's brothers could brag about such things in her presence, who knows what else they might do. Is there any hope that we could take her back to her mother's family?"

"From what Adalisa told me, no." Solomon winced at the memory of the sad face that had smiled on him for only one night. "She was a bastard daughter of the count of Blois, from before his marriage. Her mother was a well-born woman from Ponthieu so she had to be acknowledged, but I gather that with the count's religious conversion and her mother's marriage, everyone was glad when Adalisa was given to a lord at the edge of the world."

"Count Thibault, her father?" Catherine was amazed. "She had nothing of him in her that I could see, except for perhaps his courage. I wonder if he will grieve at her death?"

Solomon didn't care.

"Margaret is Edgar's sister," he said. "He can also become her guardian. I'll pay for her raising."

"Saint Barbara's three-windowed tower!" Catherine exclaimed. "You're offering to take on the care of a 'stupid Christian girl'?"

"She's not annoying like you were," Solomon answered. "She's bright and lively and I don't want her shut up in a convent or sold to some oaf who will mistreat her as her father did Adalisa."

"I'll stand by you, of course," Catherine told him, once she'd recovered from the shock. "My only condition is that if Margaret should desire, on her own, to enter a convent, you'll not forbid it."

Solomon and his conscience had a long bout. At last he gave a sigh and nodded.

"But only if it's her choice. And not until she's eighteen and able to know her own mind."

"Fair enough." Catherine gave him her hand. "Now all we need to do is convince Waldeve to give her up."

"One step at a time." Solomon yawned. "And my next step is to my lonely narrow bed."

"Don't look for sympathy from me." Catherine yawned in response. "Mine is equally lonely or else overcrowded with children who've had bad dreams."

They bid each other good night. Catherine was tempted to wake James and feed him again in the hope that he wouldn't rise with the monks at Matins, howling with hunger. But he slept so sweetly that she didn't have the heart. She crawled into her bed next to the cradle and tried not to imagine Edgar's warmth beside her. By now she had resigned herself to remaining on the island until he arrived.

But the next day brought news that would change all that. Solomon appeared at the door to her room at first light, having just returned from his daily tour of the island.

"We have to leave here at once," he said with no preamble. "The last group of peasants has brought the spotted fever."

"Oh, my God." Catherine crossed herself. She picked up James, who had slept all night. "Margaret, Willa, you haven't been near those people, have you?"

The girls sat up in their bed, rubbing their eyes. Willa answered. "No, Mistress. We were at the other end of the island all day yesterday and with you the day before."

"Thank the Virgin for that." Catherine let herself breathe again. "Are others going, as well?"

"The monks have told all those who haven't associated with the new people that they should leave, especially if they have children. Riders have been sent to Jarrow, asking if they will take us in."

"I'll pack at once," Catherine said. "Not that there's much to load. What of Lazarus?"

"Brother Hugh thinks he'll be safe enough here," Solomon told her. "Lazarus doesn't leave the cloister where he's being cared for. We can come back for him when the danger is past."

"Perhaps by then someone will know who he is." Catherine was busy folding the few pieces of clothing they had been given, along with combs and swaddling. "Girls, come help me, please. It seems we're about to become refugees again."

Sixteen

Outside Durham. Friday, the ides of August (August 13), 1143. Feast of Saint Radegunde: captive, queen, runaway wife, deaconess, peacemaker.

With hwostan: nim huniges tear 7 erces sæd 7 diles sæd. Cnucan tha sæd smale, mæng thice wih thone tear 7 pipera swithe. Nim ðhry sticcan fulle on nihstig.

For a cough: Take drops of honey and marche seed and dill seed. Crush the seed small, mix thoroughly to thickness with the drops and pepper. Take three spoonsful after the night fast.

—Old English Lacnunga

*T*hey say that William of Saint-Barbe has been coerced to come and try to take possession of his see." Duncan laughed. "That should put Bishop Cumin in a rare temper."

Urric smiled as a good lieutenant should, but he didn't see the humor. It seemed to him that God had sided against them. Urric remembered all too well the Battle of the Standard five years before, when the Scots had had more men and weapons but the Northumbrians had faced them with the relics of their saints and routed them completely. Some advisers had said that the defeat was caused when the Gallowegians were allowed to attack first although they were the most poorly armed. Others spoke of stupid deployment and fights among those who followed King David south, but Urric and most of the other regular soldiers knew that Saint Cuthbert and his fellow saints had personally petitioned the Lord to see that the Scots were defeated.

This time Urric had thought Saint Cuthbert, at least, was on his side, despite the pronouncement of excommunication from the bishop of York. Now he wasn't so sure.

He wasn't the only one. Most of the barons who had sworn allegiance to Cumin had deserted him. The land within a day's ride had been scoured so thoroughly that the rewards due any keen-eyed, enterprising foot soldier were scarce. The grumbling in the ranks was increasing. Duncan and Waldeve were formidable enough to keep their own men in line, but it was clear that William Cumin would need to find a strong ally if he hoped to keep his seat in the bishop's palace.

Edgar, who had been thwarted in every attempt to leave Durham, hoped that all Cumin's men would desert and that the end would come soon. When the final attack came, he had every intention of hiding among the monks. Much as he had disliked Brother Lawrence when he was a student, Edgar didn't believe that the canon would betray him now.

But, as with most things, Edgar's hopes for a quick defeat were crushed. That afternoon a party rode up to the palace. They were greeted with trumpets, ceremony and by William Cumin, himself.

"Who is that man?" Edgar asked Robert, who had been dragged from his vigil only by the onset of the elf-shot fever. He had recovered quickly once out of the marsh and was as fervent as Edgar in contemplation of escape. Robert squinted at the leader of the party.

"I'd say it's Alan, Earl of Richmond," Robert decided. "It looks like his standard. If Cumin has convinced the earl to join him, then we're in for a long war. He keeps a private army."

"Damn," Edgar said. "My son will be grown before I see him again if we don't do something."

"Suggestions are welcome," Robert said.

Edgar slammed his fist against the tree they were standing under.

"If I had any suggestions, I wouldn't be here," he said through clenched teeth.

Robert leaned back against the tree. At his feet, three-legged Lufen slept. Robert was careful not to disturb her.

"Edgar, why did Father bring us here in the first place?" he asked.

"To find the people who killed Alexander, Egbert and young Edgar and then cropped the horses," Edgar answered. "Though I've noticed no sign of investigation on Father's part since we've been here."

"Exactly." Robert gave a sharp nod. "I have a theory about that."

Edgar waited.

"I think Father knows who killed our brothers." Robert watched for Edgar's reaction.

Edgar raised one eyebrow skeptically. "And what do you base that on?" he asked.

"His behavior since we came here, and his character as we know it," Robert answered. "Along with something you don't know. Father and Alexander hated one another."

"Robert, none of us are known for our devotion to Father, or his to us." Edgar wasn't impressed.

"This is more," Robert said. "I heard them arguing, all of them, Duncan, too. They had stolen something from someone and Alexander was threatening to reveal the whole thing."

"What was it?" Edgar was becoming interested.

"I don't know. They stopped when they saw me. But Father and Alexander had both drawn their knives by the time I came in."

"So you believe our father had his two eldest sons and his first-born legitimate grandson murdered because he feared some petty theft of his would be exposed?" Edgar still found the whole idea preposterous.

"I think that was only the beginning," Robert said. "He wants all of us dead, except, maybe, Duncan."

"So you believe he burned down the keep, as well?" Edgar scoffed. "Just to continue the illusion of a mythical enemy."

"No, I think he wanted to be sure that both you and he were widowed." Robert's voice was hard. "Adalisa had only a daughter and then no more. I think the old goat wants to start over, perhaps even legitimize a couple of his bastards."

"Robert, you're insane." Edgar laughed. "I almost wish it were true. It would mean this whole business is done with. Father can be brought to justice and I can find my wife and son and go home. Although I wouldn't like to think I carry the blood of such an unnatural monster."

He paused, wondering what part of his father was now running through the veins of his own son. Even though Robert's theory was nonsense, there was enough truth in his assessment of Waldeve to worry Edgar.

Robert stooped to pick up the dog, then turned back to face his brother.

"Someone wants all of us dead," he said quietly. "Enough to kill even those we love. But Father hasn't been attacked. Nor has he made any attempt to continue his search for the murderers. Think about it. What other answer is there?"

He walked away, leaving Edgar more determined than ever to leave the place, whatever the risks.

The weather had stayed clear for the time it took for the refugees to reach the monastery at Jarrow, although the wind was fierce. The monks were prepared for them and had found pallets for everyone. Catherine and the girls found a corner to themselves in the guest lodge while Solomon was given a place in a hastily emptied store-room where the men would sleep. They were fed on bread and a thin vegetable broth, all the monks could offer. For many it was the best meal they had eaten in weeks.

Afterwards, Catherine went back to care for James and help the girls settle in. Solomon followed the other men, who had settled themselves on benches outside the monastery. They overlooked an inlet that seemed perfect for a raiding party to land. Solomon mentioned this to one of the men who spoke French.

"It is perfect," the man told him. "The Northmen thought so. Used it for years. See the fire damage to the stones, here." He pointed to dark streaks on the side of the church. There were bits of pebbles that had been turned almost to glass by the heat of the flames. "The monks fled or were killed during the invasions. They've not been back long."

A leather bottle of ale was being passed. Solomon started to drink, then stopped. He wasn't sure why. He'd spent most of his adult life eating unclean food and drinking anything inebriating. But, as he passed it on, he caught one of the men at the other end of the bench looking at him.

The man was fair and well built, not as light as a Saxon but still obviously of northern stock. He was muscular, as if he'd spent years swinging heavy objects around. Solomon hoped he was a smith rather than a warrior. Either way, he seemed a good man to avoid.

So he was more than a little alarmed when he got up to relieve himself and found the man following him.

Solomon wandered down to the beach, thinking to add his bit to the salt sea. The man came and stood next to him, untying his *brais* and lifting his tunic. Solomon began to panic. He hadn't had to deal with anything like this for years, not since one of his first trips to Spain. He tried to move away from the golden arc the man was sending into the water. He meant to avert his eyes, as well, but happened to glance down. His heart stopped.

The man was circumcised.

The man finished his business and tied up his *brais* again. Then he grinned at Solomon. "*Chaver!*" he greeted him in Hebrew. "It seemed the best way to convince you quickly that I was a brother."

Solomon looked at the man. He could be a Flemish trader or an English farmer, but no one would have imagined him a Jew.

"Are you a convert?" he asked.

The man laughed. "My name is Samson," he said. "And I was born in London of good, Jewish parents. My grandparents came from Rouen. They were good Jews, as well. Before that, I refuse to guess. The Northmen were active in our part of the world, too."

Solomon hadn't realized how lonely he was for one of his own. He nearly hugged Samson, then remembered his original reason for coming out to the shore. Samson waited for him to finish, then suggested that they find someplace to sit and share a flask he had brought from home.

"Those others are going to think we're up to improper acts," Solomon pointed out.

"As long as they don't think I'm proselytizing, I don't care." Samson laughed. "Do you?"

"No," Solomon decided. "But I'm sleeping with my back to the wall tonight."

"Always a safe plan," Samson agreed.

When they had settled and drunk the beer Samson's wife had brewed, Solomon started questioning him.

"I didn't know we were trading this far north," he started.

"We don't much," Samson told him. "Although there's talk of starting a community at York. The war between Stephen and Matilda has unsettled everyone. Add to it the struggle up here with the Scots king and the anarchy in general and trade becomes unappealing. Why are you here?"

"I have a Christian friend who was coming home and my uncles thought it would be worth it to see if we could get some of the wool trade before the Flemings grab it all."

"You were welcomed into a Christian home?" Samson seemed amazed.

Solomon fidgeted with embarrassment. "My friend's family thinks I'm one of them."

"I'll not pass judgment on you for that, as long as you didn't participate in their idolatry," Samson said. "But I assumed the woman who came with you was your wife. It seemed strange to bring her along."

Solomon shook his head. "It would take too long to explain. She's not my wife, but my cousin, and a Christian. Her father is one of us but was forced to endure baptism by the soldiers of Christ when he was a child. I beg you not to betray us. It might mean her life as well as mine."

Samson gave Solomon his hand. "It's hard enough for us to live among the Edomites without having dissension among ourselves."

"*Todah robah.*" Solomon thanked him. "Have you been away from London long? I was hoping for some word of our people in Paris. Things weren't well when I left."

"I'm sorry to hear that," Samson said. "I've always thought of Paris as a haven, not like Narbonne or Toledo, but better than England."

"Then you know nothing?" Solomon pressed him.

Samson scrunched his forehead in thought. "There was something a few weeks ago. A distant relative of ours was called before the bishop for being too familiar with his Christian partner or something. But I believe he was able to prove his innocence. At least there was no word of expulsion or hangings."

Solomon hadn't realized that he'd been holding his breath until he heard the gasp as he exhaled in relief. "That was my uncle, I think. I believe he sent me away to keep me from danger, the old fool."

"Then we're *mishpocha* as well as brothers." Samson handed the beer to Solomon. "If there's anything I can do to help you, let me know."

"Not unless you can arrange a safe way for my cousin to reach her husband in Durham." Solomon took the beer gratefully. Samson's wife was an excellent brewer.

"Durham?" Samson puffed his cheeks in consternation. "No one sane goes near the place these days. Even the new bishop is reluctant to visit. Still, I'll see what I can do. I speak the English of the South but most of these fellows can make out what I'm saying and I don't always bother to mention my faith. Like you, I can be cautious, if needful. But for some reason, most of these people think we have horns, like a ram. It makes it easy to pass as one of them, if necessary."

"Horns? That's a new one," Solomon made a note to ask Catherine or Margaret about it, when there was time. "Where did they get that from?"

"I have no idea," Samson answered. "All I know is that when my family came here, the Saxons insisted that they couldn't be Jews because their books said all Jews were horned."

"I don't suppose it was a reference to sexual ability," Solomon said wistfully.

"Sorry." Samson grinned again.

They walked back to the monastery, ignoring the sidewise glances of the other men.

Despite the hardness of the pallet and the snores from all around him, Solomon slept better that night than he had since they came to Britain. He hadn't admitted to himself how alien he felt among these people. Samson was a revelation. He was decidedly English and yet undoubtedly Jewish, as well. He felt as comfortable in Britain as Solomon did in France. That wasn't saying much. No place was completely safe. But it eased Solomon's mind to be with someone who knew the language and the customs here. He began to feel better about their chances of survival.

Catherine didn't share his optimism. She was worn from worry and travel and the need to produce enough food for her continually ravenous son. She realized that Willa had been taking on too much, as well. The girl seemed to have grown taller in the past few weeks and, while thinner, her body had curves in it that alarmed Catherine. Willa was almost a grown woman. Men would certainly regard her as one and, as a servant, easy prey.

Catherine let her head fall back against the wall. She closed her eyes. Every time she had ever resented her parents forbidding her to go someplace, all their lectures about not wandering off alone, came back to her now. She vowed to apologize to her father the moment they reached home.

But just now Willa was in no danger from lascivious men. She and Margaret were asleep in the corner, curled together, spoon fashion for warmth, as Catherine and her sister, Agnes, had once slept. Willa's braid had fallen across Margaret like a rope binding them together. Every now and then she half woke, coughing, and then settled back again.

Catherine was exhausted but not able to sleep, yet. She watched the other women in the room as they soothed children and set out blankets to mark the boundaries of their space. Catherine realized that she had done the same.

How odd, she thought. Even without walls, we need to create a sense of a home.

Catherine knew that if they stayed more than a day or two, each small space would develop its own personality, revealing the nature of the woman who controlled it. She wished she could speak with them. She felt how foreign she looked to them and knew they were curious about the girls with her, so clearly not her own and the baby that so obviously was. The curiosity could easily turn to fear and animosity if it came about that one of them had brought the fever with them. The spotted sickness could kill a child or leave him blind or deaf or with a hundred other infirmities. Catherine had no illusions about what she would do to someone who brought such a danger near her James, and none about what these women would do to her if they believed her family had contaminated theirs.

Willa was still coughing when morning came. Catherine kissed her forehead and was relieved to find it cool. The two spots on her face were only those that come with the change from girl to woman.

"I feel fine," Willa insisted. "Mother told me I'd had the spotted sickness when my brother did. They say if you survive, you can't get it again. My throat just feels sore from the coughing."

Catherine decided to find a leech at the monastery anyway.

"Sister Melisande used to make a tonic for the cough," she told Willa. "Perhaps someone here has a similar draught."

There was no one at the monastery but they were directed to a woman nearby who was reputed to have skill in such things. Mindful of her fears the night before, Catherine collected Margaret and told Solomon where they were going before they went to see her.

They found the woman in her garden, hoeing. She was not much older than Catherine and had a baby a little younger than James in a basket on the ground next to her. Margaret explained the problem. The woman laid the hoe aside, dusted her hands on her apron and beckoned Willa to come closer and open her mouth in the direction of the sun.

Willa coughed again as the air hit her throat. The woman listened and peered inside her mouth for a moment. Then she said something to Margaret, picked up the baby and went into the house.

"She says it looks like a dry cough, from dust or demons in the wind. She's going to get something for it."

The woman returned with a small covered clay pot. She gave it to Catherine, all the while explaining to Margaret.

Finally, Margaret turned to Catherine. "She says to give her a spoonful of this morning and evening. Afterwards draw a cross on her forehead and say, what was it?"

The woman chanted a few lines. Margaret listened, then repeated, " 'Matthew, Mark, Luke and John, cast the demons to the four winds and heal this child.' Then say a paternoster."

Catherine listened and nodded. "I can remember that. *Thanc ðe*," she said to the woman, who smiled and nodded back.

Catherine opened the pot and sniffed it. Honey with herbs steeped in it, something pungent. Much like what she had been given as a child.

"We have nothing to pay her with," Catherine told Margaret. "But I can finishing the hoeing, if that will be enough to repay her."

Margaret's eyes lit up. "May I help? That would be fun."

It was settled that the payment was satisfactory and the woman returned to her house while Margaret and Catherine hoed and weeded. Willa took a dose of the medicine and was told to sit and watch James.

The task soothed Catherine's rumpled spirit, reminding her of the days when someone else was responsible for her. The familiarity of the work also comforted her and she was almost sorry when they had finished and the woman had sent them off with a gift of a thick slice of ripe cheese.

They returned to the monastery to find Solomon and his new friend, Samson, in discussion with another man. Margaret took one look at the newcomer and ran for him with a cry of delight.

"Alfred!" She said as she leapt upon him. "Did Father send you? Are we going home? Is everyone all right?"

The old man returned her hug with some embarrassment.

"I'm glad to see you, my lady," he said. "Though heartily grieved at the news of the tragic death of your mother. Fortunately, no one from the village was killed in the attack, although some were wounded and will be some time mending. I was telling Solomon that I was sent down to find your father, as we've had no word from him. Many of us would like him to bring our men home so that repairs can be made before winter sets in."

Solomon greeted Catherine, commenting on the smudge of dirt on her nose. She rubbed at it with her sleeve as he explained what Alfred was doing in Jarrow.

"He's going on down to Durham with a party from King David that's on its way to York. We should be able to accompany them in safety."

"Oh, Solomon." Catherine was radiant. She bounced the baby on her hip. "Do you hear, *mon doux*? We're going to find your father at last."

James gave her a big, toothless smile. She was sure he understood every word.

In Paris, Catherine's uncle Eliazar and his wife, Johanna, sat alone in their chamber. Outside there were the sounds of people enjoying the warm summer evening. From a tavern in the next block, they could hear swearing that might soon erupt into fighting. Johanna put her hand on Eliazar's knee.

"You needn't worry so," she said. "This will pass; it always does."

"Not always," he answered.

"In Rouen or Speyer, not Paris," she argued, but her voice held a note of uncertainty.

"Things have been different ever since King Louis burnt the church in Vitry last year," he muttered. "People need a reason to excuse him. He's the king, after all. There have always been those who say that he and his father have been too lenient with the Jews."

Johanna snorted. "We pay him to be lenient. How else do they think he can give his fancy wife all the baubles she wants?"

"My dearest." Eliazar cut off her argument. "The truth doesn't enter into this. Hubert and I have been treading an icy path ever since we became partners. It was only a matter of time before someone started asking questions."

"But he's been to the bishop's palace twice now and was able to satisfy all their doubts."

"This time." Eliazar sighed. "Johanna, my pearl, we must consider leaving Paris, for the good of all of us, Solomon, Hubert and dear Catherine and her family. You know our friends have also complained that we spend too much time with these Christians."

Johanna looked around at the house she had lived in for thirty years. Then she turned back to her husband and tried to smile.

"I'm your wife," she said. "My home is where you are. And until the Temple is rebuilt and Jerusalem free, I suppose one place is as good as another."

Eliazar kissed her. Then they both sighed. Now they would need to find a place to take them in.

"Perhaps when Solomon returns, he'll tell us if England would be suitable." Eliazar ran his fingers through his beard. "I've heard there's talk of new settlements in the north of the country."

Johanna shivered. "I know we have many friends from Normandy who've gone, but unless Solomon tells us it's a second Eden, I'd rather go somewhere not quite so full of blonds."

Now that Cumin had the backing of the earl of Richmond, there was an increased air of confidence among the soldiers, along with increased activity. Rumors were so thick that they contradicted each other in midair. If Edgar had given credence to all of them, he would have expected to see an army of thousands, led by the earl, King David and his niece, the empress Matilda, marching across the bridge, heralded by the archangel Michael waving a flaming sword, with perhaps all the knights of Arthur bringing up the rear. There was even speculation that Cumin had obtained a special salve to protect his men from the elf darts that had been plaguing them with fever since the siege in the marshland.

"I want an ointment against human arrows before I join this army," Robert said sourly.

He and Edgar were back in the tavern along the road up to the castle. Through the open door, they could see as much as they desired of the activity going on among the defenders.

Edgar got up to refill his bowl. At least the beer here was as good as he remembered it. He had never adjusted to the flavoring the French used in theirs. He stuck his tongue in the foam and suddenly was overwhelmed by a vivid image of Catherine using the point of her sleeve to strain out the pieces of herbs and other flotsam from her beer. It was one of her more irritating affectations. In retrospect it seemed almost erotically endearing.

He was shaken from his maudlin memories by the arrival of his father. Both Edgar and Robert came to attention at once. Waldeve had never before bothered to seek them out. If he wanted them, he would send for them and woe to the son who took his time about appearing.

"Father?" Edgar tried to smile.

"I've finally found a use for you two," Waldeve growled. "You! Beer! Now!" he shouted over his shoulder.

The bowl was in his hand as soon as he reached it out. Waldeve drained it and held it out for a refill. When that was poured, he drained it, as well. Only then did he direct his attention back to Robert and Edgar.

"I told the bishop that both of you would carry messages for him to Bishopton. Word is that Saint-Barbe is there now and the barons of the district are falling over each other to be the first to pay him homage. They trust you there, God knows why. They'll believe what you tell them." Waldeve wiped his mouth and signaled for more beer. "Don't think you'll have a chance to do anything heroic, though. I'm sending guards with you and not for your protection."

Robert stood. "Perhaps I don't wish to be your page, Father," he said with dignity.

Waldeve glared at him. "Perhaps you'd prefer eating for the rest of your life toothless and tongueless."

Robert didn't back down. "I've done with you, Father. I'll make my own way now. I'll sell the house in Berwick that Mother left me and go up into the high lands to farm."

Edgar was astonished to see a flicker of panic in Waldeve's face. It passed quickly.

"I see," he said. "Then I'll give you another option. Do as I say or I'll have that crippled dog of yours hanging from the eaves along with the men who defied William Cumin."

Robert looked down. Lufen was gone. She had been investigating the mouse hole in the corner a moment ago. Waldeve moved aside and Robert saw the dog in the arms of one of the soldiers. Another half brother of his, by his looks. He lunged across the table at his father. Edgar stopped him before his body landed on the old man's swiftly drawn sword.

"Robert, he feeds on your hate," he hissed in his brother's ear. "Look at him. You can almost see his strength grow."

"If you do anything to Lufen, I will cut your throat with joy," Robert threatened as he struggled in Edgar's grip.

Waldeve laughed. "I'm almost glad Æthelræd stopped me from shooting you. I assume this means you will do as ordered. And you, Edgar, don't you want to defy me, as well?"

Edgar's shoulders sagged as he released Robert. The look he gave his father was of total weariness.

"If it will help bring this ordeal to an end, I'll do anything you like," he said. "When we've done here, I'm returning with my family, my real family, to France and I pray never to see or hear news of you again."

Edgar's weary contempt seemed to upset Waldeve more than Robert's outburst. He opened his mouth to sneer, but nothing came out. Instead he clenched his teeth and the look he gave Edgar was more cutting than his sword.

"So be it," he stated. "Be at the gate of the palace tomorrow at dawn."

He wheeled about, dropping another half-finished bowl of beer to the floor, and stalked out of the tavern. His men followed, Lufen whining in the arms of her captor.

Robert stood for a long time after they had gone, his hands clenching and unclenching at his side. Finally he sat again. Edgar had gotten him more to drink. He drained the bowl with the same gesture Waldeve had used.

"I don't think I'll cut his throat, after all," Robert said, his voice calm and considering. "Poison would be better. Something that takes years and makes his life drizzle slowly out his asshole. Yes, that would be good. Either that or find a way to give him leprosy."

Edgar regarded him with caution, trying to decide if this were madness or the family trait of biting humor in the face of adversity.

"I've heard that there is a charm to make a man's cock fall off," he said conversationally. "It's supposed to flake away. Takes weeks."

Robert pursed his lips. "I like it. Where can we find this charm?"

"It's Irish," Edgar told him. "All the best charms are."

Robert shook his head. "I don't have time to go hunting it. It will have to be leaking shits and leprosy."

"Fine," Edgar agreed. "But what do we do right now?"

Robert got up again and headed for the door. Edgar followed.

"We're going to carry the old *naddrenes* messages and try to find a way to rescue my dog," he said as they came out into the street.

Edgar looked wistfully toward the Northwest, imagining that he saw Catherine coming up the street toward him. But none of the women there resembled her at all. He wondered what the fate of the women of Durham would be, or had been already. It was just as well that his family was all safe on Holy Island.

At that moment, Catherine was trying to keep her cloak from blowing away in the coastal wind.

"How much farther?" she shouted at Samson, who was only a step ahead of her.

"We'll be turning inland soon," he shouted back.

James squirmed in his sling. He seemed to have grown much heavier over the last few days. "Soon!" she shouted down at him.

Why had she thought the pilgrimage to Compostella hard? Then she had been surrounded by family and other pilgrims, ridden a horse and most nights been sure of a warm bed and hot water. Even the morning sickness that had tormented her the last half of the trip seemed nothing compared to the endless slogging between the sand and the tree line, with the wind blowing cold off the North Sea un-remittingly, causing them to bundle as if it were January instead of the middle of August.

At last the men leading the party turned from the coast and into the woods, following a narrow road leading up though the trees.

For some time Catherine still felt the howl of the wind in her ears. Then the early-evening warmth began to penetrate her cloak and she took it off with a sigh of relief.

"Samson," she asked in a more normal tone, "when will we reach Durham?

"Sometime tomorrow," he told her. "The king's men will pass to the east of the city, but you will have only a short journey from the place where your paths diverge and Alfred knows the way."

Catherine bent over James and whispered. "Tomorrow, *leoffæst*, tomorrow we'll be with your father at last."

James belched up a few clots of sour milk. Catherine wiped his chin and decided not to take it as a personal opinion of their chances. One more day. She could do it. Tomorrow everything would be all right again.

Seventeen

The road from Durham to Bishopton. Wednesday, 15 kalends September (August 18), 1143. Feast of Saint Helena, mother, devout convert, pilgrim, finder of the True Cross but not British, despite what Geoffrey of Monmouth said.

Recole nunc, ut dixi, corruptiones meas cum exhalaretur nebula libidinis ex limosa concupiscentia carnis et scatebra pubertatis, nec esset qui eriperet et salvum faceret. Verba enim iniquiorum prevaluerunt super me, qui in suavi poculo amoris propinabant mihi venenum luxuriae . . .

Remember, as I told you, my corruption, when a cloud of lust breathed forth from the murky swamp of my body's desires and the gushing passions of youth. And no one would rescue me. The words of iniquitous ones swayed me, those who in the sweet goblet of love offered me the poison of dissolution . . .

—Aelred of Rievaulx,
Advice to a Recluse
(his sister), pt. 32

I can't believe I'm doing this," Edgar kept repeating under his breath. "What's wrong with me? I should have taken a horse and made a run for it the first day out. I can't believe I'm doing this."

Robert, riding beside him, hoped all those muttered words were prayers. They needed some divine help at this point. He wasn't thinking of the reaction of those at Bishopton to the defiant messages they were carrying, but of the possibility of losing Lufen to his father's wrath. Even more, he was fearing and hoping that among the supporters of William Saint-Barbe he would find Aelred. Perhaps they might even manage a few minutes alone together. Robert needed more than the pathetic note he had been sent informing him that his best friend in the world had renounced that world and would never see him again.

So between Edgar's subvocal fretting and Robert's thousand imagined reunions, the ride from Durham to Bishopton was unnaturally silent. Even the soldiers accompanying them, uncertain whether they were an escort or a guard, refrained from the usual banter.

Edgar had anticipated some difficulty in reaching Roger Conyers and the Bishop, but when they arrived, they found the gates they had spent weeks trying to breach thrown open and a stream of people coming and going.

Robert raised himself up in the saddle, trying to find one face in the mass of men.

"Is there anyone there you know?" Edgar came alert to ask.

"I don't see him," Robert answered vaguely, then he forced himself back to their task. "Yes, I recognize some of them. There's Geoffrey Escolland talking to Bernard de Balliol and I think that standard belongs to Aschetin of Worchester. It seems as if the barons of Durham have decided which bishop to support."

"Now that Saint-Barbe has been elected and consecrated, I don't see that Cumin has any choice but to surrender," Edgar said. "The barons must know that, as well."

Robert shook his head. "As long as Cumin has the chapter seal and control of the silver mines, he has a chance. Saint-Barbe's consecration is only a minor obstacle. Remember, a bishop's office lasts only as long as he lives."

They joined the throng entering the gates. Almost immediately Robert was hailed by one old friend and then another. One of the men with Bernard de Balliol saw him and ran over, catching him in a bear hug as he dismounted.

"Robert! Where have you been?" he shouted. "We all heard you'd turned hermit, either that or gone to Denmark for hunting dogs."

"It's good to see you, too, Erik." Robert continued scanning the faces in the courtyard. "I did neither. This is my little brother, Edgar."

Erik gave Edgar his hand. "I don't remember you. Are you the one who went to France and—" He stopped, reddening.

"Yes, I am." Edgar took the outstretched hand. "And I've never regretted it, especially the 'and . . .' "

"Well, good!" Erik said. "Have you come to give your support to the bishop?"

The question was addressed to Robert but he was still looking for Aelred. Edgar answered for them both.

"We'll give such support as we can," he said. "But our principle charge is to deliver messages from William Cumin to Bishop William. Do you know who we should approach to get an audience with him?"

"Hmm, let me think." Erik scrunched up his face, almost grunting with the effort. "There's no real order here, but I'd say that Archdeacon Rannulf is the one who could get you in to see the bishop. I hope Cumin is surrendering. I want to get home to my wife. We've only been married four months."

Edgar winced. "I'm only the messenger," he told Erik. "But I'm with you. I want to see my wife, too, and we've been married four years. Can you take me to the archdeacon?"

Erik led them through the bustling courtyard to an even busier meeting hall, so new that the floorboards were still sticky with sap from the green wood they had been cut from. Edgar soon had bits of straw and leaves attached to the bottom of his boots. Robert bumped into him every time he stopped to scrape them.

"Will you stop gawking and give your mind to the task at hand?" he complained the third time this happened.

"If you'd keep moving, we wouldn't collide," Robert snapped back.

They had barely managed to regain their dignity when Erik brought them to a corner that had been curtained off. He stuck his head around the side and said something indistinct to the person behind.

The curtain was pulled aside and the archdeacon appeared.

"Edgar! Good to see you again!" He smiled at them both. "We thought you'd been swallowed up by that dragon's lair in Durham!"

"We were." Edgar didn't return the smile. "And we must return to it as soon as we receive the reply to the messages we carry."

"You've joined forces with the enemy?" Rannulf frowned.

"We are with Saint Cuthbert," Edgar answered. "But our father has sent his men with us to assure our good behavior, and my brother has left a hostage at the bishop's palace against our return."

Beside him, Robert gave a sudden gasp. He turned quickly to the archdeacon.

"Edgar will tell you all you need to know," he said rapidly. "I must beg to be excused. It's very important."

Without waiting for permission, Robert vanished into the mass of people, following a hooded figure in a plain white robe. Rannulf raised an eyebrow at Edgar.

"My apologies," Edgar said, "but Robert is right; I can give Bishop William the message myself. When might he be willing to see me?"

The archdeacon moved closer to Edgar and lowered his voice. "Between us, he'd be just as glad not to see you at all, unless you bring Cumin's complete and abject submission."

He paused and looked at Edgar.

"I thought not," he continued. "Well, I'm prepared to do whatever necessary to regain my home and free Saint Cuthbert from his captor. As you can see—and be sure to report this to your master—every day more of the barons of Durham arrive to pledge their swords and their followers to our aid. Even David of Scotland wants no more to do with Cumin. How long does he think he can hold on?"

Edgar, mindful of Urric standing just behind him with open ears, only shrugged. "I'm not one of Cumin's inner circle," he said. "He hasn't told me his plans."

With his eyes he tried to indicate the problem. Archdeacon Rannulf nodded understanding. "Very well," he replied. "I'll tell the bishop of your arrival. I'm sure he'll send for you shortly. There's water for washing in the trough by the gate and you and your men are welcome to food and ale along with our other guests."

Edgar bowed and backed out of the alcove. He whirled around quickly enough to come nose to nose with Urric.

"Tell the others they can wash and eat," he said. "And leave Robert alone. He's not going to betray anyone. He cares nothing for this squabble."

"That's obvious," Urric answered. "Duncan told me to stay with you."

Edgar wasn't surprised.

Robert had forgotten about the reason for their coming. The only thing his world consisted of was the man walking rapidly away from him. He wanted to call out to him, but feared that would cause Aelred to vanish, as he had done in so many of Robert's nightmares.

Finally he was close enough to catch at Aelred's robe. He gripped the folds of cloth at the shoulder, causing the hood to fall back. The monk froze still as death. Then he bent his head in resignation and slowly turned around. Robert found that, after years of planning what he would say, he couldn't make his tongue move at all.

The two stood for an eternity, unaware of anything around them. Finally Aelred spoke.

"Robert, forgive me."

Robert opened his mouth, closed it, swallowed and tried again.

"No," he said. "Not until you tell me why. Your letter said nothing, only a cruel farewell. What did I do to be treated so? What reason could I have given you to flee from me?"

"Oh, Robert!" Aelred raised a hand to the other's face, but stopped short of touch. "I didn't flee from you; I fled to God."

Robert caught Aelred's hand in his own. "I don't believe you.

What am I, Satan incarnate? It was never a choice between me and
God. If you'd told me your plans, don't you think I'd have gone
with you?"

Aelred tried to free his hand. "Robert, you don't understand."

Robert tightened his hold. "Then explain it to me. You owe me
that. What kind of man of God have you become to leave a friend
alone in the darkness of desolation?"

The last words came out as a tearful cry. Aelred bit his lip, then
bent his head over Robert's hand.

"Yes," he said softly. "I've been selfish. I found a way to peace,
and perhaps salvation. It was wrong of me to cast you off with my
old life. I will let you see all that lies in my heart. Meet with me
tonight. There's a boulder just outside the bailey that was too large
to move. It has a cross painted on it and I go there in the evenings to
pray. I'll wait there for you. Now, please, let me go. I see your
brother approaching."

Edgar was going to pass them without interrupting, but Aelred
called to him and greeted him warmly.

"Have you learned anything more about the death of your
brothers?" he asked.

"Not enough," Edgar told him. "Robert has a theory about it
that I find dubious, but no one else has even that. Have you been
here ever since we came from Rievaulx? I'm surprised the abbot let
you stay that long."

"I've come and gone and come again," Aelred said, carefully not
looking at Robert. "I needed to see to my charges. We have some
novices who would falter in their conversion without guidance. I've
only just arrived again, to represent Rievaulx in a matter we would
like Bishop William to address."

Edgar thought this odd. "Don't you think it could wait until the
poor man sleeps his first night in the bishop's palace?"

"Durham has been too long in anarchy," Aelred reproached
him. "Work must be done now, if there's to be anything left for
Bishop William to govern. Also, this is something I have personal
knowledge of, due to my visit to Rome last year. It needs to be decided before I go to my new abbey in Lincoln."

"What!" Robert burst out.

Aelred still didn't look at him. "Yes, William of Roumare has
given land and funds for a daughter house at Revesby. I'm to be
abbot there."

"That's wonderful, Æthelr . . . Aelred!" Edgar said. "And you barely into your thirties. Will we be addressing you as the Venerable Aelred now?"

"Not if you want me to answer." Aelred took Edgar's arm and started to lead him back to where trestle tables were being set up to seat all the visitors for the evening meal. "But, Edgar, I have a favor to ask. Of you, too, Robert." The glance he gave Robert was brief and pleading. "If you can keep your entourage away from me this evening, I'll give Robert a message from Bishop William to the monks of Durham. It will have to be memorized, but both of you should know the contents, in case only one of you can reach them. We've heard terrible stories of how they're being treated there."

"I'll do whatever I can," Edgar promised. "I've been allowed to enter the cloister on occasion. We'll let the monks know your plans if it's humanly possible, won't we, Robert?"

"Aelred knows I can be trusted to carry out any charge he sets me," Robert answered.

"Thank you," Aelred answered, looking straight at Robert. "Both of you."

When he had gone, Robert dropped to the nearest bench. Edgar watched him with pity.

"Why don't I get you some ale?" he suggested.

"That won't help," Robert said.

"You never know until you try," Edgar went to the communal cask and filled two cups. He held one out to his brother. "My throat is coated with road dust and my temper is frayed. This will improve both conditions."

"I thought that if I just saw him, everything would be like it was." Robert sighed and emptied the cup.

"He's different now, Robert," Edgar said softly. "I noticed it as soon as I saw him among the monks. I don't know if he'll ever be completely happy in this life, but he may at least find peace in the cloister."

Robert wouldn't be convinced. He put down his cup and got up again.

"I don't believe he can ever find peace or happiness without my friendship, and I'm going to tell him so tonight."

Edgar gave up and went to get more ale. His brother and his friend would have to make their own way through this thicket. He was all out of advice.

∞

Apart from the difficulty of keeping up with men on horseback, the small party from Wedderlie, along with Samson, had an uneventful trip inland.

Away from the coast, the day was cool, but not chilling. The trail was gentle through the woods. Occasionally, they passed through a clearing where peasants had built a cluster of huts, surviving by making charcoal until they had burnt enough of the trees to plant crops. The inhabitants stopped work when they arrived to greet them and trade news of the world. Catherine and Solomon stayed back at these times, not sure how foreigners would be welcomed.

They parted from the king's couriers a few miles east of Durham and a much smaller group headed for the town.

The holdings appeared more often now. Some almost attained the status of villages. But there were also signs of recent strife: burnt buildings, fields half trampled, doors shut tight in the middle of the day. Even though the travelers appeared harmless, no one approached them, but watched stolidly as they passed, clutching a hoe or sickle like a weapon.

Once in a while, one of the English speakers would be sent to ask for directions and information. They always did so at a safe distance and with their hands visibly empty.

Samson came back from one of these encounters looking worried.

"These people say that all the bridges over the Wear are blocked and guarded and the one land gate has been shut and obstructed with stones and piles of refuse," he told them. "Only those with passes are admitted to the town."

"How do we get a pass?" Catherine asked.

Samson twisted his face, trying to come up with the best way to put it.

"It seems," he said carefully, "that the only way to get the pass to enter is to be inside first and take it with you when you leave."

"What?"

"That's what they say," Samson defended himself. "Apparently only those whom Cumin trusts are allowed out or in again."

"Then we'll just have to order the guards to send for Edgar and have him vouch for us," Catherine said. "We haven't gone through all this just to be turned away at the gate."

Solomon hid his smile. Catherine occasionally teased Edgar for his lordly arrogance, which didn't assert itself often. But she was the daughter of a rich merchant and the granddaughter of a minor lord of Blois. Standing in the road in borrowed clothes, her shoes worn and her hair a tangle, the poise that only came with knowledge of privilege was a startling contrast.

"We'll rely on you to do the ordering," he told her. "A pity you left your crown and scepter in Paris."

Durham, when approached from the east, wasn't as looming and impressive as it was to those who came upon it from the west or south, but the first sight of the cathedral and fortress on the escarpment were still formidable enough to daunt Catherine more than she would admit. It seemed as if it had risen from the rock, its golden brown stones simply brushed free of dirt as they broke from the earth and reached toward the sky.

"Edgar used to live there?" she asked Solomon in wonder.

"He stayed there four years, didn't he?" Solomon tried to imagined being imprisoned within that stone. He shuddered, then added hopefully, "So he should know all the possible ways out."

"That's true." Catherine hadn't considered that point. "But all I care about now is finding the way in."

"I suppose it's time for you to impersonate Empress Matilda," Solomon suggested.

"This is no time to scoff," Catherine answered. "But what if they don't speak French?"

This turned out to be the case. Either that or, as Catherine suspected, it was convenient for them to pretend ignorance. Alfred and Samson both tried to convince the soldiers to send word up to the castle that the family of the lord of Wedderlie had arrived. This pronouncement was met with stark disbelief and jokes that would have scandalized Catherine if she had understood them.

The gestures were clear enough to make her furious. James sensed her mood and woke suddenly, shrieking in fear. The sight of the baby provoked more mirth among the guardians of the gate. This only heightened her wrath.

"Pigs!" she shouted at them. "Ugly donkeys!"

Still they laughed, the smirking, arrogant beasts! Catherine pointed her finger at them, narrowed her eyes and intoned loudly, "*Ut bufones evolent ex ano tuo quandocumque bumbulum facis!*"

Solomon pulled her hand down, ignoring the mocking guards.

"It won't upset them a bit if you curse them in Latin, Cousin," he said.

"It will if Saint Genevieve grants my plea," Catherine said darkly, scowling at the men, who only laughed the more.

Solomon couldn't help joining them, though he knew the risk he was running.

"My dear, I'm shocked!" he said, over James's crescendo. "Asking your saints for petty revenge? Most unchristian. Come away, Catherine," he added more gently. "We can't overpower them. We'll have to outwit them. That shouldn't be hard."

"Come where?" Catherine didn't realize how close she was to breaking. The journey was telling on her.

"Samson says that the church of Saint Giles is only a little ways from here. There's a hospital there that will shelter us until we can arrange to get a message to Waldeve."

Solomon took the reins of the mule on which Willa and Margaret were riding, although in Margaret's case riding meant lying sound asleep across the mule's neck. Willa, ever watchful between coughing spasms, saw that she didn't fall off.

As they approached the hospital gates Solomon and Samson, after conferring, put themselves on either side of Catherine.

"Cousin." Solomon cleared his throat. "Just for the increase of our knowledge, what exactly did you wish upon those vigilant guards."

Catherine blushed, a deep red that rose from her neck to her forehead. "Nothing," she said.

"Catherine?"

She mumbled something. Solomon leaned closer.

Catherine was now flaming like a sunset. She spoke toward the ground but both men were close enough to hear.

"I said, 'May toads fly out your assholes every time you fart.' "

"Catherine!"

She pushed ahead of them and pounded with the door ring much harder than was necessary.

Behind her Solomon beamed with pride as Samson collapsed in laughter.

There was laughter among those assembled in the courtyard of Roger Conyers's keep, as well. The lords and their retainers were confident that now that a true bishop was in Durham, all would soon be well. Then they could turn their attention back to the war between Stephen and Matilda, knowing that the taxes would once again flow from the North.

Edgar had been steadily refilling his ale mug since the afternoon and was in serious danger of sliding under the table and being swept out with the refuse in the morning. He was tired of playing soldier. He didn't care who won the crown of England. He was beginning to wonder why Saint Cuthbert didn't settle the contest for the bishopric with some old-time smiting. He had realized sometime during the sodden evening that he had forgotten the shape of his son's face. In a tide of self-pity, he attempted to get his horse and set out for Lindisfarne. He was astonished to find that his body hadn't followed his command and that his feet were still under the table.

Robert paid him no attention. As the light of day turned opalescent, he left the rowdy diners and made his way to Aelred's outdoor chapel.

The boulder was easy to locate. It was at the rear of the bailey, hard against the wall. There wasn't much space between it and the deep motte, which at this point was being used as a midden. The odor of it wafted through the night air.

Aelred was standing before the painted cross, tears streaming down his cheeks as he prayed with closed eyes. Robert hesitated, not wanting to interrupt his devotions but also because he needed a moment to fix the image of his friend in his memory forever.

There was a soft "amen" and Aelred's eyes opened. He held out his arms to Robert who came to him and embraced him, laying his head on Aelred's shoulder as he sobbed out his loneliness and grief.

"I'm sorry, so sorry," Aelred crooned as he smoothed Robert's hair. "Please understand, please forgive me."

"But why?" Robert cried. "We were inseparable. Never an argument, no attempts at preferment. No jealousy or pettiness. Of all the men I knew at court, you were the best, the noblest, the truest friend."

"No, your love has erased the memory of my faults." Aelred lifted Robert's head and moved a step away. "I was none of those things. I was vain and proud and weak, very weak. And, oh, Robert, it pains me to tell you, I was ashamed of our friendship, of the . . . passion I felt for you."

Robert straightened and lifted his chin. "Edgar told me that Saint Augustine of Hippo believed that true friendship only happened between men."

"That's so; he did say that." Aelred nodded. "But we went beyond friendship to an attachment of the flesh that enslaved us."

"No!"

"Yes," Aelred said softly. "How could I worship God when all I saw was your face, when all I longed for was your body?"

"Why not?" Robert pleaded. "Every day I thanked God for sending you. I worshipped him all the more because I had you as a friend."

"Oh, Robert, I wish I could have your sort of faith!" Aelred stepped back farther and laid a hand on Robert's shoulder. "All I can tell you is that I was lost in disgust and shame. But I loathed myself, not you. You were the most selfless friend I ever had. And I was taking you to Hell with me."

"If so, I went gladly," Robert interrupted.

Aelred shook his head. "Don't you see that made it worse? Please, my dearest friend, believe me when I say that my prayers now are that you should forget me and start life afresh. I *must* try to forget you or at least make my body forget you, for the sake of my soul, and yours."

"Damn my soul!" Robert threw Aelred's arm off him.

Aelred smiled, "Oh, no, never that, Robert. We shall meet again in Heaven, where our impure desires will no longer exist. If my prayers and penances have any effect, that is what I wish most. And I wish it with all my might."

In Robert's heart a great iron door slammed shut, with a finality that surprised him. The hope that he had kept burning for nearly ten years was extinguished forever. He felt no more grief or yearning, only a vast hollowness. Still he made one last feeble attempt.

"I could join the White Monks, too," he said bravely. "I know it means chastity and a hard life, but I would be near you. That's all I want."

"Oh my dear!" Aelred started to hug Robert again, but curbed his impulse. "I think you believe that. Perhaps you could, but I'm not yet that strong. As it is I sit in icy water for hours at a time to discipline my stubborn flesh. Don't you understand, it's because I love you and desire you that I mustn't see you? Not for a long time, perhaps never. One day God may grant me grace enough to sit with you and not want to lay with you, but that day hasn't come."

"Aelred?"

"One more thing, then we'll turn to the business at hand," Aelred took a deep breath. "I was upset when I learned that Edgar had married rather than continuing in the Church. But I reasoned that he had decided to marry rather than burn. Only that option was never open to us. I knew that I must be celibate or burn. I don't believe I had really admitted it until then. That was the darkest day of my life. But God gave me comfort and is teaching me the worth of spiritual friendship. I don't deserve it, but your blessing would be a gift I would treasure forever."

He stopped speaking and Robert waited. "Are you finished?" he asked when Aelred said no more.

"Yes."

"Good," Robert said dryly. "My foot is asleep." He balanced against the boulder and shook it, keeping his face down until he had mastered himself.

"I'm not reconciled to your conversion," he told Aelred. "But I believe now that you are sincere. I thought for a long time that your sudden decision was because you had become enamored of one of the monks at Rievaulx. I know better now. I'll not try to see you again. And of course I give you my blessing, worthless though it may be. I will never forget you, no matter how hard you pray that I should. And I shall never have another friend that I care for as I do you." He took a deep breath and expelled it slowly. "Now what does Bishop William want me to say to the monks of Durham?"

Aelred was relieved by his friend's acceptance of his decision and said so.

"You should know me better than that, Aelred," Robert said. "Growing up in my father's house taught me to take any blow and remain standing. We'll speak of it no more."

"Thank you, Robert." Aelred became again the official of the Church. "Here are the instructions for the monks. The first is for Brother Lawrence. . . ."

Robert listened and remembered. He repeated the messages faultlessly and bid Aelred good night without trembling. Then he went and dragged his baby brother out from under a table, brushed him off and put him to bed.

∞

At the hospital of Saint Giles, Catherine was grateful to find a real bed instead of a straw pallet. She was also amazed that there was a physician there who wasn't even a monk. Master Herbert spoke good French and bad Latin so that, by using both, Catherine was able to explain her worry about Willa's persistent cough and James's perpetually red bottom.

"Let the infant lie naked as much as you can and rub oil on the rash," he dismissed the second complaint. Willa's long convulsive sounds made him grave at once.

"A dry cough," he muttered. "No phlegm. Raw throat. She may need bleeding."

"No," Catherine disagreed. "She has reached the age of womanhood and her purgations are regular. I believe the change from her native climate has upset her humors. What would you recommend to increase the heat and moisture in her body?"

"Ah, yes, well, it's possible that is the case." Herbert was used to dealing with townspeople or suffering pilgrims, none of whom ever dared to contradict him. Even Bishop Geoffrey had listened respectfully, right up until his death. What did she think she was, an abbess? Catherine answered the question on his face.

"I assisted in the infirmary at the Paraclete," she explained. "Sister Melisande explained about the different kinds of coughing. We normally saw the cold and moist kind that comes with winter. But I know about this one, too. The honey and herb only soothes her for a time. She's getting little sleep. Do you think we should add strong wine?"

Master Herbert thought a moment. "Yes, and warm it. Give her a small cup morning and evening. I'll consult my books for other options. Also, I know she's a servant, but she needs rest and shouldn't be allowed near the other children until we're sure this is an illness peculiar to her."

"I understand," Catherine said. "As my servant, I'm responsible for her welfare. And, as for your fee, whatever is reasonable, I shall pay."

Master Herbert suppressed a grin. This bedraggled refugee woman, speaking as if she ran a county! "I promise my fee won't be beyond reason, my lady." He bowed in what was intended as mockery, but she responded to the gesture so naturally that he was forced to revise his estimation of her again. One never knew whom one would encounter in these days of turmoil!

Catherine busied herself taking care of her charges. The thought of having to survive without Willa's help was dreadful. She bent over the girl's bed and tucked the blanket under her chin. Willa tried to apologize.

"No, *ma doux*." Catherine kissed her forehead. Still no fever. "I'm sorry to have brought you along on this nightmare. You've been brave, uncomplaining and indispensable. Your mother will be very proud of you."

Willa started to thank her, but the cough interrupted. Catherine went to make the wine, honey and horehound drink strong enough to let the girl rest the night. She repeated the prayer the woman had told her as she stirred.

The next morning Catherine awoke refreshed and ready to battle the guards at the gate, physically if necessary, to reach Edgar. She sat up in the bed and stretched, shaking out the damp spot where James had lain against her. She unwrapped the soiled swaddling and pulled off his long tunic, setting him naked on a blanket on the floor. After a complete investigation of his fingers, toes and penis, he rolled himself over, almost sitting up.

Catherine was sure it was a good omen.

She had just managed to get him, herself and Margaret dressed and ready for the day when there was a clatter and a blare of horns outside the building. Soon there was the stomping of heavy boots in the corridor.

"Now what?" Catherine sighed.

She checked to see that Willa was still sleeping, then she took James and Margaret out to see what was happening.

A crowd had gathered alongside the road. Catherine hadn't realized that there were so many people in the town. She pushed their way through until she found Samson.

"What's going on?" she asked. "Where's Solomon?"

"I saw him a few moments ago, but lost him in the crowd. The word is that the new bishop is coming to take back the city," Samson told her. "He's bringing an army to do it. He'll need one."

Catherine felt a tug on her skirts.

"I can't breathe down here," Margaret complained. "And I can't see."

Samson crouched down next to her.

"I'm not as tall as these Saxon men, but if you sit on my shoulders, you should be able to see everything. Will you permit me, Lady Margaret?"

Margaret gave him her hand. "You have my permission to lift me."

He swung her up and she held on to his ears, using them to direct him.

"Careful!" he cried. "I'm not a donkey!"

"Sorry!" she said from her perch. "Look at the sumpter horses, all draped in gold cloth! Which man is the bishop? Why isn't he wearing his mitre? Are these the soldiers who are going to fight Father? They don't look so fierce to me."

She kept up a running patter as the procession went past.

"There are a lot of them. I see Bernard de Balliol's standard. He visited us once. Now, that's strange, those horses look like ours, too. Do you think they all had the same sire? I'm sure that's Barnabas, Robert's horse." She lifted herself up to see better. "It is! It is! Robert! Over here! Robert! Edgar!"

Catherine's head came up at once. "Edgar! Where?"

Margaret was beating the top of Samson's head in her excitement. Robert heard her and spotted her at last, then pointed her out to Edgar.

"Margaret!" Edgar nearly fell from his horse in surprise. "Margaret, where's Catherine?"

"Here!" a voice called. "Get out of my way!"

He looked down. A ripple passed through the crowd and emerging from it. Like Venus from the waves, only dirtier and fully clothed, was Catherine, James in her arms.

It was one of those moments when the earth becomes silent. Edgar no longer noticed the procession he had just halted, or the people in the crowd. He slid from his horse and onto the ground, his knees having refused to support him. Catherine knelt, too, facing him.

"You're alive," he said.

She nodded. "I've taken good care of your son."

He touched James's head in wonder. "I thought you were dead."

"I feared you were, too." She felt tears start.

"I won't ever let us be parted again."

"No, you won't."

They came together, their foreheads touching first, then their lips, both of them supporting their child safely between them. There were those among the people who watched who said that one ray of sunlight shone just on them. Later some reported that an angel had hovered above the family. That is the way legends begin.

Eighteen

The hospital of Saint Giles, outside Durham. Friday, 13 kalends September (August 20), 1143. Feast of Saint Oswin, last king of Deira, who disbanded his army rather than shed blood and was martyred for it.

I ne can ne i ne mai tellen alle the wunder ne alle the pines ðat hi diden wrecce men on this land. And ðat lastede tha xix wintre wile Stephne was king, and æure it was uuerse and uuerse. . . . Tha was corn dære and flec and cæse and butere; for nan ne waren sum rice man. Wrecce men sturuen of hungær . . . And hi sæden openlice ðat Crist slep and his halechen.

I can not tell all the wonder and all the suffering that these men did wreak upon this land. And it lasted the nineteen winters that Stephen was king and it grew ever worse and worse. . . . Corn was dear then and meat and cheese and butter for no man was wealthy. Wretched people died of starvation . . . And they said openly that Christ slept and also his saints.

—*Anglo Saxon Chronicle*, 1137

$\mathcal{E}$ventually Catherine and Edgar were recalled to the fact that they were blocking the road. The first notice was when Robert's horse nudged the back of Edgar's neck, causing him to yelp at the sudden coldness. He was deeply embarrassed when he saw all the eyes concentrated on them. He stood quickly, helped Catherine up and took the baby from her. They moved out of the way of the procession and those watching moved their attention elsewhere.

"We're staying in the hospital here," Catherine explained. "Willa isn't well and, Edgar, I'm so sorry, Adalisa is dead."

"I know," he said. "The brother from Lindisfarne told me,"

"Our message got through? And you didn't come to us at once?"

"The brother only arrived a few days ago," Edgar explained. "I couldn't get permission to leave. Oh, *carissima*, it's a long story. Do we have to tell it all now?"

They entered the building where the chaos was almost as bad as in the street. People were scurrying about, trying to arrange lodging for the bishop's party. There was an air of rejoicing. Like the barons, the people of Durham were sure that William of Saint-Barbe would soon restore the natural order. Knowing the disposition of those in Cumin's party, Edgar wasn't so sanguine.

Catherine threaded the way back to the single cot where Willa lay. She was sitting up now and offered to take James.

"No, thank you, Willa," Edgar said. "I need to hold him myself for a while, to be sure he's whole and well."

"You should go out and sit in the clean air," Catherine added, "as Master Herbert directed."

Willa went out and Catherine and Edgar sat themselves on a hard bench against the wall. Catherine put her arm about Edgar and laid her head on his shoulder. As far as she was concerned, natural order had already been restored.

Edgar held James out at arm's length. The baby grinned, drool running down his chin. His small feet kicked under his long tunic.

"I can't believe it," Edgar said. "I left him looking like a bundle of washing and come back to find him almost a person. Fat enough, too. Although, looking at you, I'm afraid you starved yourself to feed him."

"It doesn't work that way," Catherine said. "He takes what he wants and I get the scrapings. No, it was Solomon who went hungry to be sure the girls and I had enough. We owe him." She raised her head. "Edgar, there's so much to tell you. I'm beginning to think I know who's responsible for all the attacks on us and your family. It just seems impossible."

"You should hear Robert's solution. Yours can't be stranger than that," Edgar answered, never taking his eyes from James. "He thinks Father has planned it all."

"He does?"

"There are a hundred flaws in the theory," Edgar said. "Why would a man kill his own future?"

"I don't know," Catherine said slowly. "It sounds like the work of a madman, but Edgar, that's what I've been thinking, too."

Edgar stopped bouncing James and turned his full attention to her.

"You can't mean that."

"It's the only thing that makes sense," she answered. "Let me tell you what's happened."

As she did so, Edgar grew more and more still. He put James back on his lap so he could keep his arms around both of them. He had thought the fire was the greatest danger they had faced. It was good that he hadn't known how treacherous the journey had been. Fear for them might have been too much for his reason.

"Oh, Catherine, what have I brought you to?" He kissed her again.

"Nothing I didn't accept when we married," she said firmly. "Now, let me finish. It was the horses that made me suspicious. Margaret insisted that the men who killed Adalisa rode horses that belonged to your father. And Solomon says that Adalisa recognized one of the men. She died before she could say who, and when the tide turned and the beach was searched, the bodies were gone. But I think they were Waldeve's men. Are you listening to me?"

This last was because Edgar had been using the end of one of Catherine's braids to tickle James with.

"Yes, I'm listening," he answered. "I'm just not sure I can credit it that you and Robert came up with the same improbable conclusion. I need time to let it sink in. Even if it's true, what can our next move be? It's a serious thing to accuse one's father of a crime like this. I don't even think there's a word for it."

"I know." She put her head back on his shoulder.

For a long time neither of them spoke. The wonder of their reunion was slowly replaced by the security of familiarity, of knowing that they fit together as they always had. James had caught the end of the braid and was now using it to soothe the spot on his gums where a tooth was about to break through. His eyes slowly drooped and when Edgar next looked down, he was asleep.

"Catherine, how long do you think he'll be like this?" He whispered.

She looked around the room. "Long enough, but there's no private place here."

"Outside? In the woods, the cemetery? Anywhere!" His breath was warm against her cheek. Catherine felt her body start to melt.

"Edgar, believe me, if I knew of such a place, I would race you there." Catherine kissed the underside of his chin, then his throat, longing to work the rest of the way down.

"Wait, Catherine, stop," Edgar forced himself to say. "If that's the case, then we've got to get up and do something to distract ourselves. Now."

Catherine tried to catch her breath. "Uh, yes, what else? Oh, Margaret! We left her outside with Samson."

"Who's Samson?" Edgar asked. "Is he trustworthy?"

"I suppose so; he's a friend of Solomon's. Only he's English, no Norman, no Jewish. Well, he seems like all three. He speaks English and French with equal facility. Solomon and I think he may be a distant cousin, perhaps on our grandmother's side."

"Catherine," Edgar said. "You're babbling."

"It's either that or go tell the monks that we need a place to transact a payment of the marriage debt," she retorted. "Or use the floor here and risk being interrupted by the bishop."

"Babble away, then, if you must." He smiled. "I've rather missed it."

They were standing now, Edgar letting the baby dangle from

one arm in a way no woman would risk. Catherine knew his hold was firm. She found she couldn't think of anything more to say. She just looked at them, loving them both beyond all measure.

"Margaret," Edgar reminded her.

"Outside." She gestured vaguely.

There was no one out front in the road. After some blind alleys Edgar and Catherine found Margaret, along with Solomon, Samson and Willa, waiting for them in the garden.

"We thought you'd be longer about it," was Solomon's blunt salutation.

Edgar cuffed him with his free hand. "I decided it was more important to see for myself that you weren't too aged by the charge I left you."

His face grew serious.

"*Todah robah*, my friend," he said. "I can never repay you for the care you took of my family."

"My family, too," Solomon reminded him softly. "I only wish I could have protected Margaret's mother, as well."

"She was the only mother I remember having, although, now that I think of it, she and my brother, Alexander, were the same age. I shall miss her. She didn't deserve such a death, or such a life," Edgar said.

"She was cruelly treated by Waldeve," Solomon said, more to himself than Edgar.

Catherine glanced at him sharply. Edgar saw the look and raised his eyebrows questioningly. She shook her head.

"Speaking of brothers." Edgar filled the silence. "Has anyone seen Robert?"

"Not since we first saw you," Solomon told him. "Alfred followed him, hoping he would be able to get past the guards to your father."

"Alfred?" Edgar was surprised. "He's here, too? Robert told me the villagers were scattered over the countryside."

"Apparently the damage to the keep was worse than the damage to the village," Catherine said. "Isn't it usually the other way around?"

Edgar suddenly smacked his forehead with his palm. "Father!" he cried. "I'd forgotten. I have to go up to report to him. Robert doesn't know all that Conyers and the bishop told me. Catherine, I promise I'll return this evening."

"Don't worry." She smiled as she took James from him. "When you do, I promise there will be a place, a *private* place, waiting for you."

They ignored the hoots from Solomon.

"Now," Catherine said when he had gone. "You two can help me find one."

"Catherine, you're asking for a miracle," Samson protested. "Every private room, every curtained bed will be taken by the clergy or the lords."

"Then find me a stable," Catherine said. "If it was good enough for the blessed Virgin, it will be fine for us. We spent the first night of our marriage in a hayloft."

"I remember." Solomon grimaced. "I had to sleep under a tree."

Samson chuckled. "You may have to again. Come along, friend. I'm sure it's some sort of *mitzvah* to help perpetuate the race."

"Not of Edomites," Solomon grumbled.

"Who knows? Maybe they'll see the light one day and come to the True Faith." Samson led Solomon, still muttering, out of the garden.

Margaret and Willa had watched the proceedings with interest.

"Are you going to give James a baby brother?" Margaret asked.

Catherine blushed. "Probably not tonight." She sighed.

"Edgar must be different from Father," Margaret continued, considering. "Mother didn't like sharing the bed with him. She said I should enter a convent rather than marry. What do you think?"

Catherine thought it was a decision she wasn't qualified to make for Margaret. What she said was "God knows what's best for you. Why don't we leave it in his hands for now?"

That seemed to satisfy the child, to Catherine's relief. Time enough to be concerned with Margaret's future. They didn't even know if they could convince Waldeve to let them take her, or if she wanted to go. Although, it struck Catherine that she hadn't asked to be taken up to see her father. She wondered if he had expressed any concern for her at all.

"Margaret, how would you feel about coming back to Paris with us, if your father approves?" she asked.

Both Margaret and Willa's faces glowed like summer dawn. They hugged each other.

"Oh, please!" Margaret said. "Willa has told me all about the city. I want to see the pigs with bells and the martyrs' hill and the *pet du diable* and the donkey bishop and everything."

Catherine raised her eyebrows. "There are other things in Paris," she said. "The king's palace, churches, schools." She stopped herself.

Goodness! she thought. I sound just like Sister Bertrada!

Margaret paid her no mind. She and Willa began planning what they would do first when they returned. Catherine let them. After all, Cumin would have to surrender now that the real bishop had arrived. And, horrible though it was, they couldn't do anything to see that Waldeve was punished for his crimes, beyond informing his lord. Edgar couldn't be expected to participate in the trial of his own father, could he? They might be home well before Michaelmass.

That thought cheered Catherine enough to soothe the edge of constant fear that had been with her since they left France.

Edgar caught up with Robert before he was given an audience by the bishop. He bent to catch his breath.

"Have you seen Father?" he asked.

"Not yet," Robert answered. "And if he's done anything to harm Lufen, I swear I'll run him though."

"I liked the slow curse better," Edgar commented. "It has more time to enjoy. He likes watching others suffer so much. But I wanted to ask you, please, don't tell him Catherine and James are here."

"Why not?"

"The less they have to do with him, the better," Edgar said. "And, if you're right and he's having our family murdered, one by one, I don't want him to know they're still alive."

"Excellent sense," Robert said. "It's about time you started paying attention to me."

"Well, Catherine thinks you may be right," Edgar admitted.

"She does? I suspected you'd married above your intelligence."

Edgar ignored that. He sometimes agreed. Instead he asked about the whereabouts of Uncle Æthelræd.

"No idea," Robert told him. "I think he's convinced everyone here that he's totally mad, so they let him wander about as he wills. Of course, he's also big enough that even armed men think twice before challenging him."

"You know that when he acts the complete wild man, it means he's planning something." Edgar said.

"All too well," Robert tried not to think of certain episodes of his childhood. "Whatever it is, I don't want to be involved."

"Robert." Edgar sighed. "Nobody seems to be giving us a choice."

Waldeve was closeted with William Cumin, his steward, his loyal archdeacon, Duncan and Alan of Richmond. Edgar and Robert were sent into their presence at once.

"I sent you to get Conyers's surrender." Cumin glared at them. "Instead you bring an army back. Would you care to explain this?"

Robert shook his head. "Edgar, you're the philosopher."

Edgar bowed to the men. He cleared his throat nervously. "We delivered your ultimatum to Lord Roger and to William of Saint-Barbe. However, we also found that Saint-Barbe has acquired the support of many of the local barons. He feels that his position is strong enough to make you give up your hold on the see, either by force or through fear of the loss of your immortal soul. The message we were given is that if you turn over the keys and the chapter seal and honestly repent your actions, then you and your followers will be allowed to leave unmolested."

As he spoke, Edgar had difficulty refraining from backing closer to the door. Cumin's face grew dark with anger. He seemed about to erupt. Edgar wouldn't have been surprised if flames had poured from his mouth when he opened it to answer. The beleaguered bishop stood stiffly, his hand gripping his pectoral cross until his knuckles were white.

"This is why William Saint-Barbe has taken up residence at Saint-Giles? He believes that I'll throw myself before him and beg for mercy?"

He gave a furious jerk on the cross, bending the chain links so that it was pulled off, the chain clattering to the stone floor.

"What answer shall I give him?" Edgar asked, hoping it wouldn't be a blow.

"Answer?" Cumin laughed. "No answer at all, young man. You're my emissary, not Saint-Barbe's. Duncan, double the guards at all possible entries to the city. If Saint-Barbe or his cohorts come anywhere near them, drive them off. If that doesn't stop them, prepare to attack. How soon will your army be here, Lord Alan?"

"A few days, at most, Lord Bishop," the earl replied. "From what my spies report, we'll far outnumber the rabble Conyers has gathered."

"Good." Cumin's color had returned to normal. "Until then, we only need to seal ourselves off and let them wonder what terrible assault we're planning."

Edgar started forward to protest. "There must be some word of defiance that I could take back to Conyers and Saint-Barbe," he pleaded, seeing both his promise to Catherine and their reunion dissolve under this new threat.

Cumin regarded him with suspicion. "No, there will be no more communication between our palace and the invaders. They can stew until we're ready to smoke them out like lice. You may leave us now."

He held out his hand to them. There was nothing Robert and Edgar could do but bend over the nonexistent ring and back from the room.

"That went well, didn't it?" Robert commented. "We got out with all our limbs still attached."

"Robert, I have to get out of here." Edgar hit his palm with his fist. "I'm not risking losing Catherine and James again."

"Edgar, first of all, there's no way out," Robert said. "Secondly, if you get out and Cumin notices you're gone, he'll send men out hunting for you. And you've seen how much respect they show women and children."

"Then I'll have to get back in again, as well," answered Edgar.

"Brother mine, the only way you'll manage that is if you sprout wings."

"No, there is another way," Edgar said. "If the monks can help me. If we can get in to see them again. If they can get to the northern cliff. If I don't die of terror, I can do it."

They were at the church door. Robert gave it a push. The door didn't budge. He tried again.

"It's locked!" he exclaimed. "It's not enough that they shut up the monks in the cloister, now they're keeping the faithful from the shrine of Saint Cuthbert! Is there no offense the man will not commit?"

"Apparently not," Edgar said. "Of course, it could be locked from the inside. In fact, I think it is."

He tried to see through the keyhole. One of the pillars blocked his view of the door to the cloister on the opposite side.

"Æthelræd," he said. "We have to find him. He had the key to the north door to the priory."

"It will be guarded," Robert warned.

"Æthelræd is mad enough to find a way around that." Edgar had confidence in this aspect, at least, of his uncle's character. "Especially if we tell him that doing it will thwart Father."

After much questioning and several false directions, they at last found Æthelræd sleeping peacefully under a tree near the palace wall. They had no compunctions about waking him and little patience with the time it took him to shake the cobwebs from his mind enough to understand what they were asking of him.

"Apology first," he demanded.

"I give it willingly," Edgar said. "I beg your pardon for doubting your gift. I would have been spared my blackest hours if I had believed you."

"Nicely done. Short and sincere," Æthelræd said. "I forgive you."

"So will you help me?" Edgar asked.

"I'd have done that in any case." Æthelræd grinned. "If it will give a tweak to Waldeve's nose."

"The canons have a rope-chair and know the best place to use it," Edgar explained. "Robert and I have also promised to relay instructions from Saint-Barbe and Archdeacon Rannulf to those still locked in the priory. Can you get us in?"

"If there are fewer than four guards, there'll be no problem," Æthelræd assured him.

"With the added force at the gates and bridges, I doubt Cumin can spare more than two men," Robert said.

"Very well," Æthelræd said. "Meet me at the north door when the bells ring for Vespers. But, Edgar, are you sure you want to do this? I remember your dislike of heights. I had to come get you more than once when you'd climbed a tree and then looked down."

"I didn't need you to remind me, Uncle." Edgar looked ill already. "But my promise to Catherine is enough to overcome my fear."

Æthelræd expressed his opinion of this in one word, then added, "Don't make this a matter of personal honor, boy. What you mean is, you're willing to risk your life for a good lay. At least I presume she is."

Edgar frowned at their sniggering. "This is one subject about which you know nothing, Uncle. I need her for far more than that. I always have. I'm not going out to visit a whore, but to lie with my wife."

Æthelræd wasn't impressed. "Call it what you like; I still know what part of your body is leading you."

Edgar gave up the argument. He needed his uncle's help. And he knew it was no use expecting him to understand something he had never felt nor wanted to.

Æthelræd settled back down to finish his nap.

As they left him, Edgar was still muttering imprecations. Robert interrupted them.

"Give it up, Edgar. The old goat is more like Father than he wants to admit," he said. "He's never loved anyone. How can he know that a person can be one's whole life and the chance just to see them, to talk with them, can be worth any risk?"

Edgar felt shamed by Robert's compassion. "Thank you," he said quietly. "If I can do anything—"

"No," Robert cut him off. "I'm grateful, but you can't. No one can help me now but God."

"Catherine, we've scoured the whole village." Solomon's voice rose in exasperation. "Every place flat enough to unroll a blanket is taken."

"There must be one little corner somewhere." Catherine wasn't ready to give up.

"Not for those who aren't celibate," Solomon explained. "Or unless you want to rent yourself to the soldiers. Sorry, but that seems to be the two ends of the situation."

"I just hate to disappoint Edgar." Catherine sighed.

"Of course, my dear," Solomon said. "Such a good wife, putting her husband's desires before her own."

Catherine shut her eyes. "I'm just so tired," she said.

Solomon put his arm around her. "I know you are," he said gently. "There is something about lying with another body between you and the door that makes one sleep better. I don't believe you've had an uninterrupted night since we got here."

"Actually, not since James was born," she said. "But that was done for love. I'm sorry, Solomon. I shouldn't complain. You've had the responsibility for all of us on your back and had hardly any time to do the work you were sent here for. I should be kinder to you."

"I'd collapse from the shock," Solomon assured her. "And right now the wool trade doesn't seem very important. If someone doesn't restore order in this land, there'll be nothing left but burned fields and empty towns."

"When both the secular and clerical rulers are in dispute, how can anyone be sure of what the right order is?" Catherine said. "It's the same thing that happened when King Louis refused to appoint a new bishop for Reims. A few years of that and the town was in chaos. No wonder the merchants took things into their own hands and founded a commune."

"That brought the king around quickly enough," Solomon remembered. "Odd that it hasn't happened here."

Samson overheard the last part of the conversation.

"The individual lords are too powerful," he told them. "What we have instead are a hundred kings, each gouging as much as he can from the land while he can. Only Londoners have any say at all in how things are done. Did you hear how we kept Matilda from the throne?"

"Yes," Catherine said. "It's said it's because she treated the citizens like serfs."

"Exactly. We don't allow that from anyone," Samson said.

" 'We'?" Solomon asked. "You consider yourself one of the English? I thought you said they hated us."

"Not so much in London," Samson tried to explain. "It's complicated. The English hated Jews before we even came here, but in the way they hate demons and monsters or Danes. We only existed in stories. Like the idea that we have horns. In London, our neighbors know that we're just people. But outside of it, we're legends and it's hard to convince people that their folktales aren't true, especially when they're repeated by the priests."

"Horns?" Catherine was puzzled. "Like a cuckold?"

"Of course not!" Samson said. "More like a devil."

"How strange," she said. "I'm sorry you don't. You might be able to frighten someone into giving up their bed tonight."

"Catherine, can't you think of anything but getting you and Edgar a bed?" Solomon asked.

Catherine pretended to consider this. "No," she said. "I can't."

Æthelræd's subtle plan for getting past the guard at the door had been to start a brawl with two passing townsmen and pull the soldiers into the dispute. While they were occupied, Edgar and Robert used the key and entered the priory.

"I've no idea what he'll do when we need to get out," Robert said.

"One problem at a time," Edgar told him. "Now to find Brother Lawrence."

"That should be easy enough, seeing that the bell for the end of Vespers is still ringing," Robert reminded him.

"Right, they'll be coming out the door nearest the choir."

Now that they were inside, there was no worry about being seen. Robert and Edgar hurried to the covered walk where the monks were filing out."

"Brother Lawrence!" they called, causing all the men to stop. "We bring news from the bishop."

Instantly they were surrounded. A dozen people spoke at once, all asking the same question. "When will he be here to free us?"

Edgar regarded the men, some of whom he'd studied with, some whom he'd learned from. They were all much thinner and their robes showed holes and ragged edges that would never have been allowed previously. William Cumin had sworn he had done nothing to harm the monks, but he had made sure that they only received enough supplies to sustain life.

"William Saint-Barbe is even now at the church of Saint Giles," he told them. "He leads an army to take back Saint Cuthbert's shrine. He sent me to tell you to barricade the church from possible depredations and to pray constantly for their success."

"Nothing more?" Brother Lawrence asked. "We're prepared to do anything necessary, short of spilling Christian blood."

"He would never expect that of you," Robert said sternly. "But he doesn't want your martyrdom, either. Only take courage and be assured that your trial will soon be over."

The reaction to these words was close to miraculous. The air, itself, seemed less oppressive and the faces of the men brightened with hope.

"Now I beg you to loan me the rope-chair that you used to send messages down the cliff side last year," Edgar said. "Do you still have it?"

"Yes, but we haven't been allowed out since it was discovered," Brother Lawrence explained. "We'll make the attempt if you wish, though."

"If you could create a disturbance that would allow us to leave, that would be enough," Edgar told them. "My brother and uncle will lower me down and, with God's help, will pull me up again. Give me any missives for the bishop or Archdeacon Rannulf and Prior Roger, who are with him, and I'll try to return before dawn with their replies."

Brother Lawrence placed his hand on Edgar's head in benediction. "My son, I hereby forgive you for leaving us, for I was very disappointed in you when you did."

"Thank you, Brother," Edgar said. Inside he thought, I forgive you for making me listen to your inept imitations of Vergil. You're not the ass I took you for.

The riot inside the priory was just as effective as the brawl outside had been. The guards never made the connection between the two. All too soon for Edgar, he, Robert and Æthelræd were standing at the northern rim of the escarpment, looking down at a narrow path the fishermen had used in the calm days of King Henry.

He looked over the side. His head was spinning. Part of him wanted to get as far away from the cliff as possible; the other part felt a great compulsion to step off into the air.

"You don't have to do anything," Robert told him. "We'll throw the rope over this tree limb and let it out slowly. Just close your eyes until you feel the ground beneath your feet. Will you have any trouble swimming the river?"

"I'm afraid of height, not fish," Edgar answered. "And the current is slow this time of year. Get on with it."

He would have liked to have kept his eyes closed, but Edgar soon discovered that he had to balance with both hands and feet to keep from being constantly thrown against the rock wall. He tried to focus only on that. The few times he forgot and looked down caused him to grip the rope with both hands and pray to make his stomach stay in place until the ordeal was over. Then he would be suddenly dropped another few feet and jerked still, which terror distracted him from nausea.

When his feet did touch solid ground it was a moment before his knees would support him. He knew he'd have to repeat the process to get back up. He told himself it would be easier the next time.

It was nearly dark when he reached Saint-Giles, but no one seemed to be settling down for bed. The place was surrounded by soldiers. He only was able to get by them because Catherine had been watching and shamelessly pushed them aside and threw herself upon him.

"Beloved!" she wept. "I believed you had abandoned me to my fate, after all your sweet words. How could I tell my father you had broken faith?"

She dragged him into the church grounds. The guards didn't even challenge him, believing that he was about to receive more punishment than they might inflict.

"What was that about?" he asked, after he had kissed her soundly.

"The emissaries sent by the bishop to Cumin have either been beaten or driven off," she explained. "The soldiers have orders to treat anyone coming from Durham in like manner. Why are you all wet?"

"I swam the river," he said absently. "You mean Cumin won't even treat with the bishop?"

"Apparently not," she answered. "They're preparing for battle."

"Attack that citadel? It can't be done," he said.

"I agree but no one asked me," Catherine said. "All I know is that it's madness here and there's not one kind soul in the whole place who will loan us a bed for the night."

"Oh, *carissima!*" Edgar moaned.

"Exactly my feelings," Catherine lamented. "I'm so sorry."

"Never mind," he tried to convince the both of them. "We'll have the rest of our lives. Well, then, I might as well try to tell someone in authority that I've told the monks to prepare for rescue. I only hope I wasn't bringing false encouragement."

He left Catherine in her small space on the women's side of the hospital. She settled gloomily to wait. She told herself that her disappointment was nothing compared to the horrors being done to people all around, but it didn't cause her mood to lift.

Edgar came back a few minutes later with Solomon and Samson and wearing a most peculiar expression.

"Catherine," he said, "it appears that Master Herbert, the physician, has been convinced to let us have his chamber tonight."

"What?" Catherine held her breath. She couldn't bear to learn he was joking. "How can that be?"

Samson shrugged. "It's amazing what one can do with coin in this degenerate age."

"But we have no . . . oh, Samson. Thank you. We'll repay you, I swear, with interest," she promised.

"Solomon and I have arranged that," Samson said. "We do not practice usury between cousins. I only ask that, should there come a time when my people need help, you remember your debt."

"We shall," Edgar said. "Catherine, get your things and James."

"Why don't you leave him in the care of a woman here?" Solomon smirked. "We wouldn't want him to keep you awake all night."

"He won't be the cause of our wakefulness," Edgar said.

"I'll not let us be separated again," Catherine added.

Master Herbert's chamber was sumptuous. But delightful as freshly lavendered sheets and thick goosedown mattresses were, Edgar and Catherine only cared that they were alone at last.

"I haven't been able to wash as often as usual," Catherine warned him as she removed her clothes.

"Me neither," Edgar said, as he struggled with his wet leather boots. "The only bath I've had for the past two weeks was in the Wear this afternoon. I'll endure the smell if you can."

"*Libenter.*" Catherine stood before him, wearing only the ribands in her braids. She held out her arms.

Edgar glanced at the box in which James lay, sucking his thumb.

"He'll sleep soon." Catherine smiled. "What are you waiting for? I can see you're ready."

"Overly so," he answered, moving into her arms.

A moment later they fell onto the bed with a vigor that caused the mattress to rise at either end, releasing a cloud of lavender seeds and feathers.

Catherine knew that this had to be a foretaste of heaven.

Nineteen

Durham. Tuesday, 9 kalends September (August 24), 1143. Feast of Saint Bartholomew, apostle, who was flayed alive, thus making him the patron saint of tanners.

Sainte Nicholas, godes druth
tymbre us faire scone hus.
At thi burth, at this bare
Sainte Nicholas, bring us wel thare.

Saint Nicholas, God's beloved one
build us a fine house soon.
With thy birth, by thy direction
Saint Nicholas bring us rightly there.

—Hymn of Godric of Finchale

*D*o you think Edgar got back safely? There's been no word for days." Catherine had found Solomon and Samson standing at the wall overlooking the river. Across from and above them the castle loomed. It seemed to Catherine that the masonry itself scowled down in defiance. She was beginning to think of it as some sort of sleeping leviathan, with human beings trapped alive in its bowels.

Solomon grinned at her. "He wasn't walking too steadily when we met him that morning, but we saw him make it across the river just as the fog began to lift. If his brother and uncle were there to haul him up, he shouldn't have had any trouble getting back in. Of course, he's probably still recovering from the night. Was it fair to work him that hard, Cousin?"

Catherine had no quarrel with anyone on this radiant day. The sky was clear and Edgar would soon be back. She felt wonderful. "Yes, I did," she told Solomon smugly. "He was a great deal behind in his payments."

"Wanton woman!" Solomon laughed. "How far we've come from the convent!"

"Not so far," Catherine said. "Mother Heloise told me that if I were to marry I should devote myself to the task with all the energy I would have given to my devotions."

"In that case, your God has been deprived of a dedicated disciple." Samson laughed a little hesitantly. It was never wise to make light of the Christians' God.

" 'We all serve in our own way,' " Catherine quoted. "It will be only a few days now, won't it, until we can go home? The bishop's men are packing. Cumin's surrendered, hasn't he?"

Both men straightened, their easy demeanor changed at once.

"What do you mean?" Solomon asked. "There's been nothing out of Durham at all, as far as we know."

"Not that we'd be the first ones told. I'll find out." Samson hurried toward the bishop's temporary quarters.

Catherine felt all her joy evaporate.

"They're not preparing to move up to the town, after all, are they?" she said.

Solomon looked worried. "I doubt it. There was a rumor yesterday that a huge number of men, both mounted and on foot, were only a few miles away. No one knew who they were serving. Now it's obvious."

"Cumin has bought himself a fresh army, that's what you're saying!" Catherine's face drained of color. "Oh, Saints Genevieve and Denys, can't you protect us any more? Solomon, I thought we were finally safe. Where can we go now?"

Solomon had no platitudes to give her.

"I don't know," he admitted. "To venture on to the roads would be suicide. Who knows what we might get caught up in? We seem to have gone from a small family war into an enormous regional one and there's one even larger tearing the rest of the land apart. I'm sorry, Catherine, I'm not used to caring for other people. Getting out of trouble with my own skin intact is about all I'm good for."

Catherine rubbed his head affectionately, the curls twining around her fingers.

"I'm glad of that," she said. "You must continue to do so, for I'd miss you dreadfully. Now, we should have a plan. Since you and I know so little about this country, we need to ask someone to help us."

"Samson speaks the language," Solomon said. "But he doesn't know Durham well."

"Actually, I was thinking of Edgar's friend, the monk," Catherine said. "He grew up around here. If there's a place where we can find sanctuary, he would know."

Solomon grimaced. "If we go to him, then you'll have to do the talking. I'm quite used to dealing with Benedictines, but Cistercians make me nervous."

Catherine promised him that she had no fear of White Monks and went off alone in search of Brother Aelred.

Edgar, contrary to Solomon's assumption, had been given no chance to rest up after his sleepless night. Æthelræd and Robert had managed to pull him up the cliff, greeting him with yawns and pointed humor.

"The things you do in the service of Saint Cuthbert," Robert said. "Did you tell the bishop about Alan of Richmond's army?"

"Yes, Brother, I did that first," Edgar said. He had been relieved to find that it really was better coming up because the fog made it impossible to see how far down the river was, but he was still shaking.

"Does he have the men to fight Cumin off?" Æthelræd asked.

"I don't know," Edgar said. His teeth were chattering. "They didn't invite me to their council. Could we go inside somewhere? I'm soaking wet and freezing."

He did have a few hours' sleep, once he had drunk hot wine and found dry clothes, but those were the last for the next two days. When he awoke, he found that someone had informed Cumin that the canons had been able to communicate with William Saint-Barbe and after that, the hounds of Hell were set loose on the church of Saint Cuthbert.

"The monks have barred and barricaded all the doors to the church," Robert told him even before he had rubbed the sleep from his eyes. "I'm surprised the bells didn't wake you."

Edgar could hear them now, a constant tolling, not calling men to their prayers but summoning them to defend their patrimony.

"Cumin wouldn't invade the church," Edgar said.

"Right now, the soldiers are just standing by to see that no one gets in or out," Robert answered. "But they are only awaiting the order to break down the doors. It's a good thing you didn't try to get back into the cloister."

"Robert!" Edgar rubbed his forehead. "Remind me how all this happened to us. I was happily sitting by the window in Paris. Then you showed up and brought me and my family back to Scotland to avenge a murder. The usual kind of murder, nothing difficult. Just a little dispute between families. We've all been killing each other for generations. Right?"

"I suppose," Robert answered, not sure where this was leading.

Edgar reached up and pulled his brother's face down to his.

"So," he asked, "just when did I get pulled into Armageddon?"

Robert shook himself loose and handed him his boots. "You'll feel better when you've had some ale," he said.

Edgar didn't. The day only got worse and the day after that was even more unpleasant. Cumin had spent the past three years in a battle of wills with the canons. He had bullied, cajoled, threatened and bribed them, but he knew that if he was ever to have real control of the see, he would need their support. Now he seemed to have given up on them entirely.

Edgar thought of the friends he had inside. None of them had a weapon. They had survived all that time on faith and bloody-mindedness alone.

The next day Duncan and Waldeve and their men went on a raiding expedition. Edgar and Robert were not invited.

"They're safe at Saint-Giles," Edgar said, trying to convince himself. "The bishop and his men are there."

"Who's safe? Catherine?" Robert was sitting in the tavern with Lufen on his lap. They were sharing both meat and drink. Of the two, Lufen seemed the more alert. "Don't worry, even if the hospital is taken, Father will recognize her."

They both thought about this. Edgar stood up.

"I'm getting out of here," he said.

He rushed from the tavern and into a mass of soldiers, all rushing up the street and across the green toward the guards at the cathedral.

"What's going on?" he shouted to the man nearest him as he was carried forward on the wave.

"We're finally going to throw the monks out!" the soldier yelled back.

"What?" Edgar was horrified. "But the church doors are barred."

"Who needs doors?" The soldier laughed.

Edgar soon saw that he was right. Somehow he had thought that proper respect for the saints would have stopped the attackers, froze them in their tracks before they could do any damage. But the saints didn't seem to be at home.

The bell still tolled, as it had for the past few days, but as they drew closer, Edgar could also hear the chanting of the monks, interspersed with cries of fear and pain.

"They're unarmed and men of God!" he cried. "You can't mean to kill them!"

"Orders." The man shrugged cheerfully as they were swept apart.

"No," Edgar whispered.

"No." Louder. "Saint Cuthbert, Saint Bede, where the hell are you?"

"*No!*" he shouted at the top of his lungs.

Ever after Edgar was sure that the power of the saints had entered into him for mysterious reasons not his to dispute. How else could one explain his subsequent actions?

He grabbed a pike from someone and followed the horde as they entered the church. Not through the doors, which remained solid, but through the beautiful windows. Edgar's craftsman's heart twinged at the sound as the glass shattered and the soldiers climbed in. He followed them.

He couldn't believe the scene. Saint Cuthbert's sacred shrine was surrounded by monks, prostrate, imploring his help as soldiers ran toward them. Other monks tried to stand in the way of the invaders and were roughly pushed aside. One of the men drew his sword and caught a defiant monk under the chin.

Edgar ran him through with the pike.

The soldier fell, howling in pain and rage. Edgar let go the weapon and stared in astonishment at his own hands.

"*Gratias tibi ago, Egardus,*" the monk said as he scurried off to join his brethren at the shrine.

The soldier was still squealing, which led Edgar to realize two things. One, that he had managed to drive a pike through a man and yet not hit anything vital. Two, that this was the same man that he and Uncle Æthelræd had encountered their first day at Durham. He left him to his friends and hoped fervently that they wouldn't meet again.

The place was in chaos. The soldiers were taking delight in shattering everything they could, even breaking pieces off the carvings and chipping at the columns. The monks were dragged away from the shrine by their hands and feet, still praying. Edgar stood frozen with horror at such sacrilege.

Brother Lawrence was carried past him. The monk's eyes were shut tight and Edgar thought he caught the words of the psalm "*Miserere mei*" as he went by. He threw himself on the man carrying the monk's feet. Brother Lawrence dropped with a clunk as both his porters were knocked over. The one Edgar had tackled hit his head on the floor. The other one, however, was up in a moment. The soldier's eyes lit at the sight of someone he could hit with impunity. Edgar stared in stunned fascination at the fist as it closed in on his face.

And heard the howl of anger as the man was lifted by his armpits and thrown through the broken window.

Edgar felt his nose. It was still the same shape. There was no blood. He looked up. Uncle Æthelræd stood over him, his face more alive that Edgar ever remembered seeing it.

"A glorious day!" Æthelræd shouted, tossing another soldier over his shoulder.

"Uncle, we can't defeat them all," Edgar reminded him as he was helped up. "Some of Father's men are also my brothers, you know."

"Even worse, some are my sons," Æthelræd complained. "At least, I think so. Who's your mother, boy?" he called to a tall red-head bearing down on him.

The man's face was a mirror of consternation.

"Oh, shit," he said and lowered his sword. "Æthelræd, she'd kill me if I hurt you. Get out of here! I have work to do."

He moved on.

"You see my problem?" Æthelræd sighed. "I'll have to leave the country to get a good fight. Come along."

He took Edgar by the arm and tried to lead him away.

"Uncle, you've got to help me stop this!" he yelled above the increasing din.

"It's too late!" Æthelræd yelled back. "The monks are being evicted. They're the ones who need us. Saint Cuthbert will have to look after his bones for himself."

They climbed back through the broken windows, leaving behind the jubilant noise of the soldiers as they took possession of the church. Before them the monks were being driven across the green and down the hill. As they watched, one older man fell, clutching his knee in pain. He was roughly lifted and set on his feet, but the knee wouldn't hold him and he went down again. Edgar and Æthelræd ran to him. Edgar gave him a shoulder to lean on while his uncle grabbed the two soldiers tormenting him and knocked their heads together. They slumped to the ground.

"Amazing!" Edgar said. "I've heard of that in a hundred *gestes* but I never believed it worked."

"I didn't either," Æthelræd admitted. "But I've always wanted to try it. Now, Brother," he said to the monk, "you won't limp far on that. Let me carry you."

∞

At Saint-Giles everyone came out to the roadway when the bells started their summoning. Catherine had not yet found Brother Aelred but reactions of the people around her drove out every thought except her need to get to James.

"What's happening?" she asked the first person she saw.

She was greeted with a stare of incomprehension.

No one seemed to speak French. She hurried on to the sleeping room, where she found that Willa had gathered up the few things they had and was waiting for her with Margaret and James.

"Oh, Willa!" Catherine said. "What would I do without you?"

She took the baby and the four of them followed the throng out to discover the cause of the tolling.

They were jostled about by the crowds. The bishop's men were hurrying forward to see what was going on and the townspeople were moving away, back to what remained of their homes or into the forest to hide. Between them, Catherine and the girls made little progress.

"Hold on to my skirts!" Catherine ordered. "Don't let go for anything or we may never find each other again."

She had all she could do to keep hold of James. The tumult frightened him and he was screaming with all the force of his lungs. Catherine tried to calm herself enough to soothe him, but it was no use. In another moment, she was sure she would start screaming, too.

Margaret tugged at her from the right.

"This way," she said.

Catherine couldn't see where they were going, but she caught a glimpse of a hand holding Margaret's. She hoped that whoever was attached to it was a friend.

They were being led in back of the hospital, through the graveyard and up onto a wooded path. It was there that they left the stream of people at last and Catherine saw the face of their rescuer.

"Oh, Brother Aelred!" she said in relief. "I could kiss you. Thank God for sending you to us. Have you seen my cousin? Do you know where Edgar is?"

The monk shooed them farther out of the way of the fleeing families.

"I've had no word from him," he told her. "Nor have I seen your cousin. Lord Roger told me that the soldiers were taking down the barricade at the north gate. At first we hoped that the bells were of rejoicing and that the time of trial was over, but the tolling was irregular, as if another man took over whenever one fell. Then they stopped altogether."

He looked in that direction, but the forest around them was too thick.

"Now I can only imagine what might be happening to the body of the holy saint," he said. "And to the men who guard it. I was going down to the gate when I saw you."

"Thank you for stopping," Catherine said.

Aelred didn't answer her for a moment. He was still facing Durham.

"My father was a priest of Saint Cuthbert," he said. "And my grandfather and on back as far as my family remembers. From one generation to the next we were charged with protecting the saint. It was our sacred duty. It's not something one gives up lightly. I heard the bells and my first thought was to save Cuthbert."

He looked at Catherine and smiled. "Then I saw your poor little band and I knew, just as if a voice had spoken, that it was more important to see to your safety. Cuthbert wouldn't want a servant who ignored the needs of the living."

Margaret had not let go of his hand the whole time. Now she let go to reach up until he bent down and let her kiss his cheek. Aelred hugged her and smoothed her hair.

"I shall pray every night that Saint Cuthbert might bless you," Catherine told him. "Can you take me to my husband?"

"No, and he wouldn't want me to, the way things are there," Aelred said decidedly. "But, if you'll come with me, I know a place as secure as any is in this sad land. Godric is a friend of mine and Edgar's, too. He'll take you in. Follow me. The way is steep but not long."

He led them up and down through the woods. They stepped stone by stone over rushing streams and then through thickets where Catherine would never have believed a trail could go. At last they came out onto a clear spot of land, surrounded on three sides by a rushing river. On the other side of the river were steep cliffs. There were a few huts of wood or daub and wattle placed here and there, a vegetable plot and also two proper buildings, one of wood and the other of stone, linked together by a passageway made of latticed hazelwood and covered with a thatched roof.

Aelred went up to the doorway of the stone building and rang a bell that was hanging there.

"This is Godric's chapel," he explained. "It's dedicated to Saint John the Baptist. You're free to go in here. The other building is his oratory and it's private."

"I understand," Catherine said. But she wasn't sure she really did.

There were other people about. They seemed to be in family groups, mostly the old and young, with several women of middle age and two or three men. By their weary looks, Catherine assumed they had come here for refuge, too.

"Are you sure we'll be welcome here?" she asked. "There may be too many to feed."

"Godric will see that you have enough," Aelred assured her. "He wouldn't turn anyone away. Ah, here he comes. I only hope this isn't one of his silent days." ·

Catherine's eyes grew round with astonishment as she was introduced to the hermit. She saw a little old man, older even than her mother's ancient father and much more stocky. His hands were gnarled and his bare arms thickly muscled. His face was half hidden by a thick white beard and bushy eyebrows. He wore only a long hairshirt, and Catherine tried not to back away from the stench of it. His feet were bare, callused and scarred. His eyes were gentle, a mild blue.

Aelred spoke to him for a few moments. Catherine thought she caught Edgar's name. Godric continued to look at them as he listened to their story. At one point, he put out a filthy finger to touch James.

"*Povre enfes*," he said.

His accent was thick, but Catherine understood.

"*Godes man?*" she asked.

His smile was broad. "*Ic treow.*"

Catherine looked to Aelred for the meaning.

"He says he hopes he's a man of God," the monk told her. "I believe he is. He'll make a place for you until Edgar can come get you."

"Thank him for us," Catherine said. "Tell him we have been running for weeks now and are grateful for a safe haven."

Aelred did so. Godric's face grew serious. He spoke for some time. When he had finished, Aelred turned back to Catherine.

"He reminded me that while his hermitage is considered a holy place by many, there are also those who have no respect for sanctity.

He's been robbed of the little he has several times and was beaten and left for dead by marauding soldiers five years ago. They believed that the people of the district had left their treasures in his keeping."

"I understand," Catherine said, and this time she did. "Please tell him that I am aware there is no place that is completely protected but that I place my faith in Our Lord and accept whatever He sends. Ask him, also, if there is anything we might do to help make ourselves less of a burden on him."

"I can tell you that, as he won't," Aelred said. "Respect his privacy. He eats and prays alone. Other than that, take what you need from the garden and the fish traps. He'll help you if you need it. Now, Godric will show you where you can sleep. I shall return to Durham and, I hope, locate either Edgar or your cousin."

"Thank you, Brother Aelred," Catherine said. "We are in your debt."

When he had left, the old man led them to one of the huts. It had no windows or firehole, but there was fresh straw on the floor and a door one could latch from inside. Catherine tried not to think of how easily a torch could set it ablaze. It was warm enough and out of the weather. She nodded her gratitude and she and the girls went in.

When Solomon saw the monks being driven from the town, his first reaction was incredulous delight. Then the reality of what was going on hit him.

"Samson," he said, "the whole damn army is heading for us!"

There was no reply. Solomon turned around. Samson wasn't there, but a line of guards from the bishop's retinue was. Solomon waved at them with both hands clearly open and empty. He smiled in what he hoped was a friendly, supportive fashion.

"Good work, men," he said as he made his way through the lines. "Crossbows at the ready. Swords newly sharpened. I have complete confidence in you."

They paid no attention to him. That was fine with Solomon.

He was also caught in the press of panicked citizens. By the time he reached the hospital Catherine had gone. Another woman was sitting on Willa's bed, nursing one infant while another child slept at her side. She regarded Solomon with deep suspicion.

Outside, he searched the area behind the soldier's blockade. It was only when he was certain that they weren't in any of the other buildings that he allowed himself to rest against a tree. After a moment he slammed his fist into it with painful force.

"I can't believe it!" he exclaimed. "I've lost her again."

A dagger came skittering across the cobblestones, hitting Edgar's foot. He grabbed for it. In front of him, Æthelræd carried the monk. The two of them made up a rear guard of sorts between the black-robed outcasts and the soldiers. Ahead of them there was a narrow passage that the monks were being pushed into. The other side meant exile for them and they continued to protest as they were shoved along. For Edgar it meant freedom. He was determined to reach it.

Someone came at him from his left; Edgar twisted and jabbed at the attacker. There was a squeal of protest.

"Lord Edgar! No! Please. It's me, Alfred!"

Edgar lowered the knife. "Alfred, I'm sorry," he said. "What is it? Hurry. They're getting away from me."

He pulled the old man along, stumbling in his rush to catch up. Æthelræd and his burden were in the passage now. The crowd was closing between them. Edgar felt like the last Israelite racing to get across before the sea closed in on him.

"Lord Edgar!" Alfred cried.

"Not now, Alfred." Edgar shoved his way through. He was almost there when he was hit from behind. For a moment he stayed upright in the crush of bodies, then he slid gracelessly to the ground.

When he opened his eyes again, it was to see the soft green of leaves above. The wind rustled them and a stab of sunlight shot through, causing him to moan and put his hands over his face.

Robert's voice was far too close and loud.

"Awake again, are we?"

Edgar uncovered his eyes. They were back on the edge of the palace green. The battle seemed to be over. From the church there came the sounds of a song that was once a hymn to the Virgin. What words Edgar could make out were in praise of another sort of woman entirely.

"Damn," he said. "I was almost out. How did I get back up here?"

"Alfred brought you," Robert said. "It was either that or leave you to be trampled."

"What's going on now?" Edgar asked. "Did Æthelræd make it through?"

"So Alfred said," Robert told him. "I stayed in the tavern until the shouting was over. Father has taken his men with Cumin's, and last I heard, William de Saint-Barbe was on the run back to Bishopton. He's probably wishing he could just continue on to York."

"Does that mean we can leave, too?" Edgar brightened.

"In principle, I would say yes," Robert answered slowly. "But there are five well-armed men stationed casually between us and any of the roads leading out. All of them are carefully not looking directly at us. I recognize them all. They're not just father's retainers; they also come from Wedderlie, itself."

"I don't suppose we could prevail upon family feeling to get them to let us go?" Edgar asked.

Robert felt his head. "Why would they want to help us? We're legitimate. They're not."

"We used to play with them when we were boys," Edgar said. "It didn't matter then."

"Yes it did, Edgar," Robert said. "It always mattered. Robert of Gloucester could be king of England now if his mother had held out for marriage. Instead he's supporting the claim of his half sister. Don't you think he sometimes resents her? These men have less cause to help us. We can't even offer them patronage."

"But what purpose would Father have in keeping us under guard now?" Edgar was slowly coming awake. "We have no information to betray him with. He's made it clear that he doesn't consider us a military threat. He doesn't know you suspect him, does he?"

"Of course not," Robert answered. "Do you think that's why he hasn't killed us, that he sees we're no danger to him? Maybe it's over then. He wanted Duncan to be his heir. Now that he is . . . no, then he'd let us go. You're right. It makes no sense."

Edgar cautiously sat up. His head ached and he was nauseated. He swore to himself that if they ever returned to Paris he would never leave again and that it would be a long time before Catherine and James ever left his sight.

"I'm not going to sit here debating imponderables," he said. "Father may want us held captive but I'm not going to wait for him to decide what to do with us. I've got to get back to Saint-Giles and find Catherine."

"Edgar, she's not there." Robert caught Edgar as he tried to stand. "The place was cleared out. She's probably with the other villagers. Or Solomon will have taken them with him."

Edgar had to be content with that for the time being.

Robert wasn't as indifferent to his situation as Edgar supposed.

"We can get out of here and go hunt your family again," he said. "But we need to evade the guard."

"How?" Edgar asked.

"I'm working on a plan," Robert told him.

"Is there any reason you can't work on it in the tavern?" Edgar wanted to know.

"None at all, if they'll let us," Robert said. "It might help matters."

"Then let's go," Edgar said. "I can make my legs take me that far."

Their guards seemed perfectly happy to follow along.

"Catherine, look what James can do!" Margaret proudly moved out of the way to show the baby sitting upright, only slightly supported by a rolled up tunic at his side.

He grinned soppily at them all, showing the tooth that had just broken through his upper gum.

Catherine looked up from the grain she was grinding between two stones. She wiped the sweat from her face with her loose hair and smiled back at them. It amazed her that despite the primitive living conditions, all three children were thriving. After hearing one of Willa's coughs, Godric had brought her a wad of herbs stuck together with something that smelled vile. Willa had gagged but swallowed it, and within a few hours the cough was fading. Obviously this place was sanctified.

She went back to her work. In the heat, none of the people there were wearing more than their tunics. Some of the younger children went about naked, their pale northern skin slowly turning to tan. Their host only appeared from time to time, but his voice could often be heard from his little oratory raised in prayer or song. Catherine wondered if the others found it as comforting as she did to know that they were a part of his constant devotion.

She examined the results of a whole morning bent over the stones. It was barely a few handfuls of flour and all of it coarse. Godric had given them all a barrel of grain but it hadn't been ground. Catherine wondered why there was no mill nearby. The river was certainly strong enough. Perhaps it was too unpredictable. With those high cliffs, it might be inclined to flood.

Her mind went back to the wind-powered mill that the men at Lindisfarne had been struggling with. The design was impractical but if it could be made more secure to the ground and still be turned to catch the wind, she brushed back her loose hair again, what a blessing it would be to the women who still were forced to make flour with a hand quern.

Catherine knew it was Sunday only when the priest came to say Mass in the chapel. The man seemed awed by the number of people attending and made several mistakes, once reversing the order of the ceremony. Catherine was tempted to correct him, but held her tongue. With maturity comes wisdom.

The priest also brought news from the outside world. Saint-Barbe had been forced back to Bishopton and the town of Durham was open once again. At that, several people immediately began to prepare to return.

Catherine wasn't sure what to do. All this dashing about meant that Edgar might not know where to find them. And where was he? Had he gone to Bishopton or was he still at Durham? If Aelred had told him where they were, wouldn't it be best to stay there? It was so easy to miss someone.

It was late the next afternoon before she had made up her mind to stay where they were, if Godric would permit it, when Alfred appeared. Margaret ran to him and leapt into his arms. He carried her over to Catherine.

"Alfred says that Edgar and Robert are waiting for us at Durham," Margaret said. "We should come at once."

Catherine thanked the man with her small English and went to once again gather up their things, stuff them in a sack and prepare to set out.

Godric was unavailable but they left a message with one of the local people to give him their thanks and tell him where they had gone.

Alfred led them through the thicket and onto a road.

The sun slipped lower. It seemed to Catherine that they had been walking a long time. She wondered if Alfred were taking them by a more-traveled route. Finally she became worried.

"Margaret," she said. "Would you ask Alfred if he's sure we're on the right road?"

Margaret did. It was then that two things happened. The first was that four men came round the bend in the road ahead. The second was that Alfred drew his knife. Catherine prepared to run. Alfred was no match for four young thugs.

Margaret gave a gasp and then a cry of disbelief. Catherine saw that Alfred's knife was against her throat.

Twenty

A camp in the forest near Durham. Tuesday, 2 kalends September (August 31), 1143. Feast of St. Aidan, missionary, founder of Lindisfarne, friend of kings, whose prayers could turn the course of the wind.

Maledictus sit ubicunque fuerit, sive in domo, sive in agro, sive in via . . . sive in silva, sive in aqua, sive in Ecclesia. Maledictus sit vivendo, moriendo, manducando, bibendo, . . . Maledictus sit in totis viribus coporis. Maledictus sit intus et exterius. Maledictus sit in capillis, maledictus sit cerebro.

May he be cursed where ever he may be, whether at home, in the fields, in the road, . . . the wood, the water, or the Church. May he be cursed living, dying, eating, drinking. . . . May he be cursed in every part of his body, inside and out. Cursed in the blood; cursed in the brain.

—Tenth Century Excommunication Formula,
Capitularia regum Francorum

*C*atherine cursed herself roundly for her stupidity. Why hadn't it occurred to her that this kindly old man had been a servant of Waldeve's for all his adult life? She had been so careful not to trust a stranger, so sure of her judgment. Now they were all going to be killed because she hadn't the sense to stay put.

What she didn't understand was why they weren't dead already. There was one slim hope that they were being held for ransom, but that made no sense, for Waldeve was the only one in Britain who could pay it.

At least no one had tried to harm them, although a couple of the men were giving Willa looks that made Catherine want to grab a knife and destroy any chance of their accomplishing what they were so obviously thinking.

She wished Margaret would tell them what the men were saying, but Margaret had retreated into herself. The shock of having her old friend threaten to kill her on top of the calamity of her mother's murder was more than the child's mind could bear. She lay in Willa's arms, sucking her thumb and keening softly. No one disturbed her.

"Mistress?" Willa said over Margaret's steady sorrow. "Do you think someone will come save us?"

"I don't know, Willa," Catherine answered. "I don't see how, since no one knows where we are. It may be that Alfred is under orders simply to hold us for some reason. We may soon be taken on to Durham or back to Wedderlie."

"But why are they holding us at all?" Willa asked. "Are we important? I mean, you and Margaret and James."

"I don't think so." Catherine had been trying to puzzle that out. "Unless Waldeve plans to send to my father for a ransom. I'm sorry, but I don't understand this any more than you do. There's really only one thing we can do for now."

Willa nodded. "I haven't stopped praying since we came to Britain." She sighed. "Do you think we're too far away for the French saints to hear us?"

"Of course not, silly." Catherine was certain of this. "In Heaven they can hear you anywhere you pray."

Willa was comforted by this, but Catherine wasn't so easy in her conscience. Perhaps she had done something so bad that she didn't deserve the intercession of the saints She couldn't think of anything so awful that retribution would fall on these children.

James wiggled in her arms. Now that he was beginning to want to move about, it was becoming increasingly hard to keep him quiet while he was being held. Catherine realized that she had been clutching him over her breasts, using him as a shield. It was irrational to think that the fact that she had a baby would keep these men from hurting them. She knew all too well that the bodies of women and children were left behind like refuse after an army passed through.

James was beginning to fuss. Catherine looked around at the men, trying to judge if there would be any danger if he were put down.

Their captors weren't watching them closely. Alfred kept one eye on them as he directed preparations for the evening meal. There was a chill in the air that was a reminder that summer would soon be ending.

She put the baby down in the space between herself and Willa. He immediately rolled over to his stomach and then to hands and knees, rocking like a hunting dog straining at the leash. Alfred got up and came over to them. Catherine snatched James back to the security of her lap, to his great annoyance.

The old man looked down on them with what seemed to be pity. That frightened her more than malevolence would have. It was the expression someone might give a favorite calf before sending it to the butcher.

He took off his cloak and laid it on the ground for James. Then he backed away.

Willa's prayers matched the pitch of Margaret's keening.

Catherine wondered if any of them would be sane by morning.

∞

In the tavern, Edgar pushed away his bowl of ale. He glared at Æthelræd, who had returned with no news of Catherine.

"Forget it," he told his uncle and brother. "We can't outdrink
them. I'll pass out before any of them do."

"It's that weak French beer that's done this to you, Edgar."
Æthelræd shook his head in disappointment.

They were seated at a table in the loft of the tavern. Below them,
the guards seemed to have made the best of their duty and were fast
emptying the barrel the owner had brought up only that morning.
None showed signs of being the worse for it.

Edgar had just put his head on the table when Algar came in. He
greeted the guards.

"Have you been here the whole day? What's the matter with
you? Grandfather would be furious with you, not to mention Lord
Waldeve. I suppose that means Grandfather isn't back yet?"

One of the men tried to shush him, but Algar was annoyed and
wouldn't be quieted. "He said he'd be back from Finchale last night.
What if there was trouble?"

Edgar lifted his head. Why had Algar's grandfather gone to Finchale? Alfred had no business with Godric there that he knew of.
What was his father up to now?

He opened his mouth to shout down to them. Æthelræd
clamped his hand over it.

"Algar doesn't know we're here," he whispered. "Wait. See if he
spills any more before they can shut him up."

The men were trying to, still under the illusion that their presence hadn't been noticed by the three upstairs.

"Sit down, Algar, have some beer," one said.

"Don't be an ass," Algar answered. "Grandfather may have been
set upon by bandits or fallen and broken his leg. I don't know why
one of you couldn't have gone, instead."

"Did that last time," another muttered, slurring a bit. "But the
bitch wouldn't trust me."

"Widsith, you fool!" The other whacked him on the head,
which caused Widsith to slide off his stool and into the matted straw
on the floor.

"What's he talking about?" Algar glared at the ones still upright.

"He's drunk; it means nothing," the first man said.

He looked up at the loft, Robert waved. Algar followed the
glance. He stopped and bowed apology.

"Lord Robert," he said in a milder tone. "I didn't realize you were there. Are these men in your company?"

Robert shook his head. "I just came for a nice bowl or two with my brother and uncle, and Lufen, of course."

"Have you seen my grandfather, Alfred?" Algar asked.

One of the men put his head down and pounded it against the table.

"Not today," Robert answered. "Gone to Finchale, has he? The roads aren't safe, you know."

"I know," Algar said. "But Grandfather didn't seem to agree. He said there were people from Wedderlie there that he needed to contact. But he should have been back by now, so I suppose I'd better find someone sober and go out searching him."

"Oh, don't waste time with that; we'll help, won't we?" Robert said.

Edgar and Æthelræd both instantly expressed their enthusiasm for locating Algar's grandfather.

The soldiers made one last attempt.

"You can't bother their lordships," the leader said. "They've better things to do."

"Not a bit." Æthelræd came down the ladder from the loft. "We weren't allowed to join the chase of Saint-Barbe's army to Bishopton. We could use an outing. Do you have a horse, Algar?"

"Yes, in the stables with the others," Algar answered.

"Then let's be off." Æthelræd put an arm around the young man's shoulders. "No doubt we'll come across him along the road. Probably just taking his time coming back in this bright weather."

They left the tavern. Inside four soldiers began pummeling a fifth, passed out on the floor. Each of them was trying not to think what would happen if Edgar discovered what Alfred was doing.

At that moment Alfred was on his hands and knees, trying to make Margaret stop wailing and take notice of the world again.

"*Swetnes*," he pleaded. "I wouldn't have harmed you, *deorling*. Hasn't old Alfred always been good to you? Please, please come back, Margaret. I need you to talk to the Lady for me."

Margaret paid him no attention. Her eyes were glazed over with sorrow. Willa held her ever more protectively.

Catherine understood the tone, if not the words. It confused her even more. He didn't seem to want to hurt Margaret or any of them. But then why had he threatened them? Why were they being kept here?

"Please, Saint Catherine, Holy Mother Mary, please don't let them be waiting for Waldeve to come," she begged. Even more, she feared it would be Duncan, this brother who according to Edgar was even more of a monster than his father. What kind of family declared war on itself? Well, unless a crown was at stake, or property, or . . . Oh, dear. Now that she considered, internecine warfare was fairly common, even in France.

Catherine understood at last why having an apostate Christian for a father-in-law hadn't been difficult for Edgar to accept. His father behaved as if there were no divine justice at all.

Alfred gave up on Margaret and tried, by means of gestures, to explain to her that he didn't want to kill her, either. She need only be patient and she would soon be home.

Catherine had no idea what his hopping about and pointing signified.

"Mistress?" Willa's voice made Alfred stop in his dance. "Mistress, can you hold Margaret now that James is asleep? I need to relieve myself."

"Of course," Catherine held out her arms for the child. "Go behind the tree here. If one of those beasts makes a move, I'll scream loud enough to shake the birds from the branches."

Willa had less trouble making her needs clear than Alfred. He nodded. Willa vanished into the brush behind the tree as Catherine glared threateningly at the men.

Time passed. Margaret fell asleep. James woke. Willa didn't return. Catherine began to be worried. She counted the men. They were all there.

Willa wouldn't have gone far. Could she have become ill and be lying unconscious? What if she had tried to run for help? Despite the throb of hope that thought caused, Catherine hoped she hadn't done anything so foolish. A young girl alone on the road, unable to speak the language, would be more likely to find death than assistance.

Eventually Alfred also noticed that Willa hadn't come back. He told one of the men to go look for her. Then added another command that wiped the eager grin off his face. He went into the brush where she had vanished.

Time passed. The sun began to set. Margaret woke. She didn't make any more noise, only curled up into a fetal ball on the cloak next to James. The baby patted her nose but she made no response. The man Alfred sent didn't return either. Catherine became even more alarmed. Eventually Alfred did, too. With a sharp expletive, he sent the other three men in search.

There was a surprised cry, cut off suddenly. Catherine threw herself over the children. Alfred picked up his staff and stood over her. Whether he meant to protect them or keep them from escaping, Catherine couldn't tell.

The brush behind the tree rustled and was pushed aside. Alfred raised his staff.

Algar stepped into the clearing.

"What the hell are you doing here?" Alfred demanded.

"I came looking for you," Algar said. "What are you doing with this woman?"

"It's nothing to do with you," Alfred said.

"Yes, Grandfather, it is," Algar answered.

There was more rustling.

"Catherine."

Catherine raised her head slowly. She wasn't ready to believe in this miracle.

"Catherine." Louder, nearer. She looked up.

"Edgar!"

Alfred saw him, dropped the staff and sunk to the ground sobbing. Edgar stepped over him and lifted Catherine.

"I'm sorry," he said. "I never should have—"

"I'm sorry," she said. "I should never have—"

They both stopped at the same time.

"Are you all right?" he asked.

"No one has hurt us, but Willa is missing," Catherine said.

"We found her. Everything's fine, now," Edgar told her. "I'm taking you back to Durham with me. Then we're going to Wearmouth and take the first boat home."

"Margaret, too, Edgar," Catherine said.

"Yes, of course, if she wants." Edgar would have agreed to anything.

Catherine buried her face in his musty tunic. It smelled of damp and mold and Edgar. She inhaled deeply. Then she forced herself to address the situation.

"What happened to the men with Alfred?" she asked.

"Trussed up and thrown over horses," he answered. "Robert and Æthelræd are guarding them."

Alfred was still weeping in his grandson's arms. Algar gave them a pleading look.

"I can't get any sense out of him," he said. "He just keeps begging me to take him to the sanctuary."

"Which sanctuary? Durham?" Edgar asked. "It's overrun with soldiers. No one will find sanctuary there. But Algar, tell him I won't have him punished. He was only doing what my father ordered and no one here was hurt. He doesn't need sanctuary from me."

At this Alfred's grief only increased. He clawed at Algar's sleeve.

"Make them give me safe conduct to Hexham," he said. "Sanctuary there and I will tell him everything."

Algar looked at Edgar, who shrugged.

"Very well," he said. "But I'm taking my family back to Durham now. My uncle and brother can escort you to Hexham."

"No!" Alfred switched his pleading to Edgar directly. "You mustn't go back there! The danger is too great. You don't know what they have planned for you."

Edgar lost patience.

"Then tell me!" he commanded.

Alfred leaned back on his heels.

"Sanctuary," he said.

Edgar explained to Catherine what the old man had said.

"Alfred must be terrified of what my father will do to him," he concluded. "But I won't have you spending another night in the open just to indulge him."

"We could go back to Finchale tonight," Catherine said. "Isn't Godric's church a sanctuary of a sort? The journey won't hurt us. It hasn't so far. James can sit up now, you know. And Willa's cough is almost gone. Alfred says that Durham is dangerous and I agree. Your father and brother Duncan could be planning some sort of ambush for you."

Edgar thought.

"Yes, it seems the most sensible plan," he decided. "Algar, will you tell the others?"

A cry from near his feet made Edgar look down. Margaret had put her arm over James to keep him from rolling away and he was resisting with all his might.

Edgar picked him up.

"Well, he doesn't seem to have been starved," he commented. "Thank you for watching him, Margaret. Margaret?"

"She's been like that since Alfred drew his knife," Catherine said quietly. "She won't speak to us. We can't get her to eat. I don't think she should go to Durham, either. The hermit helped Willa. Perhaps he knows something that will soothe your sister's poor spirit."

"Take the baby," Edgar said. "I'll carry her."

He bent down. "Margaret? I'm going to take care of you. Catherine and I won't let anyone hurt you again."

He picked her up, wrapping Alfred's cloak around her.

"Alfred did this to her? He does need sanctuary. If I hadn't promised it to him, I might make him account for this tonight."

"Edgar, not now. When everything is sorted out, then we can assign blame," Catherine said. "There's too much we don't understand. He didn't mean to do this, I'm sure of that."

At that moment, with his sister lying stiffly in his arms, Edgar didn't care what the intention was. The result was all that mattered.

They followed Algar and Alfred to the spot in the woods where Robert and Æthelræd waited with Willa. The four men that had come with Alfred were now trussed across two horses, hands and feet tied with the rope looped under the horses' bellies to hold them on.

"They turned green when they saw us." Robert laughed. "I don't think they were expecting a fight."

Æthelræd wasn't so cheerful. He kept walking around the men, shaking his head.

"I don't know them, but they're all of our blood," he said. He poked one of them. "You. Bastard. Did my brother promise you could have Wedderlie when he died?"

The man just groaned.

"Perhaps it was Duncan," Edgar suggested. "Alfred, are these the men who killed Adalisa?"

"Sanctuary," Alfred said. "I'll tell you what you want to know at Hexham, in the church."

As they set off again Catherine remembered the most important question she wanted to ask Edgar.

"What's happened to Solomon?"

Solomon and Samson had been swept up in the general exodus from Saint-Giles. They found themselves in the uncomfortable company of various monks and secular clerics sent ahead to Bishopton along with household goods and accounts. They landed in the courtyard there, safe but unable to get through the attackers outside.

"Edgar is going to kill me when he learns I've misplaced his wife again," Solomon repeated.

"It's not your fault if she insists on wandering off all the time," Samson insisted. "I can't believe she was even allowed on such a journey. Our women stay home and manage the business instead of taking to the road like wantons."

"At the time it seemed safer than leaving her in Paris," Solomon said. "We thought she'd have stone walls about her for most of the stay here."

"From what I've seen of that one, they'd have to be door-and windowless to keep her in." Samson snorted.

"True enough." Solomon winced as memories rushed at him. "But, to her credit, except for the sail here, I've never heard her complain about the inconvenience of travel. She likes seeing new places."

"Perhaps this trip will cure her of that," Samson said. "Do you see her husband among the soldiers there? All these people look alike to me."

Solomon scanned the crowd. He didn't expect to see Edgar with the defenders. He hoped his friend would have the sense to stay behind the parties that had emerged from Durham to harass Conyers and Saint-Barbe as they worked their way back to Bishopton. There was no one among the people around him that he recognized.

Wait. That man.

"Samson, do you know who that is?" he asked. "No, not the one unloading the packhorse, the one on the other side, trying to keep out of our sight."

"I don't think I've seen him before, although," Samson said, scratching his chin through his beard, "there is something familiar about him. Why?"

"That's the man who was on the boat from France with us," Solomon said. "I saw him in Berwick a few weeks ago."

"Well, what of it?"

"I'm not sure," Solomon answered. "He said he was going to York for trade, but I think he's been following me."

Samson was alert at once.

"You've been posing as a Christian," he said. "What do you think they'll do to you if they find out you're one of us?"

"I don't know," Solomon told him. "I've never been found out before. I'm more worried about what would happen to Catherine and my Uncle Hubert if this man returns to France with the information."

"The situation is getting worse there, then?" Samson asked.

"Paris is unsettled these days," Solomon said. "Since the king's war with the count of Champagne, people are more inclined to suspect their neighbors of everything from theft to heresy. We need a strong ruler and Louis isn't it."

"At least you know who the ruler is," Samson grumbled. "We have a king one day and a 'lady of the English' the next. No wonder people are thinking of putting their own faces on the coins. So, what should we do about this man?"

"Just watch out for him," Solomon decided. "And help me keep up the illusion of being an Edomite."

Samson grimaced. "You want to spit on me? That might convince him."

"I might," Solomon said. "Even better, I think I'll leave you and consort with monks. I see that friend of Edgar's that Catherine went to find. He may know where she is. Keep an eye on our friend, would you? I want to see what he does when I move."

Solomon strode over to where Aelred was conversing with another Cistercian. He waited until he was noticed, then introduced himself and asked after Catherine.

"You needn't fret about her anymore," the monk told him. "I, myself, saw her safely to the hermitage at Finchale before we left Saint-Giles. By now she should be back at Durham with Edgar. I told his father where she was."

"You did what?" Solomon asked. "Where did you even see Waldeve?"

"I was behind the rest of the bishop's party and some of the soldiers stopped me," Aelred explained. "It would have gone badly with me if Waldeve and Duncan hadn't arrived. They vouched for me. I gave them the information to take to Edgar then. What's wrong?"

This last was at the sudden change on Solomon's face.

"Everything," Solomon answered. "But how could you know? You may have delivered her to her death."

He went on to explain their growing belief that Waldeve or Duncan had plotted against the rest of the family and were responsible for all the murders. Aelred was horrified at the possible consequences of his helpfulness.

"We need to return to Finchale at once," he said. "I pray we're not too late."

"You do that," Solomon said as he went to get his horse. He told Samson where he was going."

"There's an army out there," Samson remonstrated with him. "Either side could kill you."

"I know," Solomon told him, "but I'll be traveling with a cross."

"What makes you think that will help?" Samson grunted. "Oh, the man was certainly watching you. He seemed nervous while you were with the Cistercian. I wonder if he's fool enough to go after you now."

"I hope so," Solomon answered.

The monk had not forgotten how to sit a warhorse and those they met were reminded that he was not only a man of God but had once been an official at the court of the king. Solomon was impressed at the authority this humble man could command. He was reminded of Abbot Bernard in France.

They arrived at Finchale only to find that Catherine had come and gone, come back and gone again.

"But Edgar and his family were with her the second time," Godric told them. "And I sent Lord Waldeve and his man after them. They'll be well protected."

Solomon and Aelred looked at each other, thanked the hermit and set off for Hexham.

Alfred's refusal to say anything until safely within the sanctuary limits at Hexham was equally true of the men with him. No matter how many times Edgar explained to them that he wouldn't judge what they had done in his father's service, no matter how many threats Æthelræd menaced them with, none would speak.

Edgar carried Margaret before him, while Æthelræd took Catherine and the baby. James was enchanted by the handfuls of hair he could pull on his great-granduncle and enjoyed the ride more than any of them.

It was late in the day when they arrived at the town. Alfred was swaying with exhaustion. Meldred, the porter, came out to see what the commotion was.

"Grandfather!" he cried. "What have they done to you? Why are you bound? Algar, what's the meaning of this?"

Æthelræd lowered Catherine to the ground. "That crafty old goat," he said to the world. "Well, now we know why he wanted to come here."

As Meldred fussed over Alfred, the other men were untied and led into the churchyard. Someone sent for Prior Richard.

"Yes, they may have the traditional thirty-seven days of sanctuary," he said when the situation was explained. "Do they understand that they may not step from the precincts of the church for any reason during that time?"

Alfred nodded. He leaned against Meldred. As they made their way to the church, Meldred bent over him and whispered, "What went wrong, Grandfather? I thought we were going to win."

"We may still," Alfred answered. "But a sacrifice is needed and I'm the one laid upon to make it. I want no interference from you. That is my wish and my command. I've let the others know, and you shall obey me as they do. Do you understand?"

"Yes, Grandfather," Meldred said. "For the others, I will do it, but I don't like this."

"Edgar," Catherine said as they left the church to find a place for the night. "Do you think it would be possible to find a bath and a bed without fleas?"

Edgar smiled in incredulity. "Is that why you've been so silent? I thought you were pondering how you could leave me behind after all I've let you go through."

"Of course not." Catherine sighed. "I know it's frivolous, but I can't ponder anything when I feel like this. I itch all over and my hair hasn't been washed in weeks. James is the only one of us who's been tended to at all and you wouldn't believe the things we've had to oil him with. Also, I think it might help Margaret."

Edgar looked at the curled bundle in his arms.

"If there's even an empty barrel in Hexham, I'll see that it becomes a bath for you. I promise."

He didn't have to appropriate a beer barrel, to Catherine's relief. There was a small but respectable bathhouse. The owner even al-

lowed them sole use of it and guarded the door while she and Willa
washed themselves and James thoroughly and then gently undressed
Margaret, bathing and oiling her, massaging her body just as if she
were a baby, too. Her tight muscles relaxed under their care, but she
showed no other sign of being aware of them.

"Is there nothing we can do for her?" Willa asked as she rocked
the fed-and-warm James in her arms.

"It may be that she just needs time," Catherine said. "I wish
Master Herbert could see her. He might have some preparation that
would help."

"I never thought I'd feel sorry for a nobleman's child," Willa
said. "Of course, Mother says I may well be one, myself, but that
hardly counts, does it?"

"I'm afraid not," Catherine said. "You know, it's odd. That's
the way the people at Wedderlie treated her, as if she should be
pitied. I thought it was because she had such a dreadful father, but
now I wonder."

"Do you mean she isn't Master Edgar's sister?" Willa asked.

"Oh no, I'm sure she is," Catherine said too quickly, thinking of
Solomon and wondering if he had been the first to test Adalisa's fi-
delity. "But how long do you think the people knew of this plot?"

"Edgar's brother would have killed her?"

"I don't know." Catherine splashed water all over the floor as
she lifted Margaret out and began to dry her. "Margaret? Do you understand us?"

"Oh, I'm sorry," Willa said. "I didn't think."

She set the sleeping baby in a box of linen while she helped
Catherine. Her hands faltered as she fussed with the neckstring on
Margaret's *chainse*. Catherine suddenly noticed how thin and drawn
she was.

"Oh, Willa, you poor dear!" she exclaimed. "What will your
mother say when I bring you back so worn?"

"She'll say, 'welcome home.' " Willa gave a sad smile. "Forgive
me, Mistress, but I do hope it happens soon."

"Oh, Willa, so do I."

Somehow Edgar had managed a bed that didn't have fleas and did
have curtains.

"Meldred found it," he explained to Catherine. "I think he's
trying to soften me so that I'll speak up for Alfred."

"Clean linen is a potent bribe," Catherine agreed, snuggling against him and sliding one leg over his body.

They were silent for a while and still, just holding each other and reveling in the solace. For once, Edgar was the first to speak.

"None of this makes sense, you know," he said.

"That's true." Catherine kissed his shoulder. "But God gave you to me and I won't question it if you won't."

He kissed the top of her head, smelling the rosemary water she had rinsed out the soap with. With one hand he reached down and tickled her.

"Edgar!"

"In a minute." He stopped her hand from retaliation. "I'm serious. From the beginning, this followed no logical path. If there were someone who wanted to revenge themselves on my kin, they're not doing it according to any custom I know of. If you've bested a man, you want him to know it. Yet, it's just as illogical to think that my father would or could plot such an elaborate way to rid himself of family members who opposed him. Why bother to bring me back? He knew I wanted nothing more to do with him. There's something missing."

Catherine's fingers made a spiral on his chest as she thought about it. Edgar closed his eyes.

"Edgar?"

"Mmmm?"

"What would you say if I told you that I think I was mistaken?"

"That the Millennium had come."

"Prepare yourself, then," she said. "I think that your father knows nothing about how these things were done. I thought Duncan might, but there was no reason for him to burn the keep. I think it's a much more convoluted puzzle. And I think Lazarus is the key."

"Lazarus? Who's that?"

"The boy your father kept chained in the storeroom."

"Saint Mungo's misery!"

Catherine tilted her face to see his.

"You didn't know, did you?"

"Of course not," Edgar said. "Why would he have done such a thing?"

"I'm not sure," Catherine said. "At first I thought he was being held for ransom, but there would be no reason to keep that a secret from me. I think now that he was a sort of hostage."

"For what purpose?" Edgar asked.

"It would help if we knew who he was," Catherine admitted. "But I suspect it was to ensure the compliance of the people of Wedderlie, or of one person there."

"What, you mean in the castle?"

"No, the people, the villagers," Catherine said. "I know it sounds mad, but all the odd pieces seem to fit together if you take the actions of the peasants into account."

"But that's unnatural!" Edgar protested. "They know what happens to people who rebel against their lord."

"Of course they do," Catherine said. "That's why no one bragged about it. What I don't understand is what they thought they could accomplish by these things."

Edgar wasn't convinced. "I can see wanting to be rid of my father or my older brothers, but why kill Adalisa? Why hurt Margaret?"

"I'm not sure," Catherine answered. "But I'm hoping that now that he's within the churchyard, Alfred will tell us. I'm coming with you tomorrow, of course."

"It had never occurred to me that you wouldn't," Edgar said truthfully.

"The right answer, *discipulus*." Catherine rolled to lie on top of him. "What would you like for reward?"

"This will do just fine." Edgar sighed.

Twenty-one

Hexham, Saturday, 2 nones September (September 4), 1143.
Commemoration of the translation of Saint Cuthbert, although it's not clear
which translation. He moved around a lot.

*Parum etenim proderit peccatori a peccto cessare, nisi studeat ieiuniis et
orationibus elemosinisque commissum deflere, et sicut existiterat operator
malicie, ita quoque efficiatur post penitentium cultor iustitie.*

For it is of little use for a sinner to cease sinning, if he doesn't strive
to lament the act with fasting, prayers and almsgiving, so that after the
penance he becomes one who cultivates justice.

—Life of Saint Rumwold,
Part 10

*P*rior Richard had decided to give Alfred a day to rest and pray before he met with Edgar and his family. Æthelræd grumbled at this, saying that it would only give him more time to think up lies, but the prior had the final say.

Unfortunately, that gave Waldeve time to reach Hexham.

Robert was on the road, heading for the priory when he and Duncan galloped in, followed by a dozen of their henchmen. "If you've come to defend yourself, it's too late!" he shouted at them. "We know everything!"

Waldeve brought his horse to a sudden halt. He looked down at his son as if at a snake on the path.

"The only way I defend myself is with a sword, boy," he said. "And I'll be a long time in Hell before you know everything. Where's that *unbryce* brother of mine?"

He spotted Æthelræd coming out of the inn.

"What's this *flitere* gibbering about?" he shouted.

Æthelræd came within speaking distance.

"About you, Brother," he said. "Alfred has surrendered to us and is going to tell all he knows about your plans to destroy the family. And don't bother to try to silence him. He's safe within the church."

"What plans? Have you all gone mad?" Waldeve dismounted. "You." He pointed at one of his men. "Take care of my horse."

Duncan joined him. Robert looked from one to the other. Waldeve seemed genuinely surprised at the accusation. It must have been Duncan all along, he thought. The intricacy of the planning was certainly more his style.

"What do you think our father's done to destroy the family?" Duncan asked. "Besides not drowning you at birth. And what's Alfred got to do with it?"

"You know quite well," Robert said. "It wasn't enough for you to make yourself the oldest, you had to try to get rid of me, as well. I'll never forgive you for what happened to Lufen."

Duncan put a hand to Robert's forehead.

"No fever, so you can't be delirious," he said. "Therefore, I can only assume you've lost all reason."

Æthelræd interrupted Robert's response.

"This afternoon, after Tierce," he said. "Come to the church. Prior Richard has agreed to witness Alfred's confession and refer the case to the proper authorities."

Some of the conversation finally made sense to Waldeve.

"If Alfred knows anything about what happened to my horses and my sons," he said, "then the only proper authority is me and he won't be able to hide behind the skirts of the monks for ever."

His hand went to the hilt of his sword.

Robert was unconvinced. "Who outside of the family would know that I was the only one who worked in my vegetable garden? What kind of marauder attacks a castle and leaves the village undamaged? Think about it, Father. You should have been more clever."

Waldeve turned from him with a look of disgust.

"Addled, completely," he muttered. "Edana must have betrayed me. This one can't be mine. All right, Æthelræd, how long before we're allowed to hear Alfred's condemnation of me? It should take him aback to have me there to cut out his lying tongue."

"Don't even consider it, Brother," Æthelræd said. "You know the penalties for breaching sanctuary. Alfred has reached *deop friðsocne*. He's under the protection of God and Saint Wilfrid."

"They're playing dice on the tomb of Saint Cuthbert at this very minute." Waldeve sneered. "That great saint couldn't even protect his own monks. What have I to fear?"

"My wrath, Brother. Only mine." Æthelræd smiled.

Edgar woke to find Catherine next to him, James sucking peacefully at her breast. For a moment, he thought himself home again. Then he heard the shouting of English voices and remembered.

Catherine opened one eye. "Just a few more minutes," she whispered. "He's almost done."

"I'm in no rush," Edgar said. "Whatever is decided today won't matter to me. I want nothing from Wedderlie or my kinfolk."

"We don't need to abandon them utterly," Catherine said. "Your uncle is welcome to visit us whenever he likes. I think Father would like him. And I'm getting rather fond of Robert. Of course, Margaret will be ours now, won't she?"

"I hope so," he said. "In her condition, I can't see that Father will protest. He never could bear infirmities. But what do you think your father will say if we bring another child into his household?"

"We're taking her into our household, Edgar," Catherine said firmly. "She's kin. Father will make no objection."

"Kin doesn't seem to count for much in my family," Edgar said. "I wish I could work up a rage against Alfred, but I can't help thinking he had a good reason for whatever he did."

"I could feel more disposed to Alfred if I were sure he had nothing to do with Adalisa's death," Catherine said.

"It still seems senseless to connive at the deaths of the family of one's lord unless another lord were inciting them." Edgar stroked James's cheek, telling himself he would never give his son reason to hate him the way he did Waldeve. "What could they gain but their own destruction? And what good would come of my stepmother's death?"

"I don't know," Catherine answered.

Edgar rolled closer to her. "Solomon seems more upset about her than you do." He made the sentence a question.

Catherine wanted to tell Edgar all she suspected, but she couldn't. Adalisa had been his stepmother. How far would his tolerance stretch? And anyway, she had no proof. It was Solomon's secret, not hers to share.

"I think he is," she told Edgar. "Adalisa helped him in his business dealings. They became friends. And I think he still feels guilty that he couldn't save her."

"From what you say, there was nothing he could have done. I'll tell him I don't blame him," Edgar promised. "I wish I could have seen this Lazarus you left at Lindisfarne. You aren't thinking about adopting him, too, are you?"

"The monks seem to think he would be happy with them and perhaps regain his speech," Catherine said. "But I wish I knew who he really was and why your father chained him for so long."

"We can ask Father." Edgar yawned. "Though I doubt he'll answer. Tell me about this machine you saw on Holy Island."

"Oh, the windmill. That was what started me thinking about the villagers," Catherine said.

"Right." Edgar was doubtful. "A house with sails stuck on a pole. I'd like to see such a machine outside of a *scopes* tale."

"I didn't describe it well. I know you'd love it," Catherine told him. "But the point is that the people of Wedderlie believe it can work. And they don't want anyone else to know about it. Why? No, don't interrupt. I'll tell you. Because with a windmill they don't need to take their grain to your father's mill. They don't have to pay the tithe. It's one step toward being free of his yoke."

"But there are a hundred other duties," Edgar argued. "*Sac* and *soke*, fees to marry, many more. At Wedderlie, the villagers are only one step above serfs. Some of them are serfs. They hardly own more than their own bodies."

"And the women not even that, if the faces of your father's men are any indication," Catherine said. "Would you tolerate that from your lord?"

"Of course not!" Edgar said. "What do you think I am?"

"I know what you are, *carissime*," she said. "It's what they are that I wonder about. You know how upset your friend John is about the situation here in England?"

"Of course," Edgar said. "But his family at Salisbury has been hurt by the wars."

"It's not just personal," Catherine said. "He feels that when the order at the top of society is unstable then the whole pattern is disrupted. There is no law in Britain now, not really. When that happens the common people may decide to be their own law."

"You're talking anarchy!" Edgar was shocked.

"I know," she answered. "But that's all I've seen since we've been here. It's like the commune at Reims. The citizens never would have formed it if King Louis hadn't wanted to collect the revenues from the empty bishopric. There was no bishop at the head of the town, so the people were forced to rule themselves."

"My father was always there to rule!" Edgar said.

"But how well?" Catherine asked. "If the ruler is corrupt and abusive, then he breaks faith with his people. It's their obligation to overthrow a tyrant."

"John explained all of this to you?" Edgar said.

"We had a lot of good conversations last winter, while you were carving wood," she said. "He likes my soup."

"That's all very nice, theoretically." Edgar made a move to get out of bed. "But I doubt that Alfred has heard John's ideas."

"No," Catherine admitted, detaching her son and pulling a *chainse* over her head. "But he might have thought of them himself."

If Alfred and the other four men were daunted by the family ranged against them, they didn't show it. He sat on Saint Wilfrid's stone chair, the *friðstol*, next to the altar, and they sat on the floor on either side of him. His grandsons, Algar, the soldier, and Meldred, the monk, stood to one side.

"Why didn't you tell me?" Algar whispered to his cousin.

"You're not of their blood," Meldred answered. "We weren't sure where your loyalty lay."

"Idiots," Algar muttered. "I'll bear the retribution with the rest of you. You might have let me share the guilt."

Prior Richard entered and was seated on a folding stool. He signaled to Alfred that he could begin.

"Be sure to tell me every word he says," Catherine said to Edgar.

Alfred took a deep breath.

"First of all, I confess here that all blame for what has happened must be mine."

His friends started to protest, but he cut them off with a gesture.

"The plan was mine," Alfred continued. "If it failed, if deeds were done that I didn't wish for, the men who did them were still following my orders. I will not have them punished."

"A man like you has no right to tell me who I'll punish." Waldeve sneered. "I'll hang every damned *neyf* on my lands if I feel like it."

Prior Richard held up a hand to quiet him.

"Perhaps you'll feel differently when you hear the rest of his confession," he said to Waldeve sternly. "I'll only remind you one time that this is sacred space and I won't tolerate violence in deeds or words within the church. Do you understand?"

Waldeve nodded grudgingly.

At that moment there was a clatter outside. Everyone turned toward the door as the porter ushered in two more people.

Robert drew his breath in sharply. "Aelred!" he cried. "Thank God you're here!"

The other man was more hesitant to enter the church.

"Solomon," Catherine called. "Just this once. Please."

Reluctantly, he came over to where Edgar and Catherine stood. Aelred made his obeisance to Prior Richard, who greeted him warmly.

"I'm glad to have you here to consult with on this, whatever the reason for your visit," he told the monk. "Meldred, fetch another stool for Brother Aelred."

They settled in again. Aelred gave Robert an encouraging smile. The prior nodded to Alfred to begin again.

The old man watched the expectant faces before him. Then he started speaking, clearly and slowly enough that Edgar could translate without missing anything.

"Now that I've had time to think about it," he said. "I know it started long ago, before any of you but Lord Waldeve and I were born. He seduced my sister, got her with child. My mother nearly killed her for it. She finally told my father that my sister wasn't his, but the child of Waldeve's father, that my sister's child would be born of a double sin."

Waldeve chuckled. "Good breeding stock. Doubly blessed, I'd say."

No one else laughed. Prior Richard frowned at him and Waldeve subsided.

Alfred continued. "My sister killed herself and the child. We buried her by the old standing stones and her ghost has been there ever since, along with the spirits of too many other victims of your anger or your lust."

He glared at Waldeve, who shrugged.

"There are a thousand other tales of Lord Waldeve, his father and then his sons," Alfred said. "They have abused the powers God gave them. They have raped and tortured for sport. They have abandoned us to starve in famine and drown in flood, never fulfilling their duty to protect those in their service.

"My lord, your sons and grandson died while chasing human beings across the fields, whipping them until they ran and running them through when they fell, as if they were game. They had the mischance to chase their quarry to the woods where the fowlers were setting their nets. Hearing the pleas for help, they circled the hunters and cast their nets over them. Your sons were dragged from the horses. I believe it was blind fury at their actions or perhaps fear of their wrath, that made the peasants beat and hack them all to death."

Waldeve was shaking with a fury of his own.

"I don't believe it!" he shouted. "No baseborn filth could have murdered my sons. They were warriors!"

Alfred ignored him. "When it was discovered who the men were, word was sent to me at Wedderlie. The peasants were terrified but I promised to protect them. I was the one who decided to cut off their right hands. My own pride wanted to tell the world that these men were no better than common thieves. We all worked to move the bodies. After that, it was as if the whole village had been awakened. People like us had rid themselves of the ones who were oppressing them. I thought we might be able to continue as they had begun."

"What about my horses?" Waldeve growled. "What harm had they done you?"

Catherine was amazed when Edgar told her what he had said. Waldeve was being told of a plot to eradicate his entire family and he still dwelt on the insult done his horses?

"Their tails and manes had become tangled in the nets," Alfred said wearily. "It was the only way they could be released quickly. I sent them to Hexham so that they wouldn't be traced back to us."

"Edgar," Catherine said. "Ask him why they had to set fire to the keep. What harm could those of us left do them?"

Edgar wanted to know this, himself.

Alfred closed his eyes, and rubbed his forehead. "That's where it all began to go wrong." He sighed. "Too many of us were making decisions. We hoped that it would keep Waldeve from returning. It was never intended that the women should die, only to keep up the illusion that some strong adversary was trying to destroy you. But the fire spread more quickly than we expected. I lost more than anyone by it."

"Lazarus?" Edgar asked. "The boy in chains. Who is he?"

"Ask him." Alfred's face hardened into a stone likeness of hatred for his lord.

All eyes turned to Waldeve. "Lazarus? My prisoner? Who called him that? He's scarcely able to rise from his ashes. So you think our bargain has ended because the boy died? I've only been saved the trouble of executing him at last."

He explained to the others. "I caught the boy in the forest, releasing the traps we had set for wolves and game. I could have killed him then. He ruined a month's work. But he was Alfred's youngest and so I brought him back."

"He was an innocent!" Alfred exploded. "One of God's chosen. He couldn't speak. He didn't understand the rules of the forest; he only hated to see things in pain. And you made him the price for my betrayal of my own people."

Now his men reacted. Alfred faced them, his hands clasped in supplication.

"I was to keep the rest of you in order, to report any signs of rebellion," he confessed in shame. "He knew already how much his outrages were resented. I did it for my poor Kenelm. I did it because I was already old and had spent my life being afraid of these men. But no longer."

He turned back to Waldeve. By some trick of nature, the afternoon sun slit the long, thin windows sending down shafts of light that hit only Alfred and Waldeve, as if they had been lifted to another world and were untouchable by mortals.

Alfred drew himself up proudly.

"I am a man," he said. "Made in the image of God, just as you are. I'll not die a traitor to my own, nor with the shame of my family unavenged."

"Oh, but you'll die!" Waldeve shouted. "And then I will hang every member of your family, down to the babe born yesterday and leave them to rot in the trees, like worm-ridden fruit."

He drew his sword and raise it above his head.

There was a moment of stunned immobility. Edgar recovered first.

"Father, no!" he screamed. "Not in the church!"

He threw himself forward, trying to stop Waldeve's arm from finishing the arc. The heavy sword fell, passing through Edgar's left wrist and slicing deep into Alfred's neck.

Edgar looked down at his empty arm. Blood gushed forth.

"No!"

The scream wasn't his, but Catherine's. She threw herself against the torrent, feeling the pulsing of Edgar's life as it gushed against her stomach, soaking through her clothing and running down her legs.

"No!" she screamed again. "Put it back! Somebody put it back!"

Edgar clutched at her with his remaining hand. He was shrieking now in agony. She looked into his eyes, watching the light in them fade, willing him to stay alive.

Someone tore off a sleeve and tied it around Edgar's arm, reducing the flow. Someone else was shouting for fire. It was an instant before Catherine realized what it was for.

"No, no, no," she said. "Not that. They have to put it back on. He needs it. Don't do this! Get it! Put his hand back!"

Someone took her shoulders and moved her away, as others lowered Edgar to the floor and bound the stump of his arm.

"Catherine." Solomon's voice was thick with tears. "Catherine, they can't do that. It's impossible. It has to be cauterized or he'll die."

"No, no." Catherine wept into his chest. She looked around. "Where are you taking him?"

"To the infirmary, Catherine." Solomon held her firmly.

"Let me go!" she wrenched herself free. "I'm coming with him. He's not going to die."

Prior Richard watched them go by. "We can't let a woman in there," he said, grasping at the one thing he could understand of the events of the past moments.

Aelred turned his head as he passed, carrying Edgar's legs. "We can't keep her out," he said. "It's her right."

The prior turned back, forced to comprehend the scene in the church. The transept was a pool of red, reflected in the sunshine. Alfred's body lay in it, his head almost severed. His grandsons knelt next to him, weeping and praying.

In another pool lay Edgar's severed hand, fingers still splayed, now palm up to Heaven as if begging mercy.

Waldeve stood motionless. The sun had moved, leaving him in shadow. Everyone else just stared at him, as if afraid to touch someone so unclean.

"Damn you, boy," Waldeve said softly. "Never where you're supposed to be."

He dropped the sword.

The sound freed the others from their shock. Æthelræd bent and picked up the grisly weapon.

"Bind him," he ordered. "Prior, is there a place we can hold the prisoner?"

"Prisoner?" Waldeve screamed. "I'm the master here! I was executing my own justice. It's my right."

Æthelræd stepped back from him.

"You have committed murder in front of the holy altar, on a man given holy sanctuary." He spoke loudly so that all could hear. "Your life is forfeit."

Waldeve spit at him. "Don't spout holy law at me, you *heoruwearg*. You never had any more use for it that I have. Men, prepare to ride. We're going to Wedderlie this very night and I'll make good on my promise to Alfred. I only wish I'd let him live long enough to see it. Now!"

Nobody moved. Waldeve stared at his men and, too late, realized his mistake. Duncan had been watching from the sidelines with no show of emotion. Now he nodded to Urric, who stepped forward and took Waldeve's arm. Æthelræd took the other and they tied his wrists with his own leather belt as the lord of Wedderlie shouted obscenities at the assembly.

"You're all of my blood, every one of you bastards! You owe me your very lives! Betray me now and you shall be damned for eternity, and your sons and theirs!"

His sons, nephews and grandsons, bastards all, helped drag him away.

The monks helped Meldred and Algar carry Alfred's body out. Æthelræd and Robert were left alone. They both looked down.

"We can't leave it there," Robert said.

"I know. After all, it's part of Edgar," his uncle agreed.

Neither made a move to pick it up.

"He was a craftsman," Robert said. "Always carving on something. What will he do now?"

Æthelræd shook his head. "Live, please God. Just let him live and after that, what fate wills."

Catherine watched as the infirmarian heated the metal over glowing coals. The cloths wrapped around Edgar's arm were bright red. His face was paler than she had ever seen it, even his lips bled almost white. He was mercifully unconscious.

She sat on the floor beside his cot. Every now and then she would reach up to take his hand, and then remember. Each time, it horrified her.

"Live," she repeated over and over. "You must live, or I'll die, too. Edgar, don't leave me. You can't leave me alone."

She should have been praying, beseeching the saints, bargaining with God. But the only one she could see or think of was Edgar, and he was the only one she implored to answer.

Solomon knelt beside her. He held her tightly as they both watched Edgar's ragged breathing.

"Catherine, you need to come out for a while," he said. "James is crying for you. He's hungry."

"Bring him to me," Catherine said, never taking her eyes from Edgar.

Solomon saw that the iron cautery was almost red hot. His voice took on a note of panic.

"No, dear. You need to go to him. This is no place for a baby."

Catherine looked straight at him. What he saw in her face made his heart pound in terror.

"I'm not leaving, Solomon," she said. "I know what they're going to do and I won't let him endure it alone."

"Catherine . . ."

Solomon gave the infirmarian a gesture of helplessness.

The Norman monk set his mouth in a determined line. "I can't have her in the way. What if she tries to stop me? What if she screams and faints?"

"I won't get in the way," Catherine said dully. "It's the only way to save him."

"And she won't faint," Solomon said. "She's stronger than you think."

The monk stood firm.

"She's his wife," Solomon added. "She has the right." He kissed Catherine's cheek. "Willa can give James some broth. I'll bring him to you when it's over."

Catherine nodded, too busy gathering up all her fortitude to hear him clearly.

With much grumbling, the infirmarian directed his assistants to unbind the wound and hold the patient steady. He stoked the coals and pulled out the cautery iron.

"Woman, you so much as move and you'll risk being scarred for life," he warned.

"I understand," she said.

They had to peel the last of the bandages off. Catherine saw the white bone amidst the sliced red bits of flesh, muscle and nerves. She watched as the glowing metal came closer and closer, finally pressing against the open wound with a horrid sizzling and a smell that she would never forget.

Edgar cried out and subsided.

Catherine started to reach for him.

"I said don't move!" The infirmarian took the iron off. He was perspiring freely. "He's not dead, if that's what you fear. If anything, the pain should be less soon. I don't know why but it seems to help."

"Will he survive?" This came out as a croak from her dry throat.

"I don't know," the monk said more gently. "I've seen men live after worse injuries. There is hope."

That one word dissolved the last of Catherine's strength. She crumpled beside the cot in tears.

By the time Solomon arrived with James, they had wiped her face and given her strong wine with honey and vervain to calm her. The infirmarian looked at the baby in amazement.

"I didn't understand," he said. "Yes, they should all be together. I'll have the brothers set up another cot and string curtains across the corner for her. But only until he can be moved."

"How long will that be?" Solomon asked.

"A few days," the infirmarian said. "Either to the inn or the graveyard. There's no way now to say which."

Solomon left in search of Aelred, the only person left who could help him amidst all these foreigners. Going to a white monk for help! He hoped his friends never learnt of it.

Aelred was in the prior's receiving room. Æthelræd and Robert were with them.

"How is he?" they asked.

"The bleeding has been stopped," Solomon answered. "Beyond that, only the Holy One knows. What will happen to Waldeve?"

"He thinks he can appeal to William Cumin and be released with no consequences," Aelred said. "What he's forgotten is that Hexham is a dependency of York and Archbishop Thurston isn't about to be so lenient. Of course, he can appeal to King David, but I believe I can convince the king that his pardon wouldn't be appropriate here."

"But Alfred admitted that he had plotted against his lord, and he sent the men who killed Adalisa," Solomon said.

"It doesn't matter," Prior Richard said harshly. "Sanctuary is inviolable. What Alfred and his people did was a mortal sin and an affront to authority. What Waldeve did was an insult to God, himself. He must pay."

"With his life?" Solomon said hopefully.

"In a way," Aelred explained. "The least he could be made to pay is Alfred's *weregild*, his man-price, but as he was only a peasant, that's not very high. However, Waldeve could be sentenced either to perpetual imprisonment or, which I prefer, to life as a *grithman*."

"A what?"

Prior Richard smiled. It did not bode well for Waldeve's future. "It means he becomes a serf of the church. He must stay here for the remainder of his days. If he leaves, his life is immediately forfeit."

"That's diabolical," Solomon said in admiration.

"That is justice," the prior corrected.

"But Duncan will still get Wedderlie," Solomon remembered.

"Until his oldest nephew is of age to fight him for it," the prior agreed. "That is also justice."

Catherine hadn't realized how much of Edgar's blood had spilled onto her until she started to feed James and saw that she had to wash it off herself before he could nurse. Even then it was the next day before Willa, along with a woman from the town who spoke French, could convince her to come with them to be cleaned.

"I must stay," she protested. "What if he wakes?"

"He won't," the infirmarian said. "Not with the inhalant I put under his nose. Go. You stink and are an offense to my sight. Don't worry. I'll readmit you."

Catherine squinted in the bright sunlight. In the churchyard the monks were setting up a table hung with altar cloths.

"What's that for?" she asked.

"They can't say Mass in the church until it's been cleaned and purified," the woman told her. "Don't think about that now."

"Edgar's hand!" Catherine stopped. "Where is it? What did they do with it?"

"I have no idea, dear." The woman pushed her to get her moving toward the gate again. "It's better not to know."

"No, I must know," Catherine insisted. "I have to ask Prior Richard."

"Not now; it's Sunday." Another gentle shove. "A fine way to greet the Lord, with your clothes stuck to your body and your hair uncovered."

"Please, Mistress," Willa begged. "Come with us. If you could see yourself, you wouldn't argue."

It wasn't until her head came out of a dunking in the warm water that Catherine thought to ask, "How is Margaret?"

Willa grinned. "Awake again," she said happily. "Solomon came looking for us last night. The moment she heard his voice, she opened her eyes and stretched out her arms to him. I don't suppose he'd wait a few years until she's of age and convert for her sake?"

"It seems impossible, but greater miracles have happened," Catherine said. Then she grew sober again. "If only we could be granted one now."

It was late that night when Edgar finally regained consciousness. He was first aware of the sharp headache, a result of the opiate. Then he felt the deep throbbing pain in his arm and hand. He lifted his left arm and opened his eyes. He saw the bandages wrapped around the end of his arm and the void beyond.

"Oh, God no," he said, dropping his arm. "I thought it was a nightmare. It is a nightmare. I've got to wake up."

Catherine was next to him at once murmuring wordless syllables of comfort, wiping his face with a cool cloth. He tried to kiss her fingers as they passed over his mouth, then fell back into a stupor.

Slowly he came alert, but not alive. When he understood the permanence of his injury, he retreated into an apathy that not even James could rouse him from.

"Edgar, please, eat something," Catherine begged. "You have to get strong again so that we can go home."

"Home to what?" Edgar answered listlessly. "What good am I to anyone now?"

Catherine tried pleading. She tried cajoling. She tried anger and seduction. Nothing would bring him round.

"I don't know what else to do," she wept to the infirmarian. "If he won't live for us, what more is there?"

The monk shook his head in worry. "I've seen cases like this before. Sometimes the patient develops his own desire to heal, others . . . well, it's still early. He's young and has a devoted family. That would be enough for most men."

"He's a craftsman," Catherine said. "He's happiest when making things, carving bits or shaping jewelry. See the cross he made for me?"

She pulled it out of her tunic. The ivory tusk had been turned into a piece of white lace, with swans and spirals. It was a work of art and love.

"He'll never be able to do that again," she said.

The infirmarian wasn't impressed.

"A man of his birth shouldn't have been doing anything like that in the first place," he stated.

One afternoon Robert came to the infirmary and offered to sit with Edgar while Catherine went out for some fresh air with Solomon and Margaret.

"You're looking paler than he does," he told her.

Catherine didn't want to go, but Edgar waved her away with a gesture that hurt her deeply and so she went.

Edgar turned his face away as Robert sat down.

"If you're going to give me a lecture on self-pity and the sin of despair, you can leave right now," he warned. "I've heard them all."

"Actually," Robert said. "I was going to tell you how Lufen is doing."

"Lufen?" Edgar was vaguely insulted. "Very well, how is your dog, Robert?"

"She's recovered as far as she's going to," he said. "She trips now and then and can't go up stairs the way she used to. She'll never hunt again, of course."

"Sounds fairly useless," Edgar said.

Robert pursed his lips, considering. "To most people, yes. Duncan would have let her die when she was hurt. But I couldn't. Do you know why?"

"Because you have a soft head and a soft heart," Edgar answered, sensing a moral coming.

"That too," Robert admitted. "But I had a much more selfish reason. She loves me. I think she's the only one who does. For that love I will carry her up and down stairs and pick her up when she trips. As long as she lives, I don't care if I ever hunt again. I didn't want her to survive for her sake, but for mine."

"I understand your point, Robert." Edgar sighed. "But Lufen is just a dog. I'm a man."

"That is my point, Edgar," Robert said. "Lufen is nothing but a dumb creature and yet I would die without her love. You're human. Think how much more you have to offer."

Edgar was silent for a long time. He thought of Catherine and how little he felt he could give her now, of how he hated the idea of being dependent on her father. Then he turned it about and looked at the situation from her side. How could she face going back to Paris alone, with a small child to care for? No, he knew her better than that. It wasn't a time for false modesty. He knew perfectly well what he meant to her, what would happen to her spirit if he died.

"Oh, Robert!" he said. "You are a complete ass."

"So I've been told." Robert smiled.

Edgar felt a weight rise from his heart, he smiled back at his brother, then fell onto his pillow.

"All right, go on and gloat," he said. "Then go tell my wife that I've decided she's worth living for."

"I suspected it all the time." And Robert ran to get her.

Epilogue

Paris, the home of Hubert LeVendeur, merchant. Friday, 9 kalends July
(June 23), 1144. Saint John's Eve.

Forð ic gefare, frind ic gemete . . .
Bidde ic nu sigeres god godes miltse
siðfæt godne, smylte and lihte
Windas on warothum. . . .

I fare forth, friends I shall meet . . .
Now I pray to the god of triumph to God's mercy
that the journey be good, a mild and light
wind from the shore. . . .

—A journey spell,
MS 41 Corpus Christi College,
Exeter Book

*E*dgar didn't heal all at once. There was no miraculous cure. His recovery was slow and there were many days of despair. They left Hexham for Berwick in the middle of October. Robert made a deal with Duncan to recover his house in the town that had been illegally ceded to William Cumin. They settled into it with Margaret and Willa to wait out the winter. James took his first steps in Scotland and his first word was "Cuddy," the nickname for the birds that gathered in their garden each morning.

Solomon left soon after they settled to head south to London. Margaret was devastated.

"You'll come back, won't you?" she asked.

"I promise I'll be here in the spring and we'll all sail home together," he said.

He and Edgar had a long discussion the night before he left.

"My friend Samson has sent a message," Solomon explained. "The man who came over from France with us, the clerk that I thought was following me, seems to have become interested in Samson. The man has been seen in London. They say he's asking questions about Samson's connection with the French. There's something wrong in this and I don't think it bodes well for the Jews."

"Has there been any word from Hubert?" Edgar asked.

"Not directly, or I would have told you," Solomon said. "But I heard that Uncle Eliazar has petitioned the community at Troyes to be allowed to settle there. I fear his connection with Uncle Hubert has become too suspect."

"And what about you, then?" Edgar worried. "Will you relocate, as well?"

"I don't know," he said. "I can't risk the lives of my people for my own friendships. Perhaps it won't come to that."

"Margaret would never forgive you," Edgar reminded him.

"Take good care of her," Solomon said. "Let her be a child."

"That won't be hard with Catherine around," Edgar said. "She forgets too often that she isn't one herself."

"One of the reasons I love her."

After he left Edgar absently raised his left arm to scratch his ear. It was still a shock when the leather-covered stump touched his flesh. He could almost feel the missing fingers still wiggling. Prior Richard told him that they had buried the hand so that on Judgment Day it would be ready to rejoin his resurrected body. This didn't give him a great deal of comfort.

It was a long time after he was well enough that he felt he could make love with Catherine again. Her patience was sorely tried. Finally one night she had grabbed his left arm and run the end of it up and down her naked body.

"There," she said. "I'm not disgusted. I'm not repelled. Are you? It there something wrong with me? Have I aged so? Do you find my swollen, drooping breasts repulsive? Your son certainly doesn't. Edgar, I can't wait any longer. Don't you love me anymore?"

She looked at him in exasperation.

Edgar didn't know how to answer. Then he realized that he didn't have to. His body was doing it for him. Catherine noticed. She grinned in anticipation.

"Oh, Edgar, I have missed you so."

"I'm sorry, *leoffest*." He pulled her closer. "I'll never go away again."

Solomon came back from London in the spring looking more worried than Catherine had ever seen him. When questioned, he would only say that there had been some sort of trouble in the town of Norwich but that he was sure it was an isolated incident. He didn't want to talk about it but busied himself with the interrupted negotiations with Robert, taking Margaret with him to translate as her mother had.

The arrangements for taking Margaret to France with them weren't as difficult as Catherine feared. Waldeve was too concerned with fighting the judgment of the archbishop of York, that he became a serf of Hexham to live out his days in penance for the double crime of maiming his own son and attempting murder in a place of sanctuary. He felt no guilt, only rage. He had no interest in what happened to his daughter.

Duncan, as her eldest surviving brother, was relieved to be free of the responsibility.

"Just so you're responsible for her dowry," he told Edgar. "I don't want you applying to me for funds to marry her off."

He returned to Wedderlie, to rebuild the castle with the king's permission. By the winter of 1144, even Duncan had realized that following William Cumin was hopeless. It was only a matter of time before he would be forced to turn over the keys to the palace to William of Saint-Barbe. Duncan decided to stay on land he could be sure of.

He tried to get Robert to help him.

"The villagers can't be trusted not to put a knife in my back," Duncan pleaded. "You're not good for much, but I know you won't murder me in my sleep."

"Only because you're not worth the trouble," Robert answered. "No, they're your people now. You deal with them. I'll stay on my own land, thank you. I don't want to be lord over anyone. I can't even master my own soul."

Duncan rolled his eyes in disgust. "Sweet Saint Sidwell's bloody scythe! You should be enslaved to Hexham instead of Father. You'd never know the difference."

He went back to the ruins of Wedderlie, determined to make life miserable for everyone there. The villagers, in turn, planned to do the same to him.

No one ever told Duncan about the windmill, and he spent the next twenty years wondering why revenues from his mill on the river were so meager.

It was almost summer before they boarded the boat to take them back to France. Catherine spent the entire voyage with her head in a bucket again, but this time she suspected her stomach problems might be compounded by morning sickness. It didn't seem a good time to tell Edgar, though. She decided to wait until she was certain and they were settled at home again.

Hubert had been warned in a letter from Catherine of what had happened to Edgar. He kept his doubts to himself and greeted them with all appearance of delight, genuinely rejoicing at his healthy grandson. He showed Edgar sympathy but no patronage.

"No work has been done on the extension since you left," he

grumbled instead. "A year I've had the back of the house torn up. Do you think you can get it completed before the rain comes this year?"

"I'll see if the men I hired are still available," Edgar promised. "We can start work within the week. Are you sure you want to commit to rebuilding? Are matters here settled?"

Hubert pursed his lips.

"The bishop seemed satisfied that the rumors about me were slanders, spread by competitors," he said "But Eliazar and Johanna have received permission to move to Troyes and they intend to go. It grieves me greatly, but it may be for the best. Things in Paris are too unsettled. There's even talk of King Louis taking the cross and mounting an army to the Holy Land in penance for the fire at Vitry."

Edgar knew what had happened to Hubert's family the last time a great army was raised to take back Jerusalem. He could almost read the memory in Hubert's haunted eyes.

"Well, then," Edgar said, "returning pilgrims often bring back a taste for foreign goods and spices. Business should increase."

Hubert smiled. "I'll need help, you know. A trader only needs his right hand, after all. Don't be offended, man. You can't fight and you can't carve toys, thank goodness, but you can shake hands to seal a pact and raise your hand to Heaven to swear to your promise. You may not think you have much of a future, but you can be of use to me, if you will."

Edgar thought a moment, then nodded. "I've cut all the bonds to my family, except my sister, who is now under my care. For her sake, and that of my son, I accept your offer."

He held out his good hand. Solemnly, Hubert took it.

Margaret was welcomed into the household and soon knew all the corners of Paris almost as well as Willa. There were still nights when she woke up crying for her mother. Catherine realized that there would always be such nights, as long as Margaret lived. But the joy of living in a place where everyone was fond of her and each other helped the child recover. Catherine and Edgar fretted over what would become of her but for now it was enough to let her heal and be a child. Everything was fine, except for Eliazar's proposed move to Champagne. One night Catherine started to put James in his own cradle and then realized that he had outgrown it.

"We'll put him in an open chest for now," she told Edgar. "But you'll have to make him a new bed soon. Oh, it's so good to be home."

Edgar lay awake long after she had gone to sleep, thinking of her unconscious comment. A year before he could have made a child's bed in a day. Now . . . now the only work that gave him joy was gone. He heard the bells of Paris toll the hours calling the various monks and canons to their prayers. Finally, he slid quietly out of bed and down to the back garden.

It was still there, propped up in a corner. James's Trojan horse. There were a few dried walnuts in the basket next to it. Edgar sat on his stool and stared at it for a long time.

At last he picked it up with his good hand. It slipped and he caught it against the stump of the other. He swore. Then he pushed the basket of nuts across the floor with one foot. He sat back on the stool and wedged the horse against his chest with his left arm.

He picked up a walnut and began to rub the wood smooth, tears streaming down his face.

Afterword

This book is a work of fiction. Catherine, Edgar and their families are made up from my own imagination. However, the world they live in is real and so are many of the events and people. William Cumin did attempt to take over the bishopric of Durham at this time, and the story of it is much more complex than I could capture in this book. Alan Young has written a thorough history of Cumin, published by the Borthwick Institute, York.

Aelred was in 1143 a monk and later an abbot of Rievaulx. His history is in his own writings and analyzed in a fascinating study by Brian Patrick McGuire called *Brother and Lover*, Crossroad Press, 1994. Godric of Finchale lived as a hermit near Durham for more than half a century and was over a hundred when he died. Unfortunately, as far as I know there is no good translation of his life story.

For further information on the books mentioned above and for a bibliography of the other sources used in this book, please write to me in care of the publisher. Usually, less than ten percent of my research is actually used in the story, and I would love to direct those interested to the rest of it. But my goal, as always, is to entertain. If I have done that, it even makes the horror of reading Lawrence of Durham worthwhile. Thank you.

—Sharan